In the Hall of the Dragon King

In the

HALL

of the

DRAGON
KING

Stephen R. Lawhead

CROSSWAY BOOKS ● WESTCHESTER ILLINOIS
A DIVISION OF GOOD NEWS PUBLISHERS

In the Hall of the Dragon King copyright © 1982 by Stephen R. Lawhead.
Published by Crossway Books, a division of Good News Publishers,
9825 West Roosevelt Road, Westchester, Illinois 60154.

Cover illustration: Chuck Gillies

Banner illustration: Michael Carroll

Eleventh printing, 1989

Printed in the United States of America

Library of Congress Catalog Card Number: 82-71942

ISBN: 0-89107-563-1

For
Ross
My golden one
With all my love

Mensandor
7 Mystic Islan
Corithy
Gerfallen The Sea
Woodsend
Flatlands
Lindalia
Wilst River
Malmar Inlet
Worsto
Carthwait
Pelgrin Forest
Askelon
Malmar
Bellavee
Wilst
Ervin
High Temple
Celbereo Wall
Herwind
Narramor
Toryn River
Hinsenby
Erlott
Fiskill Mountai
Sipleth
Manerlin
Wilderlan
Endonny
Holy Island
Persch
Gerfallen
Suth lan
Garre
Dorn
Kelkin Mts.
Drin
Heradrin

Bestow

Tildeen

Tuck

brey

Ruined
City
Dekra

Dekra Mts.

Andraj

Obreyson

Wilderlands

Manderlin

Wilderlands

Elsendor

Flinn

Lower Flinn

Wilderby
(Walled
City)

Harsh

Andraj

Mansandor

Valdai

Halidom

Elsendor

ONE

THE NEW snow lay deep and undisturbed beneath the silver light of a dawning sky. Overhead, a raven surveyed a silent landscape as its black wings feathered the cold, thin air. The bird's rasping call was the only sound to be heard for miles, breaking the frozen solitude in irregular staccato. All around, the land lay asleep in the depths of winter.

Every bear, every fox, hare, and squirrel was warm in its rustic nest. Cattle and horses stood contented in their stalls, heads drooping in slumber, or quietly munching the first of the day's provender. In the country, smoke drifted from peasant huts into the windless sky from rough-hewn chimneys, sent aloft from hearth fires tended through the night. The village, clustered close about the mighty walls of Askelon Castle, slept in pristine splendor, a princess safe in the arms of her protector.

All through the land nothing moved, nothing stirred, save the raven wheeling slowly overhead.

Quentin lay shivering in his cell, a huddled ball topped by a thin woolen blanket which he clasped tightly around his ears in a resolute effort to keep out the night chill. He had been awake, and cold, long before the sullen sky showed its drab gray through the lone slit of a window high up in his cell. Now the gloom had receded sufficiently to make out the dim outlines of the simple objects that furnished his bare apartment.

Next to the straw pallet where he slept stood a sturdy oaken stool, made by the hand of a local peasant. A table of the same craft stood against the wall opposite his bed, containing his few personal articles: a clay bowl for his supper, a candle in a wooden holder, a small bell for his prayers, and a parchment scroll on which was written all the rules and observances of his acolyte's office and which, after almost three years, Quentin was still struggling to memorize.

From somewhere in the inner recesses of the temple the chime of a bell sounded. Quentin groaned, then jumped up in bed, pulling the blanket around his shoulders. Today was the day, he remembered. The day of a great change. He wondered what it would be, for as closely as he had followed the portents he could not guess it.

All the omens had pointed to a change: the ring around the moon for three nights before the snow, the storm itself coming on his name day, a spider he'd seen busily constructing a web across his door (although that had been some time ago, he hadn't forgotten).

There was no doubt—a change was forecast.

Its exact nature remained a mystery, but such was often the pleasure of the gods to leave part of the prophecy hidden. He had at last deduced the date of the change by a dream in which he had climbed a high mountain and then had leaped from its very pinnacle and sailed out into space, not falling but flying. Flying dreams were always lucky. His lucky day was always a holy day and this day, the feast of Kamali—admittedly a minor holy day— was nevertheless the first holy day to have fallen since his dream.

Today, without question, was the eventful day; the tokens were indisputable. Quentin reviewed them in his mind as he hurriedly threw his coarse, heavy acolyte's robe over his head of close-cropped brown hair. He stuffed his feet into baggy stockings and laced the thongs of his sandals around them tightly. Then, grabbing his prayer bell, he dashed out of the cubicle and into the dark, chilly corridor beyond.

Quentin was half-way down the high-arched passageway when another bell sounded. A deep resonant peal rang out in three short intervals. A brief pause. And then three again. Quentin puzzled the meaning of this bell; he had not heard it before that he could remember.

Suddenly it came to him. Alarm!

He stopped, confused. As he turned to run toward the sound of the bell he collided blindly with the round, fully padded form of Biorkis, one of the elder priests.

"Oof lad!" cried the priest good-naturedly. "No need for panic."

"That was the alarm bell just now!" cried Quentin, inching around the puffing priest. "We must hurry!"

"No need. The servants of Ariel do not run. Besides," he added with a wink, "that was a summons bell. Not the alarm." Quentin suddenly felt very foolish. He felt his face coloring; his eyes sought the stone flagging at his feet. The jovial priest placed a heavy arm on his young shoulders. "Come, we will see what drags us from our warm slumbers so early on this chill morning."

The two moved off down the corridor together and shortly came to the vast entrance hall of the temple. A cold, stinging wind was rushing through the huge open doors at the entrance. A priest in a scarlet cassock, one of the order of temple guards, was already pulling the giant wooden doors closed. Three other priests stood round a large, shapeless bundle lying at their feet on the floor. Whatever it was, the dark bundle, uncertain in the dim morning light, had been recently dragged in from the outdoors— a trail of snow attested to the fact, as did the snow-encrusted bundle itself.

Closer, Quentin saw the bundle was that of a human form wrapped heavily against the cold. The priests were now bending over the inert shape which to all appearances seemed dead. Biorkis placed a warning hand on Quentin's arm and stepped slowly forward.

"What is this, good brothers? A wayward pilgrim early to the shrine?"

"This is no pilgrim by the look of him," said the guard

rubbing his hands to restore the warmth. "More likely a beggar for our feastday orts."

"Then he shall have them," replied Biorkis.

"He is past nourishment," observed Izash, the eldest priest of the temple whose symbol of office was a long braided beard. "Or, he very soon will be, I fear." He tapped his sacred white rod and stirred the air in front of him, indicating that the man should be turned over the better to see his face.

Two junior priests knelt over the lifeless form and gingerly tugged at the wider part of the bundle which formed the man's shoulders. The priests, overly careful not to defile themselves lest they should find themselves touching a dead body, ineffectually jerked at the corners of the rough fur skins the man wore for warmth. Biorkis watched the timid struggle with impatience, finally exploding, "Get out of the way! I'm not afraid of Azrael; my hands have touched worse!" He stooped over the body and rolled it into his arms.

Quentin, moving around the perimeter for a better look, gasped at the sight. The man's face was ashen white and his lips, pressed together in a thin line, were blue. He appeared completely frozen. But even as Quentin looked on fearfully the man's gray eyelids flickered. Biorkis, noticing the remnant of life, ordered one of the junior priests away. "Bring wine, brother. Hurry! And a vial of unction." And to the rest he directed, "Here, now! Help me loosen his wraps. We may pull him back from Heoth yet."

The priests fell upon the motionless figure, carefully unwrapping the layers of clothing. Their astonishment showed visibly in their faces when they had finished, and in the face of the priest who had just then returned with the wine and unguent.

There on the floor before them lay a knight in rude battle dress. His head was encased in a leather helm with criss-crossed bands of iron. His torso carried a breastplate of the same make and material, but studded with short spikes, and his forearms and shins were sheathed in studded guards.

Biorkis, still holding the man's head, tugged at the strap fastening the helmet. It rolled free, clanking upon the stone floor, and a murmur went up from those surrounding. Quentin looked away. The knight's head was a mass of blood. An open wound gaped just over his temple where skin and bone had been crushed by a sharp blow.

The kind priest knelt with the knight's head on his knees and pushed the man's matted hair from his forehead. He gently loosed the bindings of the breastplate and two priests set it aside. A groan emerged from the man's throat, shallow at first then gaining in strength.

"The vial," Biorkis ordered. Snatching it up and dipping two fingers into the salve, the priest smoothed the healing ointment upon the man's face. Its aromatic vapors produced an immediate result, for the soldier's eyes flickered again and then snapped open as those of a man struggling out of a dream.

"So, he is to be with us a little longer," said Izash. "Give him some wine. He may tell us of his errand." The old priest stepped closer and leaned low on his staff to better hear what might transpire.

Biorkis administered the wine as the knight, without strength enough to tilt his head, allowed the liquor to be poured down his throat. In Biorkis' hands the wine seemed to have a magical effect. Color seeped slowly back into the man's face and his breathing now deepened where before there had been no discernible breath at all.

"Welcome, good soldier." Izash addressed the knight respectfully. "If you feel like talking perhaps you could tell us whence you come."

The fair-haired knight rolled his eyes and attempted to twist his head in the direction of the speaker. The effort brought a wave of pain that washed full across his features. He sank back into Biorkis' lap.

By now other priests had gathered close about, drawn by the summons. They spoke in low voices with one another, speculating upon the strange visitor that lay before them. The knight opened his eyes again and they shone bright and hard as if strength or will was returning. He opened his mouth to speak; his jaw worked the air but no sound came forth.

"More wine," Biorkis called. As the cup was handed to him

the plump priest tugged out a pouch from the folds of his robe. He dipped into the small leather bag and sprinkled a pinch of the contents into the drink. He then lowered the cup to the knight's lips once more. The prostrate man drank more readily, and finishing, paused before attempting to speak again.

"Now, sir, enlighten an old busybody—if you do not have good reason to conceal your office." Izash inclined his old head; his white beard fell almost to the floor. A slight smile creased his lined face as if to coax the words forth with kindness.

"I am Ronsard," the knight's voice cracked. Another sip of wine followed that exertion. His eyes, steel gray in the silver light, looked around at the tight circle of faces bent over him. "Where am I?" he asked quietly.

"You are among friends, sir," said Biorkis. "This is the holy temple of Ariel, and we are his humble servants. You may speak freely. No harm can befall you here."

As if reassured by the soothing words the knight licked his lips and said with as much strength as he could muster, "I am come from the King."

The words were simple, but they struck the ears of the listeners like thunder. The King! He comes from the King! The murmur rose to echo from the high vaulted arches of the temple.

Only Izash, still leaning upon his rod, seemed unimpressed. "Our king? Or someone else's?" the elderly priest asked.

"King Eskevar," the fallen knight answered with spirit.

The name sent another ripple through the gathered priests. The King had been absent so long, his name unheard among his own countrymen, that hearing it now brought hope to all gathered there.

"And what of the King?" the old priest continued. His probing had a method to it; he was occupying the knight, making him forget his wounds and the pain which twisted his rugged features.

"That I cannot say—it is for the Queen's ears. I am duty bound to deliver my charge to her alone." The fighting man gulped air and licked his lips again. "I was waylaid last night. Ambushed by outlaws who now sleep with the snow."

The knight looked up at the faces of the priests bending over him. Fresh blood oozed from his wound, opened again by his exercise.

"Worry not," said Biorkis soothingly. "You will remain with us until you are able to resume your errand." He motioned to several of the younger priests to help him lift the soldier onto a pallet which had been brought. "No one will bother you for the details of your mission. Your secret is safe within these walls. Rest now. I like not the look of that wound."

"No!" the knight shouted hoarsely, his face contorted in agony. Then in a queer, rasping whisper, "I'm dying. You must deliver my message to the Queen. It must not wait."

Biorkis stooped with the knight's head gently in his hands as the man was carefully transferred to the pallet. The knight clutched the wooden sides of the bed and raised himself upon his elbows. Blood ran freely down the side of his head and neck, staining his green tunic a dull, rusty gray.

"You must help me!" he demanded. "One of you must go in my stead to the Queen." With that he fell back in a swoon upon his bed. The color had run from his face. He appeared dead to those who looked on in fear and wonder.

The priests glanced from one to another helplessly. Biorkis stood, his hands dripping with the knight's fresh blood. He searched the faces of his brothers and gauged the worry there. Then he stepped close to Izash who motioned him aside.

"Here is an unwanted problem," the old priest observed. "I see no help we can offer, save all that is in our power to heal his wounds and send him speedily on his way."

"The delay—what of that?"

"It cannot be helped, I'm afraid."

"Yet, we may do all in our art to restore him and still he may die," Biorkis objected. "If it is not too late already." Something in the knight's voice, his look, spoke to Biorkis. The man had certainly overcome crushing odds, and even now refused his deathbed on the strength of his message alone. Whatever the tidings, this news of the king was of the highest importance. More important than life itself.

At that moment the knight regained consciousness. He was now too weakened to raise himself up, however. A low moan escaped his clenched teeth. "He is with us still," said Izash. "How persistent this courier is."

Biorkis and the old priest placed their heads close to the knight's. "Good Ronsard," Biorkis whispered. "Do not tax yourself further for your life's sake. We possess great power over disease and injury. We have often delivered a soul from Manes' hands. Rest now. We will do all to heal your wounds and strengthen you to your purpose."

"No!" the knight objected with surprising force. "There's no time. One of you must ride to the Queen." His eyes implored the priest.

"Sir, you do not know what you ask," Izash answered. He waved an arm to include the whole of the assembled priests. "We are under sacred vows and cannot leave the temple, except on pilgrimage, or matters of the highest sacred import. The fate of nations, kings and powers concerns us not. We serve only the god Ariel; we are his subjects alone."

Biorkis looked sadly down upon the dying man. "He speaks the cold heart of the oath we have taken. My own heart says, 'Go,' but I cannot. For to leave the temple on this errand would mean breaking our sacred vows. Any priest who did that would forfeit his whole life's work and his soul's eternal happiness. There are none here who would risk that, nor would I ask it of them."

The priests nodded solemnly in agreement. Some shrugged and turned away lest they be drafted to the task, others held out their hands in helpless supplication.

"Will not one of you match your life with mine? Will no one risk the displeasure of the god to save the King?" The knight's challenge sounded loud in the ears of those around him although he'd spoken barely a whisper.

"I will go," said a small, uncertain voice.

Biorkis, Izash, and the other priests turned toward the voice. There in the shadow of an arch stood the slight figure belonging to the voice. The figure stepped slowly forward to stand by the side of the dying knight.

"You, Quentin?" Biorkis asked in amazement; the others whispered behind their hands. "You would go?"

TWO

THE MIGHTY horse carried his insignificant rider with tireless ease. Trained in the hard school of combat, Balder was used to bearing the weight of grown men in full armor upon his broad back. Quentin, clinging like a cold leaf to the magnificent animal's neck, was scarcely a burden at all.

The day was young and although still overcast as on the day previous, the low cloud covering showed signs of breaking up before long. The wind had freshened, sending whirling white clouds across the tops of the drifts with every fitful gust. Each blast sent a shiver along Quentin's ribs. He wondered whether he would ever be warm again. But he did not greatly mind the discomfort, for at last the change long foretold was in motion. Where it would lead, what it would mean, he did not know. For the present he was caught up in the adventure of it, yet he kept his eyes sharp to any omen which might present itself.

Nothing presented itself to his gaze except a vast expanse of white, unbroken except by irregular dark lumps mushrooming out of the snow. These were the peasant huts, and sometimes he saw a face peer at him from around the corner of a doorpost, or a timid wave acknowledged his presence as a bent form hobbled through the snow under a burden of firewood.

In his seven years' cloister within the temple, the land, it seemed to Quentin, had changed little. Yet it had changed.

There was something unmistakable in the eyes of the peasants he met, something which struck him fresh each time he saw it. Was it fear?

The thought gave him an uneasy feeling. Was something loose in the land which caused these simple people to be afraid?

The great chestnut war horse plodded steadily on, his hooves silenced by the cushion of snow. Billows of steam spouted from the animal's nostrils as its hot breath touched the icy air. Quentin turned his thoughts back on the brief procession of events which had placed him in the saddle of Ronsard, the King's knight.

There had been a long, intemperate discussion following his spontaneous offer to assist the knight in accomplishing his mission. Everyone concerned—Biorkis, Izash, the other priests, and even the knight himself—had been against it. And still, when all the facts were laid end to end, there was no better plan. Quentin would go at once allowing only a day's rest and feeding for the horse. The animal had been found patiently standing in the outer courtyard of the temple where his master had left him before climbing and then collapsing upon the outer steps. It was the horse's whinny to his fallen rider that had alerted the temple guards who then discovered the wounded, half-frozen knight.

Reluctantly, Biorkis had given his approval to the enterprise, for although his young age was against him, Quentin was the only logical choice. He was merely an acolyte, not a priest, as yet not having taken his vows or completed his initiation—a process which normally encompassed twenty years or more. Quentin had completed only seven years of instruction. At fifteen he still had years of study ahead of him; others his own age were already novitiates. The road to becoming a priest was a long one; most began it while still small children. Quentin, although dedicated to his calling at age eight, had come to it late.

Now that career was behind him. Never again would he be allowed to return to the temple, except as a dutiful worshipper begging some boon from the god. Ariel was a jealous god; once you had turned away he knew you no more. Only by distinguishing himself in some act of great heroism could Quentin hope to regain the god's favor. That he vowed he would do—just as soon as he could.

The journey from Narramoor, the holy city, to Askelon, the King's stronghold, was a matter of two days by horse. The temple, according to the most ancient customs of the realm of Mensandor, was built in the high foothills overlooking the land it sheltered with its prayers. In the spring and early summer pilgrims came from all over the country to ask prayers for good crops and healthy livestock. Each town and village also had a small temple or prayerhouse which was presided over by one or more priests depending upon the need, but most worshippers preferred to make the pilgrimage to the High Temple at least once a year, more often if it could be arranged.

The road, winding down from the steep hills beneath the jagged old mountains of the Fiskill, was not overwide but it was well maintained—at least it had been up to the time of the King's departure. Quentin remembered nothing of the King's leave-taking, being but a babe in arms at the time. But, in the years since, he had heard retold the vivid accounts of the splendor of that parting.

The King, dressed in full battle regalia emblazoned with the royal insignia—a terrible, twisting red dragon—had led his loyal warriors out through the giant gates of his castle. Amidst a thousand fluttering banners and the call of a thousand trumpets from the high battlements, the King's army marched through streets lined with cheering crowds and out onto the plains of Askelon. It was said the procession lasted half a day, so many men followed in his train.

The entourage had traveled to Hinsen-by-the-sea, or Hinsenby as it was usually known, had boarded sturdy warships awaiting them in Hinsen harbor, and had sailed forth. The ships were provided by King Selric of the small island country of Drin, whose people were known to produce the world's greatest sailors.

Other kings from other lands joined them, swelling their forces beyond anything ever before seen or imagined. They were going to meet the barbaric Urd, a race of creatures, one scarcely dared to call them human, so savage, so brutal their very existence imperiled all other men. The Urd, united under their king Gorr, had risen in defiance of all civilized order vowing to extinguish or make slaves of other nations. They would rule the world.

The twelve kings of the civilized nations had met and declared war upon Gorr, sailing to meet and join battle with him in his own lands before the evil lord had time to mass his army against them in theirs.

The fighting had begun in early spring and by summer it looked as though the campaign would conclude before winter set in, so successful were the united kings' first encounters. The wily Gorr, seeing his warriors melt before the terrible onslaught, retreated to his massive walled fortress, Golgor. There the stubborn renegade dug in, establishing himself with a strength and fervor no one could have foretold. From Golgor the raving giant taunted the valiant forces of the kings; his raiding parties, though often beaten back with heavy losses, continually wore down their defenses. Winter found the enemies deadlocked.

The war, so easily won in the spring, dragged on and on. Years passed and the war continued. Thousands of men died in that hideous country never to see friends or loved ones again. Several of the kings pulled out in the seventh year, returning home with the tattered remains of their once-proud armies. But Eskevar, Selric, Brandon, Calwitha, and Troen fought on.

For all Quentin knew they fought on still.

Quentin raised his eyes to the horizon. He could see, it seemed, forever; the land fell away on every side unobscured except for the occasional looming shape of a gigantic boulder or jutting escarpment which rose abruptly at intervals throughout the hills. But the slim rider was leaving the hills behind, and the dark line of the forest drew ever nearer as if by magic.

Askelon, his destination, stood on the far side of the forest. Beyond that to the west lay the flatlands and the farming towns, and cities of the plains, Bellavee being chief among these.

To the far north was Woodsend, a substantial village of farmers and craftsmen firmly planted on the banks of the Wilst River, a long, lazy branch sprung from the Arvin whose headwaters originated, as did all the rivers which flowed throughout the realm, in the high Fiskill Mountains above Narramoor. At his back rose the imposing mountains themselves, and beyond them the regions of Suthland to the south and Obrey to the north.

These were the Wilderlands, remote and virtually uncharted areas inhabited only by wild animals and even wilder men, the Dher, or Jher as they were often called.

The Jher were the lingering descendants of the most primitive dwellers of the land. They still clung like moss on weathered rock to their obscure ways, changing not at all since anyone could remember.

They were said to possess many strange powers—gifts which more disposed them toward the wild creatures with whom they shared their rough lands than rendered them acceptable companions for civilized human beings. The Jher kept to themselves for the most part, and were alike left alone by one and all. Quentin, like most younger people, had never seen one. They existed for him as characters out of children's stories, told to frighten and induce obedience in youngsters showing reluctance to behave themselves.

Quentin stirred from his meditation on these and other things to notice that it was approaching midday. He began looking for a sheltered place to stop where he might eat a morsel and rest the horse, who appeared not the least bit taxed for his exertion. The weak winter sun which had been struggling to burn through the hazy overcast all morning suddenly flared high overhead, like a hot poker wearing through sackcloth. Instantly the landscape was transformed from its ghostly pall into dazzling brilliance.

With the sun, although seemingly small and distant, came heat. At least Quentin imagined that he felt warmed, felt the heat spreading over his back and shoulders and seeping through his thick, fur-lined cap. Ahead he spotted a small stand of birch trees encircled by a tangle of forlorn shrubbery and several small ever-greens. The site offered a slight shelter from the biting wind which, now that the sun was out, whipped more sharply.

Quentin found the sun good company as he reined the horse aside and tied him to a nearby branch. Clambering down from his steed, the boy fumbled in the shallow rucksack which Biorkis had had made up for him and filled with provisions for the trip. He fished out a small loaf of seed cake and, throwing his cloak beneath him, sat down to eat his meal.

The sun played upon his face, warming the frozen tips of his nose and ears. Quentin removed his hat and turned his face to the thawing warmth. His mind skipped back once more to the bustle and confusion of his leaving; he rehearsed again, as one hundred times before, his instructions. Go to the hermit of Pelgrin Forest. Do not stop, except to eat and to rest the horse. Do not speak to anyone. Do not deliver the letter to anyone but the Queen.

That last order would be the most difficult. But Ronsard, in his final act before losing consciousness, had given his dagger to be used to gain audience. The knight's golden dagger would be recognized and would speak for the gravity of the occasion.

Quentin was not as distracted by his impending reception at court as he might have been. He was far more curious, and frightened—but curiosity held the better of his fears, to be sure—over the mysterious communication which was now sewn inside his plain, green jerkin. He absent-mindedly patted the place where it lay next to his ribs. What could it contain? What could be so important?

And yet, as intrigued as he was by the enigma he carried, a part of his mind was worrying over another problem like a hound with a gristle bone—an item he did not want to consider in any form at all: his future. He avoided the thought like a pain, yet it gnawed at the edges of his consciousness never far from remem-brance. Quentin delicately pushed the question aside every time it intruded into his thoughts . . . "What are you going to do after you have delivered the letter?"

The lad had no answer for that question, or the hundred others of a similar theme which assailed him at every turn. He felt himself beginning to dread the completion of his mission more with every mile. He wished, and it was not a new wish, that he had never stepped forward—he had regretted it as soon as he had done it.

But it was as if he had no will of his own. He felt compelled by something outside himself to respond to the dying knight's plea. Perhaps the god Ariel had thrust him forward. Perhaps he had merely been caught up in the awful urgency of the moment. Besides, the omens had foretold . . . Ah, but when did omens ever run true?

Eyes closed, face to the sun, Quentin munched his seed cake, pondering his fate. He suddenly felt a cool touch on his face, as if the sun had blinked. And high above him, he heard the call of a bird. Quentin cracked open one eye, and recoiled from the brightness of the light. Squinting fiercely and shading his face with an outstretched arm, Quentin at last determined the source of the call. At the same instant his heart seized like a clenched fist inside his chest.

There, flying low overhead was the worst omen imaginable: a raven circled just above him casting flittering shadows upon him with its wings.

THREE

THE BLUE, cloud-spattered sky had dissolved into a violet dome flecked with orange and russet wisps, and the shadows had deepened to indigo on the white snow before Quentin found his rest for the evening: the rough log hut of Durwin, the holy hermit of Pelgrin Forest.

The hermit was known among the lowly as one who gave aid to travelers and cared for the peasants and forest folk who often had need of his healing arts. He had once been a priest, but had left to follow a different god, so the local hearsay told. Beyond that nothing much was known about the hermit, except that when his help was required he was never far away. Some also said he possessed many strange powers and listed among his talents the ability to call up dragons from their caves, though no one had ever seen him do it.

It seemed strange to Quentin that Biorkis should know or recommend such a person to help him—even if the aid was only a bed for the night. For Biorkis had given him a silver coin to give the hermit, saying, "Greet this brother in the name of the god, and give him this token." He had placed the coin in his hand. "That will tell him much. And say that Biorkis sends his greetings," he paused, "and that he seeks a brighter light." The priest had turned hurriedly away adding mostly to himself, "That will tell him more."

So, Quentin found himself in the fading twilight of a brilliant winter day. The hut was set off the road a short distance, but completely hidden from view, surrounded as it was by towering oaks, evergreens, and thick hedges of brambly furze. It took Quentin some time to locate the hut, even with the precise directions he had been given.

At last he found it, a low, squattish building which appeared to be mostly roof and chimney. Two small windows looked out on the world and a curious round-topped door closed the entrance. The homely abode was nestled in a hillock at the far end of a natural clearing which gave way to a spacious view of the sky overhead. The ground rose to meet the house on a gentle incline so that one had to climb slightly to reach the front door.

Quentin rode quietly up to the entrance of the hut. Sitting on the horse he could have leaped from his saddle onto the roof with ease. But he chose instead to slide off the animal's broad back and rap with the flat of his hand on the heavy oaken door. He waited uncertainly; his hand had hardly produced any sound at all, and except for the smoke curling slowly from the stone chimney he would have suspected the place abandoned. But someone had been there—the clearing was well trampled with the foot-prints of men and animals in the snow.

Quentin slipped the knight's dagger from its place in his belt beneath his cloak. Holding it by the blade, he banged again on the door, this time with a more satisfactory result. He waited.

The sky was darkening quickly now; the sun was well down. He could feel the cold strengthening its hold on the land. No sound came from inside.

Plucking up his courage, Quentin tried the crude latch and found that with some force it moved. He placed his weight be-hind the door and shoved. The rough-hewn door swung upon its hinges and opened readily. Quentin stumbled quickly in with more ceremony than he had planned, bumping over the threshold as he entered.

The room was a good deal larger than he would have guessed from the outside, and it was sunken well below ground level. Stone steps led into the room which was warm and cozy, lit by the flickering fire left burning in the wide, generous fireplace. About the room stood an odd assemblange of hand-made furni-ture: chairs, tables large and small, stools, a large lumpy bed, and something which surprised Quentin and strangely delighted him: books. Scrolls were heaped upon the tables and stuffed onto latticework shelves. More scrolls than he had ever seen—even in the library of the temple.

All this Quentin took in as his eyes adjusted to the relative gloom of the dark room. He also saw the place was empty of its chief inhabitant. Durwin, apparently, was absent; perhaps on some mercy errand in the forest nearby. Quentin decided to slip in and await the hermit's return, dragging a stool up to the fire burning low upon the hearth.

Quentin did not know whether he was awakened by the sound or the smell. Voices seemed to drone into his conscious-ness from far away. No words could be understood, only the monotonous buzz of two voices talking quietly, but with some enthusiasm. Close by the smell of food, warm and heavily laced with garlic, drifted into his awareness. He opened his eyes.

He was covered by his own cloak and laying a little away from the hearth. Two large figures sat near the fire. One knelt at the edge of the fire stirring a large black pot with a long-handled wooden spoon. The other sat on a stool with his back to him, revealing nothing of his features or stature. Both men were dressed in dark, flowing cloaks. As they talked, their long shadows danced on the far wall of the hut like the animated puppets in a shadow play.

Quentin rolled cautiously up onto his feet. The movement at once caught the eye of the man busy over the bubbling pot. "So it is! Our young friend lives. I told you, Theido," he winked at the other man who twisted round to regard the youngster with a quizzical eye. "I told you my soup would bring him round. Enchanted—bah!"

Embarrassed to have fallen asleep at his post, and now to be the center of such attention, good-natured though it was, Quentin stepped timidly to the fire and addressed himself to both men simultaneously. "I am Quentin, at your service, sirs."

"And we at yours," came the standard reply.

He fumbled at his belt for the silver coin. "I bring this to you with greetings from Biorkis, senior priest of the High Temple." The greeting sounded very stiff and formal, which suited Quentin, unsure as he was about what kind of reception he should expect. Yet, he knew as he placed the silver coin into Durwin's hand that he had nothing to fear from this man.

Durwin's face radiated a kindly light. Bright blue eyes winked out of a hide creased and lined like soft leather, and browned by the sun. Great bushy brown eyebrows, which seemed to have a life of their own, highlighted the hermit's speech and were matched brush for bristle by a sprawling forest of a mustache and beard. Beneath his cloak he wore the simple robes of a priest, but grey rather than brown.

"So it is! The old weasel sends you with this? Does he indeed?" The hermit turned the coin over in his hand thoughtfully. "Well, I don't suppose it can be helped, can it?" Then he turned to Quentin and said, "There is a wider path than many know, though I'm sure you don't have an inkling what I mean." Quentin stared back blankly. "No, of course you don't. Still, he sent you here," the hermit mused to himself.

"Did he tell you anything else?" the holy man asked.

"Only this: that he seeks a brighter light."

At this both men exploded with laughter. The other, who had remained silent, was obviously following the exchange closely. "He said that, did he?" Durwin laughed. "By the gods' beards, there's hope for him yet."

Quentin stood mystified at this outburst. He felt awkward and a little used, relaying jokes of which he knew less than nothing to strangers who laughed at his expense. His frown must have shown them he did not approve of the levity, for Durwin stopped at once and offered the silver coin back to Quentin. "This coin is the symbol of an expelled priest. See," he dug into his clothing and brought out a silver coin on a chain around his neck. "I have one, too."

Quentin took the two coins and examined them; they were the same in every detail except that Durwin's was older and more worn.

"They are temple coins minted for special occasions and given to priests when they die or leave as payment for their service to the god. Some payment, eh?"

"You used to be a priest?" Quentin wondered aloud.

"Yes, of course. Biorkis and I are very good friends; we entered the priesthood together. We grew up together."

"Enough of old times," said the stranger impatiently. "Durwin, introduce me to your guest in proper fashion."

Quentin turned and eyed the dark man, ignored for the most part until now. He was above average in height, Quentin guessed, for squatting on the stool with his limbs folded across themselves he could not tell. His clothes were of a dark, indistinct color and consisted of a long cloak worn loosely over a close-fitting tunic and trousers of the same dark material as the rest. He wore a wide black belt at his waist to which was attached a rather large leather pouch.

But the man's features commanded the better of Quentin's attention. The face was keen in the firelight, bright-eyed and alert. A high forehead rose to meet a head of dark, thick hair swept back and falling almost to his shoulders. The man's sharp nose thrust itself out over a firm mouth that opened upon a set of straight, white teeth. On the whole, the appearance bespoke a man of action and movement, of quick reflexes and perhaps quicker wits.

"Quentin," the ex-priest was saying, "this man whom you are staring at is my old friend Theido, a much welcome and often missed guest in this humble house."

The man dipped his head low in acknowledgment of this courtesy. Quentin bowed stiffly from the waist out of respect. "I am glad to meet you young sir," said Theido. "An expelled priest, I have found, makes a good friend." At this both men laughed again. And though he did not know why, Quentin laughed, too.

The three dined on a thick, tasty soup and black bread, washed down with a heady nut-brown ale which Durwin brewed to perfection. After the day's exercise, Quentin held his own in appetite with the two men and remarked on several occasions that he had never tasted food so good.

After they had eaten they talked. The wandering conversations roamed the length and breadth of the world. It seemed to Quentin that no subject, from bees to bodkins and books, was left untouched. Never had Quentin been party to such fellowship; the temple's strict regulations kept contact between priests very formal and extremely refined. Although he mostly just listened, Quentin found this new realization of friends around the board with good food and conversation fairly intoxicating. He reveled in it and soaked it up. He wished in his heart the night would stretch on forever.

At last Durwin stood and shook his tired head. "Merry men all! We must to bed. We will talk some more tomorrow."

"I must leave tomorrow," said Quentin, having entirely forgotten his mission. He peered apprehensively into the faces of the two men who regarded him carefully.

"So soon?" replied Durwin. "I thought you would stay a little. I would like to show you what I have been doing since I left the temple."

"And how will you be going?" Theido asked.

"My horse!" Quentin shrieked. He had also cleanly forgotten about his animal in the friendly interchange around the hermit's table. He dashed to the door and heaved it open, peering outside into the frigid, black night. There was nothing to be seen of the horse. With a look of horror he turned to the men. "I have lost him!"

"What did he look like?" Theido asked with a wink.

"He was a chestnut; the most beautiful horse I have ever seen. Now I have lost him."

"Follow me," Durwin commanded lightly. "I think we will find he has not wandered far." The hermit turned and disappeared behind a standing partition lined with scrolls. Quentin ducked behind the partition and discovered that it concealed another room, the entrance of which was draped over with an immense bearskin. The room was dark and quiet, but warm and smelling strongly of hay and horses. Durwin carried a stubby candle and with it lit a pitch torch leaning in its holder on the wall. The sooty flame guttered and smoked furiously, then took hold and threw a steady light into the room.

This annex to the hermit's lodge was a small cave. Durwin's house had been built right up against the cave's entrance, which explained the smooth stone floor of the hermit's cottage. In the pale light of the torch Quentin could see his steed alongside two other slightly smaller animals, nose down in a heap of sweet fennel that had been thrown down for them. Relieved and somewhat embarrassed, Quentin thanked his host for his thoughtfulness.

"We guessed you were no true horseman," remarked Theido good-naturedly, "when we saw him standing in front of the cottage unbound. A lesser animal would have wandered off in search of refreshment. Your horse is well-trained, and I surmise you are not his master."

Quentin shook his head sadly. "He belongs to another—or did . . ."

"Enough! We will sleep now and talk of these things in the morning—which, unless I miss my guess, is not far hence."

FOUR

IT HAD been decided, quite without Quentin's opinion but not altogether against his approval, that Theido would accompany him on the remainder of his journey. This had been discussed over a cheerful breakfast of hot porridge and milk, with bread dipped in honey. Quentin ate with unusual alacrity, his high spirits charged by a renewed sense of adventure.

The two men had shown considerable surprise that Quentin had made it this far through the forest without incident. Theido had said, "Hereabouts, Pelgrin shelters outlaws of every description. Some there are who might set a high value on your horse," he chuckled, and Durwin added, "And not so much on his rider."

"They wouldn't dare touch me," Quentin announced carelessly, full of himself and his own high spirits. "I carry a letter for the Queen."

At this news, the first bare hint of Quentin's clandestine errand, both men nearly jumped from their seats. Quentin's jaw snapped shut in alarm when he realized he had ruined his secret. "The Queen?" said Theido, recovering himself instantly. "What business might you have with the Queen, my boy?"

Now Quentin became guarded and secretive. "That is my

business and none of yours," he said a little angrily, though the
anger was for his own carelessness and not his questioner.

"This letter might not be from the King?" Theido pursued.

"I'll tell you no more about it, sir," Quentin retorted.

Here Durwin interposed. "Young sir, while it may not occur
to you at once, my friend and I have known for some time that
you were about a matter of some importance. Your horse, for
example, is a champion's own, and not the mount of an acolyte.
I'll wager that your expulsion from the temple was due not to any
willful breach of your sacred vows, but rather out of necessity to
the very errand you engage." Durwin paused to regard Quentin
carefully. Quentin colored somewhat under the hermit's scrutiny
and the sudden knowledge that he was so transparent. "I see I
am not far wrong in my address."

"Lad, you can trust us. We mean you no harm. I think you
will find no two better men who would hold your secret as their
own though their lives were forfeit." Theido spoke quietly and
with deep assurance. Quentin believed the tall stranger, but sat
in sullen silence, not knowing whether to speak further or hold.

"You possess a strength of purpose and bravery enough for
any two your size," Durwin continued. "But there are events
afoot against which bravery and strength alone are no match. I
think Biorkis realized this and sent you to me, hoping I would
guess the seriousness of your mission and help you if I could.
Perhaps the god himself prompted you to spill your secret in our
hearing just now, to save you from harm."

"Is it so dangerous, then, for a subject to confer with his
Queen?" Quentin asked sullenly.

Both men nodded in silence. Theido replied, "Seeing the
Queen is but a trifle, providing you were able to obtain entrance
to the castle alive. There are those who would keep her ignorant
of outside affairs, the better to plant their own evil seeds."

"Without our help you might never reach the Queen. Prince
Jaspin would get you if an outlaw band did not."

"Prince Jaspin?" Quentin wondered that he had never heard
the name.

"Prince Jaspin," Durwin explained, "is King Eskevar's younger brother. He has designs upon the throne of Askelon; already he foments deeds of great impudence and treachery with increasing boldness. Honest men are afraid for their lands and lives if they dare stand against him. Many nobles have lost all to the greedy hound, who did not willingly join in his intrigues."

Quentin turned all this shocking information over in his mind, but found himself at a loss to know what to do. He at last decided to trust the former priest and his unusual friend and share with them the rest of his secret.

"I am going to see the Queen," he stated slowly, "to give her a message of importance. Two days ago a wounded knight came to the temple demanding our aid. He had been set upon by outlaws and was dying. I volunteered to take the message which was written in secret and sealed. It is his horse I ride, and this is his dagger." Quentin drew back his cloak to reveal the knife's gold handle.

"The knight—do you know his name?" Theido asked quickly.

"It was Ronsard."

"Ronsard! You can be certain?"

"Yes, I saw everything. He said his name and asked for someone to take the message to the Queen. I volunteered."

"Then you are even braver than we thought," said Durwin.

"The message—it comes from the King, then," said Theido. "Ronsard is one of his personal bodyguards; a knight unequaled in strength and valor." He looked at Quentin sadly. "He is dead, you say?"

"Yes—that is," Quentin hesitated, "I think so. I dared not wait to see the end, but he was very near death when I left." Quentin fell silent remembering vividly the events that had brought him hither. He felt afraid and very alone. "I can trust you . . . you'll not deceive me? I promised not to tell . . ."

Durwin rose from his seat and came around the table and placed his hand upon Quentin's shoulder. "My son, you have done the Queen a great service by sharing your secret with us. Quite possibly you have rendered your King an even greater

service. Ronsard, I think, would be no less pleased with this
outcome if he had thought of it himself."

"The hermit speaks the truth," said Theido. "But now we
must make plans to deliver your message. The outlaws will be
the least of our worries."

Theido and Quentin left the hermit's cottage about midday
as a light snow of fitful flakes drifted down to lose themselves in
the whiteness already deep upon the ground. Durwin remained
behind to tend to his usual affairs saying, "I shall be waiting with
hot soup and a cold drink when you return; I would only slow
you down otherwise." As they led their horses back along the
narrow track to the road they heard his voice loud in the winter
stillness calling, "The god be with you and speed your safe return!"

"Who is the god Durwin serves?" Quentin asked after they
had ridden several minutes in silence, each lost to his own
thoughts.

Theido seemed to consider this question and answered at
length, "I do not know that Durwin has ever spoken his name—
it may be that he does not have one."

A nameless god? The thought occupied Quentin for a long
time.

They rode through the forest, a dense, old tangle of ancient
oaks that wove huge branches overhead in a stark, intertwining
canopy of bare limbs. Here and there a stand of finger-thin pines
shot upward through the spreading branches of the oaks to find
the light above.

The horses moved easily through the snow which had not
drifted to any depth upon the forest floor. Theido rode ahead on
his quick, brown palfrey and Quentin, astride the mighty Balder,
followed not far behind at his right shoulder. Quentin listened to
the forest sounds: snow sliding off the branches of trees with a
soft *plop*, the creak of a bough shifting in the cold, a lone bird call
sharp and distinct in the distance. Even the quiet was full of
sounds when one listened.

"Do you think we will meet with any outlaws?" Quentin asked after awhile, remembering what had been said earlier.

"We should hope that we meet nothing but the trees and the snow. But there are some outlaws here who are more honest than you or I, men driven to the refuge of the forest by Prince Jaspin and his thieving rascals." This was spoken with a quiet defiance which Quentin could easily apprehend. However, there was something else in the dark man's tone that he could not guess. "If we chance upon anyone in this wood pray that he serves no lord but the Dragon King," Theido continued. "I am not without reputation among such men."

"Perhaps the snow will keep them inside today," Quentin observed. Yet, even as he spoke the clouds overhead showed signs of scattering. The last few flakes drifted down slowly.

"Yes, perhaps. Although, a traveler is a welcome sight these days. Many who once traveled abroad on business have taken to hiring armed escorts, or banding together in the hope that numbers alone will daunt the robbers. Most avoid the forest altogether, and those lucky enough to pass unharmed are nonetheless marked well. You, my young friend, were very lucky to have escaped notice thus far. Were you not afraid?"

"I did not know they had become such a serious problem—these robbers."

"News does not travel to the mountaintop, eh? The gods and their servants care not what takes place in the world of men?" he laughed strangely. "Mensandor is besieged by trouble; once-honest men turn upon one another; innocent blood is shed by day. These are grave times."

"I had not heard . . . ," replied Quentin, as if to defend himself. Although from what he did not know.

"I suppose not. Maybe it is better that way—innocence is a gift. Who knows, you might never have volunteered for such an errand if you had known what lay ahead."

At last, with only an hour of daylight left, the forest began to dwindle, becoming more sparse and open. Then quite unexpectedly the two riders were free of it. And there, across a broad valley cut through by a deep, narrow stream, rose the soaring battlements of Askelon.

The King's stronghold sat upon the crown of a hill glittering in the fading light. Its tall towers commanded a view clear to the horizon and could in turn be seen for miles in every direction. With the crimson evening light behind it, the mighty fortress loomed dark and menacing, itself a fantastic dragon curled upon its stone couch. Quentin shivered in his saddle. Long had he dreamed of this sight; now he was seeing it.

"They say this castle is the oldest thing upon the land made by men," said Theido. "Of all the ancient wonders only Askelon survives. King Celbercor, when he came to this country, laid the cornerstone himself. It was not finished until a thousand years later. It will house fifty thousand fighting men, and horses for half that number; there is not another fortress made by man that is its equal. It has weathered siege upon siege and war upon war. Those walls stood when our father's fathers were babes, and they will stand when we are dust in our graves."

"Has it never been conquered?"

"Never, at least not from without, not by force. But intrigue—the fighting *within*—has laid many a king low. Even those great walls cannot stop deceit."

The two descended the gentle slope of the hill and splashed quickly across the stream. Already the last light of day failed them. But lights were twinkling in the village that crowded close beneath Askelon's protective ramparts. As they moved closer the great dark shape above them became lost to the night, a mountain vanishing behind a shadow. The lights showing rosey from the windows drawing nearer with every step threw warm light upon the snow. Quentin heard voices from within the houses they passed, and occasionally the yeasty smell of hot bread would meet his nostrils or the tang of meat basted over an open hearth fire. Suddenly he felt very tired and hungry.

"Will we go to the Queen directly?"

"No, I think not. Tomorrow will be soon enough. I want to find out how things sit at court these days. It has been some time since I was here." He paused, reining up his horse so that Quentin could draw abreast of him. He spoke in a lowered tone, "Tonight, you are my nephew—if anyone should be curious. Speak only if spoken to, and say nothing about the Queen or the King to anyone at all. Watch me at all times, do you understand?"

Quentin nodded quickly. "All right, then," continued Theido in a more relaxed voice, "How about some supper?"

Quentin glanced up and saw that they had stopped outside an inn of some size. A weathered sign hung over the door which bid travelers welcome, and it sported the painted likeness of someone or something Quentin could not quite make out.

As they dismounted, the door burst open and a short man in a short tunic and pantaloons with a white cloth wrapped around his bulging middle came bustling forward. "Welcome! Welcome!" the man chirped. "Supper is just being laid. If you hurry you may yet find places at the board! Quickly now! Never mind, I'll take care of your horses."

"Very kind of you, Milcher," said Theido with a chuckle. "You're as blind as ever—you don't even know who it is you're dragging in out of the night. Nor do you care!"

"By the gods! Is that Theido?" The man came closer and peered into the tall traveler's face. "Yes, of course. I knew it was you. Recognized your voice. Come in, come in. Too cold out here to be wagging the tongue. In with you! In with you both!" He took the reins from their hands and led the horses away behind the large, rambling structure. "Hurry now, supper is just being laid!" he called out as he disappeared around the corner.

Theido and Quentin stepped up to the entrance and as Theido shoved open the broad door he placed a hand on Quentin's shoulder. "Remember what I told you." He laid a long finger to his lips. Quentin nodded with a furtive smile.

"Yes . . . uncle."

FIVE

THE ROOM was loud with voices raised and the clink of pewter ale jars. Smoke from the candles upon the table, from torches on the wall, and from the improperly-drafted fire in the huge fireplace filled the low-beamed room. The scene was at once jolly and reckless, boisterous and enthusiastic. Quentin found himself grinning heartily not ten steps inside the door.

Theido propelled them both toward a long table standing just a few paces from the hearth. Contrary to what Milcher had insinuated, there were plenty of places at the table; most of the guests were taking liquid nourishment this evening. But the innkeeper had been right—they were just in time. No sooner had they settled themselves upon the rough bench at a further end of the table than platters of steaming food appeared. The heaping plates of meat and vegetables and several kinds of bread and cheese were served by a stout woman with a ready smile and red cheeks and a thin, gawky boy who lurched clumsily as he smacked the pewter plates down. "Careful, Otho!" called the woman amiably. "You've had your supper, now let these fine gentlemen eat theirs in peace."

The comical pair retreated to the kitchen then, only to reappear at frequent intervals to pester the diners with more food and drink. "Eat!" the woman scolded. "Eat, eat, eat! Please! You're not eating!"

As the diners finished they left the board to others who sat down in their places. Theido and Quentin, at Theido's command, ate leisurely and with slow deliberation. Theido's watchful gaze swept over the roistering scene, alert to any hint of discovery. But even his quick eyes failed to see a small, dark man appear at the door like a shadow and slink into a darkened corner. The spy left moments later, undetected.

After a while Milcher, the busy little proprietor of the inn, stepped around to see how his newest guests were accommodated. "You'll be staying the night with us this time, I trust?" he asked.

"Yes, you have us at your mercy," replied Theido with a grin.

"Good. So I thought—I've already bedded your horses for the night. But who's this?" he exclaimed, noticing Quentin's benevolent stare. "I don't think you've introduced me to your friend, Theido." He beamed down upon the boy with a face red from running on his endless errands.

"Haven't I?" said Theido casually. "Well I thought you knew. This is my nephew, Quentin."

"Oh, of course! I knew it all along, didn't I? But my, so big already. Hasn't he grown." With that the little man was off again buzzing like a bee in some other corner of the noisy, crowded room.

"Let us hope no one else takes an interest in my family life tonight. Milcher can talk more than any twenty women. I would rather our little visit was known by as few as possible."

"You think someone might be looking for us?" The thought had just occurred to Quentin.

"It is likely. Whoever killed Ronsard, or had him killed, must know by now that the secret he carried did not die with him. Although we cannot be sure. Maybe they did not know about the message."

"You mean he was not attacked by outlaws?"

"No, lad. Or, at least not altogether. Outlaws may have been hired for the deed, but they would scarcely have gone up against a King's knight without better reason than his purse. Even an outlaw values his life more than that, I think. No, it was probably someone who knew what he carried, or suspected his mission."

"Prince Jaspin maybe?" The intrigues of court were new to Quentin, but he found himself irresistibly drawn to them. His quick mind leaped ahead to all sorts of possible collusions, a fox in a yard of plump chickens.

"Maybe. It would not be the first time he has used others for deeds he would not do himself. But I think there is some other— I cannot say why. I feel it here." He pointed to his stomach. "And now, if you are well stuffed we might as well be off to bed. We must still find a way to guarantee our private audience with the Queen tomorrow."

Milcher returned and bustled them off to their room where his wife, the jolly, red-faced woman, had laid aside the bed clothes of a high sturdy bed. A smaller, more portable pallet had been placed near the fireplace which warmed the apartment. The chamber was square and plain, but private and cozy enough. There was no window, a feature Theido had requested.

"Sleep sound tonight, good guests," said the innkeeper, closing the door to their chamber and tip-toeing quietly away.

"I should just loosen my belt if I were you," warned Theido, as Quentin, seated on the edge of the pallet, began pulling off his tunic. "Tonight we must be ready for anything."

Not far distant, high up on the hill in Askelon castle, a candle burned low in a spacious and richly appointed bed chamber. The floors were of white marble and the walls hung with exquisite tapestries depicting the occupant's favorite pastime: the hunt. A magnificently carved table spread with a vast cloth of dark blue embroidered with thread spun from silver supported a surface littered with maps and scrolls of parchment. At one end of the domed room—for it was the uppermost chamber of the east tower—a crackling fire burned brightly in an ornamented fireplace overhung by a heavy oaken mantle carved with the crest and blazon of a previous resident.

A melancholy figure sat hunched in a great chair with a high back and wings on either side to keep off the draft which seeped through the old castle walls. The chair, more a small throne, was drawn near the fire, but its tenant seemed to draw neither warmth nor comfort from the dancing flames. Instead he stared dejectedly into the blaze, with a tall horn cup of wine, untasted, in his hand.

Prince Jaspin scarcely stirred when the sound of a sharp rap reached his ears from the outer door of his private chambers. A breathless chamberlain presently returned with the news that a certain knight wished audience with him. Upon learning the man's name, Prince Jaspin exploded.

"Send him here directly, you old fool! I have been waiting days to hear his news and you keep him cooling in the corridor like a side of beef. I should have you flayed!"

The chamberlain, well accustomed to his master's fits, did not hear what was said in his absence, leaving at once to bring this most desired visitor before the angry Prince.

"Tell me, Sir Bran, what news? Have you found him yet?" Jaspin leaped from his chair as the knight entered.

"Yes, he is here—in the village," the knight said, bending low from the waist in a quick bow.

"In the village! Where? I shall seize him at once!"

"I would caution you against such a move, your grace. It would attract too much attention. We do not know how many there are—he might have brought some of his men with him. Anyway, 'twere better done in the morning."

"Yes, I suppose you are right." The Prince settled back into the silk cushions of his chair, much pleased by the news. "We must not blunder this opportunity as we did the last." He paused and asked casually, "Are you certain Ronsard is dead?"

"Quite certain." The knight, dressed in a fur-lined cape and gloves over a rich tunic of fine brocaded linen, began removing his gloves. The chamberlain brought a chair and took away his cloak. The powerfully built knight poured himself a goblet of wine from a standing flagon and downed half of it in one swallow. "You do live well, my Prince," he said as he sat down opposite Jaspin.

"Those who support my cause will not need neglect their appetite for finery, I can assure you. Have I told you, Bran, I am thinking of giving you Crandall for your efforts? What would you do with it, I wonder?"

"Give it me and you shall see," retorted the knight.

"You *are* anxious, aren't you," the Prince laughed. "Yes, by and by we shall see. I would give it to you now, only that spoiler Theido—or whatever he calls himself—is still loose and roaming about. We cannot have him coming forward and pressing his claim . . . how awkward that would be."

"I can deal with him," sneered Bran, pouring himself another goblet of wine.

"As you dealt with Ronsard?" the Prince jibed.

"You will remember we did not know it *was* Ronsard until the very encounter. Anyway, with his wounds and the freezing cold he did not go far. That I know."

"But you never found the body, did you?" the Prince said firmly.

"It was snowing, by Zoar!" the knight snapped angrily. "Do you not believe me? The snow covered everything within the hour. His horse wandered off and left him where he fell, and the snow covered him . . ."

"Yes, yes. I know. The snow—you watched the ambush from some distance . . ."

"And by the time I got there I could find but two of my own men!"

"Well it is over. Now to put an end to our other problem, this outlaw leader—what do they call him?"

"The Hawk," said the knight sullenly.

"Yes. Strange this Hawk suddenly showing himself—and so close at hand. How do you explain it?" insinuated the Prince in a sly voice.

"I do not explain it!" The knight banged his silver goblet down upon the arm of the chair; wine sloshed up over the rim, wetting his hand. " 'Tis a coincidence, nothing more," he said more evenly, straining to control his temper. "Or mayhap one of the worthless robbers I hired for this . . . this transaction returned to his den and wagged his tail for his master."

"Possibly, possibly. There is no honor among dogs, you know," Jaspin quipped.

The Prince sipped his wine and sat silent for a time, gazing into the fire now beginning to dwindle. "I suppose we shall have to ask our friend Hawk tomorrow."

The knight smiled quickly and took another deep draught of his wine. "Aye, we shall certainly find out tomorrow."

SIX

THE KNIGHT, Sir Bran, after finishing his wine, exchanged a few words with the Prince regarding the impending capture of the outlaw Hawk the next morning. The Prince dismissed him then and waited until he had gone before calling his chamberlain and discharging him for the night as well.

As soon as he heard the door to the outer chamber creak shut he got up and, taking the candle from the table, made his way to a darkened alcove across the room, hidden from view behind a lower portion of one of the giant tapestries. Slipping behind the tapestry Jaspin entered the alcove and, fishing among the folds of his clothing, brought out a key with which he unlocked a private door set back and cunningly secreted at the further side.

The Prince stepped silently into his secret chamber and placed the candle upon a small table waiting there and settled himself into a chair before the table.

Upon the table sat a small box resting on an elegant cloth of velvet. The box, richly enameled in fiery red and inlaid with gold tracery and pearls gleamed, its fine artistry shimmering in the flickering light of the single flame.

Prince Jaspin wasted no time but placed his hands upon

either side of the box and lifted it away. On the table before him remained a curious object resting on the cloth—a pyramid of gold incised with strange hieroglyphs. The entire surface of the pyramid had been inscribed with queer and fantastic runes which were, he considered, the source of its unusual power.

Prince Jaspin gazed upon his prize with an odd glint in his eye, as if lit by some unnatural source from deep within. The pyramid always had this effect upon him; he felt bold, invincible, and clever beyond human cleverness.

The golden pyramid was the gift of Nimrood, known as the Necromancer, a cunning old sorcerer whom Jaspin employed as a partner in skullduggery. Many a night did Jaspin draw upon the secret of his strange object and the knowledge of its inventor. But of late, Jaspin received less and less assurance from his accomplice and felt seeds of deep distrust beginning to sprout.

Placing his hands on two sides of the pyramid, Jaspin closed his eyes and murmured a soft incantation. Slowly the pyramid, pale in the dancing light, began to glow with a ghostly luminescence. The glow became brighter, casting Jaspin's features into high relief and throwing shadows of his hunkered form upon the wall. As the unearthly illumination reached its apex the sides of the pyramid began to grow indistinct and hazy, although they remained solid under the Prince's touch. The pyramid, now lit with an almost piercing light from within, became translucent; Jaspin could see his own hands dimly through the sides. In a moment the strange device had become completely transparent, almost invisible, and Jaspin looked long into its crystal depths.

A pale green mist shrouded the interior from view, but as Jaspin watched the mist began to thin into stringy, straggling wisps. Now the form of a man could be distinguished, walking, as if from a great distance, toward Jaspin. But even as the man walked he drew closer with alarming speed so that instantly Jaspin was face-to-face, as it were, with his old sorcerer.

It was not a face to be admired. Twisted. Cruel. Two piercing eyes burned out from under a heavy, menacing brow. Despite the wizard's obvious age, wild, dark hair shot through with streaks of white formed a formidable mane around the man's large head. The face was creased with interwoven wrinkles, each crevice representing an evil its owner had contemplated.

"Ah, Prince Jaspin!" The necromancer hissed rather than spoke. "I was expecting your summons. I trust everything is as I said it would be?"

"Yes, your information is always good, Nimrood," the Prince replied, his eyes gleaming. "The knight Ronsard appeared just as you predicted, and was intercepted before his work could be completed. Unfortunately, we may never know what that errand was—he was killed in the ambush."

"A pity. He could have told us much, no doubt. But we have other ways."

"And another of your seeds is about to bear fruit, wizard. The outlaw Hawk has surfaced again—as you suggested he would. This time we are ready for him. By noon tomorrow that irksome band of renegades will be without a leader."

"Do not make the mistake of underestimating him once again," the conjurer warned. "He has outfoxed you before, you well know." The necromancer grimaced in what on anyone else would have been a hearty grin.

"Do not think I will let him slip away again. My headsman's blade is thirsty, and an outlaw's blood is just the refreshment I shall recommend. His head shall adorn a pike in the village square. Those bandits will see how lightly I consider their threats.

"I shall have no opposition when the Council of Regents meets and I shall be named king. The petitions are already signed." The Prince rubbed his hands in greedy anticipation of the event. "All is ready."

"What about the Queen?" the wizard asked slyly. "Will she agree to step down so easily? Is her power already so diminished?"

"The Queen will agree to see things as I see them. She is strong, but she is a woman. Besides, if offered the choice between the King's head or the King's crown I rather believe she would choose his head."

"She may lose both, however—as will the King. Ha! Ha!" cackled Nimrood.

"That is your concern, not mine. Leave me out of it. You get the King and I his crown—that was our agreement. I do not want any difficulties. I cannot afford to arouse the suspicions of the people; I need their support for the while."

"I am your servant, Prince Jaspin," the wizard replied. "Is there anything more you require?"

"No, I think not. All is ready, now," the Prince replied, and added, "Is my brother comfortable?"

"Oh, yes, Eskevar is after all the King." The necromancer laughed suddenly and Jaspin felt an unaccountable anger spring up inside his breast.

"But not for long!" he cried. "Soon there will be a new monarch on the throne. That I promise!"

The sorcerer appeared to bow low and suddenly the pyramid went dim, its sides becoming once more opaque and cold. Jaspin replaced its ornamented cover and, taking up the candle, left the room at once. He did not know why, but the mere mention of his brother's name upset him. That night it troubled his sleep with dreams of doubt and fear.

Quentin awoke with a start in the strange room. He glanced to Theido's bed and saw that it was empty. He threw off the coverlet and raised himself off the pallet and took up his cloak and went off in search of his friend.

Theido was discovered in the stable behind the inn, looking to the horses. "Good morning, lad. I am glad to see an early riser. I have only just come down myself." He straightened from his work of strewing fodder for the horses. "Well, that is done. Let us fend for ourselves as well."

They ate together at a small table in the kitchen, for Theido wished to have privacy, although none of the other guests, if there were any, had stirred.

"I have a plan that will do for us," Theido said, speaking in low tones. Quentin ate quietly and listened to the plan as Theido outlined it.

The plan was simple: they would enter as furriers just arriving from trading in the wilderlands, and would offer to show the Queen the finest of the treasures they had obtained.

"We have no furs," Quentin had objected, and Theido countered by telling him they would not need any. They were merely to be admitted in order to make a proper appointment and to receive any garments which the Queen might wish to have adorned with their wares. Such appointments were not uncommon with craftsmen of high repute. However, once in the Queen's presence they would discard the ruse and make known the real purpose for their visit.

"Now, if something goes wrong," Theido continued, his voice steady and his eyes hard in earnest, "you get out any way you can. Do not stop to think or look around, just run. Go back to Durwin and tell him what has taken place. He will know what to do. Hear what I say, and obey. Understood?"

Quentin nodded solemnly. He had not considered the possibility that they might indeed fail. But Theido, noticing the boy's somber mood smiled and said, "Fret not, young master. It is not the first time I have been hunted by Jaspin's men. Besides, my plans seldom fail." Quentin was not comforted by the thought.

They finished breakfast and left by the kitchen entrance, crossing the yard to the horses. Upon reaching the stables Theido threw open the wide doors and froze in his tracks. "Run! Get away!" he shouted to Quentin, at the same time throwing his cloak aside and drawing out a short sword from a hidden scabbard. Quentin stood rooted in terror. Theido turned on him and shoved him away, saying, "Run! You must get free!"

In the same instant two riders bolted from inside the stable. Both had swords drawn and small arm shields, or bucklers, held at ready to ward off their captive's blows. Quentin turned and fled, looking back over his shoulder as he ran. He saw Theido thrust beneath the shield of one of the armed men who knocked the blow aside just as the other, while pinning their quarry between their horses, raised his sword to deliver the fatal stroke.

"Don't kill him, you fool!" a voice rang out in the yard behind Quentin. He turned just in time to avoid colliding with another man on a horse. This one was a knight by the look of his finely wrought armor. The knight called out again, "He must be taken alive!" And the next instant Quentin felt a hand grab his cloak in a powerful grip, jerking him nearly off his feet.

Quentin, without thinking, lashed out at the horse's leg and landed a sharp kick. The spirited animal tossed its head back and raised its forefeet off the ground as it jolted backward. The knight instantly lost his hold on Quentin and the boy dashed beneath the rearing horse's belly and away. He gained the corner of the inn just in time to see one of the riders swing the pommel of his sword down upon Theido's head. He heard a dull crack and Theido slumped to the ground.

SEVEN

QUENTIN ran blindly down the narrow streets—some little more than footpaths between shuttered dwellings. He cast a hasty glance over his shoulder as he ran, expecting the man on horseback to come charging into view at every turn. His strong legs dodged and turned and flew as fast as his fear carried him away from the scene.

Presently he became winded and ducked into a close passage between two buildings on what might have been the main street of the city Askelon. He stood out of view of the street and waited to catch his breath and to think.

"Go back to Durwin," he remembered Theido's voice saying, "he will know what to do." But he had no horse, and Durwin was a day's ride away. He could not make it on foot, alone, without provisions; those he would need to secure. He had no idea how or where that might be accomplished.

Not wanting to remain too long in one place he began walking along the streets; he had not the slightest idea of where he was going—unaware that he was approaching the castle until he happened to look up and see its high walls soaring above him. He seemed to be drawn to it. For although he twice changed directions purposefully to avoid coming too near it, lest he be spotted and straightway taken captive, each time he looked again he was closer than the last.

In the meantime, the shops in the merchant district, through which he was walking, had begun to open to their daily trade. Although roofs hung heavy with snow and icicles dangled from the eaves, merchants threw wide their shutters onto a bright, cloudless morning and signalled the beginning of another business day. Soon the cobbled streets began to hear the tramp of busy feet and the strident voices of shopkeepers, patrons, and street vendors exchanging greetings, hawking their wares, and haggling over prices. A number of farmers had braved the cold to set up stalls in which to sell their winter commodities: eggs and cheese, and several types of ale and cider. Large braziers filled with charcoal burned before the stalls. Quentin loitered before these, warming himself and trying desperately to come up with a suitable plan for outfitting his journey.

In the end he decided to risk going back to the inn to recover his horse, providing that it was still there and the kidnappers had not taken it. He turned down a street, by the look of it the craftsmen's quarters; Quentin saw several artisan's dwellings—a smith's forge, the chandler's, the furrier's. The furrier—something drew him closer to the place. He stood at the entrance for some time, just looking, wondering why he felt like he belonged there—an unaccountable feeling. He had never seen the place before in his life.

Quentin paced along the outside of the building and gazed at the bright-painted sign with the picture of a red fox with an exceptionally long, bushy tail. Finally he turned to move on before someone within, noticing his shameless loitering, urged him away. As he swung away from the door a small, two-wheeled, covered carriage drawn by a shaggy brown pony drew up. The coach wore a coat of shiny black paint with an insignia on the door—a red, twisting dragon outlined in gold.

The driver, walking ahead, steadied the horse, frisky in the cold morning air, and the hansom's door swung open. A lady sat within, bundled in a thick robe with a hood over her head. The lady seemed about to disembark when she noticed Quentin standing just before her. She smiled and said, "Boy, come closer." She threw back her hood to reveal a fine-featured face and long dark tresses spilling over her shoulders. Quentin thought he'd never seen anyone so beautiful in all his life. What is more, she appeared to be his same age, for all that he could tell, or if not, only a year or two older. But her manner and bearing let him know that he was no doubt in the presence of royalty.

Quentin stepped woodenly nearer the carriage, and placed his hand upon the door. "Yes, Your Majesty."

The girl laughed and Quentin's face colored deeply. "I am not the Queen," the girl replied. "I'm only Her Majesty's . . . companion. My Lady wishes to be called upon this afternoon by your master." The girl nodded to the furrier's shop. "Take this," she said, handing the surprised Quentin a small folded parchment enclosed by a ribbon and sealed with wax. "It will usher you directly into my Lady's apartment. What time shall I tell her you will call? She suggests after the midday's repast."

Quentin, remembering enough of his court etiquette, bowed low and replied none too certainly, "Your gracious servant will attend, m'lady." He'd mixed the reply, but the spirit was right. The Queen's companion laughed again. Her voice was the joyous bubbling of a happy heart.

"I am certain you will bring your finest furs." Quentin bowed again and the driver, looking neither right nor left, took the bridle strap and led the carriage away.

Quentin stared at the summons in his hand, wondering at his remarkable fortune. The god Ariel, a deity among whose many attributes was serendipity, had fortuitously arranged for Quentin to have his audience with the Queen after all. Quentin considered the serving maid's mistake a miracle of the highest order, and stuck the letter into his tunic next to his skin. He moved off quickly, with purpose renewed, forgetting altogether Theido's command to seek help of the holy hermit Durwin.

With several hours to employ until he should have his audience, Quentin decided to make his way to the gates of the castle, there to be ready for the appointed hour. He planned to use the time to his benefit, arranging precisely what he would say and do in the Queen's presence: how he would confess his subterfuge, deliver his message, and most especially plead for the release of his friend—although he did not know why Theido had been taken, he assumed it to have some connection with the secret communication secured to the inside of his jerkin.

Quentin forgot his fear of the armed men and the skirmish in the stable yard at the inn earlier in the day, believing his mission to be aided by the gods. He strutted forth boldly as if wearing the invincible armor of a king's knight. The sight of this young master in his ordinary brown cloak and dark green tunic, his slightly overlarge trousers and outer stockings with heavy peasant sandals laced high against the winter cold, swaggering down the center of the street like a whole regiment of king's men, delighted the townspeople.

Had Quentin noticed the mirth that accompanied his sally to the gates of the castle he would have slunk away embarrassed. But he did not, so occupied with high deeds and fair fortune had he become.

His attitude changed abruptly, however, upon reaching the gates of fortress Askelon. They were mammoth iron-and-timber constructions wide enough for a whole company of knights to ride through a dozen abreast. They stood as a challenge to anyone who would make war upon King Eskevar to do his worst; the gates had defied fire, axe, and battering ram in siege after siege. From the foot of the long incline of the ramp leading up to the gates Quentin stood with mouth agape in wonder at the magnificent sight. The castle rose in sweeping lines to tower high into the bright blue winter sky. Red and gold pennons fluttered in the breeze from a score of towers and turrets; Quentin heard the crisp snap of the flags in the icy wind.

Of the five ancient wonders only Askelon remained. The others—the Fire Fountains of Pelagia, the Ice Temples of Sanarrath, the Cave Tombs of the Braldurean Kings, the Singing Stones of Syphria—all had crumbled away, lost in dim ages past. But Askelon, mighty City of Kings, with its dragon curled and sleeping under the hill, stood and would endure forever.

Askelon's foundations were carved out of the living stone of the hill upon which it rested, itself a mountain of strength and grace. The massive stone curtains had been raised by the brute effort of two thousand quarrymen and laborers under the direction of two hundred masons. That work progressed for one hundred years uninterrupted. Once the outer curtain was raised, the towers were completed and construction on the gatehouse begun. The gatehouse, the most vulnerable point of the fortress, was itself a singular engineering feat, established and refined over the next fifty years. The work started on the inner curtain, the walls which would enclose the actual working and living spaces for the royal retinue of soldiers, servants, cooks, keepers, warders, stewards, and the whole host of functionaries necessary to the proper maintenance of the empire.

The inner curtain, like the outer curtain, was formed of a double wall; hollow, the interior was filled with earth and loose rubble to withstand the ruinous blows of the battering ram. Once the inner curtain and its towers were enclosed, work began on the apartments and barracks within. In time the configuration of these inner chambers was to change endlessly, each new occupant directing reconstruction to his own personal tastes and the fancies of the time. The outer structure changed also, if more slowly, as new innovations in offensive strategy demanded defensive updating as well. The castle had grown and changed over a thousand years to become the thing of dreadful beauty that Quentin saw as he stood gazing skyward, trying to take it all in with a single prolonged gape. It was all he had ever dreamed and more.

After a time he stepped onto the ramp and began the long, sloping climb to the gates themselves. On his upward journey he was passed by several ox carts and wagons bearing supplies to the castle. He noticed them not at all; his eyes were on the looming battlements and soaring towers of the fortress which surpassed all his most daring imaginings, and, in Quentin's mind, rivaled the exaggerations men told about it. The walk took much longer than it might have.

When at last he attained the end of the ramp, right up to the end of the drawbridge—that retractable platform spanned a mighty gap from the end of the ramp to the gates at a bonecrushing height above the rocky rubble of the dry moat—Quentin paused. Not wanting to attract the attention of the fierce-looking guards of the gatehouse, he lingered in the shadow of one of the houses built along the ascending ramp in stair-step fashion. The last house furnished a shelter out of the wind, so he settled himself beside a friendly wall to wait.

People passed hurrying to and fro on business of their own, but Quentin attended to nothing but the task before him. He tried to imagine what the Queen would be like. He'd heard stories of the lovely Alinea, but, with his extremely limited experience of women, he had trouble thinking of anyone who would be more beautiful than the maid he'd met just that morning. Queen Alinea was said to have long auburn hair that shimmered red in the sun, and deep green eyes the color of forest shade on a summer afternoon. Her voice was held an instrument of enchantment; when speaking, or singing, for which she had earned wide renown, it fell like laughing water to the ear. These and other details he'd learned around the priests' table or from the talk of pilgrims he chanced to overhear when they camped on a summer evening outside the temple awaiting their oracle.

Queen Alinea, it was said, formed the perfect complement in grace and beauty to King Eskevar's strength and restless vitality.

When Quentin adjudged midday had passed he stirred himself, glad to be moving again, for he had grown cold in waiting, and marched resolutely toward the gates. Although the main gates were closed, smaller gates—still wide enough to permit two wagons to pass one another—were open and attended by firm-jawed guards. Quentin did not know the proper protocol for presenting himself to the Queen, but he supposed he'd tell the first person he met what he intended and let the natural course carry him along.

The first person, of course, was a guard whom Quentin dutifully approached. But when Quentin opened his mouth to speak, the man waved him on with his lance. He immediately found himself in a low, dark tunnel, the interior of the gatehouse through which the road led into the castle's outer ward.

Quentin had expected, due to his lack of military knowledge, that upon passing through the gates he'd be inside the castle as one would be upon entering the temple. He found the gatehouse road to be disagreeably frightening; the dark and ominous feel was due to the massive portcullis with its sharpened teeth of iron under which he had to pass, albeit quickly.

Once through the gatehouse he stood on the perimeter of the outer ward gazing on another smaller castle surrounded by its own small city of houses, stables, kitchens, storehouses and attendant buildings. Some of these were stone; others were made of timber and wattle, as in the town below. This inner castle had its own gatehouse and Quentin made his way there at once. Here security was more stringent, and the guard at the gate demanded to know his business. Quentin produced the folded parchment. The soldier glanced at the seal and waved him on.

Upon emerging from the gatehouse passage Quentin hesitantly entered a courtyard of some size. The whole of this inner ward was given over to elegant gardens which contained every known flowering plant and tree in the kingdom and beyond. In springtime the inner ward would burst in blooms of riotous color; now it was covered over with a still, white shroud of snow.

As Quentin watched, a man dressed in a long brocaded coat lined with sable—a lord or prince, by the look of his rich clothing—emerged from a stone archway to hurry across the garden to another part of the castle. Quentin waited until the nobleman had passed and then followed him. The man scurried across the snowy expanse and darted into the castle with Quentin right behind.

Once inside Quentin lost the man when he disappeared into one of the many doors opening off of the main corridor. He was standing, wondering what to do next when a gruff voice bellowed behind him. "What be your business here, young knave?"

Quentin spun on his heel to see a square-built man bearing toward him menacingly. "I have come to see the Queen." He uttered the first words that sprang into his mind.

"Oh, have you now?" The man frowned furiously. "Clear out! You should know better than to be lurking about my keep. Clear out I say!"

Quentin jumped back and thrust the sealed packet before him as if to ward off an impending blow. "Please sir, I have a letter."

"What is the trouble here, warder?" The voice came from an open door and Quentin looked up to see the nobleman he'd followed into the castle.

"This one says he's to see the Queen. I think he's about mischief, I do."

The man stepped up to Quentin. "Let me see your papers."

Quentin swallowed hard and offered the sealed parchment to the man. He snatched up the letter and looked at the seal, broke it and read the letter with a cursory glance. "Where is your master?" the man demanded, eyeing Quentin closely.

"He—he could not come, so sent me ahead to beg the Queen's pardon."

"Hmph—tell your master that he had better value Her Majesty's requests more highly in the future or he will lose her favor—and the benefit of her trade." He handed the letter back to Quentin. "Very well, follow me."

The man was not a lord as Quentin had supposed, but the Queen's chamberlain, and he led Quentin through a maze of corridors and anterooms to a high-arched passageway on an upper level of the castle. "Sit down," the chamberlain commanded at last.

Quentin took a seat upon a low bench across the corridor from a great carved wooden door. A window of thick, frost-covered glass looked out upon the inner ward and Quentin gazed out blankly, trying to remember what he was going to say to the Queen. He had forgotten it all.

The chamberlain entered and exited the apartment several times, as did others, mostly servants and other women. Once or twice Quentin thought he must be seeing the Queen herself emerge from her chambers; these visions of beauty, Quentin discovered, were the Queen's personal attendants; however, all were arrayed and conducted themselves like enough to queens for Quentin's unpracticed eye.

After a time the chamberlain emerged once more and came directly to Quentin. "Her Majesty wishes to see you now," he said and added a further word of instructon for Quentin's benefit. "When entering the royal apartment, it is proper to kneel until Her Majesty has asked you to rise."

Quentin nodded and followed the man through the door to her outer apartment. This was a large open room hung with tapestries and richly furnished. A few women sat at looms weaving, and talking as they worked. A minstrel played in one corner to the accompaniment of several ladies singing. The room seemed filled with charming activity. Quentin wondered which of the lovely women he saw was the Queen Alinea. But the chamberlain marched him through this room to another, the Queen's private chamber.

The chamberlain knocked once upon the wonderfully carved door and opened it without waiting for a reply. He bowed low and ushered Quentin in. Quentin, not daring to raise his eyes, fell to his knees on the floor.

"Your Majesty, the furrier," the chamberlain announced and left at once. The next voice Quentin heard was the Queen's.

EIGHT

"SO YOUNG our furrier is, and so formal," Queen Alinea said. Her voice, just as the poets intimated, *was* like laughing water, Quentin thought. "Arise, young furrier," she commanded pleasantly. Quentin raised his head uncertainly, half afraid to cast his eyes upon his Queen. But then he saw her and could look at nothing else.

Queen Alinea stood before a window. The blazing blue of the afternoon winter sky formed a brilliant azure backdrop which highlighted the auburn beauty of her hair. Her comely form was wrapped in a simple hooded gown of deep turquoise which fell in gentle gathers to the floor. She wore a belt of braided gold and pearls which accented her slim waist, and round her graceful throat a necklace, delicate and dainty, of the same design. Her radiant hair was swept back, revealing a high and noble forehead adorned with a simple golden circlet. The red-brown tresses curled in dark cascades along her slender neck, framing a face at once so open and frank it disarmed the observer. Her eyes glimmered with a good humor which played at the corners of her lovely mouth, threatening always to dissolve these exquisite features into laughter.

All this Quentin took in as one bereft of his manners, gaping shamelessly, momentarily stricken speechless by this dazzling vision.

"Our young visitor seems to be enchanted by your beauty, Bria," the Queen remarked, and Quentin saw the girl whom he had met that morning sitting next to the Queen with an embroidery hoop in her lap. The Queen had been instructing her in some finer technique of needlepoint. "Again, I say 'arise, young furrier,' " the Queen repeated, stepping down from the dais and coming close to Quentin, who jumped quickly to his feet and bowed as she approached.

"Have you brought something to show me, young sir," the Queen asked amiably, "or would you have me describe my fancies for you that I may be surprised by your master's art?"

Quentin suddenly remembered with a start that he was *not* the furrier, or even the furrier's apprentice; he didn't even know the furrier's name. His trembling hand sought the letter which Ronsard had traded his life to bring. The Queen detected his tremulous hesitation and asked, "Is something wrong? Why do you tarry so?"

"Your Majesty . . . I am not the furrier's assistant," Quentin managed to stammer. And to her look of mild inquiry he added, "But I have brought you something more valuable than you know. It is . . ." he broke off, glancing at the Queen's companion. "I think you may wish to receive it in privacy."

The Queen smiled at this conspiracy, but nevertheless nodded to Bria, who removed herself with a sharp, disapproving look to Quentin.

"Now then," the Queen replied, her hands clasped in front of her, "what is it that begs my private attention?"

"A letter, Your Majesty," Quentin said and opened his cloak. He took the gold-handled dagger from his belt and sliced a thread which bound the patch concealing the letter to his jerkin.

"That dagger . . . let me see it," the Queen said with sudden interest.

She took it from Quentin's hand and turned it over, examining the golden handle carefully. "I have seen this knife on occasion," she declared at length. "I cannot say where."

Quentin had finished freeing the parchment scrap from its pouch and produced it without hesitation, saying, "He who owns that knife sends this in his stead." He watched as she took the knife and broke the seal of the letter. She unfolded the crackly parchment and read. Quentin, not knowing what the epistle contained, knew not what to expect. He watched her face for a clue to the letter's contents, remembering that one man prized its contents with his life.

To Quentin it seemed that the effect of the message upon its reader was absorbed only slowly, yet it must have been instantaneous. The Queen's face drained of color and she let fall the dagger which clattered to the floor. Her eyes seemed to grow cold and filled with terror as she thrust the letter away from her. "My King," she murmured.

Quentin stood, a granite statue, not daring to move lest he intrude in some way upon the Queen's distress. The beautiful monarch's arms fell limp to her sides as if the strength had gone out of them; her chin came to rest upon her bosom. Quentin quaked inside to see this gentle woman thrown so cruelly into such distraction. In that instant he vowed that whatever had caused his Queen's calamity that he, Quentin, would set it right. Or if it be too late for that, he would avenge her grief.

He stepped close to her, his own heart rending for her. Instinctively she reached out for his arm and clutched it. Her eyes were scanning the letter once again. She was silent for some moments. Quentin thought to run to the adjoining anteroom and summon aid, but dared not to leave her. So he stood, offering his arm, as at that moment he would have offered his life.

Presently she spoke again, though her voice was much changed from what Quentin had recognized only shortly before.

"Know you what this letter contains?" she asked. Quentin said nothing. "Then tell me how you came by it, for I fear it is no jest. I know the signature too well. And the poniard upon the floor is proof enough besides."

"I am Quentin, an acolyte in the high temple of Ariel. Three days ago a wounded knight came to the temple asking our help. He said his errand was most important to the realm—a message from the King. He feared not death, only that it would come too soon and he would not be able to relinquish his charge to you. He wrote it then; you have it in your hand."

"Ronsard—brave Ronsard—sent you in his place? A temple acolyte?" The Queen looked upon Quentin with wonder that a boy would volunteer for such a mission. Quentin, however, mistook the Queen's question.

"He did not wish me to come, my Lady. But, there was none else . . ."

"And what of Ronsard?" The Queen turned her head away as if to avoid the impact of the answer. "Dead?" Quentin again remained silent, lacking the heart to tell her.

At this the Queen drew herself up, her shoulders straightened, her head lifted. When she turned again to Quentin she was remarkably composed, revealing her singular inner strength. "He trusted you, and in so doing placed the safety of the King and the future of the kingdom in your hands. I can do no less than trust you, too."

She moved to a large cushioned chair which had been drawn up near the window. The sky beyond, so recently clean and fair, now appeared cold and far away; dimmed, as if a veil had been drawn over it.

Alinea seated herself and motioned for Quentin to follow. When he had perched himself upon the window bench nearby, she said, "Quentin, this letter portends dire events for all who know its secret. Our kingdom is in peril. The King is a prisoner of Nimrood the Necromancer—held by the treachery of his own brother, Prince Jaspin, who would sit upon the throne. More than that the letter does not say, but the consequences can readily be guessed.

"I have been as one blind these years. While I watched abroad the foreign wars, the King's power at home diminished in his absence, plundered by Jaspin and his hired thieves. I became aware too late—I myself am made prisoner in my own castle. My only hope was that the King's return would strike fear into their craven hearts, and, once restored, the King would settle their accounts.

"That will not likely happen now. I fear our cause is lost before we have sounded the alarm." The Queen turned to gaze out the window, but her eyes saw nothing of the scene before them.

Quentin, feeling at once great pity for the Queen and even

greater anger at Jaspin, spoke with quiet resolve. "Then we must save the King." The Queen turned her head and smiled sadly.

"A true man you are. Ronsard was right to trust you. But, were I able to raise a force the King would forfeit his life. You see, Jaspin would know in an instant. His spies are everywhere; not a leaf drops in Pelgrin Forest that he does not know about."

"I have friends," Quentin offered. "It may be that a few can do what many cannot." How few, Quentin had not stopped to consider—the only people he counted friends in all the world, besides Biorkis, were Theido and the hermit Durwin.

"You would go to save your King? You and your friends alone?" The Queen Alinea seemed about to gainsay Quentin's offer, but then hesitated. She looked at Quentin shrewdly, her head held to one side as if appraising him for a suit of clothes. "It sounds very like madness, but your words may be wise beyond your knowing. Who are these friends of yours?"

At the question Quentin blanched, realizing that his list was a short one, and without a solitary knight's name on it. But he answered with all the conviction he could muster.

"Only Durwin, the holy hermit of Pelgrin, and one called Theido." He was embarrassed by his lack of fellowship, but a light came into the Queen's deep green eyes.

She exclaimed, "Lucky is the man who counts the most noble Theido his friend. You know where he is?"

The question posed a problem for Quentin. He did *not* know where Theido was; in fact he scarcely knew anything beyond the fact that Theido had been captured by men early that very morning—a detail he'd forgotten until just that moment. He did not know how to answer, but as he opened his mouth to admit his ignorance, the Queen continued. "It has been some time since anyone has seen Theido. He was one of the King's best knights and a nobleman, too. The death of his father occasioned his return from the wars. But on his homecoming he was falsely branded a traitor by Jaspin and his brigands, and his castle and lands were confiscated. He escaped their trap and has lived the life of an outlaw ever since."

The Queen stood and turned away from the window, gazing

down upon Quentin with a sudden warmth. "He also would I trust with my life. I know not of this holy hermit Durwin, but if he is a friend of yours, and of Theido's, he will not be less my friend.

"But why do you look so? Is something amiss?" the Queen asked suddenly, noticing Quentin's fallen countenance.

"My Lady," Quentin groaned, forcing the words out, "Theido was taken this morning by men who lay in ambush for him. I escaped to come here, but I do not know what has become of Theido, or where they might have taken him."

The Queen's answer to this seemingly doom-filled pronouncement astonished Quentin and enormously cheered him. "That is a mystery easily solved," she said, a tone of rancor coloring her reply. "For there is only one person who so oppresses the King's innocent subjects in broad daylight—deeds for which even the most impudent rogues seek the cover of blackest night. Prince Jaspin has kidnapped our friend. There is no mistake there." She thought for a moment. "Such arrogance would not shrink from bringing the prize within these very walls."

The Queen swiftly crossed the room and threw open the door to her chamber and called for the chamberlain who appeared in a trice. They talked in whispers in the doorway across the room and the chamberlain hurried off again.

"We will soon know the fate of friend Theido. I have sent Oswald to inquire discreetly of the dungeon keeper whether a new prisoner was remanded to his keeping this morning. We shall see if I guess aright."

They waited for the chamberlain's return. Quentin fidgeted with nervous frustration. He wanted to run to the dungeon, wherever it may have been, and look for himself, then and there to grant his friend liberty. The Queen, for her part, bore the waiting with regal calm. Whatever emotions she felt were of a more determined kind, Quentin thought; they seemed to simmer beneath her placid exterior.

At last the chamberlain, Oswald, returned. He bowed low as he quickly approached the Queen, saying, "An outlaw was imprisoned this morning, Your Majesty. The keeper knows nothing else, only that he was instructed by the knight in charge to allow no one to see him and that no record was to be made of the prisoner's presence."

"The knight's identity was known to the dungeon keeper?"

"It was Sir Bran," Oswald replied. The Queen thanked her chamberlain and dismissed him. She turned once more to Quentin and said, "I think we have solved our riddle. But now another arises which will not be answered as easily: how are we to set the captive free?"

NINE

THE AFTERNOON sun had set too swiftly, it seemed to Quentin. The Queen's apartment was growing dim; any minute servants would begin lighting the many candles which stood round the Queen's private chamber. The day had been a rush of activity, especially the last few hours.

Now, however, all was in readiness and they waited. "You appear anxious, young sir." The Queen crossed the room to where Quentin was maintaining his vigil upon the window bench. She had been seeing to last-minute details and had just returned. "Do not be troubled, Quentin." He smiled weakly and turned his eyes slowly away from the window, from where he had spent most of the late afternoon watching servants scurry across the courtyard in the snow on furtive business for the Queen.

"I am not afraid," Quentin lied, "only a little." He looked at the beatiful Alinea in the dying light. She had vastly changed since he had last seen her. Where only a short while before she had been arrayed in regal finery, the fairest of the fair, now she stood before him in plainer trappings, a dark green tunic—not unlike his own—with a purple cloak, very heavy, but finely made. She wore a man's wide leather belt at her waist and trousers; tall riding boots completed her wardrobe. "So, you approve of your Queen's attire?" she laughed, trying to put Quentin at ease. "We have the same tailor, you and I."

Quentin forced a laugh and stood. "When will we be going? The sun is well down . . . will it be long?"

"No, not long," the Queen reassured. "Oswald will summon us when all is made ready. We need not fret. Our preparations are in good care."

Quentin was now more uneasy than he had been previously. He had had a taste of the danger of his mission, and had witnessed its effects in Theido's case. And that danger had been heightened and multiplied by all that had taken place in the last several hours: Ronsard's message, the hastily conspired plot to free Theido, the feverish preparations for their journey—and now the waiting.

In the waiting Quentin found time to think about all that had gone before, to doubt his newly discovered bravery, to question again his omens and wish a thousand times that he'd never left the temple and to curse the blind impetuosity that had propelled him into the midst of this dark adventure.

Quentin turned glumly once more to stare out the window; the courtyard below lay deep in violet shadow and a single star blazed bright as a beacon fire above one of the southern turrets. A good token, thought Quentin, and was himself brightened somewhat.

A quick knock sounded upon the Queen's chamber door and Oswald entered at once. Quentin had trouble recognizing him, for he was dressed not as the Queen's chamberlain, but as someone of much higher rank, although Quentin could not say who; he looked like a nobleman.

"You look a fine prince, Oswald," said the Queen. "Are you ready to play the part?" Oswald bowed again; turning his back to them he shouted thickly, "You may go! Leave!" He turned again and asked blandly, "Would you say that was sufficient for our purpose?" There was a hint of sarcasm in his voice, and Quentin realized with a start that Oswald was playing the part of the mysterious Jaspin.

"I think you will do nicely . . . I only hope I do not lose my chamberlain. He might like it as a prince—though not a rogue such as Jaspin, surely."

With that, Oswald went back into the anteroom. Quentin heard the hollow echo of his summons to the warder. The Queen turned to Quentin and said, "It is time to go. Follow the warder and he will lead you to the postern gate. The horses are waiting there with our provisions. We will come along as soon as may be. Go quickly now."

Quentin followed the warder, a short, thick bull of a man with black eyes and curly black hair. He looked every inch the soldier that he had once been. Quentin bobbed along in the man's wake as they made their way along the back ways and little-used passages of the castle.

They walked quickly, stopping to look neither right nor left, although Quentin's eyes caught flashing glimpses of rooms opulent and luxurious beyond his simple imaginings. He ached to be able to just stand and gaze upon them from the corridors. They passed various apartments, the armory, anterooms, and chambers. At one point they passed a great open entranceway with two huge carved oaken doors thrown wide in welcome. Inside a double colonnade supported an immense vaulted ceiling of concentric arches above a vast open room that seemed to contain the treasures of the whole kingdom. Quentin had never seen anything like it; the room seemed large enough to have swallowed the temple of Ariel whole. Trenn, the warder, saw Quentin's eyes grow round as they passed the room and explained, "That is the Great Hall of the Dragon King. There is none like it in all the world."

Quentin believed him.

No sooner had the warder spoken than he turned like lightning upon Quentin and seized him by the tunic at the back of the neck. Quentin was surprised and shocked. He jerked like a loosely strung puppet and struck out at the man with arms and legs flailing. "Come along, ruffian, or I'll feed you to the dogs!" the warder roared.

"Do you require assistance, Trenn?" Quentin heard a voice behind him. He spun around and saw two men, richly dressed and proceeding into the great hall. One looked to be a knight by his armor, but he was no knight like Quentin had ever seen. His armor was silver and burnished to a glittering brightness, his cloak was crimson and lined with sable, as were his gloves and boots.

The man standing next to the knight wore a richly brocaded cloak of silk with gold drawn into fine thread and woven into the fabric. His tunic was royal purple, and he wore a large golden collar from which hung his insignia: a vulture with two heads, one facing right and the other left.

Quentin guessed it was the knight who had spoken, though he had no way of knowing. "I can manage, my Lord," said Trenn, dipping his head curtly. "We caught this one in the larder, stuffing his pockets."

"Well, give him a taste of your strap," said the nobleman impatiently. Both men turned away and Trenn yanked Quentin behind one of the great doors, clamping a hand over the boy's mouth.

"Quiet, young master!" he whispered hoarsely. "We dare not be seen lurking hereabouts." Then he removed his hand with an additional caution not to cry out.

"Who were they?" Quentin whispered. Trenn rolled his eyes upward.

"Orphe, help us! It was Prince Jaspin and one of his nobles, Sir Grenett—a more foul gentleman I never want to meet."

"Then let us get away!" said Quentin, seeing no good reason to linger in the vicinity any longer.

"We cannot—any moment Oswald will walk into a trap unaware! We must do something to prevent it."

The plan had been simple enough, but not without its element of risk. The chamberlain, Oswald, was to impersonate Prince Jaspin, after secretly obtaining some of the Prince's clothing. A forged message was delivered to the dungeon keeper to place the new prisoner under guard and bring him to the great hall, which was the only place the conspirators could think of where Jaspin himself would not likely show up. But their worst fears had, as on such occasions frequently happens, materialized in force.

Prince Jaspin and one of his noble knaves had chosen this time for a private parley in the great hall where Oswald, in disguise, would momentarily appear. Only the doughty Trenn and Quentin knew of the serious mischance. "I fear the gods go against us, young master. Yonder comes Oswald and too soon the prisoner will follow." Footsteps could be heard far down the corridor, Oswald was hurrying to his place. "There is but one thing for it," said Trenn. "A diversion."

He peered around the huge door and pointed diagonally across the hall to the darkened arch of an alcove. "You see that door over there?" he asked. "That is the storeroom of tables, benches, and all that fills the hall on feast days. And also a quantity of banners and pennons, and other such frippery—set them afire!" He thrust into Quentin's uncertain hands a small flint and iron attached with a leather thong, which he carried in a pouch at his side. "I will be right after you yelling to catch their attention. Mind, when you hear me call, leave all and come out. We will not have much time, but maybe enough."

"I understand."

"Then go." Trenn pushed Quentin forward with such force that the boy fell sprawling into the entrance of the great hall, dropping the flint and iron which clinked dully as it skittered across the black marble floor not five paces from where Prince Jaspin and Sir Grenett had stopped to confer.

Quentin leaped to his feet and dived to snatch up the flint and iron. Trenn behind him shouted, "Stop him! Stop that thief!" Prince Jaspin and Sir Grenett turned just in time to see Quentin dash toward them, swoop to retrieve his lost utensil, and dart away. Sir Grenett, without thinking, made a swipe after the fleeing youth, but Prince Jaspin, considering this an ill-timed interruption in his important affairs, stood fuming in his place.

Quentin reached the door of the storeroom and smacked the iron latch with his hand. The door was secured from within. No, it gave somewhat, but Sir Grenett was upon him. Putting all his weight upon the effort Quentin managed to force the latch and barely swung the door open, squeezing through and closing it again in almost the same motion. Sir Grenett's heavy fist rattled the door as he threw the bolt.

The room was almost pitch dark; only a feeble light found its way in from an arrow loop set high up in the wall. With Trenn's excited voice and Sir Grenett's angry challenges and both men pounding upon the door, Quentin stumbled forward and found in a corner of the room banners on standards. He threw them down and set to striking the flint and iron.

The effort appeared futile; there was no edge or kindling which could catch a spark. Furiously he looked around for something else to start the blaze. On the floor he spied a single piece of parchment, a proclamation of some sort which had been read at a feast now forgotten. He picked it up and ran back to the door, crumpling the parchment as he went. He threw it down just in front of the door and struck the flint and iron to it. The spark caught on the brittle, old skin. He blew carefully and the spark leaped to flaming life. Trembling, Quentin shoved the smouldering parchment to the threshold and blew his breath on it, sending the smoke streaming under the door.

"Fire!" he heard Trenn's voice boom out. "The rascal's set the stores on fire!"

Prince Jaspin, growing more and more impatient with the impertinence of the supposed young scoundrel, came steaming up to where Sir Grennet and Trenn stood beating the door with their hands. "Call the guards! I'll have this door down at once!"

"The room will be in blazes before that," Trenn objected. "My Lord, allow me to remain here while Sir Grenett goes round to the other door through the anteroom."

"The room has two such entrances I believe," explained the exasperated Prince, quickly losing his temper.

"My Lord could see to the other," suggested Trenn.

The Prince seemed about to overrule this plan, but the

smoke was now curling about their feet. "By Azrael! I'll flay his foolish hide myself!" he swore, trotting off to find the other door, a location he knew but imprecisely. "Sir Grenett," he shouted, "take your post! Let us end this vexation instantly!"

The two left to their appointed stations. As soon as they were out of sight, Trenn called, his face close to the door, "Young master, they are gone. Let us away!"

Hearing the signal, Quentin emerged coughing from the room. The parchment was now but ashes on the floor, completely consumed. Trenn grabbed his arm, nearly wrenching it from his shoulder, and pulled him across the floor and away. At the entrance to the great hall they met a confused Oswald fearfully peeping in at the scene he had just witnessed.

"Our plan is discovered," he said as they drew up.

"No," replied Trenn in a hushed tone. "But you must not linger here all night. We have bought some time. See to your business and flee!"

Oswald appeared far from certain, but the noise or voices in the corridor behind, and a quick glance to see the dungeon keeper and his guards with their prisoner moving toward them, made up his mind. The chamberlain crossed to one side of the hall and took up his position, back turned toward the entrance.

Trenn and Quentin did not remain longer to see the drama to its end, but hurried on toward their appointed place—the postern gate.

Quentin felt the sting of the cold night air upon his face as they dashed out of the castle and into the broad expanse of the outer ward. Trenn and Quentin flitted like shadows over the snow and, stealing through a low stone archway set in a low wall, entered the small postern gateyard. There in the whitened square of the gateyard stood three horses laden with provisions. Standing nearby was a member of Trenn's gatewatch who was checking saddle and tack for readiness.

"Everything is in order, sir," the guard reported when the two came close.

"Good," said Trenn. "Go see that the plank is let down. The others will be here shortly."

The man turned and hastened off. Trenn cast a worried glance back over his shoulder toward the castle and said softly to Quentin, "We have pushed our luck this far; the gods will have to see to the rest." He paused and added in a hoarse whisper, "But listen! Someone comes!"

TEN

QUENTIN shivered in the cold. A large bright moon was beginning to show its silvery disc just above the eastern curtain between two towers. Quentin watched in nervous excitement, waiting to be off. He stood in the snow holding the reins of his mount, none other than the stout Balder, rescued by the Queen's thoughtfulness from the stable at the inn. The ambushers, having captured their man, had given no thought to the horses and left them behind.

The Queen stood nearby talking quietly to Trenn, who was maintaining a thickheaded obstinance over something she was telling him. "Good warder," she said, "I would not insist if I thought you were in but little danger. The Prince rages within, demanding an accounting. He thinks you have conspired some treason against him and he likes not the trickery played out in the great hall just now. When he learns of the prisoner's escape he will demand your head."

"How can he know that I had aught to do with his precious prisoner?" Trenn objected.

"He needs no reason to suspect anyone, who is suspicious of all. Jaspin will suspect and then, at very least, make an example of your death for those who trifle with him. It is not safe for you to remain behind."

"I have borne the brunt of his anger before. I can withstand."

"No, not this time. He will be satisfied with nothing less than your head upon the spike. You must come with us."

Just then two figures darted forth from the low archway: the leading one tall and dark; the other, his cloak glimmering in the moonlight, followed close behind.

"Theido," cried Quentin, when the two had joined them.

"Quentin, is it you?" the dark man asked in some surprise.

"Quickly now," said Trenn. "Truly, there is not a moment to lose. You must be off."

"Trenn, you are coming with us," the Queen said firmly, and called to one of the guards standing close by, "Make ready another horse!"

"There's no time, my Lady," the bull-headed warder protested. "I may be of more use to you here. Go now and do not worry after me."

"Yes, you must go at once," said Oswald. "The dungeon keeper will send for his prisoner soon and find him gone, then Jaspin will know that treason is afoot."

Quentin was already in the saddle of the great war horse; Balder snorted and shook his mane. The bridle jingled in the frosty air reminding Quentin of tiny prayer bells heard from far away. Theido mounted his brown palfrey and the horse tossed his head and stamped the ground repeatedly as if to say, "The time has come! Away!" The Queen climbed, with the help of Trenn's steady hand, into the saddle, offering last instructions to Oswald.

"Jaspin must have no reason to suspect my absence for at least two days. Play out the ruse as long as you are able. Let everyone believe I have taken to bed with a sudden slight illness and will not be disturbed. My ladies must behave as they would under that condition. And you must forget you know otherwise yourself."

Oswald bowed and Trenn signaled one of his men to lift the

postern gate, and the riders set forth. The hooves of the horses clattered upon the stone floor of the gatehouse road and thudded over the plank, the small drawbridge which had been put down over the broad ditch separating the postern ramp from the gatehouse. They wound their way along the walled road of the postern ramp which descended steeply down the rocky backside of the hill on which the castle was founded. When they had clattered over the final bridge, spanning the last dry moat, Theido turned in his saddle and halted briefly, allowing the others to draw up beside him. "Whoever else I have to thank for my freedom, I thank my friend Quentin," he said bowing in the saddle. He turned to Queen Alinea and said, "And I thank his influential friend."

"We will have you to thank for *our* captivity if we do not remove ourselves hence apace," she said with a laugh, then added in a more serious tone, "Good Theido, I am so sorry for the abuse which has befallen you, but the gods may yet have some plan to undo all the evil Prince Jaspin has done. For my own part, I am glad that you are still alive and are now by my side. There is not another I would entrust my safety to more willingly."

"My Lady, we have not seen the beginning of our course. It may be that you will have reason to curse the one you so highly honor now."

"No. I have too often seen your high mettle tested and shown true. I have no qualms whatever dangers lurk at hand."

"Still, it is not too late for you to go back. You—"

The Queen cut him off, saying, "I have made my decision and will abide. I could no longer live in that fortress knowing what Jaspin has done . . . how far he grasps. And so knowing, my life would be as fragile as the deer's caught in the brake." She took a deep breath and turned her face to the east. "No, my future lies out there. My King is waiting."

Theido snapped his reins. "Then we are off!"

The horses surged into the snow, striking up glittering diamonds in the silvery light. The shadows of the three riders wavered, sliding silently in the smooth void—three fleeting shades darting through a sleeping world. Away they flew to the east toward the darkly advancing line of Pelgrin Forest, their black shapes traced in the spun silver of a rising winter moon.

Quentin crouched low, clinging to Balder's thick neck, abandoning any hope of remaining close behind the others unless he gave his mount free rein. He was not an accomplished rider—the temple had little use for horses. That part of his education had been neglected in favor of other, more priestly studies. So he leaned into the wind, lashed by Balder's flying mane, squinting into the night and blinking back icy tears and enduring the sting of snow loosed by the hooves of the horses in front of him.

The moon hovered at its zenith when they reached the first straggling forefringe of the forest. Theido pursued a dodging course among the small trees and shrubs until at last the riders entered the deeper wood. Here, at the forest's edge, Theido reined to a halt to allow the horses a breather. All turned in their saddles to look upon Askelon, now many leagues behind them.

Quentin craned his neck to see the castle, dimly outlined in moonlight, rising like a mountain, dark against an even darker night. Overhead a thousand stars shed brilliant pricks of cold light glancing down upon them. Pale wisps of steam rose from the horses.

"We should reach Durwin's cottage with the dawn," said Theido. He turned again toward the vast expanse of white they had just crossed. "I cannot see that we have been followed. But we should expect that, I think. They will try to stop us, you may be sure. Our only hope is to stay far enough ahead of them that their attempt comes too late."

"We may be able to outdistance them, or lose them along the way," Alinea offered.

"It is possible; at any rate, it is our best course. Jaspin has many spies throughout the land and many who owe him costly favors. He will try to use them. If we can but elude them long enough we may lose them when we leave this country behind.

"We shall ride as quietly through Pelgrin as a party may go with speed. There is, however, one stop I would make along the

way, and that quite soon." He swung his horse into the forest
and the others followed close behind.

Quentin found the going somewhat easier; he was able to sit
more erectly in the saddle, although low hanging branches kept
him ducking and leaning constantly. Theido pursued a relentless
pace for nearly two hours, as far as Quentin could guess by the
position of the moon—which he struggled to glimpse from time
to time through broken patches of clear sky overhead.

They stayed just off the main track through the forest and
presently came to an ancient oak of immense girth, as large as
any Quentin had ever seen. Theido called a halt and rode a few
paces ahead by himself. Then he raised himself in the saddle and,
placing two fingers of an ungloved hand into his mouth, gave a
low whistle. He repeated it and then trotted back to where Quentin and Queen Alinea waited. He was just about to speak when a
long shrill whistle came in answer to his own.

"Come," said Theido, "we may proceed."

They turned off the path by the oak and Quentin saw a
narrow opening between two massive and impenetrable hedges.
The gap was just wide enough to admit a rider or a man on
foot—if they happened to be looking for the spot, for it was fully
concealed behind the eldern oak.

Through the hedge wall the riders entered upon a clearing
which was a bowl-shaped hollow. The ground sloped down just
ahead of them and rose again opposite to form a rocky rim
crowned with slim young birches on a small hill. All around the
circumference of the hill grew holly bushes, thick and black in
the moonlight.

Theido led the party to the center of the bowl and there
waited. Quentin could not imagine why they had come here, or
who had returned Theido's signal, for obviously, signal it was.
He had not long to wait for answers to his questions. As he sat
scanning the limited horizon of the bowl he noticed nothing. And
then even as he watched he perceived that the bushes themselves
were alive—each one a man outfitted with a cunning camouflage
of branches and twigs affixed to his back and shoulders. Quentin

watched fascinated as these walking shrubs rustled to their feet and came forward. There were sixteen in all. Their leader seemed to be a large man with a hat of dry leaves pulled low over his face. He approached easily and came to stand directly in front of Theido, bowing low and saying, "Good evening to you, Sir Hawk. Your signal stirs us out of a long winter's nap. But we are ever ready to serve you and yours whatever the time or need may be. How can we help you?"

"You are most gracious, Voss. I wish only to speak to you now and then you shall all return to your cozy cave." The man bowed again and this time Quentin saw his broad, good-natured face full in the moonlight which filled the hollow, reflecting off the sparkling snow. Voss waved his men closer and instantly the riders were surrounded by an odd assortment of heads, arms, and branches. Each man carried a short sword and a long bow. Quentin saw no arrows, but guessed they were concealed in the camouflage.

"I was taken prisoner this morning by men under Jaspin's orders."

"The dog!" spat Voss. The ring of bush-men murmured menacingly. Quentin got the impression that if Jaspin or any fifty of his men had been within bow shot right now, they would be wearing feathers. "How was this deed accomplished?"

"I do not know. But that is a matter of small importance. I am free now because of the quick thinking of my friends here." Theido nodded to Quentin and Alinea.

The bush-men bowed together at this revelation and Voss spoke for all of them, pledging, "Pelgrin will never hold ill for you while any of us are awake and breathing. A whistle thus," he whistled, "will bring help and rescue from man or beast. And if food or shelter is your lack, you have bed and board with us as long as bellies need eats and eyes sleep."

"We accept your most generous pledge, kind ranger," said the Queen. "You may be certain that if ever I am in such need I will summon you at your word."

"Please," interrupted Theido, "we will trouble you no further tonight but to say that we go directly to the cottage of the holy hermit, Durwin. Most likely we will be followed—if we are not pursued even now. I would require a watch to be placed upon our path, and a fair warning to be given when any of the Prince's men enter these woods."

"That is easily said," replied the woodsman, nodding to several of his companions who left at once, melting into the forest silently as shadows, "and done. Is there nothing else?"

"I may have need to put your craft to the test, but not yet I think. We will take our leave and thank you now for your help. I may not have time to thank you later."

"No thanks is wanted," replied Voss, with a wide smile. His eyes glittered and his teeth shone white in the dark. "We are only too gladsome to repay in kind what has oft been rendered us. Away with you!" he shouted suddenly, slapping the horses on the neck. "You may still dream before the dawn."

Theido saluted the stocky woodsman and bowed to the circle of men gathered round about them. They returned his salute, raising their long bows high in the air and saying, "May Ariel guide you!" Three men jumped forward and seized the reins of the horses and led them off into the forest. Quentin looked back over his shoulder to where Voss and the rest still watched after them. He waved and the bush-men's leader waved back. Quentin watched until they were removed from sight by the forest closing once more around them.

ELEVEN

QUENTIN awoke to the smell of roasting meat seasoned with pungent spices. The aroma teased him, bringing water to his mouth and an ache to his empty stomach. It seemed like a month since he had last eaten.

His eyelids were heavy as bobs of lead and he had not the strength to open them. So, he lay in a state of suspended animation, awake, but unmoving; dragging his scattered thoughts together and willing his reluctant limbs to move—and only half succeeding in either case.

At last, overcome by hunger and coaxed upright by the pleasant odors wafting over him, he pushed away his cloak and gleaned the straw from his hair.

He heard voices and, struggling to his feet out of the dry, straw-filled corner that had served for his bed, he approached the hermit's long table where Durwin and Theido mumbled together.

". . . Then we must use every caution. Any misstep would prove fatal. So much is at stake . . ." Quentin heard this ominous pronouncement as he drew nearer the table. Durwin was speaking. "We must arm ourselves accordingly—I see no other alternative."

"No," replied Theido softly, yet his voice carried a stern objection. "I cannot ask such a thing of you. There must be another way."

Just then Quentin reached the table and the two men cut short their conversation and greeted him heartily. "Durwin, our young acolyte saved my life yesterday. Did I tell you?" Theido said, raising a cup of steaming liquid to Quentin as Durwin hurried to place a bowl of hot porridge and bread before him.

"Yes, you have told me only three hundred times this morning, but I'll gladly hear it again," replied the hermit.

Theido recounted in glowing terms all that had taken place the last morning, from the capture to the daring escape and the moonlight ride. "Had it not been for my young friend's disobedience of my orders, I would be food for owls this day."

"Disobedience? When did I disobey you?" Quentin croaked.

"You were instructed to ride back to Durwin here, if I should have come to harm, or our plans miscarry."

Quentin remembered the order; it had been scared right out of his head in the confusion and fright of the ambush. And later he had chanced upon a better plan.

"Quentin," continued Theido, "you stand absolved of any wrong. But I must stress this to you now: you are never to disobey my orders again. Follow them no matter what may seem to you the outcome. Do you understand?"

"Yes, sir," Quentin answered uncertainly. He had only minutes before been praised for his bravery and pluck. Now he felt severely reprimanded.

"Tut," said Durwin, "Don't be so strong-headed, Theido. I think the god intervened with a command of his own. I tell you the god has a hand on this one." The holy hermit nodded approvingly to Quentin, who was glad for this affirmation.

"I will obey in all details," said Quentin. He sat down on the bench and began tearing the bread to pieces and stirring the pieces into the steaming porridge. "Now may I ask something that I have been wondering?"

"Ask away; there shall be no secrets between us."

"Why is it men call you the Hawk?"

"It comes from my family's blazon—the hunting falcon. I am known to the woodsmen and others hereabouts as the Hawk— they make me out an outlaw like themselves." He shrugged. "It suits them, and allows me freedom to go where another name might hinder." He paused and then added in a lighter tone, "My friends, as always, know me as Theido."

"And them that know the name never want a truer friend." The voice was the Queen's, now standing directly behind Quentin. She had awakened to the sound of their voices and had come silently to the table. Durwin, appearing somewhat flustered, hurried to offer her the best seat at the table, his own.

"Your Majesty," he said, bowing from the waist, "I am honored to have you in this humble house."

"Your kindness is appreciated," she said, sliding into the offered chair. "But from now on I am only Alinea—I have put off my crown and am no queen until my King returns to claim his throne and so redeems my own. So please, good hermit, stand not on ceremony for my sake."

"As you wish, Alinea," replied Durwin smoothly. He had a gift for meeting people high or low and making them feel honored and welcome in his presence. Quentin had felt it from the first. "Now, no more talking until we have all broken fast together."

Prince Jaspin stormed red-eyed through the corridors of the ancient castle. He had not slept the night and had just been informed that the Queen was abed with an illness and would see no one, nor receive messages. His opportunity to question her was foiled. The foul Prince was furious.

During the night he had sent word to as many of his nobles as were within reach to meet at midday to hear a plan he had been contemplating for some time. His anger at losing his prisoner had caused him to implement this new scheme without further delay.

He strode into the council chambers, his sharp face flushed with anger and exhaustion. Various knights and nobles, more than a score altogether, stood beneath their banners and standards awaiting his arrival. Many showed signs of having ridden hard and long to get there at the appointed time.

"My esteemed lords, please be seated. We have much to discuss." All bowed to him as he waved them to chairs at a long table. He indicated a chair at his right hand for Sir Bran, and one at his left for the brawny Sir Grenett. Nearby sat a noble with sly, narrow eyes and a puckered, pouting mouth, a man of vast holdings and extraordinary wealth who was determined to be the new king's chief minister. His name was Ontescue, a name not well liked by the helots who worked his lands and bore the brunt of his expensive ambitions.

"My Lord, you are looking ill-possessed this morning. Your sleep was not troubled, I hope." He had guessed the Prince was looking for an opportunity to launch into a retelling of his latest agitation. He wanted to provide a ready ear.

"It is true; I have had no sleep this night past. But that is a matter for another time." The Prince dismissed his chance to confide his troubles, pressing on to a subject of more immediate import. "Gentlemen all," he called, "your presence gratifies me. As we all know too well our kingdom has been for some time without a king, being governed in his absence by the Council of

Regents. I have uncovered evidence that certain nobles of that body have been aiding the outlaws in their campaign of robbery and defiance throughout the forests of this land.

"Only yesterday my men arrested the prince of these outlaws—I had him secured within these walls until he should speak out against those of his band, and other outlaw leaders which he is intimately acquainted with.

"My aim is to rid the woods and hills of these preying wolves, and so give back the roads to the people and to commerce. However, before I could myself set eyes upon this bandit leader he was sprung to freedom by companions high in rank and title. I have not apprehended the men who loosed this villain but I know now who put them up to it." He paused and all eyes and ears were his. "Lord Weldon and Lord Larcott!"

At once a cry rang out. "It cannot be!" Lord Larcott, slamming his fist upon the table, was on his feet protesting his innocence. Lord Weldon sat stunned in his chair. The other knights and nobles drowned Larcott's cries with their own demands for justice.

Prince Jaspin held up a hand and ordered silence. "You, as noble lords of this kingdom, will have your chance to answer the charges brought against you. For now, and until such time as your crimes shall be heard, you will deliver yourselves to the tower to be there confined." With a nod of his head Prince Jaspin signalled four armed guards to escort the Lords Weldon and Larcott to the dungeon. The furor continued along the meeting table as the two unlucky men were seized where they sat and marched out under the rough handling of the guards.

Lord Larcott could be heard screaming, "By Zoar, you'll pay for this outrage! I'll see your head black on the spike!" Lord Weldon went quietly with a look of deepest grief and unrelenting sorrow upon his gray face. Those who saw his look quickly glanced away; his eyes seemed to burn into the soul of any who accused him.

When they had gone and order was restored, Prince Jaspin rushed to the heart of his plan: filling the two newly vacant chairs on the Council of Regents. "Noble men, as you are aware, the people grow daily more dependent upon strong leadership to maintain order in the land. I propose we now elect two new members to the Council, and do so without delay."

"Hear! Hear!" the nobles in Jaspin's sway shouted, delighted with such a display of efficient and farsighted leadership. When once more the din had died, a figure stood at his place at the table. "I cannot accede to such a move," said Lord Holben, a knight of no small renown. He was Larcott's friend, and one who had been chosen by King Eskevar to sit at council. "For to elect new members to this council would be to declare the guilt of the previous members. There have been no writs of justice presented, and no decrees posted. As it involves nobility, this is a high matter and as such can only be judged by the King himself upon his return." With that Lord Holben sat down.

"He is right," said some. Others objected, "It cannot wait!" The chamber once again rang with the shouts of contending voices until Ontescue held up his hands and succeeded in reducing the tumult to silence.

"Surely the Prince does only have the best interests of the realm at heart. Therefore, I will abide by Prince Jaspin's decision in this matter," said Ontescue. He nodded with a sly smile toward the Prince.

"I defer as well," said Sir Bran. He was aided in his opinion by Sir Grenett who then scowled down the length of the table daring any to defy him. Most, willingly or with reluctance, came at length to their side, opposed only by Lord Holben and several of his neighbors who cared not for Jaspin.

"I maintain the King's justice in this matter. No further moves may be taken against those charged with this crime," Holben declared. "Here it rests until the King shall return."

"Very well," snapped Jaspin irritably. "The matter shall go no further for the present. However, it is equally a breach of the King's law to leave an empty chair at the regent's council. Two members must fill those vacancies. Since we are all assembled here and now I see no reason why we should not proceed to elect new regents."

Lord Holben started to his feet to make some objection, but was shouted down by Jaspin's minions.

"Very well," continued Jaspin. "Since it pleases this body I propose to put forth the names of Sir Bran and Sir Grenett for your commendation."

"I commend them," said Ontescue. His words were echoed time and again as the vote proceeded around the table, man by man. Nearly everyone commended the Prince's choice heartily; only a few abstained from Lord Holben's party. Only Lord Holben himself dared go against the vote.

"Sir Grenett and Sir Bran," Prince Jaspin beamed, "you are now regents of the realm. You will be sworn to your office within the fortnight, as is required by King's law," he said snidely, bowing to Holben who clenched his fists in his lap. "How say you, bold knights? Do you accept this charge placed upon you by your peers?"

"We do," they answered.

Just then there was a commotion in the hall. Amidst angry vows, fierce gestures, and dark, threatening looks, Lord Holben and his party stalked out of the council chamber in a great show of protest. The smile which had only moments before curled the corners of Prince Jaspin's fleshy lips now faded slowly.

Other nobles and knights now took their leave and began filing out of the chamber, attended by their pages and standard bearers, each with the banner and device of his lord. Prince Jaspin rose and called Ontescue to him. "Some of the voices were not loud enough in their approval of my new regents. Go to them and smooth any uncertainty with whatever means seems best to you. I will have these men, as many as can be won with favors, on my side."

"Of course, my Lord. You, as always, know what is best. Your cause shall not suffer for want of generosity at my hands. I will bring them around," the would-be chancellor declared. Already his shrewd eyes were stealing after the nobles as he calculated the price of fealty for one and then another.

"Good," said the Prince, adding, "Have I told you that I am

considering giving you Crandall? No? 'Tis true. It only needs a slight demonstration of your loyalty to secure that estate—one of the largest in the realm, I am told."

"I am flattered, my Lord."

"Go now and bring me word of your success as soon as may be. Other matters now beg my attention. Go."

Ontescue hurried after the departing lords, engaging each one in private conversation and pressing upon them promises, gold and royal pledges of the Prince's undying loyalty to them, greasing the machinery of state with warm words and lofty indulgences.

Prince Jaspin hurried out of the council room by a side door and went directly to his apartment where five men waited in his anteroom.

"The knaves! The fools!" he fumed as he bustled along. "They will see how Jaspin deals with troublemakers! Ah, but first to loose the Harriers upon that blasted Hawk and his miserable friends."

TWELVE

"THE NEED is great—already it may be too late. If there were another way, or a lesser cost, I would not insist. But there—the choice is mine and I say we must go to Dekra." The voice was Durwin's, and from what Quentin could tell the discussion, which had started again as soon as the breakfast table had been cleared, was a continuation of the one he had interrupted earlier. He lazed in a patch of warm sunlight, half-awake, sitting on the floor under a thick-glazed window which the low winter sun filled with streaming yellow light. Quentin basked in the light and let the warmth seep into his bones.

"No," said Theido, objecting once again—and with, what seemed to Quentin, a god's own obstinance. "We will find another way. We have time yet, and we know not what Jaspin plans . . ."

"Precisely! We know not what Jaspin plans, but it is certain to be nasty and cruel. Most likely his malice is already afoot. But what of that? He only wants a crown. Nimrood will not be so easily satisfied—he wants a world! We *must* go to Dekra."

Who or what Dekra was Quentin did not know. But the conversation had been going on so long he had lost interest in it and had retreated into the background to doze. The Queen still sat at the table with the two men, but it had been a long time since she had occasion to speak. Quentin knew that nothing would be settled until this impasse between the two men was resolved.

Presently he stood up, yawned and wrapped his cloak around him and slipped quietly outside. The cold air tingled in his lungs, and the piercing white light thrown up by the sun's reflection upon the snow brought tears to his eyes which he rubbed away with the back of his hand. For the first time since leaving the temple Quentin wondered what the kindly and plump Biorkis, his only friend among the priests, was doing at this moment. Working among his medicines, no doubt; or blistering the ears of some poor acolyte over letters unlearned or scrolls unread.

Quentin heard the door creak open and turned to see Alinea slip out beside him. She was as lovely dressed in the attire of a ranger as in the fine raiment of a queen. Her hair gleamed in the sun, and the cold brought a rosy blush to her fair cheeks.

"Do you miss the temple, Quentin?" she asked lightly. Alinea regarded him with a warmth and understanding Quentin had only rarely felt from another person.

"In a way," he replied, "but not so much. I have had but little time to miss anything."

"Yes," she laughed, and once again the music was in her voice. He had not heard it since he had given her Ronsard's message at their first meeting. "Yes; there has been little time for aught but escape." She smiled and, drawing Quentin by the arm, began to walk. "Tell me about what you did in the temple. How did you come to be an acolyte?"

"I cannot say, my Lady. I was very young. My parents were lost to the sleeping plague that swept over the land in the Spring of Death. I don't remember them or much about my home. I see a face sometimes—it might be my mother's. Mostly, I have always lived in the temple."

"Why did you volunteer to leave it then, since you have no other home?"

"I felt . . ." he hesitated, searching for the right words, ". . . felt something was pulling me. Like I was *supposed* to go . . . it was right for me. I have never felt that way about anything before."

"It must have been a very strong feeling for you to forsake all that you had known—your home, your friends."

"I have no friends in the temple. Only Biorkis, one of the elder priests."

"Was it lonely for you?"

Quentin could not think how to answer her at first. "No—that is, I don't think so. The temple is . . . the priests exist to serve the god. Acolytes serve the priests. There are rules and tasks. That is all."

The Queen nodded thoughtfully. Quentin had not been lonely because he had known nothing but the rigorous order of the temple where each had his place and his task. "What would you be doing now if you were there?" she asked after a long silence.

"Oh, studying. I had much to learn—more than I could master, sometimes. And soon we would begin making ready to receive the god back from his winter journey. He will come in the spring as he always does, and the temple must be ready. Rites of purification must be performed; the sacred stones washed and anointed. There is much to do."

"I believe you."

"But then," Quentin continued, his eyes kindling with excitement as he warmed to his story, "when everything is ready the god comes and there is celebration—it goes on for weeks.

There are feasts and games and so much happiness. The temple is opened to the pilgrims who have gathered outside the walls, and all join in the celebration."

"Yes, that is a good time for our people. I have attended some of those celebrations—when I was a little girl. I was always afraid of the priests; I thought they were the gods."

"Sometimes they think they are, too," remarked Quentin. His face brightened momentarily with a grin. "Or they'd like to have you believe it. But I think there must be more to it somehow. I don't know . . ." His voice trailed off, unable to express what he felt. They had reached the foot of the hill below the hermit's cottage.

"I know what you mean. I often think that the gods are not the least bit interested in us or our problems. And sometimes I think there are no gods at all. And yet . . . even in my doubting I feel a presence I cannot explain. A moving within. A longing in my spirit for something more."

"You have felt it, too," said Quentin firmly. "Perhaps that is why I chose to leave; I could no longer stay.

"Often I would lay awake at night burning with a strange fever. I would hear someone call my name, and yet the night was hushed around me. I used to tell the priests about these things and they said that it was the god calling me, that he had something special for me. But deep inside I knew that wasn't it. Finally, Biorkis told me not to speak about it any more with any of the other priests.

"Still, whenever I heard the voice or felt the fire, I would go to Biorkis and we would talk about it. He would ask me what I thought it meant."

"What do you think it meant?"

Quentin drew a deep breath and looked into the sun-filled sky. "I am not a priest, but I do think a god was calling me. But a god greater than any other. Higher, wiser. And he knew me."

"You are a special boy," Alinea said, raising her hand to his face. "I knew that the moment I saw you standing nervously in my chamber. I knew also that you were no furrier," she laughed.

The air seemed to grow sharper as a gust of wind spun snow around the two figures. Without another word they turned and went back up the little hill to the cottage.

The Prince slouched in his winged chair fingering a soft leather pouch full of gold coins. Sir Bran and Sir Grenett stood on either side of him, and all three gazed with some trepidation upon the three visitors in front of them. Prince Jaspin said, after a moment's deliberation, "I want them found and brought back—this Hawk and whoever his friends may be—however it may be accomplished. I care not what means you use."

Sir Bran and Sir Grenett, knights hardened in battle and fearless, shrank away from the sight of the Harriers, fierce and brutal men devoid of human compassion or mercy. The Harriers, as they were known in Mensandor, were last descendants of an ancient people in the realm, the cruel Shoth. A savage, war-loving race who killed for the pleasure of killing, and the twisted enjoyment of inflicting pain on another.

Over a long and unbroken history of war the Shoth had developed special powers which enabled them to pursue their enemies with unerring accuracy, powers the simple peasants considered supernatural: the ability to see in the dark like cats, to scent a trail, and to hone in on the intense emotions of their prey. It seemed as if they could snatch thoughts out of the air, and so many believed.

There were few of the Shoth left in the world; they were dying out stubbornly. But those who lived on employed themselves as mercenary soldiers, or as trackers of outlaws. For either service they received high rewards from their patrons—as much as ever they desired, since they were not the kind of men one wanted as enemies.

The Harriers were greatly feared by everyone who knew of them, or who happened to meet them, upon those rare occasions when one or more might be seen in passing.

Two long braids from either side of their heads were woven together and fell down their broad backs. Their features, wolf-like and hard as stone, were made more fearsome by the blue tattooed designs which covered their faces. Their clothing was rough, made of animal skins with the hair scraped or burned off; they wore soft boots made in the same fashion, laced on the outside from ankle to knee. Around their necks they wore necklaces made from the hair and finger bones of their victims. On their brawny arms were bracelets of human teeth.

To see a Harrier was to know fear. Their bizarre appearance was coldly ordained to inspire terror, to immobilize their hapless quarry.

They carried long, thin swords with serrated blades so that a wound from the thrust of a Harrier sword did not heal quickly or without difficulty. That mattered little since few who ever felt that dangerous edge remained alive to tell it. They also carried small wooden and skin shields on which were painted crude symbols of their barbaric religion—said to include regular human sacrifice.

The Harriers who sold their services as trackers also used birds, most often hawks, but also small eagles or ravens, to help them locate their human game at long distance. These birds rode with them upon the Harriers' peculiar stout, shortlegged ponies upon ornate perches built onto their saddles, usually of bones and hide—again the bones and hide of their victims. Some said the Harriers spoke with their birds mind to mind, so extraordinary was the communication between the two preying creatures.

"There are at least three of them, maybe more. I have a report from one of the guards who saw three ride off toward Pelgrin last night." Prince Jaspin stood abruptly and tossed the bag of coins to the foremost of the Harriers who deftly caught it and slipped it into an inner pouch in his clothing. "There will be more money when you return; you will be paid well." He smacked his clenched fist into his open palm to add emphasis to his words. "I want them found!"

"So shall it be done," said Gwert, the largest of the three. Then without another word or look they turned and filed out as silently as smoke drifting away on the breeze.

When they had gone Sir Bran let a deep breath whistle through his clenched teeth. "Fair Prince, I do not like this turn.

I would that you had requested me and some of my men-at-arms to bring back this prisoner for you. These Harriers—these barbarians—are not to be trusted. You will get your prisoner and his companions, if you care not how many pieces they are in."

"I do *not* care," said Jaspin angrily. "I only want them found and stopped."

Sir Grenett interposed, "My Lord, why is this man—this Hawk—such a menace to you? He is only an outlaw—and even if he were chief among them he would account you no more loss than your bounty will cost in the end. Why do you seek his end so ardently?"

"That," said the enraged prince, "is my own care, sir, and none of yours!" He turned on them threatening, "You will both keep this to yourselves. Do you hear? Besides," Jaspin continued in a softer tone, "it would not do for my new regents to entertain such troublesome pursuits. There are more important things to be done.

"Come, let us begin making plans for our next little surprise." He led them to his table and a pitcher of wine and goblets on a silver tray. "My friends, I pledge your health and continued success," he said, lifting his glass to theirs when he had poured them full. They all drank deeply, and when they rose from their cups the knights returned Jaspin's pledge.

"To Askelon's new king!"

THIRTEEN

THE OLD man lay upon the stone altar in a great darkened hall. Torches smouldered at each corner of the five-sided altar casting a strange, flickering glow which curled and eddied like water over the man's face. He appeared to be asleep, or dead, yet even in deepest repose the fierce malevolence of the features did not abate. So bent was the black soul which inhabited that body, it twisted all it touched. The face was a mask of hate, the more terrible because it was also a face of keen intelligence.

Nimrood sank, as it seemed to him, through layers of smoke, as if falling from a great height. His head throbbed; dull pains shot through his limbs. But he willed himself to continue.

The smoke thinned and then scattered completely. He looked beneath him and saw the solid earth sliding away below. Still dropping rapidly, but gliding now, not falling, the magician could make out detail in the land. Behind, a high range of snow-capped mountains, the Fiskills; to the right, the long silver ribbon of the Wilst River now frozen in its wriggling push to the sea; ahead, but still too dim to see clearly, the dark, gray-green mass of the great forest Pelgrin, partially hidden by clouds. Further ahead, but beyond sight, lay Askelon, the city on a hill.

Nimrood slowed his descent and heard the cold air rushing past him, but he felt nothing at all. He closed his eyes and when he opened them again he turned his head to see the black wing rising and falling rhythmically as the wind sang shrilly through his feathers. The sorcerer had taken the form of a raven. He flew swiftly on.

Approaching Pelgrin, Nimrood's keen raven's eyes could see the dim shape of Askelon rising in the distance. Light was failing as the world sank into the darkness of a long winter night. It would be dark by the time he reached the castle, but it mattered not. Nimrood was a friend of darkness, and of all things that loved the darkness. He used the black of night as a cloak to hide his deeds.

Nimrood had delved deeply into the hidden arts; he had toyed with secrets veiled from the foundations of the world. He had traveled widely, learning the lore of magicians and sorcerers of every race. An insatiable pupil as a young man, he had studied with every occult master until he was as powerful as any who had lived before him. He had gazed upon the heart of the unspeakable and had bartered every human emotion to gain the power he sought, and which still eluded him: the power to bend all men to his will.

When at last he reached his destination, Nimrood circled over Askelon, descending in sweeping spirals. He dived for the tower where Prince Jaspin's quarters lay, and alighted upon the narrow ledge of an arrow loop high in the wall above Jaspin's chamber. Prince Jaspin was alone, sitting in his great chair near the fire. Nimrood fluttered to the floor noiselessly, changing back into his human form as he lightly touched down.

"Prince Jaspin," he said, enjoying the fright he gave the Prince. "You are not expecting anyone, are you?"

"By Zoar! You startled me." Jaspin threw himself back into his chair, clutching at his heart. "No, by Azrael, I should say not. No one—least of all you, Nimrood. How did you get here?"

"That would not interest you very much, I am afraid. I am not really here at all. You see merely a phantasm, my projected soul-body, or what you will." The sorcerer crossed the room, and as he passed in front of the fire Jaspin could see the flames shining faintly through his ghostly form. He came to stand directly in front of the astonished Prince.

"What are you doing here? If you will not tell me *how* you got here, you'll tell me why, I'll warrant."

"Indeed I shall." The wizard folded his arms upon his breast and glared down upon Prince Jaspin, who sank in bewilderment further into the cushions of his chair. "You let him escape!" he shouted. Jaspin fancied he heard thunder crack in the magician's voice.

"He had help . . . friends within the castle. I have had the keeper of the dungeon and the guards beheaded . . . I have . . ."

"Silence!" Nimrood hissed. "Do you think spilling the blood of worthless guards will appease me? Will it bring back the prize?"

Nimrood frowned furiously and began to pace before the hearth. Jaspin watched in dread fascination. "He is mine! I want him! Twice you have let him escape. Argh!" he cried in anger.

"Twice?" Jaspin asked timidly. "Surely you are mistaken. We have only caught him once."

"Nimrood mistaken?" The wizard's eyes flashed fire, but he opened his mouth to a hollow, cackling laugh. "You little know me, Prince Jackal.

"You fool!" Nimrood shouted, suddenly loosing his temper again. "Do you not know? This outlaw Hawk is none other than Lord Theido of Crandall, the greatest military mind of this age."

"No . . . I . . ." the Prince gasped speechless.

"None other. You had him in your clutches when you arrested him upon his return from the wars. You let him slip away then, too."

"That was different," Jaspin objected, starting out of his chair.

"You raise your voice against Nimrood?" the wizard cried. The fire in the hearth billowed forth with a roar, spilling a torrent of cinders and sparks into the room. Jaspin felt the heat on his face. "I shall reduce this pile of stone to smouldering ashes, my Prince. Be careful." Nimrood ran his long slender hands through his wild hair and continued to pace.

"What do you intend to do about it?" he demanded.

"I have set Harriers upon the trail," said Jaspin sulkily. "We shall have him back before too many days have passed."

"Hmmm . . . all right. I see you *can* use your head when you are pressed to it. But notify me at once when you have him once more. Dead or alive, I want him. You have bought yourself another chance, and maybe saved your crown. But do not fail this time, or it will be your last human act. Ha!" the wicked Nimrood sneered.

He then turned and fixed Prince Jaspin with a terrifying scowl. Jaspin felt his limbs grow heavy, losing strength; his heart turned cold within his breast. "There are worse fates than death, I assure you. I know of several—all equally distressing. I reserve them for those who particularly disappoint me. You have one more chance . . . do not disappoint me." The sorcerer turned and stepped into the flaming fireplace. The deed brought Jaspin to his feet.

The wizard cackled and appeared to stretch, growing taller and more transparent. Just before he faded from view he said,

"Did you know that Ronsard lives? No? Well not for long. I have sent men to capture him." He laughed again and faded completely into the flames. Prince Jaspin heard only the thin echo of his depraved laughter and then that too was gone.

Jaspin sank once more into the winged chair. His face had taken on the pallor of a dead man.

The fire on Durwin's hearth had burned low. Quentin slept lightly, curled in a warm corner near the fire. He felt as if he had finally saturated himself with slumber; his mind drifted hazily through shifting dreams. It had been an uneventful day, spent in talk and minute preparations, of which Quentin had but a small part. He had mostly eaten and slept, and cared for the horses, making sure they all had an extra portion in payment for their hard ride the night before.

Theido and Durwin sat near the fire smoking long wooden pipes filled with aromatic leaves which Durwin cultivated. They sat in silence, all talked out. Puffing occasionally and grunting as they turned matters over in their minds.

Alinea slept comfortably stretched upon Durwin's low wooden bed. She had said little all day, but Quentin thought her eyes spoke eloquently of the turmoil taking place within. Her emerald eyes seemed to weep inside for the anguish she felt for her King. Still, she had put aside her own torment and had found kind words to say to Quentin in that moment when they were together. For that, Quentin had declared to himself, he would gladly give his life for hers at the first opportunity.

Durwin rose at last and stretched. He knocked his pipe gently against the stone mantle and turned to roll himself in his cloak in some further corner, leaving Theido to his thoughts. Quentin, who dozed fitfully, thought he heard Durwin utter a shrill whistle and thought it extremely odd behavior so late at night.

Then he heard it again and stirred himself out of his half-sleep, pushing himself up on his elbows. Durwin had stopped where he stood, listening. Theido, his chair tilted back, resting his long legs against the fireplace, stopped puffing and listened, too.

The whistle sounded again, this time closer. Theido got up and went to the door and slipped out. A cold draft washed over Quentin, rousing him more fully awake. Another signal was heard, this time closer to the cottage; it was Theido replying to the sign.

Alinea was awake now and standing near Durwin. She bent her head and spoke to the hermit, but Quentin could not catch the words. He strained every sense to hear what was taking place outside. All he heard was the crackle and pop of the fire upon the hearth, and his own breathing.

Then he heard the soft, muffled shuffle of snow-dampened footsteps returning to the cottage. Theido ducked in rubbing his arms for warmth. "Voss and his bush-men have a visitor for us," he explained. "They are bringing him along."

No sooner had he spoken these words than a soft knock was heard at the door. Theido threw it open and there stood the squat leader of the rangers. Behind him was another man held in tow by several of Voss' companions.

"Come in, Voss," said Theido. "Let us see your catch."

The hefty ranger strode into the cabin and waved his charge forward.

"Trenn!" the Queen cried as her warder tumbled into the light. He swayed uncertainly upon his feet and looked about to topple over, but Voss put out a hand to steady him. Durwin whisked up a stool and sat the man down.

"We watched him as soon as he entered the wood. When he appeared to be heading in this direction we took him," said Voss casually.

"Trenn, what are you doing here?" Alinea's eyes searched his face for a clue. "Has Jaspin discovered our game?"

"As I fear, my Lady," said Trenn, rising to his feet and bowing. "I came to warn you all: Jaspin has put Harriers on your trail. I prayed to every god I knew that I would not come too late."

At the mention of the dreaded trackers even Voss' broad face blanched. "This is dire news," he said.

Alinea's hand went to her face. She shot a hasty look to

Theido who stood unmoved. "There is our answer," said Durwin.

"How long ago did this take place?" asked Theido with forced calm. He spoke very carefully and smoothly, not allowing his voice to betray the alarm he felt.

"I saw them enter the postern gate this morning about midday, conducted by several of Jaspin's knights. There was also much activity through the main castle gate this morning—knights and nobles, some from as far away as the flatlands. Rumor has it that Jaspin had called a hasty council to catch those that helped you escape."

"What? The man is mad," said Theido.

"That was just a ruse," explained Trenn. "Prince Jaspin accused two nobles of lending aid to your escape. I got it from the jailer—the new jailer," a quick chopping gesture showed what he meant, "that two nobles were being held—Lords Weldon and Larcott."

"The snake!" said Theido quietly. "He is using my escape to alter the Council of Regents. I suppose he wasted no time in having two new regents enfranchised. Do you know who took the others' places?"

"I cannot say positively, but I think Sir Bran and Sir Grenett," answered Trenn. "It was said that Lord Holben stood up to him—saved the lives of the lords. The Prince wanted them bound over for treason. Lord Holben appealed to the King's law."

"He saved their lives for the time being, and probably lost his own," replied Theido.

"Does Jaspin dare so much?" asked the Queen, shocked that such bold effrontery should take place in her own court. "I had no idea."

"We cannot help Weldon and Larcott," said Theido, sadly. "We must help ourselves now."

"Trenn, how did you get here without the Harriers seeing you?"

"I left before they did, and as I knew where I was going had little trouble in making good time, though I must have nearly killed my good horse."

"They will have followed you," pointed out Voss. "It'll make their task so much the easier."

"I hope I have more wits about me than that," sniffed Trenn. "I had some of my men ride out with me to muddle the trail. They rode with me a way and then each split off to a different direction. It was all I could do in the time I had."

"Good," said Theido, jumping forward. "That will buy us some time."

"My comrades and I can purchase some more," said Voss. "I will put them to work at once confounding the trail. We can lead the fiends through the forest for days."

"These are Harriers, not ordinary hunters," said Theido.

"And we are not ordinary game," boasted Voss. "Don't worry. They will never see us nor learn our trick until you are well on your way. But we won't be able to stop them forever."

"We could fight them," suggested Trenn.

"And die trying," replied Theido. "No, our only hope is to stay ahead of them until we cross the Wall. I doubt if even Harriers can find us once we have crossed over into the Wilderlands."

"So it is!" replied Durwin, triumphantly. "You admit it now. We *are* going to Dekra."

"Yes, we are going to Dekra. You have your way, my friend. And it is our only hope. We go to Dekra . . . and we leave tonight."

FOURTEEN

FROM DURWIN'S cottage in the heart of Pelgrin Forest, under night's dark wing, the unlikely rescue party set forth on their quest. They little dared hope for the success of their labors, nor scarce conceived a plan by which they might obtain their goal of freeing the King from the malignant magician, Nimrood.

In a fortnight upon the trail, heading north and east through the furthest reaches of Pelgrin and the low foothills of the Fiskills, they had encountered no other living soul. This, however, was accounted as an auspicious tiding for it meant they had not seen what they feared most to see, and that which kept them all peering over their shoulders when they thought no one else was watching—they had not seen a trace of the merciless Harriers.

Led by Durwin, and urged on by Theido, they pursued a course that would skirt the treacherous mountains and lead them instead across the hilly woodland regions of Askelon, bending ever eastward toward Celbercor's Wall.

Once over the Wall—traversing that formidable obstacle would be an ordeal all its own—the rescuers would make straight for the Malmar inlet, crossing it on foot over the ice. Safely across Malmar they would have a brief rest in the small fishing village of Malmarby, one of the few outposts of human habitation in all of the vast peninsula of Obrey. They would have time, it was hoped, to replenish their supplies and to obtain a guide who could be induced to lead them to Dekra.

Quentin had at last learned that Dekra was not a person, but a place: the forgotten city of a mysterious people long ago vanished. No one now remembered what had happened to the city's strange inhabitants; but they had left behind a fantastic dwelling which had grown rich and wonderful in song and legend, although few men had actually ever been there to see it. Fewer still believed its existence, regarding it as mere glittering fancy spun by bards and minstrels to tickle the ears of the gullible. Some though, insisted that it did exist and was a very evil place where men were not welcome—those daring to search for it never returned, so it was told.

"Never heard of Dekra, my boy?" questioned Durwin. His bushy eyebrows arched in a quizzical look when Quentin ventured to ask him about it. "No, I don't suppose you have. The priests of Ariel do not willingly admit that it exists. Well, you shall have a chance to do something most men never do: you shall see it with your own eyes."

"Is it a very bad place, then?" asked Quentin. "Is that why Theido wished not to go there?" He was riding Balder abreast of the hermit, having left his usual position at the rear of the train just ahead of Trenn. Quentin liked to ride up ahead with Durwin whenever the trail permitted.

"No . . ." Durwin replied, after a pause in which he tried to think of the correct words. "Dekra is not an evil place, though many believe that it is. It is one of the seven ancient places of power on the earth. And though the power is mostly gone now, remnants still linger for those who know where to look.

"But it is not an evil place—that is not why Theido argued against our going. He knew it to be a dangerous journey and a long one for nothing if we should fail to obtain what we seek."

Quentin had had to content himself with that answer, for Durwin would say no more about the ruined city, or their reason for going there. Yet, the hermit was withholding more than he would say—Quentin sensed it in his voice. Something there Durwin avoided telling, and Quentin, his youthful curiosity piqued, itched to find out what it was. So he listened constantly for any clue which Durwin or Theido might let fall at meal times or around the fire at night. He was most often disappointed.

Theido spurred the party forward at a relentless pace, never stopping long or allowing a fire by daylight. Nights were short by design—stopping at dusk, sleeping only a few hours and then moving on well before dawn. Quentin had mastered the art of sleeping in his saddle when he could no longer keep his eyes open. In fact, he had found himself rapidly becoming a better horseman all around. He reveled in the new skills he was developing day by day and the woodland lore he was learning from Durwin, who proved an inexhaustible source of knowledge.

Quentin could now name thirty different kinds of tree and shrub. He could tell the tracks of every forest creature that stirred in the dead of winter. And he could read the weather signs with some small degree of accuracy. Quentin considered this far more useful information than anything he had learned in the temple, although he had to admit his temple training was useful in other ways.

For these and other reasons, arising mainly out of the kinship formed of a group dedicated to a common purpose, Quentin felt a deep sense of joy in the rigors of the journey, forgetting easily the innumerable discomforts of living on the trail. He had also quite nearly forgotten the danger dogging their every step—the Harriers. Yet, there seemed to be nothing to indicate the presence of the hated trackers.

Theido, however, continually dropped behind the group, leaving it for hours at a time to watch and wait, scanning the forest for any sign which might indicate they were being followed. Each time he returned to report that he had seen nothing of the Harriers. But each day he grew more worried.

"I am afraid they are waiting for us to run out into the open," Theido told them one night. The sun had just gone down and they sat around the fire wrapped in their cloaks and thick robes made of animal skins which Durwin had furnished.

"You don't think we might have eluded them?" asked Trenn hopefully, "that Voss and his rangers put them off the trail . . ."

"No," Theido replied gravely, shaking his head slowly from side to side. "I fear not. Voss may have put them off for some short time, and by the fact that we are still awake and moving, I'd say that was likely.

"But, each day I feel their presence stronger. I seem to sense the fingers of their minds reaching out for us, drawing closer. They may not have found our trail as yet, but they are closing upon us."

"Why do you think they will wait for us to break and run into the open?" asked Alinea. "Why would they not take us in the forest?"

Theido again shook his head. "That I do not know. There is something preventing them, though what it is I cannot say. But once we are free of the forest, which we shall be in two days' time, they will have no trouble seeing us. The hills beyond offer little cover in the summer, and less in the winter, for those who need shelter from preying eyes."

"Yet, if we can but cross the hill country as far as the Great Wall we will then have a chance," interjected Durwin. He alone looked hopeful.

"We still have to find a way to cross the Wall," reminded Trenn. "That could take many days. Unless my horse sprouts wings I do not see how we are to cross."

"There must be a way," said Alinea. "The Wall is old, perchance there is a breach . . ."

"Pray there is no breach, my Lady," said Trenn. "Any advantage we receive, our captors will benefit the more."

"The Harriers are not our captors," said Quentin oddly. The others stopped and looked at him, raising their heads from the fire to see his face. He wore an expression of fear and wonder, his dark round eyes looking beyond the circle of light thrown out by the campfire. "These men are."

Theido was the first to follow Quentin's gaze outward and to see what he saw: a ring of faces—almost invisible in the darkness but for the firelight glinting in large eyes—circled them in. They were surrounded.

FIFTEEN

THE JHER village, if that word could be applied so loosely, was as nearly invisible as could be made. Shelters for fifty or more people had been erected out of limbs and branches, bark and leaves. Each was dug into the earth and was shaped like a shallow dome. If there had been no people standing in front of these simple abodes, or peering from the narrow slits of doorways, Quentin could have passed right through the rude village and never had an inkling he had been there.

The footprints in the snow on the ground told a different story.

The snow had been compacted by the constant trammeling of many feet. It appeared that the Jher had been living in this part of the forest all winter, as indeed they had. Hunting and trapping in the northernmost reaches of Pelgrin, they had established a winter camp in the forest. They would move again in the spring when they returned to their usual habitat—the Wilderlands of Obrey.

Seeing them now in the full light of day, Quentin wondered what he had feared from them in the long night when they had stood at the edge of the campfire's light. All night they had held their strange vigil, faces shifting only slightly as one would go and another appear to take his place. He had imagined all sorts of horrible tortures at their hands. But looking now at their broad, brown faces, their finely formed yet sturdy features with their clear, untroubled brown eyes which seemed wise and all-knowing, Quentin was ashamed he had thought ill of these simple folk.

When dawn had come, the leader, who called himself Hoet, had advanced to the campfire where Theido and Durwin stood waiting to receive them in whatever manner they presented themselves—in war or in peace. Then, quite inexplicably, Durwin had startled everyone, not the least the Jher tribesmen who hooted in amazement, by speaking a few halting words in their lilting, sing-song tongue.

Durwin had turned to the others then and addressed them sheepishly. "I am sorry, my friends. I should have told you all sooner that we had nothing to fear from the Jher. But I thought it best to remain on our guard, for it has been long since I encountered any of them about in this part of the forest, and many changes have taken place in the world. I could not be certain what reception we faced. But it is as I hoped—they welcome us as friends." He then faced the Jher leader and spoke again in that strange tongue.

Hoet signalled excitedly to his companions, about a dozen in all, and they had advanced murmuring together in astonishment at the strange wonder they beheld—a member of the white race speaking their language.

And wonder it was. The Jher were a wandering people. Simple, uncomplicated, their ways had not changed much in a thousand years. They built no cities, erected no altars, neither read nor wrote their own language. They were older even than the hated Shoth; older than the land, for all anyone knew. Where they had come from was a mystery long past discovering—one of the many which, like bark grown thick around an ancient oak, surrounded these shy people.

They were seldom seen in the region of Askelon anymore. Civilization forced them further and further north and east into the Wilderlands. Few city dwellers ever encountered the gentle Jher, but the peasants living close to the northern edges of Pelgrin glimpsed them on rare occasions. Sometimes they would not be seen in a region for a generation or more, and then suddenly appear just as before.

The Jher were a peaceful, timid people who had no enemies, except the brutal Shoth whom they hunted like the deer they lived upon. It was a marvel these unassuming beings could fight at all; they did not seem capable of conflict. But they had among their surprising traits an inbred hatred for the last of their ancient enemy.

Durwin sat in consultation with Hoet, the Jher chieftain, in the midst of the small clearing. Quentin could tell the going was very slow. The same words were repeated over and over, with many gestures and lapses into confused silence. But Durwin seemed to be making headway. He nodded more frequently and seemed to ask questions less often. All this Quentin wildly inferred, since nothing in the Jher speech seemed like words in the ordinary sense. It was more a random uttering of forest sounds and nature imitations than real language. And yet, to Quentin's ears it was strangely beautiful and even moving, for in it he heard the gentle sounds of the earth as it moved through the seasons, of trees in the wind, of water slapping stone, of animals playing. The language of the Jher was filled with the beauty of the forest and its creatures.

While the two leaders tried to understand one another, Quentin established contact in his own way: gawking unashamedly at the strange people who had gathered around them. The Jher just as boldly stared back, pointing at the outlanders (their term for anyone who was not another Jher) and coveting their horses and steel knives.

The Jher, Quentin decided, were a compact race, tending more toward grace than bulk. They possessed smooth, well-formed bodies, lithe rather than muscular—again, like deer. The Jher had so long lived with the deer, they had become like them; it struck Quentin that they even looked like deer, with their large, dark, fathomless eyes, deep as forest pools and as calm.

They wore deerskin clothing, sewn of deer-gut thread with

deer-bone needles. They ate venison, burned deer fat in their lamps made from skulls of deer. The race had become wholly dependent upon the deer for survival and followed them wherever the nimble animals went, running with them through the seasons.

On any of the crudely decorated items of clothing or personal possessions Quentin happened to see were usually pictures of deer, painted, scratched, or carved into the item. Or, perhaps a representation of the sun, which they also revered.

And the people had the same quick instincts and lightning reactions as the shy forest creatures. That, coupled with their acute awareness of their surroundings, made them invisible to the loud, clumsy white races who tramped through the forest unaware that there might be other living souls as close as the larch they passed under.

Quentin was engaged in making hand signals with several of the braver Jher children who had gathered around, when Durwin rose and shuffled back to where the rest were seated on deerskins in the snow, awaiting the outcome of the parley.

"Hoet says that we are marked for death," announced Durwin, who quickly realized his blunder by the stricken looks of anguish appearing on his comrades' faces. "Oh, no! Not by the Jher. Oh, my!—no. Forgive me—I have been trying to piece together the story and did not realize what I was saying.

"Hoet says that we are being followed by Harriers, which we know. However, the Harriers were closer than we had guessed. Last night should have been our last. He said that was the reason they stayed with us through the night watching, lest the Shoth try to take us. Without our knowing it we have stumbled very close to their winter village, and they did not want any Shoth coming so close to them.

"So they protected us through the night, did they?" said Theido. "I am grateful for their aid. But what will happen when we leave here? The Harriers will be waiting for us as soon as we enter the forest."

"We have discussed that," replied Durwin. He smiled and inclined his head toward Hoet, who stood a few paces away. Hoet repeated the gesture. "Hoet says he will give us a bodyguard and a guide to lead us away from the Shoth by ways known to them."

"How many men will go with us?" asked Trenn. His eyes scanned the group for likely conscripts. "Five or six of the bigger men should be adequate, I think." In his soldier's brain Trenn had already formed them into a fighting contingent and outfitted them with the helmets, bucklers, and hard leather armor of foot soldiers.

Durwin looked a little confused. "I cannot say how many Hoet intends to send with us." He turned and went back to where the chief was standing, arms folded, chin resting on his breast. They put their heads together and began discussing again, hands groping as if to pull words out of the air. Finally, Hoet turned and whistled and waved his hand toward a group of men who were standing by the horses, admiring the animals, tack and gear. A slender young man, not much older than Quentin, came gliding over and presented himself to Hoet, who presented him to Durwin.

"Here is our bodyguard and guide," said Durwin, returning with the youth.

"What?" exploded Trenn, flabbergasted. His eyes started out of his head and his mouth hung open. The young Jher did not seem a fair match even for one of his own people, let alone three blood-lusting Harriers.

"This is Toli," said Durwin, introducing him to the others. Then he went around the group saying each person's name. Toli did not attempt to duplicate the sounds. He merely smiled and nodded politely.

"When do we leave?" asked Theido with a sigh. He too had his doubts about the Jher bodyguard. He cast a quick glance overhead to see the once-clear sky had become overcast while they had waited for Durwin and Hoet's deliberations to run their course.

"Hoet suggests we sleep for a few hours. We can leave tonight. He also says not to worry; Toli will show us a secret way past the Wall which he claims the Shoth do not know."

SIXTEEN

THE KING sat in darkness in the deep dungeon of Kazakh, Nimrood's walled mountain keep. Around him lay the scattered pieces of his armor, now rusting in the dank jail's seeping damp. His once-proud head fell forward dejectedly upon his chest and his sunken eyes were closed against the disgrace of his surroundings. His long, black hair and well-kept beard, once curling with vitality, now hung in limp tangles, filthy and matted, graying at the edges.

Inwardly he cursed himself for his own stupidity and lack of foresight. So intent had he been upon returning home, so full of good spirits, he had dismissed his men to his commanders and, taking only a small bodyguard of knights, had set off straightway to catch the last boat before the raging seas of fall brought an end to the shipping season. They had boarded the ship and had, with some misgiving of the captain, sailed forth upon a sea running to chop and a sky glowering with pent-up fury.

The storm had broken the fourth day out and the captain had made for the nearest port, the harbor Fallers at the far southern tip of Elsendor. The captain had wisely refused to go further, so Eskevar and his knights struck out crosscountry. A day and a night out of Fallers they were attacked. A force of armed men had been waiting to take them as they entered a narrow canyon.

The King and his knights fought valiantly, though greatly outnumbered, but at last had been overpowered. They were bound and thrown into wagons and covered with sailcloth and traveled for many days through rocky country. One of the knights, Ronsard, had been able to work free of his bonds and had escaped, recovering his horse and weapons, but having to leave behind his King and comrades.

Ronsard had followed the wagons to their destination, a ship with black sails standing off a lonely stretch of coastland. He had followed hoping to seize an opportunity to free his companions. But when he espied the dark ship and its stout occupants he despaired of loosing his friends with his lone sword and had turned toward Mensandor with his message for the Queen.

The months had passed, each day more unbearable than the one before it. King Eskevar refused to surrender to the hopelessness he felt closing around him. At first he had railed against his captor, his mighty voice kindled in righteous rage. The halls and galleries of Kazakh reverberated with his angry thunder.

Nimrood had paced his chambers cackling maniacally, his wild eyes kindled with a fierce, unearthly light.

After weeks of captivity, Nimrood had descended to his dungeon to at last cast his wicked eyes upon his prize. The King had challenged him, had begged for the freedom of his knights, had promised a stunning ransom, had demanded to know the reasons for his kidnapping. To this latter demand he had been told that his brother, Prince Jaspin, had arranged to have him kept comfortably and safely locked away until Jaspin wore the crown.

Nimrood had left then, leaving his miserable prisoner alone to eat out his great heart in anger and frustration. The King had seen no other living person since that brief interview.

Eskevar heard the scraping clank of an iron latch lifted and dropped into place again, followed by the squeal of unused hinges. Then he heard the pinging echo of footsteps on the spiraling steps descending to the dungeon. The jailer comes with food, he thought.

Then he saw the flickering light of a torch playing on the rough rock walls of the narrow gallery that led along the row of cells. He listened and waited. From the shuffle he heard in the gallery he guessed there were more than the jailer alone. A torch thrust into sight, blinding his clouded eyes with its unwonted brightness. Sharp pains stabbed into his brain as he forced himself to look at the jailer.

Eskevar struggled to his feet uncertainly, to tower over the jailer and his two scurvy guards.

"You get back there!" screamed the jailer, thrusting the torch through the bars of the iron door. The old rusty door swung open and the two guards with lances at the ready stepped gingerly in. One prodded the King forward with the butt of his lance and the King tottered like an old man into the gallery. The dripping passageway was so narrow and short he had to hunch himself together, bending low to proceed. For good measure, and to remind the prisoner that he was under guard, the spear would jab him in the back periodically as they made their way to the spiral steps.

Eskevar stumbled twice as they climbed the steps, but caught himself and continued the climb slowly and with great deliberation. He was buying himself time to restore some part of his strength and allow his eyes to become accustomed to the pale light which grew brighter as they ascended upward out of the dungeon.

At last the King stepped out into fair light again; it seemed to dazzle his deprived senses. He breathed deeply, filling his lungs with cool, clean air. He found his head cleared from the confusion he had fallen into of late. He straightened with difficulty and squared his shoulders and raised his head high.

The party was ushered into the great hall where Nimrood sat waiting on his high black throne. "So, our prisoner lives still, does he?" hissed the necromancer. "Too bad; our pets will have to wait a little yet for their meat!" he laughed to himself, and Eskevar noticed the huge ugly head of a tremendous snake leering at him from beneath the throne.

"Set me free or kill me," said the King. "You shall receive

no ransom and my brother will never sit upon my throne. The regents will never allow it."

"Perhaps not *your* regents, proud King. But several of your regents seem to have come under suspicion of certain foul deeds. Two of them are even now locked away in the bowels of Castle Askelon, awaiting their impending fate."

"You fiend!" shouted the King, dashing forward. One of the guards sought to block his path with lowered lance, but the King grabbed the lance and wrenched it out of the man's grasp and shoved him back with the butt of his own weapon. He then swung the lance in a wide arc around himself, keeping the jailer and the other guard at a distance. Eskevar lowered the lance and advanced on Nimrood menacingly. The sorcerer raised his arms above his head and shouted an incantation, *"Borgat Invendum cei Spensus witso borgatti!"*

"Your powers cannot . . ." the King started, then something like a leaden net dropped upon his limbs and he felt his strength leave him. He raised his mighty arm to loft the lance, but the weapon suddenly seemed to weigh as much as the dungeon door. The throw went soft and the lance skidded weakly upon the stone floor.

"You shall see what my powers can do!" snapped the angry wizard. "I have been waiting for just this moment. Bind him! And take him to the tower."

King Eskevar cried out in rage, "Kill me now! If you miss this chance you will regret it for all eternity, black wizard!"

The guards rushed upon the helpless monarch and bound him in chains. They dragged him out of the hall and to the tower where he was locked again in a strange room, not a cell, but a high-domed room painted with grotesque shapes and queer inscriptions. No sooner had he entered the room and the door slammed behind him did King Eskevar feel himself overcome with an unnatural urge to sleep.

The heavy vapors of slumber seemed to drift out of the very floor beneath his feet. His head nodded and lolled on his shoulders, eyelids fluttering. His knees buckled and he crashed to the wooden floor where he attempted to rise again. The King gained his knees and knelt awkwardly, for his chains would permit but limited movement.

"You will find the rest here refreshing, I hope," hissed Nimrood. Eskevar jerked his head up to see the sharp, twisted face of his tormentor at the barred slits of the door.

"I curse your bones, necromancer," spat the King. But even as he spoke his tongue went slack in his mouth, and his eyelids fell shut. He tried again to rise, but his legs could not support him and he dropped senseless to his side fast asleep.

"Look your last upon the world as a mortal, great King. It is a rare gift I give you. When you awaken you'll be one of my own Immortals. Sleep well."

SEVENTEEN

IN THE four days since they had left the camp of the nomadic Jher, Durwin's party had covered ground at a tremendous rate. They were all amazed at the skill and clear-thinking of their guide, Toli—none so much as Trenn who had severely doubted that they would last an hour more in the forest.

But Toli knew the land like his own skin. He knew instinctively when a trail would veer and when to abandon one path and choose another. The forest seemed to hide no secrets from his alert eyes: in fact, this slim, brown young man read it as easily as Durwin read the scrolls he collected in such profusion. Quentin suspected that generations of following the deer had made the Jher more at home in the forest among the wild things than in the world of men. In this he shared the conventional wisdom, for the wary Jher were widely considered a people sinking back into animal ways rather than arising out of them.

But a better guide they could not have found anywhere. And

if there had been six like him, the company could not have been safer from discovery by the Harriers. Toli knew when to halt and when to move forward. He varied the times of their travel, never keeping to a determined pattern, but moving more like a cunning animal might, though still chiefly at night.

Still, none of them doubted that the Harriers were yet behind them. Toli agreed that until they crossed the Wall there would be no safety. He and Durwin were often in consultation shortly before and after each day's trek. Durwin began to grow visibly more apprehensive as they neared the great structure.

The ancient architectural wonder had protected the realm of Mensandor for a thousand years from marauders and would-be conquerors. Now it stood as a warning of the strength and determination of the people of Mensandor to live free, for no enemy had dared to cross it with an army in anyone's memory.

Celbercor's Wall as it was known of old rose to a height of four-score spans from the rocky, uneven ground to the jagged merlons which formed its battlements. The Wall was wide enough at the top for three knights to ride abreast or a column of men to move along with ease. It spanned a gray, barren stretch of land a hundred leagues in length from the inlet of Malmar where it jutted out into the water to the sheer rock curtain of Mount Ostenkell in the northernmost Fiskills.

Celbercor's Wall was intended to separate Askelon from the entire wilderland region of the Suthlands, but it had never been finished. Only the northern extremity running south from Malmar's icy finger to the treacherous Fiskills had been erected, and that at dear cost.

But it stood intact. A staggering achievement: seamless, without gap or breach imposed by the years, raised with such stonecutter's art that no mortar was used—only stone fitted to stone, interlocked and assembled with exacting precision throughout its whole length.

Quentin had never seen the Wall, but had often heard of it in stories. The thought of at last beholding it sent a tingle of excitement to his sandal-clad toes. But Durwin dashed any lighter

mood when he announced to the assembled company, "Tonight
we will cross the Wall, and most assuredly tonight the Harriers
will try to stop us. Toli thinks they are not far behind and they
probably already sense what we are going to attempt. We will be
vulnerable once we leave the shelter of the forest.

"The forest will end about a league before the Wall, but
there is a valley which runs along our course. We shall enter it
and follow as long as we may."

"What then?" asked Trenn, his soldier's ethics offended. He
considered it a disgrace to slink away by night like cowardly
dogs. Yet, he did not relish putting his sword to the test against
three such formidable blades as those of the Harriers.

"What then? Why, Toli will lead us to the Jher's secret
crossing. If we make it, I doubt if the Shoth will pursue us
further. It would take them weeks to find a means to cross the
Wall with their horses, and months to ride around it."

"How will we get *our* horses across?" asked Alinea.

"Yes," said Theido. "Are we to take our horses, or no?"

Durwin called Toli to him and they spent a few moments
together in discussion of this problem. Durwin turned with a
grave look upon his face. "He does not know. The Jher do not
have horses, so have never considered whether it is possible to
bring them through. You see, the secret way is not over the Wall,
but under it—a tunnel."

"Blazes!" muttered Trenn. He liked the scheme less and
less.

"Is it so bad to continue without horses?" asked the Queen.

"It would be very difficult," replied Theido.

"Impossible," put in Trenn.

"Not impossible," Durwin said. "Remember, Toli and his
people live in the Wilderlands. He will show us how to get
through them. They travel the land continually."

"The main thing is the loss of our horses will slow us down
considerably. Dekra is still weeks away—longer on foot."

Quentin listened to this talk with a sorrowful feeling. He
hated the thought of leaving Balder behind to become the prey of

wolves—or worse, the Harriers. He turned away and went to the animal he had grown quite attached to in the short time they had been together.

"They say you may be left behind, Balder. I would rather they left *me* behind," he sniffed, a tear forming in his eye. "I don't want to leave you." He put an arm around the huge animal's neck and pressed his cheek into the horse's thick shoulder. Balder nickered softly and swung his head down to nip Quentin on the arm.

"You are fond of this animal." Quentin turned to see Theido standing near him, reaching up to pat Balder's white forehead.

"I did not realize it until just now." He smeared the tear across his cheek with his sleeve.

"It is nothing to be ashamed of. A knight must have a thought for his mount—in battle you are partners. And this sturdy war horse knows best how to protect his rider in a fight, I'll warrant."

"He will be able to fend for himself, won't he? When we turn them loose?"

"Yes, he will manage—better than we will, I should think. But I have no intention of turning them loose if it can be helped. We need our horses too desperately." Quentin saw the look of strain in the tight lines around his friend's eyes.

"Is it that difficult, this road through the Wilderlands?" Quentin had not considered that it would be very much different than what they had experienced in the forest.

"Yes. Worse than you can imagine if you have not seen it. There is no road, nor path nor even trail. The whole region is naught but thickets of brush and bramble resting on a queasy bog. At least we shall have the benefit of snow to firm our footing. But even with that we must be careful—many of the bogs are fed by warm springs underground. They do not freeze in winter, though the snow will sometimes cover them over. There are few more hazardous places for a company of travelers."

Quentin took this news glumly and wished the journey was at an end. He was beginning to tire of the constant making and breaking of camp and the long cold intervals between. He had long ago stopped thinking about the Harriers and the terrors they held; after days of fretting constantly and lying awake through the night clutching his dagger, he had simply refused to consider them anymore. Now he was once again forced to wonder what they might do to him if he were caught.

At dusk the party once more set out. The forest thinned around them as they pushed ever nearer the Wall. And so too did the awful dread increase. What lay behind them was not to be dwelt upon for any length of time.

Quentin felt only partly more secure. For this run to the Wall Toli had been mounted with him on Balder, the largest of the horses. The two sat together comfortably, Toli occupying the place behind Quentin. Although the Jher had no horses of their own, they seemed to be unafraid of them, and tolerably able to handle them when given the chance. But Quentin, being the better horseman of the two, held the reins, and Toli directed the course.

The group traveled a league and more single file behind Balder's lead. The sky was dark overhead, moon and stars obscured by low, scudding clouds. So much the better, thought Quentin; maybe the Harriers would not see them at all.

Finally they reached the edge of the forest, and without hesitation Toli led them out on to a wide expanse of barren hills where standing stones lurched out of the ground sharply and at odd angles. The landscape was a desolate waste, the exposed roots of the subterranean rock shelf that pushed up inland to form the Fiskills. To Quentin it appeared a lonely, forsaken place, bare and forbidding.

Picking up the pace, Toli led them down a steep incline to the bottom of a broad gully which had been formed by the icy waters of spring cutting through the loose soil. Above them on either side rose the banks of this dry steam bed. Long icicles hung down from the lips of overhanging rock, and the slight wind which had risen behind them whispered over the craggy fissures.

Ahead or behind they could see nothing, overhead only the

blank, dark sky. But each of them began to sense a deep foreboding, almost a loathing to continue. Each step became a labor, and each turn in the way a thing to be avoided. In spite of Toli's urgings the party slowed and began feeling its way along haltingly.

Quentin felt the fear wash over him and knew that it did not come from within. He had, as an acolyte, witnessed possession rituals where a priest would call upon the god to inhabit his body for a brief time to espouse the god's oracles. He had felt the same sensation on those occasions when the supercharged emotional atmosphere gave vent to the strange proceedings.

This impeding force Quentin knew was foreign, and with a jolt realized its source: the Harriers. They were coming at last.

In the same instant Quentin framed the thought he felt an icy tingle skitter along his ribs and he swiveled in the saddle to peer behind him. He saw nothing; then, even as he turned to look away, he caught a glimpse of a dark shape melting into the background some distance away. What it was could not be seen, but Quentin knew in his heart that the Harriers were upon them. He jerked the reins sharply. Balder stopped dead and Theido nearly collided with him as his animal lurched forward in the dark.

"I saw something behind us just now," Quentin whispered hoarsely. He saw Theido's face only as a dark mask in the darkness around it.

"How far back?"

"I cannot tell," said Quentin, breathlessly. "I only saw something move back there. Listen!" As he spoke there came the patter of a stone falling into the ravine, somewhere far behind them. The thin, rattling echo was lost instantly in the void.

"Away!" whispered Theido. The urgency in his voice made him sound small and far away. He wheeled his horse around and passed the word back. Quentin slapped Balder and let the animal have his head. They dashed into the darkness with a clatter.

Through the twisting gorge they rode, Toli holding onto Quentin with a stubborn grip. He shouted something unintelligible into Quentin's ear, and Quentin looked forward to see the banks on either side sloping away as they began to climb a shallow incline. A final burst and they were out of the valley.

Rising in front of them was the massive, undulating shape of Celbercor's Wall, a looming rampart of astonishing dimensions. Quentin urged the horse forward as overhead the moon broke through the low overcast. Now he could see the vast bulwark of the Wall towering above them, although they were still some distance from the foot of it.

The moon disappeared again as they turned, following Toli's instruction, and began running along the face of the Wall at an angle toward it. From the sound of hooves behind him Quentin knew the others were close behind.

They galloped down another steep ravine and started up the opposite side. They had just gained the top of the further bank when the moon again peeped out, scattering light across the wild landscape. To Quentin's horror he saw in that fleeting stream the glint of steel and two riders wheeling toward him. Toli tugged at his arm and he threw the reins to the side and headed straight for the Wall.

A piercing shriek cut the night; at first Quentin thought it a woman's scream and then recognized it as the hunting cry of a hawk. A rider bolted past him and he heard Theido shout, "To the Wall! Lead the others to the Wall!" He saw the moonlight shimmer on the thin line of Theido's uplifted blade.

Toli yelled and waved his arm for the others to follow as they started upon the Wall.

"They're upon us!" cried Trenn. His horse stumbled on the loose rock and he went down.

The Queen just ahead of him turned and started back, but Durwin propelled her forward, saying, "I shall look to him—go on!" Her quick horse flew over the uncertain footing as nimbly as a shadow, and in an instant she was beside Quentin and Toli.

Just ahead, but hidden from them by an outcropping of rock, Quentin could hear the clear, cold ring of steel upon steel and the wild cry of the horses as they engaged one another. They reached a sheltered hollow and Toli threw himself to the ground and ran directly up to the very face of the Wall. Quentin blinked his eyes, for in the shifting moonlight he thought he had seen the young Jher disappear right into the huge foundation stones of Celbercor's Wall.

He was back almost at once, shouting and pushing them forward. Quentin heard the scream in the air above him once more, this time very close. He spun around instinctively throwing an arm over his face as Toli, leaping like a cat, caught his other arm and pulled him to the ground.

There was a rustle in the air and a tearing sound as he went down. Then he felt a sharp pain high up in the arm he'd thrown over his head. He saw Durwin come pounding in and Trenn, hanging sideways over the back of his horse, slumped to the ground. Quentin rolled his eyes and saw two white wings lifting away in the night. He looked at his arm and saw that his tunic had been ripped and blood was oozing out of the wound.

"Here is the tunnel!" someone called. Quentin felt hands lift him to his feet and then he was running for the wall. A rider thundered up from behind them and he heard Theido's voice bellowing. Quentin suddenly thought it strange that he should be running like a scared deer; he wanted to sit down. The voices around him buzzed and the air became warm. He slowed and turned. Theido said something and Quentin cocked his head, puzzled, for Theido had begun speaking in an unknown language.

He stopped and looked up at the twin moons hovering just overhead. He reached up to touch one, as if to pluck it and hold it in his hand. He heard music: the ringing of temple bells far away. Then the black sky turned blood red. Quentin blinked his eyes and sat down marveling at this queer wonder. He felt his head slam down against the smooth stone of the Wall and the last thing he saw was Durwin's face peering down upon him as if from a great height, speaking to him in a confused tongue. A tear rolled down Quentin's cheek and he knew no more.

EIGHTEEN

THE TWINKLING, shifting light spun in bright globes. Quentin could see them even though his eyes were closed. He traced their play on his eyelids for hours, half-waking, half-dreaming. From somewhere far away, in another room or in another world perhaps, he heard music. High-pitched bells tinkled sharply, pricking his ears with their thin melody.

How long he had lain watching the dancing lights and listening to the crystalline song of the bells he did not know. Maybe hours. Maybe days. Maybe forever.

Quentin, in his twilight world between darkness and light, drifted in and out of consciousness almost at will and was aware of nothing but the shifting globes of light, sometimes red or blue, but most often a rosy golden hue. He perceived nothing but the lights and the intonation of the tiny chimes.

The room where Quentin lay commanded a western view of a range of low, forested mountains. They rose and fell in gentle folds like the thick, bristly fur of some mythical beast sleeping peacefully through the ages. From the balcony's high parapet one could look to the west and the fiery descent of the setting sun.

And every afternoon the earthward trail of the falling sun brought the light full through the arched double doors which opened onto the balcony. The light washed over Quentin's inert form, transfiguring him from a pale, waxen image into a creature of living light. A wind chime hanging at the apex of the arch danced in the light breeze which capered now and then in through the open doors.

An old woman in a white woolen shawl sat near Quentin's high wide bed. She held in her hands a small jar of aromatic unguent which she periodically applied to a spot just over Quentin's heart, and to his temples. At these intervals she whispered a few brief words under her breath, holding her hands over the young man's still, barely breathing form.

A steady train of visitors throughout the day came to stand at the foot of Quentin's bed, or merely to step inside the door. They looked to the old woman, always with the same question in their eyes, and always they left with the same reply in kind: no change.

Durwin relieved the old woman from time to time, sitting for hours gazing upon the motionless body stretched before him. In the evening he brought a cup of lukewarm broth which he administered to Quentin by means of a short, hollow tube of bone. Durwin let the broth trickle slowly down Quentin's throat, careful not to choke him. There was never any response.

Durwin had just administered the broth one evening when Theido came to the room.

"Still no change?"

"None. He hovers between life and death. Sometimes I think he might awaken; he looks about to rise up—but the moment passes away and he is the same."

"Can he recover, do you think? It has been nearly two months."

"I do not know. I have never seen this kind of illness before. Certainly no one recovers from the poison of the Shoth. Still, the people of Dekra have many powers unknown in the world abroad. And had his wound been deeper, or closer to the mark, this old woman's art would not have mattered—he would have died within the hour, or out on the trail."

Durwin sighed as he looked sadly at the boy's thin body. "We came for nothing. It is my fault that he is stricken so."

"Do not blame yourself, sir. If fault is to be found we need not look further than Jaspin's door. 'Twas he loosed the Harriers."

"Still, our purpose in coming here has come to naught, and our number has already been diminished. It was my willfulness and pride, Thiedo. That is why young Quentin suffers now."

"It was your healing skill, good hermit. That is why he still draws breath."

Thiedo did not speak again for a long time. Then, hastily, as if fearing what he must say, he blurted, "We cannot wait any longer, Durwin. We must leave by week's end. The ships will be sailing soon from their winter's harborage in Bestou on Tildeen. We must secure a ship to take us to Karsh."

The hermit lifted his eyebrows in surprise. "You think you will find a merchant who will endanger his ship so?"

"For the King, yes."

"For no king or kingdom. The fate of a king matters little to these sailors. They care nothing for the rise and fall of nations. Their loyalty swings by the heft of your purse."

"Then the captain that enjoins our enterprise shall have a king's ransom for his troubles. I can guarantee that—the Queen herself will vouch it."

"Do not be so sure. They are a wild, superstitious lot. Worse than peasants when it comes to charms and sacrifices. Karsh may hold a power over them which even the love of gold cannot release."

"We shall see. Anyway, we have no other plan—we cannot fly."

"No, I suppose not. I doubt if even old Nimrood could foresee that," Durwin laughed.

It had been meant as a joke, but Theido remained grave at the mention of the magician's name. "Do you think the necromancer sees so much? Does he know of our enterprise?"

"Undoubtedly he knows—whether by art or by spies he knows we are abroad. But I do not think he considers a party of five . . ."

"Four," corrected Theido. Durwin was about to continue

when he heard a rustle at the door and Alinea stepped into the room. She went to the bed and placed a warm hand on Quentin's cool forehead. She looked sadly upon his upturned face and then stepped over to where the men stood talking.

"Is there nothing more we can do?" Her voice lightly pleaded for the young man's release; her eyes held a touching pity for her fallen friend.

"All that can be done has been accomplished. Now we must watch and wait," said Durwin.

"Yes, I know. So you have told me often enough. I only wish there was something that could sway the balance. These weeks have not been easy ones."

"Our wait is nearly at an end," said Theido. He caught the Queen's questioning glance and explained, "We must leave at week's end to begin our journey to the island Tildeen. The ships will be sailing again soon, and I am anxious to secure our passage."

"Then we must leave him?"

"I think it is for the best," offered Durwin. "He cannot travel as he is, that much is obvious. Even if he were to recover he would be still too weak to travel for weeks to come. No, we must leave him here. The Curatak will take care of him. When he is strong enough he can return to Askelon; Toli will bring him safely as far as Pelgrin."

"Yes," agreed Theido, "it is for the best. We know not what the outcome of our mission might be. 'Twere better for Quentin that he abide safely in Durwin's cottage."

"It will break his heart to find us gone," said Alinea. "He has come this far only to be denied . . ."

"It cannot be helped, my Lady," said Theido. He too felt badly that Quentin, who had shown himself to be a stalwart and worthy companion, should now have to remain behind.

"When do we leave, you say?" she asked. "By week's end? I will compose a letter of safe conduct for him, should Jaspin's men be roaming the way."

"Do you think that will matter very much?" asked Theido.

The Queen paused and looked at the two men sorrowfully.

"No," she said quietly, "but it is the one thing I can do."

"Yes," agreed Durwin. "I shall compose a letter myself explaining all that has happened and what we intend. That should help ease his mind that we have not abandoned him unreasonably."

"Good! A fine idea. I will begin seeing to our provisions and equipment," said Theido, feeling better about their leave-taking. As with most knights, he did not like leaving a fallen comrade behind in any circumstances that he could improve. He left the room with a more resolute tread than he had entered it. His mind was at ease now.

"I do not know . . ." murmured Durwin into his beard.

"What troubles you, friend Durwin," wondered Alinea. "Is there something more?"

"More than I am telling? Yes, I do admit it." He moved to Quentin's bed and sat down on the edge. He placed his hand upon the boy's chest for a moment. "I told him once that he had some part to play in this—so I still believe. But the god I serve has not illumined me more precisely, I am afraid." He gazed fondly down upon the motionless form beside him. "It could be this is the beginning for him, not the end."

Queen Alinea nodded silently and placed her hand on the hermit's shoulder. After a few moments of silence they left together, leaving Quentin's care once more to the old woman.

NINETEEN

THE SNOW lay melting in Askelon's inner ward yard. The high windswept dome of the sky appeared spotless and clean, heralding an early spring. Servants of various rank scurried across the yard avoiding the mud and standing water as much as possible. Each was intent upon some important task. To look at them was as much as to see a column of ants hurrying about their chores with more than the usual amount of vigor.

In a constant parade to his chambers, where Prince Jaspin held court amidst the bustle of servants packing his furniture and belongings, came the knights and nobles, some of whom would ride in his train. They all came to pledge their fealty and support to his cause, and to receive some indulgence for themselves in return. The sycophant Ontescue stood at the Prince's left hand, bending close to whisper in the Prince's ear how much this noble's allegiance had cost, or what boon that knight required to satisfy his conscience.

A young knight who wished leave to take back the lands of his father (which he had squandered away in dissipation), by right of the point of his lance, entered and knelt before Jaspin. He pleaded his cause when asked, and the Prince acquiesced as instructed by Ontescue's intimations. As the knight rose to leave, bowing deeply, Prince Jaspin asked, "Will you be attending us to our summer castle at Erlott Fields?"

"If it so pleases you, Sire," replied the knight. Several of the younger knights, and a few of the less secure nobles, had begun using the royal designation as a show of deference, and it did not fail to please the greedy Prince who took it as his right. Those who knew better withheld their esteem judiciously.

"It pleases me to have your lance ever ready at my side, sir knight," the Prince replied. He did like to be attended in style when he chose to move about the country. "I dare say there will be sport and games enough to occupy a young and lively blade anxious to win some valor among his peers."

"It is my honor, kind Prince," said the knight, bowing again. He would rather have seen to the retaking of his forfeited lands, but a request of the Prince was not to be trifled.

When he had gone Jaspin turned to Ontescue. "You have sent my chamberlain and attendants on ahead to ready Erlott for my arrival, have you not?"

"Yes, of course. They left day before yesterday, and should

be even now seeing to your homecoming," Ontescue replied. Of late he had weaseled himself into a position of growing consequence in the Prince's estimation. "We may leave as soon as you yourself give the order."

"That is well. I am tired of abiding this accursed tower. I want to see my own lands again. But I like it not that the Queen has disappeared. She has been away too long and without sign or word of her whereabouts."

"Why should that trouble you, Sire?"

"Something is amiss; I can feel it. I fear not for her safety, but rather my own while she is loose about the country doing who knows what. She may stir up a faction against me."

"If she were to stir up a faction you would soon know about it. You could quell it in an instant and have her thrown into chains for her troubles."

"Throw the Queen into chains? Ho! There's a thought. I should have done it long ago if I had dared.

"Still, I would rest the easier if I knew where she was." He paused; a small dark cloud of worry crossed his brow. "I would also have some word after my Harriers. They should have returned with their captives, or their captives' bones long ere now. This bothers me more than the Queen's absence . . ."

"What could go amiss with them? Are they not proven to the task—and with cunning to spare? I warrant we will have our answer before too many days hence."

The Prince pulled on his chin and threw his counsellor a fretful glance. "I suppose you are right. But I would go to my summer quarters in a better mind if these loose threads were clipped and discarded."

"Worry not upon it. If you like I shall abide behind until I myself can bring you the news you seek." Ontescue smiled his most ingratiating and winsome smile.

"You *are* a good counsellor, Ontescue," replied Jaspin, glad to have the matter taken care of. "I will tell you this: I can use men of your abilities when I come into my power—that will not be long in coming now. Sir Bran and Sir Grenett are good men, but they are, after all, soldiers and understand not the finesse of court and government. You, though you may not admit it, have special gifts in this area, I perceive."

"You are too kind, my Lord." Ontescue bowed and looked appropriately innocent to deserve such favor; inwardly he leapt for joy that his goal was so near within his grasp.

In all the Prince took fifty knights and nobles with him to his summer palace. Counting their servants and men-at-arms, the numbers swelled to five times as many.

The pilgrimage to Erlott Fields, the Prince's private castle wherein he resided some four or five months of the year, was a drawn out affair commanding more regard than it warranted. But Jaspin would have it no other way. Being within an hour's riding distance of the sea the climate remained somewhat cooler there during the hotter months, and though many times smaller than Askelon it was nonetheless well fortified and ample for any prince's needs. Castle Erlott housed his fluctuating retinue with ease.

The coming of the Prince to Hinsenby, the nearest village, was always a gala event. People lined the roads as the royal caravan passed. They marveled at the knights and horses, the weapons and costly furniture they saw carefully packed away on the wagons. It was a show well attended with merry-making and festivity. Jaspin himself usually participated, supplying a good deal of meat and wine to the occasion.

This year Jaspin was weeks early in his desire to remove to the safety of his own battlements. Two things occasioned his somewhat premature notion: his own growing uneasiness about his alliance with Nimrood, who was showing himself to be a perverse and ambitious ally, and his wish to remain apart from Askelon until the Council of Regents should meet and declare him king. Then he planned a glorious triumphal entrance to the great city as its monarch. He did not wish to lessen the impact of his brightest moment by remaining in Askelon until the deed was accomplished. Jaspin reveled in the pomp and splendor of such events. He knew how to please the common people and wooed

them with lavish spectacle and cheap entertainment to divert
their wandering attention from their troubles, and thus silence
any defaming tongue.

A chill yet sunny day greeted the departure of the Prince and
his army of nobles and knights, servants and soldiers, and various minstrels, game masters and ladies who had been invited to
help while away the cool spring evenings. A day of good travel
would bring them south to Hinsenby, there to encamp and enjoy
a day of sport before removing to Erlott, another half-day's
march to the west.

The day proved fair for the journey, and they achieved Hinsenby well before dusk. The servants set about erecting the
bright, multicolored tents used on these occasions as they took
the broad fields just west of the town. Under the sparkling eyes
and laughter of the townspeople, the tent city blossomed. A great
bonfire sparked to life in the center of the field, and smaller fires
for cooking flamed around it and in front of the various tents.

Eating and drinking would continue through the night, and
on the morrow a mock tournament would be held among the
knights and the more adept of their sidemen. It was done for play
and practice for the knights, and for the grand sight it presented
to the people who would crowd the perimeter to see the spectacle
of horses clashing under gallant knights, dangerously armed.
Much care was taken to prevent anyone from being harmed
accidentally, for there was no renown in being wounded in a
mock tourney, and a knight indisposed was without honor or a
source of income. Like knights anywhere, most relied on their
skill at arms to secure the favor and patronage of a wealthy
nobleman—that is, those who were not themselves of noble
birth.

In his large tent, raised above the others on a wooden platform, Jaspin slept uneasily while the raucous sounds of the
roistering crowd continued far into the night. The Prince, begging leave of his merry followers, had retired early saying he
wanted to present himself fresh for the tournament on the following morning. In truth he had grown restive and disturbed, hav-

ing brooded the whole day upon Queen Alinea's disappearance and the lack of effect from the Harriers he had sent out to bring back the fugitives.

He took to his bed in an apprehensive mood and fell at once into a troubled, dream-filled sleep in which the ghost of his brother rose up accusingly before him demanding to know what had happened to his wife Alinea.

Twice during the night he awoke to the feeling of a lurking presence somewhere close by—as if someone were prowling around outside. Each time he called for his chamberlain who denied, after checking the circumference of the tent, that anything was amiss.

By morning he had all but forgotten his unpleasant night; the prospect of games greatly cheered him. All that remained of his midnight misgivings was an occasional twinge of forboding, vague and undefined, as if bad news were winging its way toward him unexpectedly.

But his disquiet vanished as preparations began for the mock tournament. The boundaries of the fighting field were drawn and marked with lances bearing red and gold pennons. Tents at either end of the field were converted for the use of the knights who would engage themselves in the combat. The weapons were readied—all sharp edges wrapped in leather and the points of the lances blunted with wooden protectors. Helmets, shields, and breastplates were shined and devices and insignias painted fresh where use had rubbed them thin.

The people of Hinsenby and beyond, some who had walked all night, assembled on the somewhat soggy Hinsen Field early in the morning. Most had brought with them baskets of food and drink to last the whole day; others bartered with the local merchants who took advantage of the sudden influx of visitors to vend special delicacies—sausages and rolls and spicy meat pies of a small, portable nature.

The midday sun, bright and warm before its season, found all in readiness. Jaspin sat under a canopy on a raised platform overlooking the field of contest; a score or more of his favorite nobles graced seats on either side of him. Ladies, their faces demurely covered from the sun, sat below just in front of the platform. Publicly these fair damsels decried the rough sport of the tournament, but not one flinched from the clash of arms, or from the issue of blood that often accompanied the games.

When all contestants, buckled and braced and mounted on their sturdy war horses, had ridden twice around the lists, the marshall of the games took his place upon the field and read out the rules of the tournament to the participants now lining either end of the field.

Lots had been drawn to decide the order of the knights to participate. Sir Grenett had won first place and advanced across the field, paused, and turned in front of Prince Jaspin's party.

"For Mensandor and glory!" he shouted. All the people returned the cry, "For freedom! Fight on!" Prince Jaspin dipped his head and Sir Grenett rode to the knight he chose as his opponent, picking him from among the mounted knights assembled in a long line at the west end of the field. He stopped before Sir Weilmar and touched his buckler with the point of his lance. The two then rode out to take their places at either end of the field.

At the signal, the Prince's falling glove, both riders spurred their charges forward, lances held high. As they closed upon one another in the center of the field, the combatants lowered their lances and made ready to exchange blows.

Sir Weilmar's aim was good. He placed his blow precisely on target in the center of Sir Grenett's chest. Sir Grenett was no less precise and the shock of the collision staggered both horses. Sir Weilmar's lance splintered like kindling as it glanced off his competitor's heavy armor. Sir Grenett would have fared no better but for the strength of his arm and his own slightly more advantageous weight in the saddle. His blow caught Sir Weilmar and lifted him in the saddle, but Weilmar's excellent horsemanship kept him at the reins, causing instead his saddle bindings to burst.

Weilmar's saddle slid to the side, and both saddle and knight tumbled over the rear of the horse to the ground. This slight advantage was accorded to Sir Grenett's favor, since neither had won a decisive fall.

All this took place in a twinkling amidst the general clamor and cheering of the crowd, many of whom had placed wagers upon their favorites. The marshall accorded Sir Grenett the victor and Sir Weilmar vanquished. The two retired to watch the rest of the games in peace, having won enough valor for the day, and the next two contestants took their places. Sir Grenett received a gold sovereign for his victory; Sir Weilmar, nothing but a broken cinch strap and fleeting disgrace.

The games moved through their course to the delight of the gathered onlookers. One after another, each knight tried his strength and skill at arms. The games continued to the delight of the spectators, when midway through the contests a murmur of alarm arose from the far side of the field opposite Prince Jaspin's canopy. The riders awaiting the signal for their turn at the joust paused and turned their attention toward the crowd to see what the disturbance might be.

"What in Orphe's name!" cursed the Prince as spectators, apparently frightened by some cause as yet unapparent, fled into the field.

"Someone has undoubtedly seen a snake in the grass," laughed Bascan of Endonny, sitting near the Prince. "Nothing to be concerned about, I am sure."

Another sought to further the joke adding, "A snake in the grass is better than rats in the cellar." Everyone laughed again.

The Prince, perceiving this to be a sly comment on his jailing of Weldon and Larcott exploded at the joker. "Who dares ridicule my judgment? Speak up!"

"I meant nothing by it, Sir. 'Twere but an idle jest . . ." Sir Bran spattered. "No offense was intended, I assure you." He was about to speak further when a gasp arose from the ladies below them and several of the knights on the platform jumped to their feet.

"Azrael!" some shouted, "protect us!"

The throng on the far side of the field had opened, clearing a wide avenue for a lone rider who took the field with a slow, dignified, and somewhat menacing gait. Prince Jaspin's face drained of its ruddy hue and his hands fluttered like frightened birds in his lap.

A lone Harrier advanced across the field and brought his horse to stand in front of the Prince. On his shoulder perched a large hawk; at his side hung an awkward bundle.

Without a word he loosed the bundle and drew out the contents of the rough sack. The defiant Harrier then raised high into the air for all to see the two severed, bloodied heads of his dead comrades.

TWENTY

QUENTIN stood at the parapet of his room overlooking a dark, mist-shrouded forest feeling useless and disgraced at being left behind. His hand hung at his side, still holding the letters left for him by his friends, and which he had just reread yet once again.

He heard a sound behind him and turned; it was Mollena, his aging nurse. She hobbled in, glancing at his empty bed and then out onto the balcony, and smiled a toothless grin when she saw him.

"Come in, young master. You will be chilled standing out there like that. Warmth comes to these old mountains but slowly. You'll be needing your cloak a good spell yet."

Quentin said nothing, but came reluctantly inside and threw himself upon the bed.

"You are feeling stronger, I can tell. But not so much is good for you yet. Your feet are anxious, but your heart needs rest." She paused and looked at Quentin's fallen countenance. "What you have read troubles your soul, my bold young man?"

"They left me, Mollena. Why?" Quentin knew why; he merely wanted some other assurance that he had not been forgotten.

"It could not be any other way. That I know." She spoke these words in a queer way. Quentin rolled over and looked at her. The Curatak were an odd people and knew many things by many strange ways.

"What do you know?" he asked, much as one would ask a soothsayer to divulge his future.

"I know that your friend Toli waits for you below. Come, the walk will do you good, I think."

Quentin slid off the bed and shuffled to the door. "Here," said Mollena as he stepped across the threshold, "remember your cloak." Quentin took it and threw it across his shoulders and went with the old woman down to meet his friend.

Under the old healer's ministrations Quentin had revived and awakened three days after Theido and the others had set out. He had opened his eyes, as if from a long night's sleep, hungry and not more than a little lightheaded. He lay for a long time trying to remember what had happened to him and how he had come to be where he was. But the attempt was futile.

Somewhere in the far recesses of his mind a shadowy, indistinct dream still lingered—a dream in which he had a part. But it seemed long ago and far removed from himself, as if it had all happened to someone else and he had only read the account of it. He had—in the letters Durwin and Alinea had left behind for him.

Quentin had gotten up to walk around the room on the second day, and had explored the whole of the upper floor the day after that. Under Mollena's tutelage he had learned something of Dekra and the mysterious Curatak who guarded the ruins.

Dekra was the last stronghold of a great and powerful civilization, a people who had vanished without trace a thousand years before Celbercor had come to forge his kingdom. The Curatak, or Caretakers, had long ago colonized the ruined city and fought back the ever-encroaching weeds and wildlife—and from time to time even discouraged squatters from settling there.

From the dust of crumbling walls and columns in the once-proud city of a highborn race, the Caretakers had rescued the memory of Dekra and its inhabitants. They had delved deeply into their past, learned their ways and customs, and had even effected restoration of much of the ancient city's common square, or the seat of the government. It was here Quentin and the others had been housed, in the lofty, many-roomed palace of the governor of Dekra, which now served as the central communal dwelling of the Curatak.

Quentin had seen but little of the ruined city, but enough to know that the aura of fear which surrounded the mere mention of the name was totally unfounded. The legends which men told each other in the dark by firelight were assuredly false—if not outright fabrications designed to protect the privacy of the Caretakers and their mission to restore the city to its original splendor—a task which Quentin learned was, to the Curatak, the ultimate in devotion to a people they seemingly worshipped as gods.

The Caretakers believed that the Ariga, Dekra's original tenants, would someday return to claim their city. The Curatak believed that in that day they would themselves become Ariga by virtue of their loving work.

Where the Caretakers had come from was less certain, for they seemed to care nothing of their own history, only in so much as it helped them to remember Dekra's. But the original number of a few score had grown into several hundred over the years Outsiders still occasionally wandered to the city and stayed to embrace the work. The Curatak did not in the least discourage visitors who held nothing but honorable intentions toward them or who wished to study the ancient ways. In fact they were always more than pleased to offer the arts of the departed Ariga to any and all who asked. This they also considered their sacred duty.

Durwin had visited the city on several occasions, staying once for over three years. He had seen and learned much in the ruins and had himself helped in the restoration of one of the main buildings—a temple to the god of the Ariga. A lone god with no name.

"Do you think I will be strong enough to leave soon?" asked Quentin when they had reached the lower floor. They entered a large area which had been partitioned off into smaller rooms, but which retained an atmosphere of light and openness in what would have been a dark, solid basement in any structure he had ever encountered. Quentin, feeling winded from his walk down so many stairs, sat on a three-legged stool while Mollena stirred herself in another corner of the room. Toli, apparently, had darted off on another of his ceaseless errands.

"Leave soon? That is up to you. You can leave when you feel you must. Or you can stay as long as you wish," Mollena answered finally. Quentin looked at the old woman's gray hair and wrinkled, stooped appearance. Anywhere else the woman would have been regarded as one of Orphe's Daughters. But here she was as much a part of the natural surroundings as the strange architecture he saw and the exotic murals which lined the walls of nearly every building. And there was something in her spirit which made her seem as young and alive as any maid he had ever seen (although for Quentin, those were few indeed).

Quentin always had the impression that Mollena was refraining from telling him too much; that she knew more than she would bear him to hear. And not only Mollena—all the others he had met in the past few days spoke in the same cryptic way.

"Would you teach me something?" he asked, after watching her busy herself with preparing some small morsel for him. She turned to eye him with a long, sidewards glance, her head held to one side as if weighing her decision.

"There are some few things I might teach you, and there are others far more learned than I. What would you learn?" she asked.

"I do not know—I mean . . . I would not know where to start. Tell me what you think I should know of this place, of the world."

"What I think does not matter a great deal. You must choose yourself how you will go," Mollena answered, setting a small table before him which contained a bowl of dried fruit and a cup with a warm yellow liquid. "Eat now. Regain your strength. Consider what will help you accomplish your purpose, and that I will teach you."

Quentin ate and did as she suggested, but at the end of his meal he was no closer to an answer to his own question.

"It's no use," he announced, pushing the bowl away from him and wiping his mouth with the back of his hand. "I do not know enough about this place or its people to decide what would serve me best to learn."

"Well spoken," said the old woman with a warm smile. "That is the first step toward knowledge. Come, I will guide you through the city and we will find the answers you seek."

Toli appeared at the doorway just as they made to leave, so the three started off together.

A firm friendship had grown up between Quentin and the quiet Jher, who seemed to hold his friend in reverential awe as someone who possessed strong mystical powers. Anyone who could survive the poisoned talons of a Harrier's hawk qualified as deity in Toli's opinion, as in the simple peasants' regard as well. He seemed determined to serve Quentin as bodyguard and cup-bearer, and he made a point of insisting upon learning Quentin's tongue so that he might know how to serve his master more efficiently.

Quentin, for his part, considered Toli's quick thinking and lightning reflexes in pulling him to the ground on that black night as the only reason he still walked among the living. The hawk had barely scratched his upper arm with its hollow, poison-filled metal talons—the bird was trained to the throat.

So, out of gratitude Quentin busied himself with teaching Toli and taking up the task of learning the gentle Jher's lilting speech. He was surprised to find that, after the rigors of temple training in the official temple code language, the Jher tongue was not as obscure as he feared. There were only a handful of basic sounds which were combined to form more complex words and sentences.

With steady work and patience Quentin and Toli began to eke out a method of communication with each other.

The old woman led them along wide, tree-lined avenues, which in another day Quentin imagined would have been jammed with carts and people bustling to and fro, buying and selling. He looked at the tall buildings of ingenious design—lofty towers which rose with a effortless grace. And although they used the same stone Askelon's builders had later used, Dekra's architects did very different things with it. Their skill was such that even the most solid, massive structure appeared airy and light, well-proportioned and elegant. A city designed by poets.

Dekra's only temple sat in the center of the city, and all lines focused upon this center. The streets ran in concentric rings and intersecting angles from the temple, which was large enough to accommodate all inhabitants of the city with ease.

It was toward the temple that Mollena directed them.

Quentin walked through the quiet streets, some of them more closely restored than others, in a kind of waking dream. The city of the vanished race was an exotic, alien place—itself a city of dreams. He stared in awe around him, gazing in wonder at the strangeness of the place. He wondered what the people themselves had been like.

"What happened to the people?"

"It is not known—oh, we find things from time to time, and there are many theories among us, but the answer to our most perplexing question remains a mystery.

"But this we know: they left all together and all at once, very quickly. We have found pots still on the ashes of the fire that burned under them with the charred remains of the meal which was being prepared still untouched. We have found, in the merchant quarters, money boxes left open and the contents inside and undisturbed. Once we found a table set with writing instruments and the fragmented remains of a letter in composition—the pen laid aside in mid-word, as if the writer were called away suddenly and unexpectedly, never to return."

The old woman stopped and looked around; her face revealed an excitement no less aroused than Quentin's own. "The answer is here, within these buildings and walls. Someday we will find it."

Quentin was silent as they continued their easy stroll. After a time he ventured another question. "What were the people like, Mollena? Were they very different from us?"

"Not so much in appearance, maybe, though they were taller and stronger than our people are. That we know from the many murals which abound in every house and public building. Among them were many artists and writers of surpassing skill.

"One of the first buildings to be restored was the library of Dekra, a vast collection of writings. Many of the scrolls were in readable condition still; many others have been preserved and restored, though it is a long and often frustrating process. But we have learned how to read their words, and many of the Curatak engage themselves fully toward learning the teachings of the ancient scholars. What we have read reveals a wise and benevolent race of high intelligence; their teachings are not easy to understand, but we have learned much. Much more remains to be discovered."

The three were moving toward the temple along one of the straight, bisecting streets. As Quentin listened to the old woman he watched in fascination as the temple grew larger with their slow approach. The holy place rose majestically over the tops of the trees surrounding it—all clean lines and pinnacles pointing heavenward.

"Who were they?" Quentin asked, more to himself than to Mollena, experiencing a growing sense of suppressed excitement, mingled inexplicably with a grief he could not place, as if someone he knew did not exist might yet appear at any moment.

"Who were they?" repeated Mollena as the three stepped onto the broad plaza surrounding the soaring sanctuary. "They called themselves Ariga—children of the god."

"And who was their god?" Quentin asked. "Do we know him?"

"Many know him, but by no name. The god of the Ariga has no name. He is one, nameless and supreme. Their holy writings sometimes use the words 'Whist Orren,' or Most High, and 'Peran Nim Gadre,' or King of the gods. Most often they called him Dekron—the One, or the One Holy. But his name, if he has one, is never written."

Without another word Mollena led them inside the great temple. Quentin saw Curatak moving quietly about their work within the temple. One section of the west wall, opposite them, had given way. Scaffolding was erected around the damaged portion, and workmen were painstakingly laboring with the rebuilding. All moved about their tasks with great reverence, it seemed to Quentin.

"We Curatak," explained Mollena, "have ourselves become Ariga in that we worship the nameless god as our own." When she saw Quentin's questioning glance she continued, "We believe, as did the vanished ones, that their god has many children."

"Where did the priests stay?" asked Quentin, looking around. Most of the inner temple was given over to a vast open area, raised at one end by a dias which was reached by stone steps ringing its circumference. He saw no place where priests could live, unless their chambers lay underground somewhere.

"There were no priests—that is, not the way you think of priests. The Ariga approached the god alone, though they had readers—men who had studied the holy texts extensively, who spoke to them when they assembled, reminding them of the various tenets of their religion. But no priests interposed for the people."

They turned to leave then and when they had returned outside once more Quentin was struck by a thought suddenly remembered, a thought he had often wondered and often had meant to ask Durwin along their journey to the ruined city.

"Mollena, why was Theido frightened of coming here? Why did he wish Durwin to stay away?"

The old woman turned a wrinkled squint upon him. "Who told you he was afraid?"

"I heard them talking about it. Durwin said from the beginning that we should come; Theido was against it. Then something happened—Trenn came with word that the Harriers were after us—and Theido relented. What was he afraid of?"

"That is not for me to say, but you may ask Yeseph, one of our leaders. He may give you an answer to your question, for I cannot."

Again the cryptic reply, thought Quentin. What was it that these Curatak were withholding from him? Certainly he had seen nothing so far to be afraid of. He puzzled on this the rest of the day and far into the night before dropping off to sleep. The next day he awoke determined to seek out Yeseph and put the questions to him. Why was Theido afraid for Durwin? And why had he changed his mind?

TWENTY-ONE

"WE HAVE luck with us yet, my friends," exclaimed Theido upon his return from the shipyards of Bestou.

"You have found a ship to take us to Karsh?" asked Alinea. She and Durwin sat in the lodge of the inn Flying Fish, waiting for Theido to arrange their passage to the island stronghold of Nimrood the Necromancer.

"Yes, though it has not been easy. I have asked fully half of the captains in the yard if we may be accommodated—always the same reply, 'We stay far away from Karsh. Not for gold, nor for the god themselves would we go nearer!'

"But one man sought me out himself, saying that he was owner of a ship that would pass near Karsh, and would be willing to land us on a friendly shore, if there be such things in Karsh."

"He sought you out, you say?" mused Durwin. "We must be suspect of any offering aid too readily. They may be in Nimrood's employ."

Theido brushed the observation aside impatiently. "We cannot always be looking under every rock and behind every tree for a spy. We must trust to our own initiative; we must act!"

"My friend, I am all for moving ahead on our enterprise. But we must be careful. Our foe is a dark sorcerer of great skill, who shrinks not from evil of any kind. And his net of intrigue is cast far indeed."

"That may be," said Theido, a little angrily. It chafed him to remain idle; a man of action, he wanted to move at once. "But we cannot wait forever for a sign from heaven—whether your god smiles or no, we must go."

"Gentlemen, please! Restrain your tempers for the sake of our cause," pleaded Alinea. She had seen the growing restlessness of Theido in the past few days as they waited for a favorable result from the docks. She had often to play the peacemaker, supplying a gentle word, or quiet touch in times of heated discussion between the two men. "I am as anxious as either of you to see the end of our journey, but not at the cost of enmity between us. That, I fear, would be disaster for us and our good King."

Theido nodded, acknowledging the reproof. Durwin, too, admitted his irritation, laying a hand upon Alinea's and saying, "You are right, my Lady. Our purpose will not be served if we are crossing swords with one another."

"Then come, good friends. Let us be resolved. Our differences are slight, and were better put far behind us." She looked long at Theido's worn appearance and at Durwin's usually cheerful countenance, now clouded over with care. "My King has never had more noble subjects, nor any half as brave. His gratitude to you in this adventure will be hard pressed to find worthy enough expression."

"To see him alive and safe once more will be payment enough for me," said Theido. He smiled, but the tight lines around his eyes were not erased.

The party had reached Bestou on the island of Tildeen after a rigorous march through the tangled forest surrounding Dekra. Their path had become surer and the way easier upon reaching the fishing outpost, hardly big enough to be called a village, of Tuck. There they clambered aboard the ferry which plied the narrow channel to the island of Tildeen, one of the larger of what were called the Seven Mystic Isles. In truth, there was nothing particularly mysterious about any of the islands in the small chain—only that the largest, Corithy, had long ages ago been used as a primitive holy sanctuary of a shadowy, secret religion. Strange events were said still to take place on that odd-shaped, often mist-shrouded island.

But Tildeen, the second largest of the seven, was the site of a fair and energetic seaport city, Bestou. This commercial center served as the winter refuge for the whole of Mensandor, due to its immense sheltered harbor which seldom froze during the coldest months, despite the island's northern lay.

Upon arriving on Tildeen, put ashore rudely by the rustic operator of the ferry, Theido, Durwin, Alinea, and trusty Trenn had before them an arduous mountain trek, up and over the hunched and twisted backbone of the island, on a serpentine path descending at last to the low-lying port on the other side.

The journey was accomplished in rather more time than Theido would have liked to allow. But, as the group came within sight of the harbor, approaching like bandits dropping down out of the high hills behind Bestou, Theido had been vindicated for his relentless push along the trail; the ships lay at anchor, their colored sails ready-furled, waiting for the first good day to sail.

As he walked the shore that first morning after their arrival, having spent the first warm night in weeks before the fire in the lodge of the Flying Fish, Theido had talked to sailors and captains of large ships and small. Each refused, some politely and others with bold discourtesy, to grant them passage to that accursed land.

Their reluctance was understandable. Karsh, a grotesque lump of earth, the tip of a huge submerged mountain, jutted out of the water far east off the coast of Elsendor, Mensandor's sprawling neighbor. The island had long been shunned by superstitious sailors, even before Nimrood had taken up residence there and built his fortress. The place was forsaken by all gentle humanity, fit only for countless sea birds, which nested in the precipitous cliffs on the western side, and the tiny land crabs which feasted upon the washed-up remains of putrid fish and hatchlings from the cliffs above.

Theido, with Trenn behind, had stalked the wharf for two days before happening upon the captain who agreed to deliver them to the hated island.

At last satisfied that his objective had been achieved, Theido did not bother with the formality of inspecting the ship or its crew, relying on the word of the captain, a rather short, oppressive-looking man who called himself Pyggin, to vouch a faithful account of its seaworthiness.

He returned to the inn humming to himself and leaving Trenn to stow their few things aboard and make any provisions which he thought necessary for their convenience on board. Trenn, after seeing to his task, also returned to the inn, much less happy than his friend Theido.

"There is something queer about that ship," he told Theido, pulling him aside after dinner that evening.

"What did you see on board—something amiss?" The knight searched the soldier's troubled features for a clue to his misgivings.

"Nothing I can say, sir. But I noticed that while all other hands aboard the ships in harbor made ready to get under sail—loading and stocking provisions, mending sails, tarring, and what not—this Captain Pyggin's men sat idle. Not one stirred a hand all the while I was on board. They stood about the deck, or sat on barrels in the hold . . . as if they were waiting for something." He frowned deeply. "I like it not at all."

"Perhaps they are ready and only waiting for the first fair wind to be under sail. So the captain told me," replied Theido, blunting the other's complaint as gently as he could.

"Aye, perhaps, but I never saw a ship of that size that didn't need some fixing, nor any captain that ever let a crew stand idle."

"Worry not on it, Trenn," said Theido. "I am sure we need have no fear. We ask only to be put ashore at our destination; surely there can be no harm in that."

Trenn pulled on his chin and scowled furiously, repeating his original pronouncement. "May it be as you say, by Ariel! But I still say there is something queer about that ship."

TWENTY-TWO

WHEN PRINCE Jaspin fled from the games, so disrupted by the sudden and unwelcome appearance of the Harrier and his grisly mementos, he flew at once to his castle on Erlott Fields. "Let the games continue," he had announced magnanimously, after disposing of his debt to the odious tracker (who demanded twice the payment he had been promised and his dead companion's shares as well). Prince Jaspin, being caught in an awkward position, careful not to offend public sentiment, which held that anyone dealing with the Harriers was as much a villain himself, paid the savage and sent him off with a minimum of show.

So Jaspin called for the contest to be resumed lest the people be too disappointed. Then he, with a handful of his esteemed confidants, left the field immediately, allowing that he had been called away on some detail of state importance.

The Prince and his cronies had run at once to the security of Castle Erlott and there held a hasty conference to discuss the situation.

The meeting availed little in terms of correcting the damage already done, and since the Prince could not reveal the actual source of his fear, he dismissed them all brusquely and retired to his own council in his inner chamber.

Once the door to his outer apartment had been secured and guards posted to make certain no intruders should interrupt, the Prince stole into his inner chamber, a small, dark room with no outside window, a nook hollowed out of the massive outer curtain of the castle.

There Jaspin sat down before the black enameled box.

Lifting off the lid and placing his hands upon the sides of the miraculous pyramid, he felt the pulse of power begin to throb as the golden object began to glow. Soon his sharp features were bathed in the waxing light. He listened to the drumming throb of his own heart pounding in his ears, and watched the opaque sides of Nimrood's invention take on a misty appearance.

Then, as always before, Jaspin looked into the clearing depths of the enchanted object, and watched the thinning mist reveal the dreadful mien of his malicious accomplice.

"Well, what portends this unexpected summons, my Prince? Lost a pin? A throne?" The necromancer threw back his head and laughed, but the sound died in his throat. He then fixed Jaspin with an icy glare.

Prince Jaspin quailed at the message he had to deliver. But having no choice, he plowed ahead and steeled himself for the wizard's awful fury. "The Harriers have returned," he said simply.

"Good. They enjoyed the benefits of a successful hunt, I trust?"

"N-no," Jaspin stuttered, "they returned empty-handed—or rather one of them did. The other two lost their lives."

"You fool! I gave you but one more chance, and you have wasted it. You are finished! Hear me, you insignificant dolt!"

Thinking quickly, and in an effort to appease the raging sorcerer and avert further threats, Jaspin seized upon the one scrap of information he had and flung it forth like a leaf against a thunderstorm. "I know where they have gone, Nimrood!" he shouted.

The seething sorcerer quieted his ranting, but, still frowning furiously, demanded, "Where have they gone, then? Tell me."

"First, you must promise . . ." Prince Jaspin started, but Nimrood cut him off.

"I, promise? Ha! Listen, dog of a prince! I give my word to no man! Never forget that!" Then the black magician changed, instantly sweetening his tone, as if speaking to an unhappy child.

"But I forgive you. Only tell me where the scheming wretches have gone and I will forget this trouble between us."

Jaspin told quickly the minute fragments of information he had been able to drag from the Harrier. "There are six and there is a woman among them—the Queen, I believe. It is fair certain they have gone to the ruins of Dekra—to hide, most like. Everyone knows there is nothing there."

"There is more at Dekra than people know," said Nimrood. The faintest trace of worry crossed his wrinkled face, but was instantly banished by his haughty leer. "They will leave that place as they must. I will ready a special surprise for these bold travelers. Yes, I think I know what it shall be." Then speaking again to the Prince he continued, "You serve me well in spite of yourself, proud Prince. And you have earned yourself a reprieve from my anger. It may be I can use you yet."

"You are forgetting your place, wizard!" Jaspin, incensed at the staggering insolence of the necromancer, rebelled. "It was I who hired *you*—you serve me!"

"I tire of your games of petty ambition," hissed the sorcerer. "Once it suited me to further your childish schemes. But I have designs you cannot imagine. But serve me well, and you shall share in my glory."

The pyramid lost its crystalline transparency and became cold and solid once more.

Quentin had begged and otherwise pestered Mollena into arranging a meeting with Yeseph for him at the earliest possible time. That meant the moment he opened his eyes the very next morning, the day after their limited tour of the ruined city.

Toli sat opposite Quentin over their breakfast, pointing at objects around the room, and demanding that his instructor supply the appropriate word that he might learn it. Quentin, although it seemed sometimes a colossal chore, beamed with pleasure at his pupil's progress. Toli could already speak halting sentences, albeit simple ones, and could understand most of what Quentin said to him, though he could not always repeat it. When others were around, however, he usually lapsed into his native tongue.

They were deep in concentration when Quentin heard the old woman's shuffling footsteps on the stone steps outside the kitchen where they were finishing their meal.

"Mollena! What news? When can I see him?" he blurted as soon as he saw her creased, kindly face poke into view.

"Not tomorrow. Not next week."

"Mollena . . ."

"Today—we will go as soon as you are ready."

"I am ready now!"

"No, you have not finished your food. You must eat to regain your strength."

Toli watched this conversation, as he did most others, in an alert silence. But then he broke in, demanding in his own tongue to know what Quentin prepared to do. "What is it that my friend requires?"

Quentin ate and related to him as well as he could the discussion between Durwin and Theido, their disagreement and the final resolution that had brought them to Dekra. Toli nodded and said, "This leader, Yeseph, he will tell us what we are to do?"

Quentin would not have put it quite that way, but after considering for a moment, nodded his head in agreement. "Yes, he may tell us what we are to do." Mollena, who had observed their talk with admiration for the growing bond between the two, now stood them on their feet.

"Let us go, you lazy young men. It does not do to keep a Curatak leader waiting."

The three hobbled together over the jumbled stones of the deserted streets. Quentin, again, was impressed by the elegance and grace of the vanished Ariga's city. Even in its crumbling state the abandoned buildings spoke of a purity and harmony of thought and function. Surely, buried here were treasures beyond material wealth.

As they made their way along, occasionally meeting a group

of Curatak workmen hauling stone or erecting scaffolding around a sagging wall, Mollena explained to Quentin who Yeseph was and how properly to address him. Quentin listened attentively, careful to mark her words so he would not offend the man best able to answer his questions.

They turned down a walkway, or narrow courtyard, lined with doorways which opened onto a common area of small trees and stone benches. "These are the reading rooms of the Ariga library," Mollena explained as they passed the open doors. Quentin peered through some of the doors to see scribes busy over scrolls at their writing desks.

"Where is the library?" he asked, realizing that he had seen no structure large enough to house the great library that had been described to him. He looked around to see if he had somehow missed it.

Mollena saw him craning his neck, looking for the library and laughed, "No, you will not find it there. You are standing on it!" Quentin's gaze fell to his feet and his expression changed to one of puzzlement. "It is underground. Come."

She led them to the end of the narrow courtyard and to a wide doorway. Inside they crossed the smooth marble floor of a great circular room, ringed around by murals of robed men. "Those are Ariga leaders," Mollena indicated with her hands spread wide. "We know little of them now, but we are learning."

In the center of the round room, which contained no other furniture of any kind that Quentin could see, rose an arch. As they approached the arch Quentin saw steps leading down to an underground chamber. "The entrance to the library," he said.

"Yes; notice how the steps are worn from the feet of the Ariga over the ages. They were lovers of books and knowledge. This," she again embraced the whole of the edifice with a wide sweep of her arm, "this is our greatest charge: to protect the scrolls of the Ariga, lest they pass from human sight and their treasures vanish with the race that created them."

Quentin caught something of the awe with which the old woman spoke; he was touched as before by the mingled reverence and excitement, as if he were in the presence of a mighty and benevolent monarch who was about to give him a wonderful gift.

"There," Mollena pointed down the darkened stairway. "Yeseph waits for you. Go to him—and may you find the treasure you are looking for."

Quentin stepped forward and placed his foot on the first stair. Instantly the darkened stairwell was lighted from either side. He turned to Mollena and Toli, who appeared about to follow him but then hung back uncertainly, and experienced the strange sensation that he might never return. Brushing the feeling aside, he said, "I won't be long." Then he proceeded down the stairs.

He had just reached the bottom when he heard a voice call out, "Ah, Quentin. I have been waiting for you." Quentin stepped forward into the huge, cavernous chamber to see more books than he had ever seen in one place. Shelves three times the height of a man held scrolls without number, each one resting in its own pigeonhole, a ribbon extending on which was written the title of the book and its author and contents. So taken was he by the staggering display he did not see the small man standing right in front of him.

"I am Yeseph, an elder of the Curatak, and curator of the library. Welcome." The man was dressed simply in a dark blue tunic over which he wore a white mantle edged in brown.

"I am glad to meet you, sir," said Quentin, somewhat disappointed. He had expected someone who looked like a king or a nobleman of stature, not a short, balding man who walked with a slight limp as he led the way along the corridors of shelves.

"Come along," the curator called after him, "we have much to talk about and much to see." Yeseph stopped, standing between two tall shelves, and said, "I can tell a book-lover when I see one—you belong here, you know."

Quentin started, as if to speak; the words seemed to fly out of his head—banished by a most remarkable sensation. It was if he had been there before . . . seen it just like this . . . somewhere, sometime—long ago, perhaps. He had been there, and now had returned.

TWENTY-THREE

NIMROOD sat brooding on his great black throne, draped over it like a wind-tossed rag. Incensed at Prince Jaspin's bumbling ineffectiveness, he nevertheless grudgingly considered that the chance encounter of Theido and Pyggin had brought about an even better possibility than he had planned—the opportunity of defeating that meddlesome hermit, that bone in his throat, Durwin, once and for all.

As he mulled over these recent developments, a new plan began to take shape. He called for his servants to bring him the keys, which they did, as they carried out all his orders, with stumbling haste lest they displease their perverse lord.

"Tell Euric I will see him in the dungeon at once," snapped Nimrood to the quaking wretch who had brought the keys. He snatched the large ring from the servant's trembling hand and flew like a bat from the throne, across the room and out.

In a further part of the dungeon, Euric, a man almost as depraved as his keeper, found Nimrood unlocking the door to a special cell. "Allow me to do that for you, master," the swarthy, gap-toothed Euric croaked. He took the keys and in seconds swung open the reluctant door. Nimrood stepped in to the darkened room. He clapped his hands and fire leaped from his fingers to a torch sitting in its iron holder on the wall. He handed the torch to Euric and indicated that he was to lead the way.

Through the chamber and a door at the opposite end they went. The second door opened onto a narrow hall lined with cells. They hurried past these cells and came to the end of the passage which terminated in a narrow flight of stone steps twisting down into a black vault below.

The two entered the vault. Nimrood clapped his hands again, and torches all around the room flashed to life. There in the guttering glare of the torches lay nine massive stone tables in rows of three. Six of the tables were occupied by the prostrate forms of six mighty knights bedecked in gleaming armor, with swords clutched over their chests and their shields across their loins. Each one appeared composed and serene, only sleeping, in an instant to join the call to arms. But their flesh bore the ashen tint of dead men's flesh and their eyes were sunken like dead men's eyes.

"Death's Legion," hissed Nimrood. "Look on it, Euric. It is terrible, is it not? Soon it will be complete, and I will give the signal and these, my army, will arise. With them I will conquer the world. Who can stand against such as these—the boldest knights the world has ever seen. He moved among the slabs calling out their names: "Hestlerid, Vorgil, Junius, Khennet, Geoffric, Llewyn . . ."

Euric indicated the three empty biers. "Who will occupy these places to complete the number?"

"One is for Ronsard, who would be here now if not for Pyggin and his men—but I have given them another chance. They bring him now by sea; the other is for King Eskevar, who shall be commander of my Legion. Very soon now he will join his new regiment. His will is strong; he lingers yet. But my will is stronger and he shall be mine ere long.

"Look how still they sleep; even death does not diminish them."

The necromancer's eyes glittered with excitement as he beheld his handiwork.

"And who is the last slab for, great one?" asked Euric. He

fully enjoyed his participation in the black arts as much as did Nimrood.

"The last I feared would have to remain empty. The great knight Marsant died in that petty war against Gorr, and the ignorant barbarians burned his body.

"But now it appears I shall not lack a full complement of warriors to lead my soldiers into battle. Theido, that troublesome renegade, will be joining us at last. He will no doubt thank me for the opportunity to serve his King in death as once he served him on the battlefield in life."

"How will this be accomplished?"

"Did I not tell you? The gods decree that I am indeed fortunate. Pyggin found him wandering the wharf of Bestou where they await the sailing season. It seems the foolish knight wishes passage for himself and his companions to Karsh—they would come *here!*

"Since they are so eager to die, I will not disappoint them. Pyggin will deliver them to their destination all right. And with a courtesy they do not expect. Ha!"

Euric's face glimmered in the dim torchlight. His eyes rolled up into his head ecstatically as he contemplated his foul lord's intricate machinations. He bowed low, saying, "You *shall* rule the world, Nimrood."

The harbor of Bestou remained wrapped in rain and fog for several long and vacant days. Then, on a quiet afternoon of damp, dripping drizzle, the sun broke through in a sudden burst of beaming brilliance and all the sailors abiding in the inns and taverns of the town streamed down to the quay with their scant belongings stuffed into rucksacks and canvas bags. They came as if on signal. That night they would sleep aboard their vessels and sail with the dawn.

When the rising sun was merely a dull promise on the eastern horizon, Theido and the others made their way down to the docks and boarded the wherry with a few other passengers to be delivered to various ships lying at anchor in the harbor.

Ships were already streaming toward the pinched opening of

the harbor to be the first to take to the open seas. Durwin and Alinea could hear sailors calling to one another from ship to ship, captains cursing their crew's winter-dulled skills as they made ready to put off, the splash of the oars in the green water.

As they pulled further into the harbor the humped back of Tildeen rose in the thin spring mist which hung over Bestou like a gossamer cloud. Gulls worked the air with their slender wings and complained of the activity in their harbor as they hovered and dived among the ships. Trenn stood in the front of the boat directing the rowers to their ship, and Theido sat in the rear pensively watching the land recede slowly behind them.

"You appear wistful, brave knight," observed Alinea. She had noticed Theido's somber mien. "Tell us, what could trouble your mind on a morning such as this? We are on our way at last."

"I slept ill last night, my Lady. A fearful dream came over me as I tossed on my bed. I awoke sweating and cold, but of the dream I remember nothing. It vanished as yonder mist will disappear when the morning sun touches it.

"But the feeling of doom lingers, though the dream has departed."

Durwin listened to his friend, nodding and rubbing his chin with his hand. "I, too, felt ill at ease last night. I take it to be a confirmation of our quest. Sometimes we must enter the course by the least likely gate—the god has his own way, often mysterious and always unpredictable."

"Well, we go and none will stop us," replied Theido, squaring his shoulders. "Come what may, the gods will not find us sitting idly by. It is good to be moving again."

"I only hope we may be in time," said the Queen. She turned her lovely face away for a moment and was silent.

"Yes, Jaspin and the regents will convene their council soon, I think. His crown is bought many times over ere now, if I know him at all," said Theido.

"Time will not be hurried," offered Durwin. "We can go only as fast as we may. I will pray to the god that our purpose will not be thwarted. He is a god of righteousness and loves justice. He will not see us fail."

"Well said, holy hermit. I am always forgetting the god you serve is of a different stripe than the gods of old. But I prefer to trust to my own arm for righteousness and the point of my sword for justice."

"Arms lose their strength and swords their edge. Then it is good to remember whence came your strength, and who holds a sword that is never dull."

Alinea, who had listened closely to this exchange said, "Holy hermit, tell me about your god. He seems to be far different from the capricious immortals our people have long worshipped. May I learn of him, do you think?"

"Why, of course, my Lady. He turns away none who come to him, and it would honor me to instruct one as wise and lovely as you. This gives a purpose to the empty hours of our voyage," said Durwin, pleased to have a pupil and an excuse to discourse on his favorite subject.

As these last words were spoken the rowboat bumped against the side of Captain Pyggin's ship.

"Passengers!" cried Trenn, grasping for the rope that dangled from the taffrail. A squinting face appeared over the rail; the man regarded them closely and disappeared again. A rope ladder then dropped over the side of the ship which was quickly secured by the rowers. Trenn clambered up the ladder and reached a hand down to the others. When they had all assembled on the deck Pyggin came wheezing up.

"Everyone aboard? Yes, well . . . excuse me, I did not know we would have the pleasure of a lady on our journey. I am honored.

"This way," the captain said, bustling them off. "I will show you to your quarters." As Pyggin herded his passengers before him he gave the signal for the crew to cast off. Neither Theido nor Trenn saw the signal, nor did they see several crew members skulking along behind them toting belaying pins in their thick fists.

"The *Gray Gull* is a small ship, but a tight one. I think you'll find your accommodations adequate." Pyggin indicated a narrow door leading to stairs descending to the ship's hold.

"Are there no other passengers?" wondered Theido.

"No, we seldom take passengers—but we have made an exception for you, my lords." So saying he opened the door and ushered them down the stairs.

No sooner had Theido, being the last of the party to enter the hold, reached the bottom step than did Pyggin throw the door shut crying, "Enjoy your voyage, my lords!" And before Theido could hurl himself up the stairs against the door, the sounds of heavy bolts being thrown and locks clicking shut let them know they were now prisoners.

Theido beat on the door with his fists. "Open this door, you scoundrel! In the name of the King! Open, I say!"

The sound of derisive laughter came through the fast bolted door, and the prisoners heard footsteps departing on the deck and they were left alone.

"Well, we are in it now," said Theido. "It is my fault—I should have listened to the counsel of our good warder, Trenn."

"Nay, do not blame yourself," said Trenn. " 'Tis true I had a boding of ill, but let us consider what best to do now."

Just then a low moaning, barely audible, drifted to them from behind a wall of stacked barrels.

"What monster lurks here about?" said Trenn in a strained whisper.

"Listen . . ." said Theido.

The sound came again, starting low and growing louder, then trailing off at the end like a wounded animal exhausting the last of its strength.

"It is no monster," said Alinea. "It is a man, and he is hurt."

Feeling her way in the dark hold, lit only by a few lattice-covered hatches cut in the center of the deck overhead, Alinea moved slowly around the musty kegs, followed closely by the others. There in the dim gray light she saw the form of a man stretched out upon a pile of dirty rags and ropes. His head was bandaged and, upon perceiving his fellow prisoners, the man slumped back on his filthy bed in a swoon.

Something about the unconscious form struck the Queen. "I know this man," said Alinea, bending close to him. She took the bandaged head in her hands and peered intently into the insensible face.

Her eyes grew wide in recognition. "Can it be?"

"Who is it, my Lady?" asked Trenn. "Do you recognize him?"

"Look," she said, pulling Trenn down beside her. The ship, already under way, dipped and turned, and for a moment the feeble light from an overhead hatch fell full upon the man's face.

"It is Ronsard!" said Queen Alinea, cradling the great knight's head lovingly in her arms.

"It *is* Ronsard!" shouted Trenn. "By the gods! It is!"

TWENTY-FOUR

"YOU STAND there blinking, young sir," replied Yeseph kindly. "Is there something your heart would say, but your tongue cannot?"

Quentin, suspended by the feeling that he had once stood in the very spot, talking to this venerable little man, could only stare in wonder.

But the feeling passed like a cloud sweeping before the sun, and Quentin came to himself again.

"I had the feeling I have been here before, that I know you," he said, shaking his head as if to clear it.

The Curatak elder smiled knowingly and nodded. "Perhaps you have—all the more reason I should treat my guest with honor." He turned and led the way between the towering shelves. "These are my life," Yeseph said, indicating row upon row of books with his raised palm. He went on to describe the work going on in the enormous library.

Quentin followed in rapt attention, fascinated by all he saw, and haunted by the lingering feeling that he belonged here, that somehow he had come home.

Presently their tour led them to a row of copy desks where Curatak scholars were hard at work over manuscripts, making notes and translating. Yeseph made his way along the desks, stopping at each one to offer some word of encouragement or answer a question. Then he reached a door which stood ajar, and Quentin entered Yeseph's own work room.

The small room was sparely furnished with a desk, piled high with scrolls, and a table straining under the weight of still more books. Generous light poured into the room from a round skylight overhead.

Two fragile-looking chairs faced each other, and Yeseph took one and waved Quentin to the other, after closing the door for privacy.

"Now then, Mollena tells me you have questions which only I can answer. I will try," he nodded, smiling encouragingly.

For a moment Quentin had quite forgotten his questions, but upon recollection they came back to him, if somewhat reduced in importance by the things he had seen around him. Quentin explained to Yeseph, who listened patiently, about the disagreement between Theido and Durwin, and Theido's reluctance to come to Dekra. He ended by saying, ". . . though I can see no reason for fear—surely there is only good here." He paused and added, "Unless the danger lay not in the destination, but in the reason for coming."

Yeseph smiled. "Your mind is quick! Yes, I could not have put it better myself.

"There is no danger here. The stories," he dismissed them with a mocking frown and a wave of his hand, "bah! Superstitious prattle—made up to scare the children. Though I admit we do not discourage them. Our work is very important; it is best that the world stays far away and troubles us only rarely.

"But that is not why Theido did not want to come, or rather, did not wish Durwin to come." He stood and began walking around the cell, hands clasped behind his back in the manner of a teacher instructing his pupil.

"Dekra is a place of power, one of the last remaining on the earth. Durwin knows this, as does Theido." He laughed, "You little know your hermit friend—a man of amazing talents. He came to us as High Priest of the temple of Ariel. On a pilgrimage, he was, seeking to further his quest for knowledge. He believed at that time that knowledge alone could transform a man, make him immortal, exalt him to the status of the gods.

"Here he found how far wrong he was—it would have crushed a lesser man. But not him. He grew from strength to strength, discarding all his previous beliefs as fast as he could embrace his new ones. In three years' time he learned all that we had to teach. He went back to the temple and renounced his position and his faith. They nearly killed him—would have, but for the scandal."

Yeseph stopped walking and placed his hands on the back of his chair and looked at Quentin. "Durwin returned to us then, but only for a short time, though we begged him to stay and join us in our work. But he had greater things to do—the god revealed that to him.

"You see, he had only come back to divest himself of all his earthly power. As High Priest he had studied long the magic of sorcerers, the wizard's art, and he had become keenly adept. But he saw that for what it was—the way of death. He put off his power—here, where he knew no one would misuse it.

"As it happened, when Nimrood was discovered to have risen against the King and his kingdom, Durwin thought to come here to retrieve his power, to take it up again in this good cause. He proposed to face Nimrood himself, alone."

Yeseph smiled sadly. "That was not to be."

The elder's words sank slowly in, but as their meaning broke fully in Quentin's consciousness he exclaimed, "Then what will become of them! They go to meet the enemy unarmed!"

"They go. Unarmed they may be, but not unguarded. We could not allow our honorable friend to take such a terrible burden upon himself. It would destroy him. Theido understood that, although imperfectly. He knew that coming here would very likely mean the death of Durwin."

"But he changed his mind—why?"

Yeseph shrugged, "He weakened in the face of the threat posed by the Harriers, and Durwin's insistence. Still, that mattered but little. We did not allow them to carry out their plan.

"The power has been put off. It is here and here it will stay."

Quentin fought his rising emotions, but fear for his friends and anxiety over their safety roiled within him. "How could you let them go!" he shouted, leaping from his chair. Quentin knew nothing of Nimrood, only that everyone around him seemed to tremble at the name. The sorcerer appeared to be the cause of all the troubles besetting the land. He had not experienced the evil of the black wizard firsthand; he had been spared that, but he had formed a picture in his mind of something grotesque and twisted in its terrible hate, less a man than a maleficent monster. It was the monster Nimrood his friends now quested, unarmed by the power which Durwin might have commanded.

"How could you let them go?" he asked again quietly, hopelessly.

"How could we prevent them from going?" rejoined Yeseph kindly.

"What will happen now?" Quentin already expected the worst possible outcome. "They cannot stand against Nimrood alone."

Yeseph smiled knowingly. "Your friends are not alone. The god goes with them." He said it so simply, so trustingly that Quentin wanted desperately to believe him. But his own doubts, and all that he had seen in the temple, stole away his seed of belief before it could take root. His face fell in misery.

"The gods care little for the affairs of men; our lives mean nothing to them," he said bitterly.

"You are right—and yet you are far from the truth." Yeseph crossed the distance between them and peered into Quentin's brown eyes intently. "The Most High God is One. The gods of earth and sky are but the chaff blown before the mighty wind of his coming. They cannot stand in his presence, and even now their power grows weak."

"But what makes this nameless god different from all the others?"

"He cares."

Again Quentin wanted desperately to believe, for the sake of his friends. But the years of temple training, all his earlier beliefs, rushed upon him and extinguished any spark of hope that what Yeseph said might be true. "I wish I could believe you."

"Do not fear for your friends," Yeseph said, placing a hand on Quentin's arm. "The god holds them in the palm of his hand."

"They will be destroyed!" said Quentin, recoiling in horror at the thought of his companions marching headlong into battle with the beast Nimrood, defenseless and vulnerable.

"They may be killed," agreed Yeseph, "but not destroyed. There are worse things than death, though I would not expect you to know about them. It would be worse for Durwin to take up again the power which he laid down years ago—that would destroy him in the end. He would become the same as Nimrood. He would become the very thing he hated. That would be worse than honorable death.

"Besides," the Curatak elder said lightly, "do you think your presence with them would sway the balance very much?"

Quentin's head fell to his chest; his cheeks burned with shame. "Who am I to make a difference?" he mocked sadly. "I am no one. No one at all."

"You feel things deeply, Quentin," soothed Yeseph. "You are young, impetuous. Your heart speaks before your head. But it will not always be so."

"But is there nothing I can do to help them?" Quentin asked. He felt helpless and cast aside, useless baggage.

"Does it mean that much to you?" The elder eyed him closely.

Quentin nodded in silence. His eyes sought Yeseph's for some sign that he would help him find a way.

"I see. The god's ways are mysterious indeed. I will puzzle on this and bring it before our council of elders. There are those among us who discern more clearly than I how the god's hand moves through time and men's lives. We will seek their counsel."

Quentin's eyes brightened at the prospect, and hope revived in his heart. As he left Yeseph to his work he felt as if a great burden had been lifted from him. He did not know what to make of the feeling.

"Quentin," the elder curator called after him as he slipped through the door, "there is more to you than meets the eye. I knew that the moment you opened your mouth to speak. When all this is over promise me you will come back again and sit at my feet—there is much I would teach you."

That night Quentin dreamed another flying dream.

TWENTY-FIVE

JASPIN called his hirelings together in the great hall of Castle Erlott. The sun was well up and warming the land to a fresh and early spring. The Prince was growing more restive with each passing day—now pensive and brooding, now sweetly polite and even jovial in company. The tight little lines around his mouth told those who knew him best that the Prince was deeply troubled.

"I have decided that the Council of Regents must be held within a fortnight," Jaspin told his assembled knights and nobles. Many had taken their leave of Erlott Fields to attend their own concerns, but many still remained at the Prince's pleasure. These murmured at the suggestion that the Council should depart from its appointed time—midsummer.

"Sire, we must protest this alteration," spoke Lord Naylor

boldly. He and his neighbor, Lord Holben, alone dared to confront the Prince openly. Naylor himself, chief regent of the Council of Regents, was no great friend of Jaspin. Others in the group demonstrated their agreement with Lord Naylor by nodding and nudging one another. "Surely, after all these years the Council may accomplish its duty in its ordained season." He laughed stiffly, knowing the danger he was in at that moment. "I see no reason to depart from our commission now."

The Prince rankled at this challenge to his ambition. "What I propose shall be done," he said firmly. "And you, my lord, shall see that it is done according to my wishes."

Jaspin fixed Naylor with an icy glare and then looked around at each of the others individually, defying them to challenge him. "And you shall have the letters drawn up and dispatched to all the members not in attendance here, that we shall hold Council here in Erlott, not in Paget."

"And if I refuse your suggestions?" questioned Lord Naylor, his own temper rising. The Prince little knew, or cared, that he was making the situation harder for himself by bullying the chief counsellor of the regents. But Jaspin was a man whose mind seized upon a thing like a mongrel with a meaty bone and would not be put off.

"Refusal would be construed as a failure of your office. You could be replaced."

Some who looked on, and who would have happily pledged their support of Prince Jaspin if allowed to do so with a show of free will, were now uneasy at the thought of electing him at his own direction—for so they surmised his plans. They were appalled at the idea of naming him king in his own castle, and not, as tradition dictated, in the traditional setting in the Hall of Paget.

Jaspin only sought to hasten the appointed meeting. And, since as the object of the meeting he would not be allowed to attend the Council himself, he thought that by simply moving the designated meeting place to his own castle he would then know the result that much sooner, and save himself a ride to Paget, a journey of several days.

His idea, however, was a solidly unpopular one. And, if not for Lord Naylor's challenge, Jaspin would have been persuaded by a cooler head such as Ontescue's to abandon his scheme. But the matter had proceeded too far. Jaspin would have it no other way.

A hasty conference proceeded between Holben and the chief regent. "I will do as you bid, my Lord," said Naylor, his teeth set on edge. "But you may regret having pressed your way in this matter." He turned and crossed the room under Jaspin's dark look. "By your leave," he said and walked out of the hall.

The captives heard nothing but the occasional curses of their captors going about their business on the deck above and the wash of waves against the hull of the ship. In four days at sea they had been fed twice—a ration of coarse bread—but as they had access to all the water aboard ship they lacked nothing for their thirst.

Queen Alinea had been able to nurse Ronsard back to his senses. With her kind ministrations and the help of Durwin's healing power, the knight swore he felt better by the hour. Alinea insisted he remain reposed on his bed, although, cheered by the nearness of his friends, Ronsard largely ignored her pleas. They had much to talk about, and he much to tell.

"It gives me no pleasure to say it, my Lady," said Ronsard, leaning upon his elbow, "but I fear for the King. Nimrood is a crafty snake; his plots are beyond reckoning. However, we may be certain there is mortal danger for any within his grasp."

"He has induced Prince Jaspin, though little enough encouragement was needed, to practice his bold effrontery in a treacherous quest for the throne," said Theido.

"And I have heard it voiced far and wide that Nimrood raises an army; though who—or what—would fight for him, I cannot but wonder. In Elsendor there are rumors of a Legion of the Dead."

"By Orphe, no!" gasped Alinea. "Oh, it is too horrible to contemplate."

"Has he the power to do such things?" asked Trenn.

"He has," said Durwin, "and we have not the means to stop him . . . of ourselves."

"We will find a way," said Theido. His eyes kindled fire against the wicked necromancer. "Nimrood will be stopped. My life is my pledge."

"Would that my arm had the strength to hold my sword," moaned Ronsard. His stony features fought against the pain which his companions could see hovering there; he sought to rise.

"Nay, brave sir. Rest and allow vigor to return," said Alinea, pressing him back down with her hands gently on his shoulders.

"Alas," wailed Ronsard, "though I could wield ten swords I have none in this time of need."

"Soon—too soon I fear—there will be no lack of blades, but of hands to hold them. You will have your chance, Ronsard. Only content yourself till then, and pray your strength recovers." Durwin spoke softly and peered deeply into Ronsard's clouded eyes. The knight shook his head and his eyelids fluttered weakly. He lay his head back and slipped off to sleep moments later. "Would that I had such power over our enemies, as I have over the wounds of brave knights," sighed Durwin.

Trenn looked at the hermit with wide eyes full of awe. "There is power enough, I'll warrant, for many purposes. Perhaps you could charm this Nimrood to sleep as you did Ronsard just now."

"Would that I could. But no, the power that remains in me is of a healing kind—though it may be turned for other purposes in time of need. Were I to think of harming someone, even the evil Nimrood, this last remnant of my power would desert me instantly. It is a law of this healing power to be used ever thus." He paused, deep in thought, and then continued excitedly, "But what may be done with draughts and potions and the mixing of rare earths—that I may still do! Oh, I have been so slow. Gather round quickly! I have a plan!"

In a little while the captives heard the tick of a key in a lock, and the sound of rusty bolts thrown back. There was a rattle as chains dropped free and a blinding glare as the cargo door was opened wide, sending a shaft of light flooding into the hold.

A rough voice announced, "I trust my fine passengers are enjoying their trip." The voice was that of Captain Pyggin, whose portly form could now be discerned descending the steep stairs followed by two of his ruffians. "Give them their food," he ordered one of the men. The other stood guard.

"By Zoar! I'll . . ." swore Trenn, jumping to his feet. The guard's long knife flashed in his hand in an instant.

"Make no threats you care not to die by," warned Pyggin. "My men are less civilized than I. They kill to pass the time."

Trenn backed away slowly. "What do you want, pirate?" asked Theido carelessly.

"Only to tell you to enjoy your final hours." He cast a lustful eye over Alinea's comely form. "We reach our destination in two days hence." He waved his hand and the sailor carrying the food set down an iron pot and tossed a couple of loaves onto the filthy floor of the hold.

Pyggin turned to leave. "Enjoy your meal!" He laughed perversely and climbed the steps. The guard watched them with hooded eyes, daring anyone to try to rush upon him.

Then he was gone and darkness returned as the door slammed shut. The locks and chains were replaced and they heard the derisive call of Captain Pyggin through the lattice, "Two days—mark them well. They'll be your last."

"To think I paid him for our passage," muttered Trenn when Pyggin had gone.

"He but takes us where we want to go," observed Durwin.

"Yes, though not in the fashion we desired," replied Theido. "But much can happen in two days' time."

TWENTY-SIX

THE LAST light of day splashed crimson into the sky and tinted the edges of lingering clouds violet and blue. Quentin walked easily, though nervously, between Mollena and Toli. Ahead of them loomed the graceful silhouette of the Ariga temple.

Mollena was dressed in a long flowing robe of white, edged in silver, and her gray hair was pulled back straight to hang down her back. Quentin gazed upon her as he walked, thinking that something of the woman she must have been was revived in her this night. She appeared much younger than her years, her skin smoothed, the wrinkles eased with a radiance he had never seen in her countenance.

"Yes, it is Mollena and no other," she replied to his wondering glance. Her eyes twinkled brightly as they approached an avenue of torches leading to the temple entrance.

Quentin, embarrassed and enjoying it at the same time, said, "You are beautiful tonight, Mollena."

She laughed, "You say that now because you have not met our young women."

Quentin realized with a wince that he would not be meeting any young women at all—he and Toli had made plans to leave in the morning. His gaze slid from Mollena's laughing mouth to

Toli's deep-set, dark eyes. He, like Quentin, was dressed in a sky-blue mantle which covered a white tunic embroidered with silver at the neck. Toli looked like a Pelagian prince with his brown skin and gleaming black hair. For all the trouble they had faced in getting him to give up his rough skins, Toli appeared quite used to such finery.

Quentin, though, was too nervous to enjoy himself—except in fleeting moments when he forgot what was about to happen. For he was to be presented in a special temple service given in his honor. Quentin was to receive a special gift, as Yeseph had explained it; he was to receive the Blessing of the Ariga.

What that might be, Quentin could only guess.

"Here you are," said Yeseph. Quentin did not see him at first. He was gazing up at the sweeping lines of the temple's narrow, finger-thin central tower. People, dressed in the same simple elegance as Mollena and Yeseph, streamed into the temple. "Follow me—I will lead us to our places."

Quentin obeyed mutely. He was much too busy taking in all the sights and sounds—a chorus had begun singing as they entered the vestibule of the temple.

Yeseph led them along quickly. Quentin could see through the spaces between the great hanging tapestries they passed that the sanctuary of the temple was already mostly filled with worshippers. They moved around the semicircular auditorium and arrived at a side entrance where three men in long white robes waited with a half-dozen young men carrying large candlesticks of burnished gold.

One of the priests, for so Quentin took them, held out a white robe for Yeseph who slipped it on over his other garments. "Now," he said, "we are ready. Quentin, you follow me and do as I instructed you earlier. Mollena, you and Toli may take your places in the front row. You may watch from there."

The three priests, or elders, turned and formed a single line. Yeseph stepped into file behind them and Quentin behind him. The fire bearers stood on either side of them forming, Quentin thought, an impressive procession.

Then they were moving down a wide aisle toward a raised platform behind which hung a great golden tapestry which glittered bright as the sun in the light of hundreds of candles.

There were seats arranged in a semicircle on the platform behind a large stone altar. Upon reaching the final step the elders went to their seats and the fire bearers placed their candles in receptacles around the altar. Yeseph took a seat near the center of the circle and Quentin sat at his right hand.

"Listen carefully and do as I say," the Elder Yeseph instructed. "There will be an invocation—a calling of the One to hear our prayers. Then Elder Themu will deliver a short message to our people. When that is done it will be our turn. We will enter into the holy place—I will lead, you will follow."

Quentin nodded his understanding and the choir began a short verse which was followed by one of the elders ascending to the device Quentin had taken for an altar—it was a large stone cube set in the center of the platform with steps at the rear allowing the speaker to climb to the top. Around it in a circle burned the candles placed by the fire bearers.

"Mighty Peran nim Perano, King of kings, you who ever hear our prayers, hear us now . . ."

The invocation continued, and to Quentin it seemed somewhat similar, and yet very different from the invocations he had heard in the temple at Narramoor. Similar in the style of speech and the words used, but very different in the way in which it was delivered. There was no fear, no self-consciousness or ostentatious display of humility. The elder spoke simply and with assurance that his voice was heard by the god, as it was heard by the hundreds who filled the sanctuary. Quentin shifted nervously in his chair, a little unnerved by the idea that the god was actually listening to them, watching them.

Quentin imagined that he could actually feel the god's presence and then surprised himself when a real surge of emotion welled up within him in response to his imaginings.

He puzzled on these things as the ceremony moved along its determined course.

Quentin started to his feet at Yeseph's example, as the words of Elder Themu's message died away in the vast hall. He had daydreamed through the entire speech—it seemed like only moments since he had been seated, and yet he had a vague recollection that there had been more singing and the reading of the sacred text. But it all ran together in his mind as one brief event. Now he was standing and moving toward the stone with Yeseph.

"My good friends," said Yeseph to the congregation. Quentin looked out at the hundreds of bright eyes glittering in the light of the candles. All he saw were the eyes. "We have come tonight to confer upon this young man, a sojourner among us, the Blessing of the Ariga." Nods of approval rippled through the auditorium. "Attend us now with your prayers."

Yeseph signaled the fire bearers who came forward, each one carrying a candle in a shallow bowl.

The fire bearers filed to the rear of the platform followed by Yeseph and Quentin and then the remaining elders. As they approached the wonderful golden tapestry, two of the fire bearers stepped up and drew the tapestry aside and Quentin saw a narrow doorway.

Yeseph entered the doorway, darkened but for the flickering glow of the candles, and they passed through a short corridor and into an inner chamber.

The chamber was much like the inside of a tomb, thought Quentin. Bare. Cut out of smooth stone with a stone ledge running the length of the further wall. No symbols or ornaments were to be seen as the fire bearers silently began placing their candles about the room.

Quentin heard the gentle splash of water and saw at one end of the oblong room a small fountain playing peacefully in a hollow bowl set in the floor.

The elders took their places along the stone ledge and Yeseph drew Quentin toward the fountain. "Kneel, Quentin."

Quentin knelt down before the fountain and felt the smooth stone cool against his legs. In the quiet he heard the breathing of the elders behind him and the burble of the fountain dancing in its bowl. Then Yeseph, standing over him, said, "This is a place of power, the center of the Ariga's devotion, for in this room each young Ariga received a blessing when he came of age.

"They received many blessings throughout life, but this was a special one, delivered not by the elder or priest, but by Whist Orren, the Most High God himself.

"This special Blessing they carried throughout life, and it became a part of their life. They did not earn it, nor did it require a ritual of purification or obedience. The Blessing is the gift of the god. All that is required is a true heart and a desire to receive it.

"Now, then, is there any reason why you should not receive the Blessing of the Ariga?" Quentin, his eyes focused on the fountain while Yeseph had been speaking, turned to look into the elder's kindly eyes.

"No," he said softly. "It is my desire to receive the Blessing."

"Then so be it," said Yeseph. Raising his hands above Quentin's head, he began to speak. "Most High God, here is one who would be your follower. Speak to him now and out of your wisdom and truth, give him your blessing."

Again Quentin was struck with the bare simplicity of the prayer—an unadorned request, spoken with calm assurance.

Yeseph stooped to the fountain and cupped his hands in the water. "Drink," he commanded, offering Quentin the water.

Quentin took a sip and Yeseph then touched his forehead with damp fingertips. "Water is the symbol of life; all living things need water to live. And so it is the symbol of the Creator of Life, Whist Orren.

"Close your eyes," Yeseph instructed, and lifted his voice in an ancient song.

At first Quentin did not recognize the words; the elder's quavering voice echoed strangely in his ears as it reverberated in the stone chamber. Yeseph's song seemed to swell, filling the chamber, and Quentin realized the others were singing, too. It was a song about the god and his promise to walk among his people and guide them in his ways. Quentin found the song moving, and as the simple melody was repeated he recited the words to himself.

Gradually Yeseph's song died away and Quentin heard a voice. Was it Yeseph's or another's? He could not tell—it could have been his own. The voice seemed to speak directly to his heart, to some part of him that he carried deep within.

Quentin then entered a dream.

In the dream he still knelt upon the cool stone floor, but around him lay a bright meadow of limitless size. The lush green valley shimmered in honeyed light. The light itself seemed to emanate from no single source, but rather hung over the meadow like a golden mist.

The air smelled of pine and the lighter fragrance of sweet grass. Overhead the sky formed an arc of delicate blue iridescence which fairly rippled with subtle shades of changing color, yet appeared always the same. No sun roamed the sky, but the heavens, as the whole of the valley, seemed charged with light.

A crystal brook burbled close by, joyfully offering up its music to his ears. The water seemed alive as it splashed and danced along, sliding over the smooth, round stones.

An air of peace breathed over the scene, and Quentin felt a surge of joy spring up like a fountain inside him. His heart tugged within him, as if struggling to break free and soar aloft on light wings of happiness.

The voice he had heard before called him again, saying, "Quentin, do you know me?"

Quentin looked around somewhat fearfully. He saw no one nearby who might be speaking to him; he was utterly alone. But the voice continued.

"In the still of the night you have heard my voice, and in the depths of your heart you have sought my face. Though you searched for me in unholy temples I cast you not aside."

Quentin shuddered and asked in a small voice, "Who are you? Tell me that I may know you."

"I am the Maker, the One, Most High. The gods themselves tremble in my presence. They are shadows, faint mists tossed on the breeze and dispersed. I alone am worthy of your devotion."

As the voice spoke Quentin realized he had heard it many times before, or had so longed to hear—in the dark of his temple cell when he cried out alone. He knew it, though he had never heard it this clearly, this distinctly before.

"Oh, Most High, let your servant see you," Quentin pleaded. Instantly the peaceful meadow was awash in a brilliant white light and Quentin threw his arm across his face.

When he again dared to peer beneath his arm he saw the shimmering form of a man standing before him.

The man stood tall, with wide shoulders, rather young, but his features bore the stamp of a wise, seasoned leader. The man's form seemed to waver in Quentin's gaze as if he were seeing a reflection in water. The man appeared solid enough, but his outline grew fuzzy at the edges as if made of focused beams of living light, or clothed in an aura of rainbowlike luminescence.

But his face held Quentin's attention. The Man of Light's eyes gleamed like hot coals and his face shined with the radiance of glowing bronze. Quentin could not remove his gaze from the dark, fathomless depths of the man's burning eyes. They held his in a sort of lover's embrace: strong, yet gentle; commanding, yet yielding. Hunger of a kind Quentin could not name burned out from those eyes and Quentin felt afraid for presuming to exist within the sphere of the radiant being's sight.

"Have no fear," said the man. The tone was unspeakably gentle. "Long have I had my hand on you and upheld you. Look on me and know in your heart that I am your friend."

Quentin did as he was bid and experienced a sudden rush of recognition, as if he had just met a close friend or a brother who had been long absent. His eyes filled with tears.

"Please, I am not worthy . . ."

"My touch will cleanse you," said the Man of Light.

Quentin felt a warmth upon his forehead where the man placed two fingertips. The shame vanished as the warmth spread throughout his body. He wanted to leap, to sing, to dance before the Man of Light who stood over him.

"You seek a blessing," said the Man of Light. "You have but to name it."

Quentin tried to make the words come, but they would not. "I know not how to ask for this blessing . . . Though I know in my heart that I need it."

"Then we will ask your heart to reveal what lies within."

A sound of anguish and sorrow such as Quentin had never heard ripped from his own throat. It was as if a stopper had been removed from a jar and the contents poured out upon the ground in a sudden flood.

The cry ended as suddenly as it began, though for a moment it lingered in the air as it faded. Quentin blinked in amazement, shocked by the intensity of his own feelings—for that was what it was, the raw, unspoken emotions wrenched from his heart.

"Your heart is troubled about a great many things," said the Man of Light. "You cry out for your friends. You fear what may happen to them if you are not with them. You seek the assurance of success in rescuing your King from the hold of the evil one."

Quentin nodded dumbly; these were his feelings of the last few days.

"But more than this you seek higher things: wisdom and truth. You would know if there are true gods which men may pray to who will hear their prayers."

It was true. All the long nights alone in his temple cell, the anguished cries of longing came back to him.

"Quentin." The Man of Light stretched out a broad, open hand to him. "My ways are wisdom, and my words are truth. Seek them and your path will know no fear. Seek me and you will find life.

"You ask a blessing—I will give you this: Your arm will be righteousness and your hand justice. Though you grow weary and walk in darkness, fear nothing. I will be your strength and the light at your feet. I will be your comforter and guide; forsake me not and I will give you peace forever."

Quentin, looking deeply into the Man of Light's eyes, felt himself falling into the limitless void of time—as if through the dark reaches of starless night. He saw, not through his own eyes, but through the eyes of the god, the orderly march of the ages, time stretching out past and future in front of him in an unbroken line.

Then he saw a man he seemed to recognize: a knight. He was arrayed for battle and his armor blazed as if made from a single diamond; he carried a sword which burned with a hungry flame, and a shield which shone with a cool radiance, scattering light like a prism.

The knight spoke and raised his sword and the darkness retreated before him. Then the knight, with a mighty heave, flung the sword into the air where it spun, throwing off tongues of fire which filled the sky.

When the knight turned again Quentin recognized with a shock that the knight was himself—older and stronger, but himself.

"I am Lord of All," said the voice, "Maker of all things." Then the vision faded and Quentin was once again staring into the Man of Light's eyes. But now he knew them to be the eyes of the god himself, whose voice he had heard in the night, who had called him by name.

"Quentin, will you follow me?" he asked gently.

Quentin, bursting with contending emotions, threw himself at the Man of Light's feet and touched them with his hands. A current of living energy flowed through him and he felt stronger, wiser, more sure than ever before in his life. He felt as if he had touched the source of life itself.

"I will follow," said Quentin, his voice small and uncertain.

"Then rise. You have received your blessing."

When Quentin came to himself he was lying on his side in the dark. A single candle burned in its shallow bowl. Before him the fountain splashed; the sound made the chamber seem empty. Quentin raised his head to look around and saw that he was alone.

As he got up to leave the inner room he noticed that his right arm and hand tingled with a peculiar prickly sensation: both hot and cold at the same time. He paused to rub them and then went out.

TWENTY-SEVEN

THE RAIN fell in a miserable drizzle from a low, gray, unhappy sky. The track underfoot had become a muddy rivulet which trickled slowly as it wound its way down the hill among the giant forest evergreens. Quentin, astride Balder, and Toli, mounted on a black and white pony—left behind by the others— slid uncertainly down the trail in a muffled silence which hung on them like the heavy hooded cloaks they wrapped themselves in to keep out the rain. The trail from Dekra to the east was a much improved version of the boggy maze which they had floundered through on their way to the ruined city. So Quentin let Balder have his head and allowed his mind to wander where it would. He thought again of their leave-taking from Yeseph, Mollena, and the others.

A sad parting it was, for in the short time he had been with them he had grown very fond of them. They had said a few brief words of farewell—the Curatak do not believe in lengthy goodbyes, since they consider that all those who serve the god will one day be reunited to live forever together—and, as the horses stamped the ground impatiently, Quentin embraced Mollena and hugged Yeseph a little clumsily.

"Come back, Quentin, when your quest is at an end," said Yeseph. "I would welcome a pupil like you."

"I will come back when I can," promised Quentin, swinging himself into the saddle. "I am grateful for all I have received of your kindness. Thank you."

"The god goes with you both," said Mollena. She turned her face away, and Quentin saw the sparkle of a tear in the corner of her eye.

He looked on them for a lingering moment and then wheeled the big war horse around and started down the hill into the forest. He looked long over his shoulder, etching the memory deep into his mind. He wanted to remember it always as it appeared then: the sun filling the sky with a joyous light; the high, bright sky scrubbed clean by white clouds; the red stone walls of the city rising gracefully into the heady spring air; his friends standing at the wide open gates waving them away until at last the slope of the hill cut them off from view.

Quentin had never experienced a more emotional departure. But then, he reflected, he had never known anything but the coldness of the temple priests who never greeted, nor bade farewell.

Inside Quentin tingled with excitement; his heart soared like a bird freed at last from a long captivity. He quickly forgot his melancholy of leaving in the overflowing good spirits he felt at being alive, being back on the trail, and at reliving again the vision of the night before.

He had found it extremely difficult to sleep at all the last night. After the feast in his honor, where there was more singing and dancing and games, which lasted long into the night, he and Toli had returned to Mollena's rooms in the palatial governor's home. He had told them of the vision. Yeseph, and some of the other elders who had also gathered there, listened intently, nodding and pulling their beards.

"Your vision is a powerful sign. You are favored by the god," he said. "He has special plans for you."

"The Blessing of the Ariga," mused Elder Themu, "is itself a thing of power, for it carries with it the ability to accomplish its own end. The Most High God grants to every pure heart a blessing in kind, and the strength to carry out his purpose. In so doing you will find your own happiness and fulfillment."

Quentin puzzled this and asked, "Then what does my vision mean?"

"That is for you to discover. The god may show you in his own time, but most often knowledge only comes with struggle. You must work out the meaning yourself, for the interpretation comes in the doing."

"This is indeed different from the ways of the old gods," said Quentin. "In the temple the people come to the priest for an oracle. The priest takes the offering and seeks an oracle or an omen on behalf of the pilgrim. He then explains the meaning of the oracle."

"That is because the oracles are but foolishness of blind men—the smoke without the fire," said Themu.

That night, when the guests had departed and he was alone in his bed, Quentin had prayed for the first time to this new god, the one he had met in his vision. The vision seemed still more real to him than the vague dimensions of his own dark room and comfortable bed. He prayed, "Lead me in the discovery of your ways, God Most High. Give me the strength to serve you."

That was all he could think of to say. After all the formalized prayers of the temple, written down to be memorized by constant repetition, Quentin's simple prayer seemed to him ridiculously inadequate.

But trusting in Yeseph's observation that the god regarded more the state of the heart than the length of the prayer, Quentin let it go at that. And he had the strong inner conviction that his prayer had been heard, and by someone very close.

Early that morning, before the sun peeped above the undulating horizon, Quentin and Toli had discussed their plans.

"It is my desire to follow Theido and the others, and perhaps catch them if we can," said Quentin, munching a seed cake. Toli looked at him with strange eyes which Quentin found unsettling. "Why do you look at me so?"

"You have changed, Kenta," he said in a low voice, struck with wonder. Kenta was the Jher word for eagle—and, by extension, seemed to mean friend, master, lord—all at the same time. It was also the closest approximation of Quentin's own name which Toli would attempt, though to Quentin it seemed his friend did not try very hard. Toli fastened on this word for his own reasons.

"How have I changed?" Quentin tried to smile his old boyish smile, but it felt forced. "I am the same as I was."

Toli saw it differently. He had watched the ceremony of the Blessing with great admiration and respect. It had appeared to him as the coronation of a king, and he was proud that his master, for so he considered Quentin irrevocably now, had acceded to such a high honor.

"No," said Toli, "you are not the same."

That was all he would say on the subject. So Quentin pushed on to other things. They would ride on to Tuck and then to Bestou, as the others had done (so Mollena had informed them).

All Quentin knew was that Nimrood could be found at Karsh, though where that might be he could not say. Mollena refused to speak of the place, saying that it was an evil island not nearly far enough away though it be half-way round the world.

So they had struck out upon the trail to Tuck, a much forsaken path through the northern forests which were home to the great numbers of red deer and wild pigs. The animals themselves kept the trail open giving it the little use that it received. The Curatak had no need of it.

The second day out Toli had awakened Quentin to a dismal dawn. Shortly after they had breakfasted on some of Mollena's specially packed provisions the rumbling clouds had begun to leak a fine mist of rain. They had thrown on their hooded cloaks and proceeded in a subdued and melancholy mood. The soaring high spirits of the day before were dampened in the cheerless rain.

As they rode along Quentin became restive, his mind made uneasy by a thought which jabbed stubbornly at his conscience. He resolved to mention it to Toli at first opportunity. So, when they stopped by a small running stream to water the horses, Quentin spoke what was on his mind.

"Toli, do you know what is ahead of us?" he asked. The young Jher squinted up his eyes and peered down the darkened trail.

"No," he answered with typical Jher logic. "How can one know what lays ahead? Even well-known paths may change. The careful hunter goes with caution."

"No . . . I mean something else. We go to find Theido and Durwin and the others—most likely we ride into great danger." He watched Toli's face for any sign of concern. There was none.

Quentin glanced down into the racing stream at his horse's muzzle sunk deep in the swirling water. "I have no right to ask you to accompany me any further. Your people sent you as a guide out of friendship. Now that we have reached Dekra, and indeed, left it behind, your task is ended. You are free to return to your people."

Quentin glanced up to see Toli's bronzed features drawn into deep lines of sorrow. His mouth turned down sharply at the edges; his dark brown eyes had grown cold. "If that is what you wish, Kenta. I will return to my people."

"What I want . . . that does not matter. But you must go back. This is my journey, not yours; you did not ask for it. I cannot ask you to risk your life—you have no place in this fight."

"You must tell me what you wish me to do," said Toli, throwing his palms out.

"I cannot," pleaded Quentin. "Do you see?"

Toli did not see. He blinked back at Quentin gravely, as if to reproach him for cruelty unimaginable.

"You may be killed," explained Quentin. His knowledge of the Jher speech was quickly becoming exhausted under the strain of trying to communicate this dilemma. "I cannot be responsible for your life if you follow me."

"The Jher believe that every man is responsible for his own life. The Jher are free—I am free—we do not suffer any to be masters over us. But a Jher may take a master if he chooses."

Toli's voice rose and the lines of his face began to ease as he continued. "For a Jher to take a master, to serve him in all to the death—this is the highest honor. For to serve a worthy master accounts the servant worthy. Few of my people ever find an opportunity as I have found." He spoke this last part as a boast, his eyes sparkling. "A great master makes his servant great."

"But the danger . . ."

"He who serves shares his master's portion—danger, death, or triumph. If the master receives honor, so his servant receives much greater honor."

"But I did not ask you to be my servant."

"No," he said proudly. "I chose you."

Quentin shook his head. "What about your people?"

"They will know and rejoice for me." Toli's face beamed with pleasure.

"I do not understand," complained Quentin, though he did not much mind his lack of understanding.

"That is because your people are brought up to believe that serving another is a weakness. It is not out of weakness that one serves, but out of strength."

"I would still feel better if I could ask you myself."

"Ask then, but I have already given my answer."

"Is there no getting rid of you then?" joked Quentin. The joke escaped Toli, whose face fell again momentarily.

"To be dismissed as a servant is a great humiliation and disgrace."

"A worthy master would not dismiss lightly one who esteems him so highly," Quentin said. "But maybe I should serve *you*!"

Toli laughed, as if Quentin had made the most ridiculous jest. "No," he chuckled. "Some are born to be masters, but a servant must be taught quite young. It is better that I serve you." Then he grew serious again. "You, my master, wear the look of glory. You will I serve. For only by your side will I find glory, too."

"Very well," said Quentin at last. "Since I would really rather not go alone, and you are determined not to allow me to in any case, we will go together."

"As you wish," said Toli pleasantly.

"My wishes seem to have nothing to do with it," remarked Quentin. Toli ignored the remark and held Balder while Quentin mounted, then mounted his own black and white.

"To Tuck, then," said Quentin. His heart was much lighter and his mind at ease. He had not wanted to give up Toli's company and would have tried to persuade him to remain if that had been the case. This master and servant situation, however, would require some getting used to. He had not known the extent of Toli's loyalty toward him and wondered if he were at all capable of being a good master. Already the responsibility weighed heavier than he would have supposed.

They rode along together through a wet afternoon and stopped to spend a soggy evening along the trail under the skimpy shelter afforded by a long-limbed evergreen whose branches brushed the ground.

Toli tethered the horses and allowed them to walk a short pace to graze on nearby clumps of grass and forest foliage. Quentin unrolled the packs under the evergreen boughs and made a dry, soft bed by piling up the aromatic needles. Toli gathered dry bark and stones and soon had a small fire going to warm them and dry out their sopping clothing.

Night fell quickly in the forest and the two lay in the dark listening to the drip of water from the high boughs and the small crackling of their little fire. Quentin stretched himself upon his bed roll and breathed the fragrant balsam deep into his lungs.

"What do you think of the new god?" Quentin asked absently, searching the darkness nearby for the glitter of Toli's eyes.

In all the time they had spent at Dekra, he had not spoken to Toli about any of the Ariga religion. Now that oversight embarrassed him.

"He is not new. The Jher have always known him."

"I did not know. What do you call him?"

"Whinoek."

"Whinoek," Quentin repeated to himself. "I like that very much. What does it mean?"

"You would say it means Father . . . Father of Life."

TWENTY-EIGHT

"IT IS a slim chance, but it is a chance," said Durwin, lifting off the first of the water barrel lids.

"I only wonder why we did not think of it sooner," remarked Theido. "Keep your ear to the door and be ready to sing out," he added, whispering across the hold to Trenn crouching at the top of the steps.

Durwin took a handful of yellowish-looking powder from a cloth which Alinea held in her hands. He sprinkled it into the water in the barrel and Theido stirred it with a broken oar and replaced the lid.

"Do you think they will come for water today?" asked Alinea. The three moved on to the next barrel and repeated the procedure.

"I hope so." Theido rolled his eyes upward to the deck overhead. "They come every second day to replenish the stoups on deck with fresh water. With any luck at all they will come today, too. Though we must be close to land by now—they may wait."

"We do what we can. Just to be sure, we will refrain from contaminating this last barrel; it will be for our use." Durwin shook the last of the powder into the keg and dusted his hands over the top.

Just then Trenn rapped sharply on the stairs with his foot. "Someone comes!" he whispered harshly. "Look quick!"

Theido stirred vigorously and replaced the lid of the keg, driving it home with the end of his oar. The three then took up their usual places at the foot of the stairs as the door to the hold opened.

". . . Bring up a goodly length," a voice called out from the deck to the two descending figures.

"Get back!" snarled one of the sailors. The other went to a corner and proceeded to sort among piles of rope. When he found what he wanted he returned and started up the stairs with the rope. The captives watched in disappointment.

After the sailors had locked the door behind them Durwin said, "Take heart; the day is yet young. Perhaps they will come again."

Trenn looked doubtful. "But we have no way of knowing how close we may be to land. We could drop anchor soon."

"Indeed we could. If that is to be, so be it. The god holds us in his hand and moves however he will."

But as he spoke there arose a commotion on the deck above and the sound of someone furiously throwing off the chains and lock that secured the hold. The door again swung open and Pyggin's scream could be heard as he berated his poor seamen. "The day's ration of water, you dolts! Fetch it! You've already fetched yourselves a flogging!"

Three forlorn sailors tumbled down the stairs, led by the sailor with the rope. They dashed straight for the nearest water keg without casting even a sideways glance at the prisoners huddled at the edge of the shaft of light thrown down by the door overhead. They lifted the keg in their brawny arms and struggled back up the steep stairs. They did not see the surprised and pleased expressions on the faces of the prisoners as they disappeared back upon the deck with the water ration for the crew.

"We still don't know whether Pyggin drinks from the same bowl as his men or no," said Trenn, when the footsteps had faded away above.

"It is a risk we will take," answered Theido. He turned to Durwin. "How long before your potion works?"

"It varies, of course—how big the man, how much he drinks . . . But I made it slow to act, though strong. When all have gone to sleep tonight, none will rise before the dawn—though tempest blow and waves beat down the masts." He laughed and his eyes twinkled in the darkened hold. "But, lest we forget, we have a more immediate problem before us . . ."

"Right," said Trenn. "If we do not find ourselves an escape from this stinking hull, it matters not how long the rogues of this tub sleep."

"What about one of the other hatches," said Alinea, pointing into the darkness beyond to one of the two dim squares of light cut in the deck above.

"An excellent idea, my Lady." The voice was Ronsard's. Surprised, all turned to see the knight standing somewhat uncertainly behind them.

"Ronsard!" exclaimed Theido, "how long have you been standing there?"

"Lie down this instant!" said Alinea, rushing over to take the wounded knight by the arm and lead him back to his crude pallet. He took one step toward them and his face screwed up in pain; a hand shot to the side of his head.

"Oh!" he said, then steadied himself. "I am not used to having my feet under me just yet."

"It will come," assured Durwin.

"Ah, but I feel better than I have in months," replied the knight, allowing himself to be sat down on a keg by the Queen's insistence. "Aside from this throbbing head of mine I feel like a new man."

"I am glad to see it," beamed Theido. "I had long ago given you up for dead—even seeing you here and looking like you did when we found you did not increase my hopes by much. But it now appears that you will live after all."

"It is all due to this wizard priest of yours," Ronsard said, grinning at Durwin.

"I did nothing—only allowed you to get the rest your body needed. You have slept these last three days."

"You said something about the forward hatch, sir," reminded Trenn. "If you don't mind my saying so," he said to Theido, "I think that is our most pressing problem."

"Of course. What do you know about the forward hatch? Is there a way out from there?"

"It may be we can make one," said Ronsard rising slowly from his keg. "I remember when I was thrown none too gently in here that the forward hatch was not secured as the others."

"Let us see." Theido led the group ahead, carefully picking his way among the carelessly stored cargo and supplies. In a moment they stood under the small hatch, gazing up through the latticework of its bars.

"It is a scuttle hatch more than likely," said Trenn pessimistically. "Too small for a man to get through."

"Though not too small for a woman perhaps," said Alinea brightly.

"My Lady, I forbid you to go running about on deck—what if one of those pirates does not fall asleep? No, it is too dangerous." Trenn spoke in an authoritative tone. Theido and Durwin were inclined to agree with him, but said nothing.

"Well, are heroics only for men, then?" Alinea's eyes snapped defiantly. "I will match my hand against any of Pyggin's herd if it comes to it, but I have stealth and surprise on my side at that. Not to mention Durwin's art."

"It may be our best plan after all," said Ronsard. "It would be dark."

"Yes, and she could move about more quietly than any of us, I will grant," said Theido.

"But we have yet to find the means to raise the hatch," pointed out Durwin. "I suggest we start there while we still have a little light on our side."

"Here," said Theido, "help me stack up a few of these casks and barrels. We will build our Lady a staircase to freedom."

The prisoners worked all day and into the evening chiseling away at the lone hasp that fastened the hatch, using bits of metal and a tool or two they found lying rusting in the bottom of the hold.

As twilight came upon them they heard sounds from on deck which gave them to know that the ship had sighted its destination, the cruel land of Karsh.

Captain Pyggin's voice, hoarse from screaming orders at his lackluster men, could be heard above the commotion of scrambling feet and dragging tackle. "You lazy gulls! You'll get no rum tonight, land or no land. Move! What's got into you! Are ye all bewitched?"

"Hmmm . . . the drug is beginning to take effect, I believe," said Durwin.

"Surely he will not try to land tonight."

"No, most likely they will wait at anchor some way out and not risk their boats against the rocks in the dark," replied Ronsard from his bed.

"Good," said Trenn. "That will give us time to work. By dawn we should be ashore and this tub resting at the bottom of the sea."

"You would not sink it with all on board," objected Alinea. She was perched upon a barrel top, grinding away at the hasp of the hatch above.

"I would caution against such an act myself," warned Durwin. "The needless taking of life."

"But this is war!"

"Even in war we must conduct ourselves in a manner worthy of men."

"Besides," added Theido, "we may need the ship later to make our escape."

"Now, *that* I understand," muttered Trenn.

Just then the clink of metal falling to the deck above them sounded and Alinea said, "It is free! The hatch is free!"

"Good. Come down now and we will wait for darkness to make our move," said Theido. "We will not have long to wait, I think."

Prince Jaspin paced furiously about his apartment in Erlott Castle. The Council of Regents had been in session all day and he had been barred from going anywhere near the meeting which was taking place in his own hall.

"Leave them to their business," cautioned Ontescue, the Prince's would-be chancellor. "They will remember their benefactor, have no fear. If you like I will send to the wine cellar for some of your excellent ale. That should refresh their senses to the task—and give them a taste of the riches to come under your reign, my Liege."

Though the selfish Jaspin did not fully appreciate pouring his best ale down the throats of the regents, he nevertheless saw the wisdom of such a move; it was a sure reminder to them who pulled the strings.

"Yes, a fine idea, Ontescue. See that it is carried out at once." He continued his pacing.

"How long have they been in there? How long will they remain?" Jaspin wailed. "What can be taking so long?"

Ontescue returned shortly with a message in his hand. "The ale is being served. The regents are in recess now for a time. Sir Bran delivered this now to me in secret—it is for you."

The eager Prince snatched the letter out of Ontescue's hand and read it at once. "By the gods' beards!" he shouted, losing control. "The Council is deadlocked. That skulking bandit Holben has talked some of his spineless friends over to his side," the Prince fumed. "They are blocking my approval with their dissent."

"How can that be? They have not the power to suggest another in your place. The right of succession goes to you."

"True enough, but they appeal to a dusty old law, insisting upon proof of the King's death beyond reasonable doubt. That proof I cannot give."

"Does such proof exist?"

"You ought to know as well as I," evaded Jaspin, covering his mistake quickly. "If the King is dead then proof exists."

"I only meant that even were the King still living—though unfit to continue his reign—some proof might be found that would satisfy the troublemakers."

"Hmmm . . ." The Prince's high brow wrinkled in thought.

"There is something in what you say, my friend. How quickly you think."

"Might I suggest that a search be made that would turn up something or someone who would provide the necessary proof?"

"Yes, that's it," said Jaspin, rubbing his hands together with glee. "Where do you propose we start looking?"

A wry look came over Ontescue's sharp features; his weasel eyes squinted up merrily. He bent his head close to Jaspin's ear and whispered.

"By Azrael," breathed Jaspin, "You are a clever fox. Let us make haste. There is no time to lose."

TWENTY-NINE

"SHHH! Make no sound!" warned Toli in a strained whisper. One hand covered Quentin's mouth and his other dripped with the water that he had splashed in his friend's face to wake him.

Quentin struggled from sleep, blinking the water out of his eyes, puzzled at first, then he caught a look at Toli's wide eyes and tight lips. Concern mingled with fear lurked there.

Toli removed his hand with another warning for silence. "What is wrong?" Quentin barely breathed. He rolled onto his side and pushed himself up on an elbow and followed Toli's gaze into the forest. There was not a sound to be heard.

He peered into the night. All was darkness; the fire had burned out and it appeared to Quentin several hours yet before the dawn. A thick overcast shut out any light from moon or stars. The forest round about lay in deepest gloom.

Just then one of the horses whickered softly, and the other answered nervously. Quentin, straining both eyes and ears into the darkness saw and heard nothing. He waited and was about to speak again when he saw a slight flicker through the trees some way off: a ghostly shape, gray-white against the black trunks of the trees. Low to the ground. Moving swiftly among the dense undergrowth. A thin, pale shape.

It disappeared almost as soon as Quentin had seen it.

"What is it?" Quentin asked, leaning close to Toli. He could see the tense expression on his friend's face and felt his rapid, shallow breathing on his cheek.

"Wolves."

The word burned itself into Quentin's mind slowly, as if it had no meaning. But then like a slap in the face he realized their danger. Wolves! They were being stalked by wolves!

"How many?" he asked quietly, trying to make his voice sound calm and unconcerned, and failing.

"I have only seen one," said Toli in the barest whisper. "But where there is one there are others."

Unconsciously Quentin reached for the only weapon he had, the gold-handled dagger of the King's knight. His fingers tightened around the hilt as he drew it from his belt.

He glanced at the smouldering remains of their camp fire, wishing that it would spring magically to life again. Wolves are afraid of fire, he thought. He had heard that somewhere and wondered if it was true. As if reading his mind, Toli leaned over and placed his face close to the smoking coals and blew on them. His face glowed duskily in the feeble firelight, and for an instant a single flame licked out. But, lacking fuel to feed it, the flame winked out again and the coals grew cold.

The horses, close behind them, but invisible in the darkness, jingled their bridles as they tossed their heads to free themselves. "We must loose the horses," said Toli, "so they may fight."

"Will it come to that?" Quentin asked. He had no experience in these things. He felt out of place and strangely indignant about it, an emotion which puzzled him.

Just then Quentin caught another flickering glimpse of a gray shape floating among the trees to the right of them. This time the animal was much closer.

"They are closing in," said Toli. Quentin realized he had been holding his breath.

"What are we going to do?" asked Quentin, shocked because he did not have the slightest idea himself what to do.

In answer to his question Toli handed him a stout branch, one they had gathered for the fire. It was hefty enough to use as a club. With the club in one hand and the knife in the other, Quentin felt only slightly more confident. "Keep low," Toli warned. "Protect your throat."

Toli stood slowly and from a long distance behind them they heard the mournful call of a wolf. Quentin's stomach tightened as if someone were squeezing it. The eerie, hollow cry was echoed by another on the right, not nearly so far away. Toli placed a hand on Quentin's arm, clenching him in a steel grip, drawing him to his feet.

Suddenly they heard a low, slathering growl from the left very close. Quentin turned toward the sound and saw a gaunt white death's head floating right at him out of the forest.

"To the horses!" screamed Toli, spinning on his heel and diving forward.

Quentin turned in the same instant and flew to Balder's side. He found the animal's head and slashed at the reins which tied him to the branch where he had been tethered for the night.

The mighty war horse jerked free and reared upon its hind legs as it spun round to face its ghostly attacker. Quentin dodged out of the way as a heavy, iron-shod hoof whistled through the air where his head had been an instant before.

Balder neighed wildly, flailing the air with his forelegs. The wolf, plunging at them from the forest, swerved and bounded aside to avoid Balder's singing hooves.

Out of the corner of his eye Quentin saw another wolf dashing in from the side. He leaped forward and swung the makeshift club high over his head, yelling at the top of his lungs as he did so. The yell surprised himself as much as it scared the wolf who hung back in its attack just long enough for Quentin to land a blow square on its long snout. The wolf's jaws snapped shut with a teeth-cracking crunch as the club fell. The animal let out a pleading yelp and backed away.

Another yelp sounded behind him and Quentin spun around to see Toli lashing with a long stick at a large gray wolf crouching beneath the ineffectual blows. Quentin started toward Toli to lend a hand. He had run not two steps when his foot caught on a root and he went down.

As he fell Quentin sensed a motion behind him and before he hit the ground with a thud he felt a weight upon his back. Without thinking he threw an arm over his head as the wolf's long teeth raked at his exposed neck. He felt the dagger in his hand and tried to wrench free his other arm pinioned beneath him.

He felt the wolf's teeth tearing at his clothing, caught in the sleeve of his tunic. He squirmed under the weight of the animal, trying to bring the knife up and into the wolf's belly.

The knife flashed up, suddenly free, and Quentin looked beneath his arm to see the body of the wolf flying sideways and folding in midair as if it had no backbone. Then he saw Balder's head tossed high above him as he prepared to deliver another, similar blow to any predator daring to come within range of his lightning hooves.

"Kenta!" Toli cried. Quentin looked around to see his friend holding four wolves at bay with his whirling branch. Three others were working at the other horse, closing in for a lunge at the frightened animal's throat.

Jumping to his feet, Quentin found his club in his hand and raced toward his friend. "God Most High, help us now!" he screamed as he ran.

One wolf broke off its attack of the horse to meet Quentin in full flight. Quentin lunged with the club, but the wily creature dodged and caught the club in its mouth. The wolf jerked backwards with such force it nearly pulled Quentin's arm from its socket as he let go of the club. He brought the knife up before him as the wolf gathered itself for another lunge.

Toli screamed something unintelligible and Quentin saw a wolf standing on its hind legs with its paws on Toli's back, jaws snapping wildly.

There was a growl before him and Quentin looked down into the wolf's evil yellow eyes. The wolf snarled savagely and bared its cruel fangs, coiling itself, snake-like, for a strike.

Then Quentin heard a squeal from the bushes beside him. Another wolf? It did not sound like a wolf. He heard more squeals and the sound of something big crashing recklessly through the underbrush.

The wolf heard it too and turned its baleful eyes from Quentin to look to the brush behind it.

All at once the bushes erupted in high-pitched squeals and the crashing sound of small hooves tearing among the branches. Dark shapes like boulders came dashing through the clearing from the far side of the forest.

The dark forms raced headlong into the wolves, squealing and snorting as they ran. The wolves, snarling in terror, turned to face this new foe.

One of the dark creatures brushed by Quentin nearly knocking him off his feet. It was then that Quentin realized the squealing shapes were those of wild pigs—boars and sows.

The wild pigs, led by a huge boar with long curving tusks, bolted with a fury into the thick of the wolves. Toli leaped aside as they came crashing into the clearing to engage the wolves.

Fur flew. The tear of flesh and the meaty crunch of living bone being splintered could be heard amid the yelp of the terrorized wolves.

The large white wolf, the leader which had begun the attack, barked once and made a dash for the forest. Those of his marauding band that could still run turned tail and followed him as the pigs snuffled after them.

In moments they were gone, and Quentin stood fighting for his breath in the center of the clearing. All that could be heard was the receding crash of the wild pigs in thundering pursuit of the fleeing wolves.

Then Toli was beside him peering into his face in quiet wonder. Toli's face was wet from sweat and blood from a small cut over his eye. "Are you all right, Kenta?" he asked, touching Quentin on the arm with his fingertips.

"Yes. I am fine. But you are bleeding."

"I am not hurt—just a scratch." He turned to where the sounds of pursuit were dying away in the forest.

"I have never seen anything like it," breathed Quentin. "Have you?"

Toli shook his head. "It is known among my people that wild pigs will sometimes fight off a wolf which threatens their young. But this . . . this is a mighty sign. Whinoek has raised his hand to protect us."

"The god must care about us very much," said Quentin, remembering his desperate prayer of only moments ago.

"Yes," agreed Toli, thankfully. "But there is something else."

Quentin waited for him to say what it was.

"There is plenty of game in this forest for wolves to pull down—deer and pigs, the old and sick. Much safer than taking on humans with horses. Wolves do not attack men—only rarely, in the deep of winter when food runs scarce and they starve."

"What made them do it?" Quentin's eyes went round. "Nimrood?"

Toli gave a cryptic shrug and raised his eyes above where the trees met overhead. The small patch of sky showed a dull iron blue. "The sun is coming up soon. We must be on our way."

Together they set about calming the horses and breaking camp as quickly as possible. Though neither spoke it was clear to both they wanted to be far away as soon as possible.

THIRTY

CAPTAIN Pyggin had threatened not to give his men their usual rum ration, a customary gesture when a ship reached port. But, as were most of his threats, it was an idle one. As darkness fell the rum pots were filled and the rowdy play of the crew began.

The captives could hear the raucous clamour of drunken voices raised in song. The wild revel would normally have lasted far into the night, but the rum, acting in harmony with the power of Durwin's drug, heightened its effect. Thus, after a few salty choruses and a drink or two the men collapsed upon the deck where they stood—a normal happenstance on a night like this, but the outcome hastened thanks to Durwin's art.

Abruptly, the singing stopped, and the snores of crew members could be heard droning softly against the wash of the waves.

"So it is!" announced Durwin, "that is the remedy. Now to business."

"Be careful, Alinea," warned Theido. "There may be one or two still on their feet. Stay out of sight until you have a chance to look around."

"I will," she said. "Do not worry, I will have you out of here in no time." Alinea, looking more like a stable boy than any queen, ascended the rude staircase of cargo and pushed open the hatch while the others gathered below.

"Oh, my Lady," moaned Trenn nervously, "I'd rather you let me take your place."

Durwin smiled, "No need. Besides you would not likely fit through that hatch in your present shape. Come, let us make ready to be off."

The three ascended the steep steps to the chained and bolted door. Presently they heard Alinea's soft footfall approaching. "What do you see?" asked Theido when she had reached the door.

"All are fast asleep, save the cook and his galley servant. They sit nodding in their cups beside a rum pot on the far side of the deck."

"Can they see us from there?"

A pause. "No . . . I do not think so. Anyway, it will soon be beyond their power to stand up, let alone draw sword against a knight."

"We must find the keys to these locks—how many are there?"

"There are two, and the door itself. Where should I begin looking?"

"The captain's lackey," suggested Trenn. "Unless I miss my guess, 'twas he that opened this hold when first we entered here."

"Good eyes, man!" said Theido. And then to Alinea, "Find the man who first greeted us. If I remember aright he wears a blue coat and a squint."

"He'll likely be found in the captain's shadow," offered Trenn.

"Yes, look for the captain."

They heard her footsteps leave and stood waiting for her return. A minute passed. Then another, and another. Each one seemed to stretch out far beyond its normal limit.

Finally, they heard her return. "I cannot find the man, though I found Pyggin. He had no keys on him."

"What do we do now?" wondered Theido.

"If I were up there I would find that pirate. Those keys are up there in a pocket somewhere." Trenn clenched his fists as he spoke.

He had no sooner finished speaking than they heard a low rumble from somewhere far away. "What was that? Listen!"

"It is thunder," said Alinea. "The sky is clear, but I can see a storm approaching from the east. There is lightning. It looks a large storm. And it is moving fast."

"We have got to find those keys," muttered Theido.

"What about the other hatch?" suggested Durwin. "The main cargo hatch. We could climb out from there with ease."

"Alinea, we are going to try the main cargo hatch. How is it secured?" As Theido spoke thunder cracked in the distance.

"Listen," said Trenn, "The wind is rising."

It was true. They could now hear the wind singing in the high rigging of the ship—fitfully, but with growing force.

"I had best wake Ronsard," said Durwin. "He may need time to gather his strength."

Alinea returned from looking at the main hatch. "It is a simple hasp with a single staple—it will require no key. They have beaten a wedge through the staple. I may remove it if I can find something to loosen it with." She hurried away again in search of a tool.

"Come," said Theido, "let us be ready to leave here as soon as the hatch is opened."

The three set about busily restacking casks and kegs, most of which were empty, in a rude stairway that fell short only a few spans from the hatch. Theido stood on the top of the pile while Trenn and Durwin handed him the items needed to construct the precarious stairway. Ronsard sat to one side, complaining, "I am fit, I tell you. I can lend a hand . . ."

"Save your muscle, brave knight," said Trenn. "You may have need of it ere this night is through."

"No more than will you, I should think."

"Perhaps not," reminded Durwin, "but none of us have been sleeping as close to death's dark door as have you. There is much to be done before our journey's end. We will need your unhindered strength when the time comes."

From above could be heard the tapping sound of Alinea working at the hasp. The teetering mountain of cargo tilted dangerously in the slow rocking of the ship with the waves which were beginning to run higher.

The three held their breath and waited.

"It is free!" shouted Alinea, and then, "Aieee!" The scream was muffled and broken off quickly.

"Something's wrong," cried Theido, clambering up the cargo mountain and heaving the hatch open.

As he poked his head above the deck he saw Alinea caught in the grasp of a hulking figure whose hands were around her throat. She struggled furiously but futilely against the superior strength of her assailant.

"Let go, varlet!" shouted Theido, pulling himself through the hatch. The Queen's attacker turned slowly, drunkenly, around to meet Theido's crouching charge. Theido sprang headlong at the man, spearing him full in the stomach like a ram butting into an unwary trespasser.

"Oof!" the man wheezed as he went down.

The pirate hit the deck like a felled timber and lay stretched full length gazing up at the sky. He made one feeble attempt to raise his sodden head and then fell back, asleep, his head thumping upon the deck.

"The cook?" asked Trenn, now standing next to Theido and ready for action if his services were required.

"Yes," said Alinea, drawing a shaky breath.

"Oh, my Lady, are you all right?" The warder took her by the arm and gestured her to sit down.

"Worry not a moment, good warder. I am unharmed. The man was so obviously drunk . . . he frightened me just a little, that is all."

"Come, everyone!" shouted Durwin as he clambered from the hatch, his eyes searching the sky. "This storm will be upon us too soon, I fear. We must away!"

Theido dashed across the deck, shouting, "Trenn, give me a hand with the boats!"

"Ronsard, you and Alinea go with them. I will join you in a moment." With that Durwin turned and climbed a low companionway leading to the captain's quarters.

Ronsard and Alinea made their way to where Trenn and

Theido were lowering the ship's long boats. They were three rickety-looking specimens of the boatwright's art long past their prime; decrepit—a state hastened by neglect. One boat was already in the water as the Queen and the King's knight drew up.

"Here, hold fast to this rope," said Theido, shoving the thick, braided seaman's rope into Ronsard's hand; the other end was attached to a small, open boat. "This one looks to be the most seaworthy." He and Trenn then dashed further down the deck to lower the others.

"I like not the look of that sky," said Ronsard. As he spoke the first fat drops of rain splashed at their feet in small puddles. The wind whipped the high rigging, and the ship began to rock against the waves. "I fear we are in for the brunt of it."

"Where is Durwin?" asked Theido as he came running up.

"He went in search of the captain's quarters, I believe," answered Ronsard.

"Well, let us get aboard while we still may." Theido threw one long leg over the ship's rail and buried his hands into the netting hanging there. He dropped down the side of the ship like an awkward spider and jumped into the boat. He grabbed an oar and pushed the boat, now bobbing like a cork in the swell, closer to the ship.

"My Queen, you come next. Trenn, Ronsard, hand her down gently."

"I can manage," she said as she threw herself over the side like an experienced sailor and shimmied down the netting and into the boat. Trenn and Ronsard stood marveling.

"Move, you two," yelled Theido.

Ronsard was next, lowering himself somewhat laboriously, a step at a time, into the boat. Trenn followed, releasing the ropes attached to the other two boats.

"Now, where is that meddling wizard!" wondered Theido impatiently.

"Let me to the oars, sir," said Trenn, settling himself on the center bench. "It may take two," said Ronsard, sitting down beside him. "From the looks of those waves we have our work before us."

Alinea positioned herself low in the center of the boat at the bow. Theido manned the rudder, casting an anxious eye up to the rail in expectation of seeing Durwin's round face peering over the side at any second. "What can be keeping that hermit? The storm is almost upon us."

Thunder crashed around them now as lightning tore through the heavy black clouds. Salty spray off the whitecapped waves drenched them, and the rain, falling faster now, pelted down in stinging pellets.

"Look!" cried Alinea, her voice lost amidst the roaring wind and thunder. The others followed her outstretched hand with their eyes.

"The gods save us!" shouted Trenn; the words sped from his mouth in the shrieking wind.

Glowing green out of the darkness, twisting, writhing like a gigantic living serpent, spun a waterspout coming straight for them. The awful maelstrom, lit by the terrible lightning that showered around it, whirled and coiled about itself, rising half a league into the sky. Behind it a curtain of rain, tossed by deafening winds, hurled into the flood. The ship beside them shuddered as the waves slammed into her. The little boat rocked violently, but stayed above the swell, descending into the valley and then climbing the hill of water on the other side.

Finally, Durwin's bewhiskered face appeared at the rail. Without a glance toward the onrushing waterspout, though the gale seemed to fill the world with its scream, the hermit threw himself over the rail and down the side of the tilting ship.

"Careful!" shouted Theido. No one heard him, though they saw his mouth form the words.

The netting, slippery now, proved treacherous for Durwin's grip. Twice he lost his footing, being saved from a plunge into the angry sea by thrusting his arm through the netting and crooking his elbow.

"Jump for it!" shouted Theido. Durwin had the same thought at the same instant and half turned, gauged the distance, and then dropped the rest of the way into the boat. As soon as the hermit had plopped into the bottom of the craft, Theido shoved them away from the hull of the ship.

Trenn and Ronsard strained at the oars and began to row furiously. The little boat bit into the water and moved slowly away from the ship.

Theido threw himself against the rudder's stout tiller and headed them toward the shore, now showing as a faint white strand against the gloom.

When they dared look again, the waterspout had grown fantastically as it swept in from the sea. Sucking more and more water into its cyclone, it wavered like a long, wicked finger tracing a course of death toward the small boat.

Blindly, the party fought the waves which threatened to swamp them at every valley and overturn them at every peak. Somehow Theido managed to keep the boat heading to shore, and Trenn and Ronsard moved them ever so slightly ahead. Durwin, gripping the gunwales with white fingers, lifted his face to the sky and prayed, "God of all creation, spare us from the storm's great wrath. Deliver us safely to yonder shore—for without your help we surely will drown."

No one aboard heard the prayer, but all knew what Durwin was doing and echoed his thoughts in their own.

A shout turned the others toward Theido, who stood waving his arms. They looked through the driving rain to where he waved and saw to their horror the waterspout looming up behind them, thrashing through the water like some agony-driven creature loosed in fury upon the sea.

Theido threw himself forward into the bottom of the boat indicating for the others to follow his example. Water hurled from on high showered down upon them in sheets. The bawl of the storm filled their ears.

Then, suddenly, inexplicably, when the terrible spout should have been upon them, there was no sound. Nothing. The rain stopped. The water grew calm.

Durwin lifted his head and peered above. "Look! The spout has skipped over us." It was true. The waterspout, which only moments before towered above them, threatening to draw the tiny boat and its occupants up into its dreadful tempest, had lifted over them, dancing back up into the clouds. They could see its green tornado spinning directly above them, twirling like a burrowing worm, and heading inland.

The calm lasted only brief seconds. Then the wind and water hit again with renewed force. The boat spun helplessly in the torrent, the rudder slammed into the stern and broke its hinges. Theido threw himself to the tiller, but it was too late. The handle flopped uselessly in his hands.

"The rocks!" Alinea screamed.

All turned to see the jagged roots of the island jutting crazily from the swell and disappearing again, only to rise once more as the water rushed around them.

The rocks formed a sharp row of teeth protecting the shallow bay beyond. In calmer weather the breakers beat upon them ineffectually, and even the most hopeless sailor could navigate them with ease. Now, however, the stony teeth gnashed furiously, driven to rage by the boiling sea.

The boat was lifted high and thrust forward with the waves. As the water crashed down a rock rose beside them on the right. Ronsard, picking up his oar, shoved against the rock as it shot up and the boat spun aside, barely grazing her fragile hull against the unyielding mass of stone.

Again the boat was lifted high on the frothing waves and thrust forward. Trenn on his side wiped the flying spume out of his smarting eyes and held his oar ready to avert another rock. But before anyone could see the warning tip shooting up out of the foam, they heard a sickening crunch as the boat dropped square upon the crown of a huge rock they had just passed over.

The hull splintered and buckled. The boat teetered, now completely out of the water, stranded upon the rock as the wave drew away. For a second the small craft hung in the air, a fish speared upon a jagged tooth of stone. Then, with a sideways lurch the boat began to tear away from the rock as the hull gave way.

A wave pounding in upon them picked up the damaged boat again and split it in two, spilling its occupants into the rolling, angry sea.

THIRTY-ONE

NIMROOD strode the high parapet of his castle, his black cloak streaming out behind him. His raven-black hair—shot through with streaks of white like the lightning flashing among the black storm clouds he watched and revelled in—flew in wild disarray. The booming cataclysms of thunder echoed in the valleys below his mountaintop perch, and the evil wizard cackled at each one.

"Blow, wind! Thunder, roar! Lightning, rend the heavens! I, Nimrood, command it! Ha, ha, ha!"

The sorcerer had no power over the storm; it was a pure thing of nature. Instead, he seemed to draw a strange vitality from its awesome force as he gazed out toward the bay where Pyggin's ship lay at anchor. Nimrood could not see the ship; his castle was built upon the topmost peak of the highest of the rugged mountains which rose out of the sea to form his forsaken island. The bay was a league or more away as the gull flew.

The storm, spreading its anvil high into the atmosphere, flew on reckless wings in from the sea. Nimrood watched, his thin old body shaking in paroxysms of demented glee; his sinister features lifted upward toward the storm, illuminated by the raking streaks of lightning. The wizard chanted, danced, and laughed, thrilling to the storm as it passed overhead.

At last the heavy drops of rain began plummeting to earth. Loath to leave, but hating the wetness more, Nimrood the Necromancer turned and darted back into his chamber.

"Euric?" he shouted, throwing off his black cape. "Light the incense. I feel like following the storm." His henchman scuttled ahead of him as he descended the spiraling stone stairs to a vaulted room below. The room was bare stone except for a five-sided stone altar standing in the center.

Euric, with torch in hand, flitted around the altar lighting the pots of incense which stood on low metal tripods, one at each corner of the altar. "Leave me," shouted Nimrood when he had finished.

Nimrood stretched himself upon the altar and folded his hands over his breast. He let his breathing slow, becoming more shallow, as the incense swirled around him. Soon he dropped into a deep trance and the sorcerer's breathing seemed to stop altogether.

As Nimrood sank into the trance his mind rose up as if through layers of colored smoke, ascending on the pungent vapors of incense. When the smoke cleared he was flying high above the earth in the face of the onrushing storm.

The wizard closed his eyes and when he opened them he had taken the form of a kestrel, soaring in the turbulent air. His body tingled with excitement as he played among the rolling clouds, diving steeply and rising again in the blink of an eye.

As he wheeled ecstatically through the rushing wind he watched the land slide away beneath him. Directly below he saw his castle, dark upon its crown of mountain. To the west, falling sharply away to the bay, the thickly wooded hills hunched like the backs of tormented beasts. Beyond them, the glimmering crescent of the bay itself.

In a sudden blinding burst of lightning his sharp kestrel's eyes spied something in the bay. "I wonder what that might be?" he thought to himself. "I will fly closer for a better look."

Nimrood dove into the wind, streaking to earth like a comet, and heading for the bay.

"A ship!" he squawked when another stroke of lightning

revealed the vessel's outline. Then he sailed out over the bay. "Could it be Pyggin's ship? So soon? I did not expect them for another week."

Then, hovering in the air above the bay, the wind whipping through his feathers, Nimrood saw far below a small boat break away from the side of the ship. "Ach!" he screeched, "my guests have arrived!"

With that he flew back to the castle on the speed of the racing wind and swept into the vaulted chamber through an arrow loop in the wall. He alighted on the edge of the altar and became a wisp of gray smoke lingering in the air before dissolving above his own entranced form beneath.

As soon as the smoke vanished, the wizard's eyes snapped open and he sat upright with a jolt. "Euric!" he screeched, "come here at once!"

"Where is that fool servant?" he muttered, swinging down from the altar. "Euric!" he shouted again, then heard his servant's quick steps in the corridor beyond as he came running to his master's call. Nimrood met him at the door.

"You called, wise one?" The pitiful Euric bowed and scrabbled before the sorcerer.

"Yes, toad. We have work to do. Our long-awaited guests are even now arriving. We must prepare to meet them. Call the guards. Assemble them before my throne; I will give them their instructions. Hurry now! No time to lose!"

It was the third inn they had tried that morning, and this one sat down on the wharf at the water's edge. Toli and Quentin stood looking at the squeaking, weatherbeaten shingle which swung to and fro on the brisk wind. It read Flying Fish in bold blue letters handpainted with some care by the owner whose name, Baskin, was also painted beneath the legend.

"This is the last public house in Bestou, I think," remarked Quentin. "This must be where they stayed. Come on." He jerked his head for Toli to follow him inside. Toli, stricken with the jittery bafflement that most Jher held for all cities of any size, followed woodenly as he gazed along the waterfront.

"Excuse me, sir. Are you Baskin?" Quentin inquired politely of the first man they encountered within.

The man looked up at him over a stack of coins he was counting, his eyes blinking in the light of the open door. "My good fellow!" he shouted, somewhat surprised.

"Are you Baskin, sir?" asked Quentin again, startled by the man's unusual manner.

"At your service. Indeed, yes! If it is Baskin you want, Baskin you have found. What can I do for you . . ." he cast a sharp, and not altogether approving glance toward Toli, "for two young sirs?"

"We are looking for a party traveling through here—through Bestou some time ago."

The man scratched his head with a quizzical look on his face. "That could describe a fair number, I'll warrant."

"They were four of them altogether . . ."

"That helps, but not much. Many merchants travel in numbers."

"One was a lady. Very beautiful."

"That's better . . . but no, I cannot think of anyone like that. Who did they sail with?"

"I . . . I do not know, sir."

"They stayed here, you say?"

"They may have . . . that is, I cannot say for certain that they did. This is the last place in Bestou they could have stayed . . . if they did."

"Let me see," said Baskin, pulling his chin. "You are looking for a party who came you don't know when, and stayed you don't know where, and sailed with you don't know who. Is that right?"

Quentin's face flushed scarlet. His eyes fell to his feet.

"Oh, don't mind me, lad. I only wanted to get the facts . . ."

"I am sorry to have troubled you," said Quentin, turning to leave.

"Are you sure there's nothing else you can think of?" Baskin inquired after them.

Quentin stopped and considered this for a moment, then said, "They were bound for Karsh."

At the word the innkeeper jumped down from his stool and came around the table to where Quentin and Toli stood. "Shh! Do not say that name in here. Bad luck! But, hmmm . . ." He rubbed a long hand over his high forehead. "I seem to remember them now. Yes.

"There were three and the lady. One tall, fidgety. Looked to be a man of quick temper. The other big, stout. Dressed like a priest somewhat, though no priest I ever saw. They had a servant of sorts with them. A sturdy man. Didn't see much of him. And the lady—beautiful she may have been, though you couldn't prove it by me. She wore men's clothing all the while. Disguised, perhaps?"

"Yes, that's them!" cried Quentin.

"So I gather. They wanted to go to . . . that place. Had difficulty—and who would not—finding any honest captain to take them."

"Did they find someone?"

"Yes, I think so. They must have. They left early the first sailing day. Paid the bill the night before and were gone, along with everyone else, at dawn."

"What day was it?" Quentin was almost breathless with relief at having found word of his friends.

"Oh, it must be a week ago now. Yes, at least that long. Perhaps longer—let me see . . ." The innkeeper turned and went back to his table. A hutch stood nearby and he fished in one of the cubbyholes for a parchment which he at length brought out. "Yes. Here it is. I remember now. They left their horses with the smith up the way. I have the record now." He pushed the paper under Quentin's nose.

"Did they say whose ship would carry them to . . ."

"No, I never did hear. But there would be those who would risk such a trip for enough gold, I would think. Though many would not, as I say."

Baskin looked confidentially at Quentin and asked, "You are

not thinking of following them, are you?" He read the answer in Quentin's eyes before Quentin could speak. "Forget it. No good can come from it. I will tell you what I told them; stay far away from that place. I told them, and I tell you. Go back to where you come from. Don't go anywhere near that evil land. Stay away!"

THIRTY-TWO

PRINCE Jaspin swept through the ample corridors of Erlott Castle on his way to the great hall where the Council of Regents sat deadlocked for the third day. He was followed by two of his own bodyguard carrying halberds with royal pennons fluttering from the halberds' long staves. Jaspin had chosen this moment to remind the recalcitrant regents of his power and prestige.

Behind him also marched Ontescue carrying a small ornamented casket. Next to Ontescue walked a man in the worn clothes of a soldier, hesitant of step, eyes darting everywhere as if seeking refuge for an uneasy conscience.

This parade arrived at the towering doors of the great hall, now locked and the way barred by three guards, one of whom was the marshall of the Council of Regents.

"Halt!" bellowed the marshall. "The Council is in session."

"The Council is deadlocked," said Prince Jaspin in his most unctuous manner. "I have with me the means they require to resolve their impasse. Let me through!"

The marshall puffed out his cheeks as if to protest when a knock on the door sounded from within. "Stand away," he warned the Prince and turned to open the door to the summons.

"Marshall, the Council will recognize the Prince," said Sir Bran as the door swung open slightly. He added under his breath to the Prince, "I am sorry. I only just received your signal or I would have given this featherbrain orders to admit you on sight."

"Hmph!" the Prince snorted. "Are you ready?" Sir Bran nodded as they moved inside the door. "Are the others?"

"They know their part. You will hear them sing when the time comes. Worry not."

Ontescue followed them through the doors, motioning for the man in soldier's clothes to remain without. The huge door closed with a resounding crash, and all heads turned to see who had entered to disturb their deliberations.

"I protest!" shouted a voice above the murmur which accompanied the discovery that the Prince had invaded the privacy of the Council. "I protest the presence of the Prince at this meeting." The strident voice belonged to Lord Holben who was on his feet waving an accusing finger in Jaspin's direction.

"I come as a friend of this body and as one offering evidence which the Council requires."

Lord Holben clenched his fists at his side and bent his head stiffly to confer with one of his friends. "The Council will provide its own evidence," retorted Holben. There were nods all around the table.

"Of course," smiled the Prince sweetly. "But the Council may examine any evidence brought before it from any source—if it so choose." More nods of agreement.

"How is it that you know this Council desires any such evidence?" asked Lord Holben. His voice was tense, barely under control. "It seems you have long ears, my Prince, but methinks they belong to a jackass!"

"That is unseemly, sir!" cried Bran. He made as if to dash across the room to where Holben stood shaking with rage.

"Good sirs, desist!" shouted Lord Naylor, leader of the Council. "The Council has the right to decide if it will admit Prince Jaspin's evidence or no." He turned to address the whole of the Council. "What say you, my lords?"

Starting with the chair on Lord Naylor's right hand each regent spoke his pleasure—yea or nay, for or against admitting an examination of the Prince's evidence. Curiosity enticed the greater number of the assemblage, and the Prince was invited to submit his proof.

"I bow to your discretion," said the Prince, bending low. He smiled, but his eyes were stone as they cast upon Lord Holben and his dissenters.

"It has reached me that this Council stands deadlocked for want of proof of the King's death. And though it grieves me—you know not how much—to render this sad account, I would be remiss if, having the power to end this dissent, I stood by and did nothing."

Again murmurs of approval were voiced around the table. Jaspin picked out his paid followers, eyeing each one individually.

"I have bare hours ago received this final proof of the King's death. And though it deals a grievous wound to us all, who have hoped against hope that we would one day see his return, it nevertheless confirms the reason for this meeting." He raised sad eyes around the room. "It does confirm our darkest suspicions."

Prince Jaspin raised a finger and motioned Ontescue to approach with the jeweled chest. Jaspin took the chest and placed it himself before Lord Naylor. He handed him the key saying, "I believe you will find the end of your questions within."

Lord Naylor took the key and without a word placed it in the lock and turned it. In all the hall only the sound of the lock clicking open could be heard. Naylor withdrew the key and carefully raised the lid. What he saw inside drove the color from his face. He closed the lid and looked away, sinking back in his chair, eyes closed.

The small gilt casket made its way around the table, pausing before each regent in turn. Prince Jaspin watched the effect of the casket's contents upon each member. Some stared down in disbelief, others in grave sadness, like Naylor, and still others expressed nothing more than a dread curiosity.

All except Holben seemed to accept the evidence as proof enough of the King's untimely death.

"Do you think, Prince Jaspin," he began quietly, "that this scant remnant will suffice our inquiry?" He drew breath. "It is a travesty!" he shouted, flinging the casket from him. The contents, a severed finger, once bloody and mutilated, now withered and rotting and bearing a great golden ring, rolled out upon the table. The ring was King Eskevar's personal signet.

"I have seen that ring on His Majesty's hand. With my own eyes I have seen it!" someone shouted.

"I, too have seen it. I swear it is genuine!" cried another.

Others joined in the chorus, but Holben stood his ground. "The ring may be genuine, my lords. Indeed, it may even be the King's finger which wears the ring. But it proves nothing. Nothing!"

"He is right," said a noble sitting to Holben's right. "A king's ring and a king's finger, though they be, does not add up to a king's death. Surely, a king may be separated from one or the other or both and that lack not prove fatal."

Doubt travelled fleetingly across several faces.

"A king does not suffer his ring—the symbol of his sovereignty—to be taken except on pain of death. King Eskevar would fight to the last breath rather than give up that ring. That is enough for me." The speaker, Sir Grenett, sat down triumphantly, as if he had carried the day.

But Lord Holben was adamant. "King Eskevar, I will warrant, would face death a thousand times rather than relinquish that ring. But King Eskevar may have had nothing to do with it." He turned to fix Prince Jaspin with a fierce, defiant scowl.

Jaspin shook his head slowly and said, with seeming great reluctance, "I had hoped to spare you the grisly details, but since Lord Holben would stain the illustrious memory of our great monarch with his morbid disrespect . . ." He turned and signalled Ontescue to produce the witness.

Ontescue, standing ready at the door, gave a sharp knock and the marshall opened the door and admitted the soldier.

"This man, this poor wretch you see before you, followed our king to foreign lands and fought steadfastly by his side. He was present at the end, when in the last battle Eskevar was killed and the ring cut from his hand by the enemy." The soldier hung his head and did his best to appear dutifully grief-stricken.

"How did this ring come to be in your possession?" inquired Lord Naylor gently.

"If it please you, sir, the sight of the King sprawled dead upon the field so saddened our men that we were overcome with a righteous frenzy and slew the enemies who had killed our King as they retreated in victory. And so we retrieved this ring."

"You saw the King fall, did you?"

"Yes, my Lord." The soldier's eyes shifted uneasily from face to face around the room.

"And how did the . . . ring. How did it come to be in your possession?"

"The wars being over, we were all returning. I was aboard the first ship to sail for home, but the last ship to leave before winter. I volunteered to bring it on ahead."

"The armies will be returning shortly?"

"Yes, my Lord. With the first ships of spring."

Lord Naylor closed his eyes again as if in great weariness. "Thank you, good soldier." He nodded, dismissing the man. The soldier backed away from the round table with a bow. Prince Jaspin waved him away with a furtive gesture.

"Where is your commander?" demanded Holben. "Why was this token not provided with an honor guard? Answer me!"

"The man came directly to me as soon as he could," remarked Prince Jaspin, ignoring Lord Holben's demands. His witness left the room.

"Yes, of course," agreed Lord Naylor wearily. Then he raised his head and in a voice filled with emotion said, "My lords, I think we have seen and heard enough." He raised a hand quickly to parry Lord Holben's objection. "Enough to make up our minds. For myself, I choose to believe what I see, and what has been told among us. I can see no other course but to do what we came here to do."

"We can wait," suggested Holben readily. "Wait for the others to return. Members of the King's bodyguard, for example. Those who buried him . . ."

"And how many will it take before you believe?" asked Sir Bran. "You would not believe your own eyes, nor would you anyone else's."

"This council has been charged with a duty that must not wait," offered Sir Grenett. "The realm daily cries out for strong leadership."

"That from you, Sir Grenett?" sneered Holben. "Since when did strong leadership become a concern of yours? You and the rest of your thieving rabble!"

"Careful, my hot-headed sir. You go too far. This is not the place to settle our differences," Grenett spat out with great control.

"You are right, Sir Grenett," mediated Naylor. "This is not the time nor the place to dwell on these things. Lord Holben, you are entitled to your vote of dissent, but the rest of this body has a right to vote as they will.

"Prince Jaspin, if you will leave us to our duty. We shall endeavor to inform you of the Council's decision within the hour."

"I think a Midsummer's coronation would suit me splendidly," laughed Prince Jaspin upon returning to his chambers. "What think you, Ontescue? I am overjoyed. At last it is mine!

"Wine! We need wine! I feel like celebrating! Send the chamberlain to broach a cask of my finest . . ."

"I have already done so," said Ontescue. "And I would congratulate you myself, and take the opportunity to remind you of certain promises upon which we have agreed?"

"Oh, pish-tosh! I am in no mood to discuss such petty trifles. We will talk again on it soon. Plenty of time for that later. Let us celebrate now."

"I would not like to be premature," reminded Ontescue stiffly.

"Premature, you say? Nonsense!" The light died in the Prince's eyes as the smile faded from his lips. "Still, if you think we should, we will wait. Yes, we will wait. Better that way, of course. I shall share the celebration with my friends. Yes, quite so."

Jaspin threw himself into his chair to spend a worried hour waiting for the news he so longed to hear. At last the chamberlain thrust his head through the door to announce a party from the

Council wished to see him. "Let them in, you fool!" he shouted at the man's disappearing head.

"Sire, good news!" Sir Bran crossed the room in a bound, followed by Sir Grenett and several others. "I am charged by the Council of Regents to inform you that you have been named to the throne of Askelon, King of the realm Mensandor."

"The Council awaits the pleasure of your decision regarding the coronation," added Sir Grenett. "Let me take them word so that the coronation may be announced at once."

"Hmmm . . . I really hadn't given it a thought," said Prince Jaspin. His fleshy lips twitched with mischief. "But I think Midsummer's Day would suit me splendidly. Yes. Let it be so proclaimed."

THIRTY-THREE

QUENTIN sat upon the cold stone of the harbor wall kicking his feet against the thick green moss. Toli stood beside him like a shadow, arms folded across his chest, gazing out into the harbor. Squawking gulls hovered in the air, noising their protest of these two humans invading their sunning spot.

"The ships are gone," sighed Quentin. He swung his eyes over the broad, empty dish of the harbor. Only two ships remained behind of all that had sailed a week earlier—both needed repairs and were going nowhere very soon. Quentin had already inquired after them.

"They will return," replied Toli. He had a knack for stating an obvious fact in a most enigmatic way.

"Undoubtedly. They will return. But it may be too late for us."

Quentin got up from the low slanting wall which, for the most part, kept the sea from running through the streets of Bestou. "I don't know what to do now." He sighed again and brushed his trousers with his hands.

"*Wisi thera ilya murenno,*" said Toli, his eyes still searching far out to sea.

"The winds speak out . . . what?" Quentin's translation halted unfinished.

"The winds blow where he directs," replied Toli. He turned to regard Quentin again. Quentin could not help noticing his servant still held a strange distant light in his eyes.

"Who directs?"

"Whinoek."

"Um," said Quentin thoughtfully. "Then we will leave it to him. Come, let us see after the horses." Casting an eye toward the sun he gauged it to be nearing midday. "I could use something to eat myself. What about you?"

The two climbed the long sloping hill upon which Bestou was built, and which ran down from the forests above to plunge into the sea. They had left the horses in the care of a farmer on the outskirts of Bestou, not knowing if horses would be welcome in a shipping town.

In no time they were through the town. Bestou cuddles the whole length of the crescent bay, but has no depth. The merchants crowd the waterfront; above them stand the houses of the wealthy ship owners who make their homes in Bestou; beyond that lay the widely scattered stone and timber dwellings of the hill folk and farmers.

The two walked back to the farmer's tumble-down house at their leisure. When they arrived, Quentin spoke to the farmer, whose wife insisted that they share their midday meal. Toli led the horses to water and turned them out to crop the new green grass around the house.

The travelers and their hosts ate huge hunks of brown bread which the farmer's chattering wife toasted at a small fire on the hearth, and great slabs of pale yellow cheese. Several times during their meandering conversation the farmer mentioned the horses with admiration, especially the surpassing strength of Balder. "I will wager he can work, that one," he said as if imparting some great truth.

"Balder is a war horse," explained Quentin. "Trained to combat."

"Aye, and such a strong one, too."

"Well . . ." Quentin winked at Toli, "have you some chore fit for a horse? Then we would see what he could do."

"Oh, no. No. I wouldn't think . . . well, but there is a stump in the field. But, no . . . Do you think he might?"

"We shall put him to the test," said Quentin rising heavily to his feet. He had not eaten so much since leaving Dekra, and that was many days ago. "It is the least we can do to repay your kindness."

"Do not trouble yourselves for us," said the farmer's wife. "We are glad of the company. A farmer's lot is a lonely one. We are only glad of the company."

But Quentin could see that they were both very pleased. He enjoyed being able to help them; it gave him a warm feeling. Serving, he thought.

"This stump has vexed me raw these two years. It sits in the middle of my new field," the farmer explained as they tramped out to the spot where it stood.

Horses, though not unknown on Tildeen, were rare enough. They were not needed for travel; there was no place to go and Bestou, being a port, had little use for them. Only a few of the better established farmers owned them for working the land. But those were very few and fortunate indeed.

They had rigged a harness for Balder made of leather straps and rope. Nebo, the farmer, carried a long, sturdy branch to use as a lever. Quentin led Balder, and Toli carried the harness. Tisha, the farmer's wife, bustled along behind them.

After several attempts, and much adjusting of the rustic harness, Balder lowered his head and leaned into his work. The ropes stretched taut and threatened to snap. Nebo, Quentin, and Toli hung from the branch nearly bending it in two. Tisha, standing at Balder's head, coaxed him on with soft words.

There came a loud pop underground and a long wrenching creak. Balder's smooth muscles bulged under his glossy coat. And then, suddenly the stump lay upon its side dangling moist, earth-covered roots in the warm spring air.

"Hoo! Hoo!" the farmer shouted. "That is the strongest animal I ever saw! Hoo! Wait until Lempy hears about this! Hoo!"

"Now, Nebo," said the farmer's wife, "remember that you promised to make sacrifice to Ariel if that stump be moved in time for planting. It be moved. The god requires his due."

"Ah, yes. So I did," drawled the farmer reluctantly. "I will make sacrifice of a silver bowl at the temple." He hesitated. "Though I would rather buy a new plowshare."

Quentin listened to this exchange with a curious sinking sensation. "Please, make no offering to the god Ariel. Such is not required. Only help another when you may; that shall be your sacrifice."

The eyes of the farmer and his wife looked strangely at him and Quentin suddenly felt foolish. He should not have spoken.

"Are you a priest, young master?" wondered the farmer cautiously.

"I once belonged to the temple of Ariel," admitted Quentin. "But I follow a greater god, now. One that is not honored by silver."

A look of relief appeared on Nebo's broad, good-natured face. "Then I will make the sacrifice you and your god suggest," he said lightly, happier than ever. He had moved the troublesome stump and had saved the price of the silver bowl, too. This new god, whoever he may be, impressed him very much. He clapped his hands in childlike glee.

"I am tired," announced Quentin. "I have eaten too much and the sun makes me drowsy."

"A nap, then," Nebo declared. "A little sleep is a good thing."

Quentin awakened with a grudging reluctance. The air was cool, the sun warm upon his face as it spun in the treetops, having crossed over the high arch of heaven to begin its descent toward evening. Toli sat quietly beside Quentin, having awakened some time before.

"Why didn't you wake me?" asked Quentin, pushing himself up. They were lying on a small grassy hill beside Nebo's small farmhouse.

"It is time to go back to the harbor," replied Toli.

Quentin looked at his friend, holding his head to one side. "Now? What makes you say that?"

Toli shrugged. "I feel that we should. Something here tells me." He pointed to his chest.

"Then we will go. We will leave the horses here for now."

"No. I think we should take them."

"As you say." Quentin was agreeable, though he did not see any point in taking the horses into town; they would only have to walk back again. Better to let them rest. But it was not worth discussing on such a bright, brilliant afternoon.

They took their leave of the kind farmer and his wife and struck out upon the rocky lane toward Bestou. Descending to the bowl of the harbor, they could see the whole of the town, the harbor, and the blue sea beyond, glimmering in the distance.

They walked along in silence, listening to the horses clopping peacefully behind them; the fresh scent of grass and growing things hung in the air. Quentin thought that in such a place, on such a day he could forget all about his task. Forget about kings and wizards and fighting and hiding. He could lose himself in these hills, in the idle drone of the bees buzzing among the wild flowers, nodding their pink and yellow heads in the breeze along the road.

Quentin stirred himself from his contemplation of the dusty tracks they walked upon. He turned with a question on his lips and drew a breath to speak. The question died at once and the air spilled out between his teeth when he beheld Toli's face.

That distant light once again burned in the Jher's dark eyes and lit his features in a queer way. It was like he stared into the future, thought Quentin, beyond this time and place, or perhaps very far into the unknown distance.

"What is it? What do you see, Toli?"

"A ship comes." He replied matter-of-factly.

"A ship?" Quentin swung his eyes to the harbor. He saw nothing. He looked beyond the harbor to the sea—nothing there. No object shown on the horizon at all that he could see. He looked long to the north and south as far as he could until the hills on either side restricted the view. "I do not see a ship," he admitted at last.

Toli said nothing more and so they continued down the hill once more in silence.

They reached the houses, then the cobbled streets where the merchants had their stalls, and then the harbor wall itself where they had sat that very morning. Quentin searched the horizon again, as he had all the way, to see what Toli apparently saw quite plainly.

The streets were brisk with activity. The fishermen in their long, low hulled boats had returned from a day's work. Women with cane baskets hurried along to gather in groups around the fishermen spreading out their catch on the stone streets. Gulls nattered sharply overhead, hoping for a morsel.

Quentin took in this activity with mild interest—he was still discovering in little ways life in the world outside the temple. It all seemed so new; he felt himself drawn like a wild creature to a domestic abode to wonder at another kind of life. Commonplace, yet foreign. Strange and ordinary at the same time.

Toli stood as a tree trunk rooted to the spot, his eyes fixed upon some spot in the distance.

There was no point in arguing with a Jher about anything, so Quentin tied the horses to a big iron ring set in the sea wall which served at other times as a mooring for ships. He hunched down to wait, and allowed himself to drink in all the various industry around him.

The sun shone low behind them and the shadow of the sea wall flung itself out into the gray-green water of the harbor. Quentin swung himself up and turned toward Toli. He had been watching a man with a barrow full of shellfish sort through his wares, separating the living from the dead.

"How much longer will we wait?" asked Quentin. His tone spoke of a mild concern.

"Not long," replied Toli with a short inclination of his head.

Quentin followed the unspoken direction and turned toward the harbor. There in the pinched mouth of the harbor, sailing slowly ahead, streamed a ship, a large ship with sails stained orange by the late afternoon light. Quentin's jaw dropped open as he gaped in amazement at his friend and at the ship.

Toli at last relaxed and smiled. "The ship is here," he announced. His voice carried a triumphant ring, as if he had conjured the ship by will power alone. Quentin believed that in some mysterious way the Jher had made the ship appear and would not have been more surprised if he had. Toli after all had many unusual abilities which Quentin was still discovering.

The ship drew closer and soon Quentin could make out the masts, the rigging, and individual sailors moving about the deck. He could also see, from the way the ship seemed to limp from side to side, that there was something wrong. The ship, now very close, moved through the water stiffly, with an awkward list— first to one side then to the other. But, instead of anchoring in the center of the lonely harbor, the ship proceeded to come up close to wharf.

Quentin and Toli watched until the ship docked full length against the wharf, then untied the horses and walked along the sea wall till they stood right alongside her.

"The *Marribo*," read Quentin.

"A good name," replied Toli, looking pleased with himself.

"It looks a good ship." Quentin knew nothing of ships, but he liked the straight lines of the rigging and the coiled ropes on the deck, the way the sails had been furled expertly along their spars. Everything seemed right and in order to him; therefore: a good ship.

The gangplank had been let down and sailors were busily engaged in various tasks, working efficiently. The captain, or so Quentin took him to be, stood at the bow and bellowed orders to the men below. There seemed to be some haste involved, which Quentin considered strange for a ship just reaching its destination.

"Captain, sir," Quentin called out. It had taken him a full ten heartbeats to pluck up his courage to speak. "May I ask . . ." he began.

"I am not the captain," the man hollered back carelessly. He jerked his thumb toward a man in a short blue jerkin descending the gangplank in close conversation with a man in a leather apron who looked to be a shipwright.

The two stood head to head for some time before the shipwright hurried off. The captain sat down upon the ledge of the sea wall and lit a long clay pipe as he watched his crew working.

"Are you the captain, sir?" Quentin asked again, this time in better control of his courage.

"Aye, lad. That's me and here's my ship. At your service."

"And we at yours," replied Quentin with a bow that included both he and Toli. "It is a fine ship, too."

"You know ships?" The captain squinted up at him, blowing smoke.

"No . . . I mean . . . I have never been on a ship before."

"That is your misfortune, sir. Ah, the sea . . . I could tell you stories . . ." He lost himself in a cloud of smoke. "I am Captain Wiggam. Who might you be?"

"I am Quentin. And this is my . . . my friend, Toli." He still felt awkward saying servant.

"What can a seafaring man do for you, young gentlemen?" The captain stuck out a wide, dry paw which Quentin shook with vigor.

"Could you tell us, sir, would you be going—"

Captain Wiggam cut him off. "We will not be going anywhere without our rudder. What cursed luck. Half day out she breaks her hinge pins. By the gods! Took us half a day to turn her about and another whole day to jog back to port." He paused and drew another long pull on the pipe. "You looking for to go somewhere?"

"Yes, sir. We would go to Karsh." Quentin spoke in a self-assured tone despite what the innkeeper had said about the place.

The captain's eyebrows shot up. "Karsh!" He squinted up again and asked suspiciously, "What would you be going there for?"

"I . . . that is, we have friends in trouble. We are going to help them." Quentin did not know for certain they were in any specific sort of trouble at the moment, but he could not have been closer to the truth.

"If they be anywhere near Karsh, they be in trouble."

"Could you take us there?"

"Me? This ship? Never!" Captain Wiggam turned a hard face away.

Quentin stood speechless; he had no other course of action planned. But the captain, puffing furiously on his pipe now, seemed to soften somewhat. "We be bound for Andraj in Elsendor. I will take you there if you think that would serve you."

"I do not know exactly where that is, sir."

"Don't you now?"

"No . . . I lived in the temple. That is, until a short while ago. I was an acolyte."

"Which temple? What god did you serve?"

"Ariel—in the high temple at Narramoor. I was going to be a priest." Quentin thought he saw a glimmer of interest in the seaman's clear, gray eyes. There was a moment of silence as the captain considered this. There came the sound of hammering accompanied by the soft slap of waves against the hull of the ship.

"Ariel is the god of fortune and fate, the seaman's benefactor. It would not do to disappoint him by turning aside one of his servants." He tapped the pipe out against the stonework of the ledge and rose to his feet. "I will tell you this—I will take you to Valdai, around the peninsula from Andraj. I dare not do more. At Valdai there are those who do go to Karsh on occasion. You may find someone there to take you further than I dare to."

Captain Wiggam looked at Quentin and then at Toli. Noticing Quentin's troubled look he asked, "Is there something else?"

"We have no money to pay our passage."

"Oh, I see. Well, think no more on it. The *Marribo* is a cargo ship—though we sometimes carry passengers."

"And we have horses." Quentin attempted to diminish their size and number with a small, pensive gesture in their direction.

Wiggam winked an eye and appraised the two horses from where they stood tethered to a mooring ring a few paces down the sea wall. "That is a problem," he said. His solemn tone pricked Quentin with doubt. Then came another wink. "But no more serious than seaweed in your scupper. We have carried horses before. We are a freighter after all." He laughed and Quentin laughed, too, in grateful relief.

The captain turned and started away. "I must see to the repair work now, my lads. Starkle will see you aboard. Tell him I said so."

"When do we leave?" called Quentin as the seaman hurried aft along the hull.

"We leave as soon as ever we can—as soon as the rudder is seaworthy. Get your things aboard. We leave tonight."

THIRTY-FOUR

DURWIN awoke with a cough, spitting sand. His face lay upon a prickly bed of seaweed rank with the fetid odor of fish. He felt a sharp, stinging pain on, of all places, his scalp. Perhaps it was the pain which had brought him to.

Another prick, and another pain. Durwin raised an arm to his head and dislodged a gull which flapped off along the beach squawking its displeasure. "Not food for the birds yet," mumbled Durwin under his breath.

He shoved himself up on his elbows and waited for the throbbing in his head to subside. He wiped the sand out of his eyes with a sandy hand and peeped around. He lay alone on the beach by a rock which poked up out of the sand like an old fang from the gums of an aging dragon. The rock was draped in stinking seaweed, as was Durwin.

The sun had not yet risen, but the rosy glow spreading over the horizon promised a new day very soon. The waves of the storm had deposited Durwin high up on the strand, and as he sat taking in his surroundings he felt strange eyes upon him. Glancing around he saw a host of crabs scuttling closer, their eyes wavering in the new light. "Go pick the bones of some other poor fish," he yelled at them. "This one needs his skin a little longer."

Durwin pulled himself to his staggering and unsteady legs. He placed a hand on the rock and looked both ways along the jagged, rock-strewn shoreline. "Ah, this *is* an evil place," he muttered. He lurched down to the water which now lapped calm and undisturbed, as if nothing could ever perturb its placid surface. He dipped his hands in and washed his face and gritty neck. He shook the sand out of his hair and beard, then started along the water's edge in search of the others, dreading what he might find.

He had not tottered more than ten paces when he spied a shapely foot sticking out from behind a low, moss-encrusted rock. "Alinea!" He rushed to the lady's side and her eyelids fluttered open.

"Durwin? Oh, what has happened? I feel sick," she frowned.

"You probably drank your weight in sea water. As did I."

Then coming to herself more fully, "The others . . . Theido, Trenn, Ronsard. Where are they? Have you found them? Are they . . . ?"

"Shh . . . in time, in time," he soothed. "You are the first I have discovered. The others cannot be far away. We shall look for them together." He hesitated and added after a moment, "Or I will seek them alone, if you would rather. You may rest here."

"No. We will go together. I can face what we may find; the waiting would be worse."

Durwin helped his sodden, sand-covered Queen to her feet.

"Sit on this rock for a moment. Breathe the air. Deeply. It will make you feel better."

"I must look like Orphe's daughter—more fit for the fishes than for human company."

"We will all require some careful grooming, I'll warrant. But to be alive—there is nothing more beautiful than that. After last night. . . ."

"Oh, Durwin . . ." the Queen gasped. Her hand found his arm and squeezed it.

Durwin turned to look where her eyes were fixed to see what he had taken to be a pile of kelp and seaweed lumped upon the beach. Now he saw that it had a human form, and then what Alinea had regarded with horror. Dozens of crabs were feeding upon the body, gathered around an open wound. Their pinchers scissored tiny chunks of red flesh from the body's flank.

"Ack!" cried Durwin, rushing to his comrade, sending the blue and green crabs scuttling in sideways retreat.

"It is Trenn!" he shouted as he rolled the body over. He placed his ear to the man's chest. "He is alive, thank the god!" Then the hermit bent to finger the wound in Trenn's side—a long, ragged gash, deep though not bleeding; the flow of blood had been stanched by the salt water.

"Will he be all right?" Alinea crept close to Durwin.

"I think so. The wound is deep, but not severe, I think. He may have other injuries we cannot see."

Alinea shivered at the memory of the crabs. "I saw them snatching at him . . . I thought . . ."

"And so did I. But look. The crabs have done a service after all. The wound is clean now; it will heal the quicker." Durwin spoke with assurance, but cast a doubtful eye upon Trenn's insensate features.

Suddenly a crash sounded in the undergrowth of the thick wooded land that fringed the shoreline. Durwin glanced up and met a ring of sullen eyes set in dull, unfeeling faces. There were perhaps twenty soldiers dressed in hauberk and helm, leveling spears upon them. Each helmet carried a crest with the insignia of the soldier's cruel master: the black croaking raven of Nimrood the Necromancer.

A rider on a spotted black horse leaped through the tangle and onto the strand. He eyed the humble survivors with a malicious glare. A purple scar cleft his face from forehead to jaw, bending the nose aside as it swept across the cheek.

"Seize them!" the rider cried. The voice was a sneer.

The impassive soldiers leapt at once to the task of jerking Durwin and Alinea to their feet and roughly binding them. The prisoners were marched, with much prodding and poking, into the woods above the beach.

"He alive?" asked the rider, jerking his head to the body of Trenn reposed upon the sand.

"Yes, he is alive," affirmed Durwin. "Be careful with him. He is injured."

"Tch, a pity. 'Twere better he were dead." The rider spurred the skittish horse past Durwin and the Queen and shouted, "Take the other one."

The three were bundled into a high-sided cart. Alinea and Durwin edged Trenn carefully to the bottom of the cart and settled, as best they could, beside him.

"Not a word about the others," Durwin warned in a whisper.

"Take them away!" yelled the rider with the wicked scar, who seemed to be the commander of the company on the shore.

The cart bumped off into the woods, rocking as if to overturn. Neither the driver of the cart nor the four accompanying soldiers paid the slightest attention. The cart passed through a thin, unhealthy wood made up of wiry trees and straggles of vines. Rocks with sharp edges thrust out of the ground making the going exceedingly strenuous. And though it was sunrise, the dire wood seemed to banish the light, steeped instead in perpetual gloom.

"This is a cheerless place," noted the Queen.

"So it is. Any place the necromancer calls his own is cheerless; and, I fear, a good deal worse."

The cart and its contents bumped and rumbled over rock and root. Eventually they reached a feeble trail scratched into the stony soil. The surrounding wood thinned as they proceeded along.

It soon became apparent that they followed a struggling brook; the splash of its churning water could be heard close by. Rude hills rose on either side covered with dense, though sickly, vegetation of unpleasant sorts. An air of quiet doom hung over the valley which they trod. Only the forlorn call of an occasional bird and the groan and whine of the wagon's ungreased wheels broke the oppressive silence.

After an hour or longer—time seemed irrelevant in this place—the cart turned onto a wider path and began a steep ascent. Alinea looked round with wide, frightened eyes.

"Do not be afraid, my Lady," soothed Durwin. "He is not so terrible that he cannot be faced. Evil always misrepresents itself. Pray instead for Theido and Ronsard; they may yet escape. That is greatly to be hoped."

"I will do as you ask, though I have not the knowledge of the god that you possess."

"It matters not what words one uses. He hears the heart itself."

After a long ascent the cart rolled to a level place, a wide ledge of stone carved out of the steep mountain. From there, peering over the cart's high sides, the unhappy prisoners could see the hunched hills through which they had been traveling. The sun was well up, and yet seemed dim and far away. A sulky mist draped the hills and gathered thick in the miserable valleys. The land seemed shroud-wrapped and forsaken.

From somewhere a keening wail rose into the air like a lost soul crying for release.

"Just a gull," replied Durwin looking above. But his tone lacked conviction.

Once more the silence crept back. And then "Ohhh . . . ohhh . . ." a low moan escaped into the air. Durwin looked at the Queen and then at Trenn. An eyelid flickered. A finger twitched.

"So it is! He is coming round." Durwin, hands tied behind him, could do nothing to ease Trenn's entrance back into the realm of the living. But he bent his head close to Trenn's ear and whispered, "Rest easy now. No need to fear. We are with you. Take your time."

Presently the warder opened his eyes and stiffly turned his head. "Trussed up like chickens, aye," he said.

"Oh, Trenn. You are all right."

"Yes . . . ohh," he winced as he tried to move to sit up. "But I may be better with some looking to."

"You have had a horrid gash," said Alinea. "Just lay back."

"Where are the others?"

"Shh!" Durwin warned.

"We do not know—could not find them this morning." He looked doubtful. "But we had no time to look."

"Where are we? Nimrood's tribe?"

"It appears we are on our way to meet him."

"You should not talk so," whispered Alinea. "Rest now while you may."

No one spoke for a long time after that. Each nursed his own thoughts and discouraged the fear which grew like a dull ache with each step closer to Nimrood's foul roost.

Finally, "There it is!" Durwin inclined his head past the driver of the cart. Alinea turned and Nimrood's castle, like a blackened skull set upon a rock, swung into view.

"What a ghastly ruin," said Alinea.

"So it is."

Black stone battlements rose straight up from the rock of the mountain. A maze of stairs and dark entrances carved in the stone like the tunneling of worms weaved throughout. Odd-shaped towers of irregular heights thrust themselves above the great domed vault of the hall. Empty holes of doorways and windows stared like eyeless sockets out from the squat jumble of apartments around the dome. Dark shapes of birds flapped through the cool air above the castle and shrieked at the approach of the cart.

The winding road to the castle had here been built upon the back of a ridge. The road, only wide enough for the wagon with a man on either side, twisted up sharply. The mountain fell away in a steep run to either side. The ridge ended in an abrupt precipice just before the long, narrow, iron-studded drawbridge.

The cart lurched to a halt before the raised drawbridge. The chasm, falling down in a sheer drop from a breathless height, stretched before them. Below, ringing like the clash of sword upon shield, a noisy cataract fought its way to lower ground.

With a prolonged groan the drawbridge began to lower. It thumped down with a hollow knock and the wain rumbled over it; each creak of the cart was magnified; each step of the horse's iron-clad hoof sounded a death knell which rolled away to echo in the chasm below.

Squeaking in protest, the cart bumped across the drawbridge and through the dark gatehouse under the baleful stare of an owl perched in the beams. The gatehouse was as dark and damp as a cave. Water dripped from the ceiling and trickled down the sides of the stone walls with a snickering sound.

Trenn, now sitting up in the cart, let out a low whistle which reverberated through the tunnel. "It is hollow beneath this road," he said after listening to the echo die away. "I would not like to find what lurks down there."

"Courage, friends. Our enemy seeks to break the spirit. Resist him. Do not give in to fear."

"I fear no mortal man," said Trenn. A tremble shook his voice. "But this sorcerer—"

"Is a mortal man like any other. He has powers, yes, but he can be beaten. He can be defied."

"The King is here," said Alinea. Though Durwin could not see her in the darkness, from the sound of her voice he knew she must be close to tears. "How long, oh, how long?—this wretched, hideous place."

"Take heart, my Queen. The King is strong and, unless I am far wrong, his imprisonment has not been unbearable. He is able to withstand."

"Your words are well spoken," sniffed Alinea. "I am his Queen and I, too, shall withstand."

The cart rolled suddenly out of the dark gatehouse tunnel and into the light of a misshapen and unkempt courtyard. A man dressed in a sable cloak, dark tunic and trousers with high black boots was waiting.

"Bring them," he said and turned on his heel and disappeared into the yawning entrance of the castle. The prisoners were handed down and marched through a maze of corridors and passageways. The castle seemed deserted, so few servants did they meet. Without ceremony they were thrust unexpectedly into the throne room of Nimrood.

The sorcerer awaited them, eyes half-closed as if in a daydream, sprawled upon his great black throne as if flung there at the height of some monstrous passion that left him limp. Oily torches behind the throne spewed thick, black smoke into the room and cast a slippery glare round about.

"Welcome to Karsh, my friends," the sorcerer mocked. He neither opened his eyes nor lifted a hand in acknowledgment of their presence. "I have been waiting for you. I have only to wait. In time everything comes to me."

"Even death and destruction—the end of your schemes," replied Durwin calmly.

"Silence, fool! I can have your tongue torn out where you stand!" Nimrood had leapt to his feet and stood glowering down at them. His hands gripped a rod of polished black marble.

"But no," the wizard suddenly sweetened. "Prattle on. Your words are the rhymes of children Noise and air. There is no power in them. It amuses me. Please continue."

Durwin said nothing.

"Nothing more to say? We shall see if I can inspire you! Take them to the dungeon!" He swung the rod over his head and the guards who had accompanied them from the wain hustled them away with the butts of their spears. As they left the room they heard Nimrood cackle, "You will soon have company—your friends, unless they are dead, cannot elude me long. Ha! It makes no difference. Dead or alive, you shall have company. Ha! Ha!"

THIRTY-FIVE

QUENTIN awoke to the quiet touch of Toli on his shoulder, shaking him gently from sleep. He came up with a start, confused. The lulling creak of the ship reassured him and he remembered they were on board the *Marribo*, making for Valdai.

"You cried out in your sleep, Kenta," said Toli.

"Did I?" Quentin rubbed the sleep from his eyes with the heels of his hands. "I don't remember . . ." Then it hit him afresh—the dream.

"Oh, Toli, I had a dream." In the dark he could see Toli's eyes, liquid pools which glittered in the reflected light of a sky full of stars. The moon had set, leaving the lesser lights of the heavens to glow and sparkle like the lanterns of the night fishermen spread upon an endless sea.

"Tell me your dream. Now, before you forget."

"Well, I was standing on a mountain. And I looked out and saw all the earth covered in darkness. And I felt the darkness was like an animal. Watching, waiting."

As he spoke Quentin again entered into the spirit of his dream. He saw again, as in the dream, but clearer, more real this time, that faraway land stretching out under a black and barren sky. An ancient land of years beyond counting and darkness huddled close like a preying creature—breathing, waiting.

He continued. "Into the darkness there came a light, like a single candle flame, falling—an ember, a spark—falling as from the very pinnacle of the sky."

Again he saw the pinpoint of light falling through space, arcing across the sky, tumbling down and down toward the earth.

"And the light fell to earth and broke into a thousand pieces, scattering over the land, burning into the darkness. A shower of light. And each splintered fragment became a flame just like the first and began burning and the darkness receded before the light.

"That was all. Then I woke up."

Quentin remained silent as he remembered the dazzling rain of light and the feeling that somehow the dream had something to do with him. He brought his eyes back to Toli, who wore a look of quiet wonder.

"This is a dream of power."

"Do you think so? In the temple I would have dreams like this—seeing dreams, we called them. But I thought the dreams had stopped. I haven't seen an omen or had a dream since I left the temple . . . not counting Dekra." He was silent again for a while. "What do you think it means?"

"It is said among my people that truth is like a light."

"And evil is like the darkness. Yes, we say the same thing. The truth is coming, maybe now is here, that will strike into the darkness and take hold against it."

"A dream can mean many things, and all of them are right."

"Do you think this might be one answer?"

"I think it is your dream and that you will find the answer within yourself."

"Yes, perhaps I will. It was so real—I was there. I saw it. . . ."

Quentin lay back down on the thick straw pallet. He turned the dream over in his mind and finally, feeling sleepy again, said, "We had better get some sleep. We come into Valdai tomorrow morning . . ." But Toli was already fast asleep.

When Quentin stirred to the smell of fresh salt air, the port of Valdai was already within sight. The sun was up, filling the sky with golden light. The sky arched royal blue overhead, spotted with a few wisps of clouds sailing across its empty reaches.

Toli was up and had already seen to the horses. Quentin found him standing at the rail looking on as Valdai neared.

"Look," he said, pointing as Quentin came to stand beside him. "Another ship is coming in, too."

Just ahead of them a ship plowed the water, dividing the waves and tossing back a harvest of white foam. The ship was stubby, squat, and low in the water—a usual enough design for a ship, but Quentin got an uneasy feeling as he watched it moving toward the harbor. There was something strange about it—what was it? Then he saw what it was that bothered him.

"Toli, that ship has black sails!"

Toli said nothing, but the quick shake of his head acknowledged the fact.

"That is odd," remarked Quentin. "I know very little about ships, but I have never heard of any with black sails before. I wonder where they are from?"

"You might well wonder." A deep voice spoke from behind him. Quentin turned to greet Captain Wiggam, who continued, "She running the black hails from Karsh, like as not. Yes. Take note of her."

The captain had become very friendly with Quentin in the few days of their short voyage. And he had become concerned with Quentin's plans to join his friends. "Forget Karsh," he said, regarding the ship with distaste. "Come with me. I will make you a sailor and show you the world."

"I cannot forget my friends," replied Quentin. It was not the first time Captain Wiggam had made the offer. "Though, maybe when we return . . ."

"Sure enough," said Wiggam, Quentin thought a little sadly. "You look me up in any port, and wherever I be you have a ride with me." The captain folded his hands behind him and walked aft along the rail.

"He would like to help," said Toli when the captain had gone, "but he is afraid."

"Do you think?" Quentin watched the retreating figure and shrugged. "Anyway, it is not his concern; it is our mission."

"It is anyone's who will accept it," said Toli with a certain finality.

Valdai shook with activity. A smaller port and harbor than Bestou, it nevertheless was just as busy. Elsendor, a far larger realm than Mensandor, had many such ports all along its western coasts. These served the whole world.

"There is the Black Ship," said Quentin, pointing across the harbor. They had come to dock at the northern end of the harbor, while the Black Ship, as they called it, being smaller had gone further in, toward the southern end. But Quentin could see the black sails hanging slack as her crew set about furling them.

The gangplank was soon down, and Quentin and Toli made their farewells. They led the horses down onto the quay and waved a final goodbye to Captain Wiggam who watched them from the deck, smoking his pipe. He waved once and turned away.

"We have to find somewhere to keep the horses," said Quentin. A plan was already forming in his head. "There is probably a smith here. We will find one; perhaps he can help us."

The search was but a short one. The task of making the smith understand what it was they were trying to ask him proved much harder. The inhabitants of Elsendor, though like their neighbors of Mensandor in many ways, had a thick dialect all their own—a fact which Quentin had not foreseen, and which taxed his meagre language skills beyond their limit. The smith, struggling to unravel the meaning of Quentin's strange (to him) request kept insisting that Quentin wanted his horses shod.

"No. No shoes. We want you to keep the horses for us, or tell us someone who will."

The burly, smoke-smeared man, smiling still, shook his head once more. Then he got up and came to Balder, patted him on the neck and reached down for a hoof. He saw the shoe, tapped it with his hammer and grunted his approval. He replaced the animal's foot and spread out his arms questioningly to Quentin.

Toli had disappeared into the rear of the smith's shop and now returned saying, "There are horses in a stable yard behind this place. Water and food, too."

"Come," Quentin told the smith. He led them back to the stable yard and pointed to the horses there. "Will you keep our horses?" He pointed at Balder and Ela, that was the name Toli had given his horse, and then he pointed at the smith and then again at the stable yard. The smith's face lit up with the slow dawn of understanding. He shook his head repeatedly up and down. Then he held out his hand and jabbed his palm with a grimy finger.

"He wants money. Now what are we going to do?" wondered Quentin.

At that moment a familiar figure appeared in the front of the shop. "It's Captain Wiggam. Hello, captain!" Quentin called.

"I thought you might need some help," he said simply. "You want this man to board your horses, I take it? Very well."

The captain turned and spoke to the man quickly. "Done," said the captain. "How long?"

"I don't know!" Quentin hadn't considered that.

The broad faced seaman dug into his pocket and handed the man a piece of money. The smith bobbed his head and thanked the seaman. "There, that should take care of them for a while. You can redeem them when you come back."

"Thank you, Captain Wiggam. I shall repay you someday, if I can."

"Think no more on it. If I was—the gods forbid—on Karsh and in trouble, I would want someone like you trying to rescue me. You are brave, lad. That you are."

Quentin reddened slightly. He did not feel brave.

"Have you thought about how you are going to reach Karsh?" The captain was already walking into the street.

"Yes, we have." He explained his plan to the captain, who listened nodding.

"Stowaway, eh?" He nodded again, considering. "It could

work. Once you are aboard there would be hiding places aplenty for smart seamen like yourselves. But how do you plan to get aboard unseen?"

"We thought to wait until dark and climb aboard over the side."

"There may be a better way," winked the captain. "But . . . Ho!" he said, looking at the noonday sun. "I say we should discuss it over a fisherman's pie. What say you to that? Ever had a fisherman's pie? No? Well, come along. The captain'll show you a wonder!"

Captain Wiggam trudged off along the narrow, cobbled street onto which opened every kind of shop imaginable. Quentin and Toli struggled in his wake. The streets were jammed elbow to elbow with sailors and merchants and townspeople shouting, jostling, and generally making it difficult for Quentin to keep an eye on the captain, who moved ahead like a ship under full sail.

At last he drew up before an inn so crowded with patrons that several sat out in the street with their ale jars. Quentin and Toli came tumbling up behind him. "Ah! Smell that, my mates. Did you ever nose anything so tasty in all your days?" With that he elbowed his way in the door and began calling to the innkeeper with whom he seemed on intimate terms.

The next thing Quentin knew they were all seated at a table together with three other seafarers—all captains, pointed out Captain Wiggam. And in moments they were eating a rich stew of fish and vegetables baked in a deep dish with a thick, brown crust over all. Jars of light ale stood on the board and Quentin drank his fill of the heady brew.

"One more stop," promised Captain Wiggam. He had promised that three stops ago. Quentin cast a doubtful eye to the sky where the sun was already well down, causing shadows to lengthen toward evening.

They had been running all afternoon, here and there, talking to this merchant and that. Wiggam, he gathered, was looking for a specific piece of information, and it appeared at last as if he had found it.

"Here's what we've found out," said the captain as they turned up a steep side street, off the main course. "The ship, as I guessed by its size, is only an island runner. A supply ship good for short trips; Karsh lies only a day and a night out, in good weather. They come often enough to replenish provisions, which is what they be doing now.

"Ah, here we are." They had stopped before an open courtyard, which, from the wood shavings on the worn stone flagging, Quentin took to be the carpenter's shop. Captain Wiggam proceeded into the courtyard calling, "Alstrop! Where are you, old friend. Come a'runnin', Alstrop. You've a customer!"

"I hear you well! No need to shout!" came the reply from behind an uncertain tower of barrels.

A curly head of white hair poked round the side of the tower to look over the newcomers. "Wiggam! Old sea dog!" cried the carpenter when he saw his guest. He came from behind the stack of barrels and Quentin saw a man, though white-headed and round of shoulder, strong and full of life, with large hands and well-muscled arms.

"Not injured that broken-down ship of yours again . . . that would be your luck." He stamped over to shake the other man's hand.

"No. Though I will admit to you I could have used your help a few days ago—rudder hinge pin."

"Aye. I told you. I told you. Give me a week with the *Marribo* and I'll put her to rights. But you? No. Too busy. By the gods!"

"She is a stout ship. Stout enough, I'll warrant, even to stand up to your moiling about."

"Bah!" The carpenter threw up his hands. "What brings you here, then?"

"I have friends here that require your assistance. Two of those firkins would do nicely."

The captain outlined his scheme for Alstrop while the

carpenter nodded gravely and scratched his chin. His bright blue eyes regarded everything in turn: the sky above, the woodshavings below, Quentin, the captain, Toli, the barrels. They took in everything, and after Captain Wiggam finished speaking they seemed to turn inward and examine the carpenter himself.

"Yes, it is a plan," he uttered vaguely. "I am certain that is *your* plan, for who else could think up such as this? Laughable! That is what it is. Not a plan but a joke!"

The carpenter turned and rumbled back to his work table and came back with a short length of whittled wood; his thinking stick, he called it. He slapped the smooth stick into his beefy palm.

"Now! The barrels might work. Yes, they'll do. But there must be some changes made. And you must let me take them down. No? All right, we go together. I have a hand cart. The rest later. We must go to work. Quickly! There is little time."

The last of the afternoon light had faded and the first evening star had risen before the two men standing next to a cart with two large barrels nodded to one another. "Here we go," whispered one of the men to one of the barrels. "May the gods smile upon you." Then they wheeled the cart around the corner and down the bumpy street to the wharf where the ship with black sails was making ready to get under way.

"You, there!" the carpenter called to a sailor aboard Nimrood's ship. The sailor glared down sullenly, but did not offer a reply. "Tell your captain that we have some cargo to come aboard."

After a long, hard stare the sailor disappeared and came back with another, a man who carried a braided leather lash.

"Are you the captain?" asked Alstrop.

"The captain is busy," called the man gruffly. "We're putting off to sea. Be off with you!"

"We have barrels here to come aboard."

"We have taken our provisions." The man jerked the lash through his fist.

"That may be," replied the carpenter calmly. "But these barrels are to come aboard. If you think better, go get your captain and let him deal with this."

"I can deal with this, swine! Get away from here!" He turned to leave, indicating to the sailors who had gathered around to continue their preparations for casting off.

The captain winked at the carpenter. "Very well, we will take them back," Wiggam called in a loud voice. "But I would not want to be the man who told my master he had forgotten two barrels, and those barrels left right here on the dock!" He nodded to the carpenter who turned and began pushing the hand cart and the barrels back up the hill.

The sailor with the lash came back to stand glowering over the rail. He whipped the lash several times against the rail. "Wait!" he bellowed. "What is in those barrels?"

Wiggam shrugged. "Nothing much. It probably is of no consequence . . ." He turned to follow Alstrop away.

"Stop!" cried the sailor. He jerked his head toward several of his crew and the gangplank suddenly thrust out from the side of the ship. Two sailors disembarked and ran up the street to the barrels. They turned the cart and in a moment had the two large kegs aboard.

"Now, be away with you," the sailor in charge snarled.

"Be careful with those barrels," warned the carpenter. "I will not be responsible for damaged merchandise. You will pay if you break it!"

The two men watched as the barrels were carried carefully aft, and the ship pulled slowly away with the evening breeze. "May a fair wind blow you good fortune, my young friends," said Captain Wiggam.

"And may the gods return you speedily home," added the carpenter.

Then the two friends turned and walked back in the deepening twilight. The evening star glimmered high on the horizon near the newly risen moon. "Ah," said the carpenter. "A good omen for their success."

"Yes," replied the captain. "But it will take more than an omen to keep them from harm now. It will take the very hand of a god."

THIRTY-SIX

"THERE IS no way out, my Lady," said Trenn in a voice fraught with despair. "I have searched every bolt and every brace of this dungeon . . . there is no way out. Except through that door and Nimrood holds the key."

The Queen, arms folded and legs drawn up, did not lift her head. "It is no more than we expected." It was the deepest of sighs.

"Do not lose all hope, my friends." Durwin had been standing in the small patch of light which fell from some unseen loophole above. He came to where Trenn and Alinea sat huddled together. "The god will set us free from this pit."

Trenn sneered. "Since when did any god care what happened to a mortal? Look at us—what has your god to do with us now? If he cared we would not have suffered as we have, as we will yet, I fear."

"The God Most High has his ways. They are not the ways of men."

"Do not talk to me of the ways of the gods. I am tired of hearing it." Trenn turned his face away. "I care only for what a man can do."

"Do not go on so," soothed Alinea. She placed a hand on Trenn's knotty arm. "We must endure in any case; let us do so with dignity."

"Do you see?" said Durwin, waving an arm overhead. "This

is his doing—this hopelessness that creeps over us, that makes us turn on one another. Cast it off; it is a trick of the enemy."

Trenn turned a stony glare upon Durwin.

"Besides, as long as Theido and Ronsard remain free on the outside we have hope. They will be even now working for our freedom, and the King's."

"If they are not dead," replied Trenn bitterly. "The storm, Nimrood's men . . ."

Durwin said nothing, but went back to his patch of pale light and his prayers.

The dungeon was a misbegotten hole in the lowest part of the castle. There was no opening, save the rusting iron door and the unseen grate of the loophole. The floor was bare earth and slimy with the dank moisture which oozed from the walls and dripped from the ceiling. Snakes could be seen slithering among the cracks and fissures of the castle foundations, for that was where the dungeon was—at the very roots of the castle.

The floor being wet and reeking of age and the obscenities practiced upon it, the prisoners had heaped together what they could of some mildewed straw which had been placed there as a bed some time long past. It was here they sat, in the middle of the foul chamber.

In the darkness of the dungeon only that thin shaft of light gave them to know the passing of the day. They watched it creep along the floor until it vanished in the gloom of oncoming night. Then they huddled close together to endure the bleak misery of the blackest of nights.

Then, on the second day, as the pale patch of light that marked the passing of the day moved closer to the far dungeon wall, there came a sound echoing down the low rock corridor which joined the dungeon, beneath one tower, to the main basement maze of cells and subterranean chambers.

"Footsteps!" said Trenn, rising stiffly to his feet, a hand pressed to his wounded side. They could be heard distinctly now. "Someone is coming this way."

It was true; the footsteps of what sounded like a whole regiment were undeniably shuffling closer. A rough, unintelligible voice could be heard grunting orders. And then, with a rattle and a clank, the bolt of the iron door was thrust back and the door slammed open.

Two of Nimrood's soldiers carrying torches stepped through the narrow opening, followed by another with a wicked-looking halberd. "Stay back!" snarled one of the soldiers as Trenn hobbled closer.

Then through the dungeon portal stumbled a tall figure, shoved rudely through from behind to fall face forward down the crude stone steps to the stinking dirt below. The man grunted as the air escaped his lungs. He lay there without moving.

The two soldiers with the torches stepped down, and each seized an arm and hauled him up to his knees. "Make our work more difficult will you?" one spat, then raised his foot and placed it in the man's back and kicked him forward. The prisoner's hands were bound to his sides so he was helpless to forestall the fall. His head snapped back and banged down upon the dungeon floor. Then the two turned and went out.

The door clanged shut and the footsteps receded again down the corridor.

Durwin raced to the fallen prisoner with Alinea who stood at his side. Trenn lurched forward and bent over the body. He looked up at the others. "Here is our hope," he said, quietly.

"Theido!" cried Alinea as Durwin rolled the man into his arms.

The knight's face had been beaten bloody and bruised; dark purplish marks swelled beneath his eye and over the temple. His eyes were open, but unseeing, cloudy from the torture he had just undergone.

"If only we had some water," said Alinea. "There is none left of the ration we were given this morning."

But Durwin was already at work. He placed a hand over Theido's forehead and, speaking strange words under his breath, made a sign with his fingers and then lightly touched each bruise. A moan of pain escaped Theido's lips.

"He will sleep now. Here, help me get him untied."

In fact, the sturdy knight hardly slept at all. No sooner had they loosed him from his bonds than did he awaken again. The cloudiness was gone from his eyes, but he seemed a moment coming to himself. He blinked and peered into the faces of each of his friends. "You are alive!" he cried at last.

"Oh, Theido, we have been worried about you," said Alinea, reaching out her hand to clasp his.

"They told me all were killed in the wreck. They said you had drowned and they had left you on the beach for the birds."

"Lies!" Trenn, his face black with rage, ground his teeth and clenched his fists.

"Where is Ronsard?" said Theido, pushing himself slowly off the filthy floor.

"Have *you* not seen him then?" wondered Alinea.

"No, I saw no one—not even my captors. I was dragged from the beach half-full of sea water and still groggy. I didn't even hear them coming."

"When was this?"

"I do not remember . . . midday perhaps, or close to."

"We were taken at dawn yesterday," explained Durwin. "They must have gone back and searched the beach more thoroughly."

"Then Ronsard is gone?" The Queen's voice quavered.

"Now, we do not know that for certain. He may still be alive—we all survived the wreck."

"But we were not injured as he was," said Trenn roughly. "Ronsard is dead."

"We will not think on it for the time being," advised Theido. "Trenn, have you made an inspection of this cursed place?" He looked slowly around in the gloom.

The Queen's warder nodded silently and spread his hands in frustration.

"I see, then . . ."

"Listen!" said Durwin. Theido, the words still on his tongue, fell silent. Far down the corridor the sound of returning footsteps could be heard. "They are coming back."

"Probably for another one of us to torture," said Trenn. "I'll go, and welcome it!"

"No, they will not take another one of us," replied Theido. "We will fight first."

The footsteps were now just outside the dungeon entrance. The sharp grating of the bolt thrust aside and the creak of the opening door on its rusting hinges filled the chamber.

Once more two soldiers ducked in throwing their torches ahead of them. Then the guard with his long halberd glinting cold and bright in the glare of the torches.

Following the guard came a short, hunched figure who stood quietly behind the others off to one side. Behind him came a dark shape that thrust itself through the door and into the sphere of light cast by the torches. The prisoners saw the black hair with its shock of white streaks.

"Nimrood!" cried Durwin.

"None other." The sorcerer smiled treacherously. "And now I see our little party is complete." He gazed on them one by one and then drew himself up to full height and shouted, "You fools! Trifle with Nimrood the Necromancer! I shall blast you all to cinders!"

He swept down the steps, his black cloak fluttering through the damp air like a bat's wings. He came to stand in front of Theido, who did not move a muscle, but stood his ground unperturbed.

"I will begin with you, my upstart knight, my 'Hawk.' Oh, yes!" he hissed at Theido's recognition of the name. "You see, I have long had my eye on you. But you'll not burn like these others. I have better plans for you. Much better. I've a special place for you, my knight."

"I will die before I serve you," replied Theido coolly.

"You will. Oh, yes. I dare say you will," cackled the evil wizard. "But not before you've watched your friends die screaming." Spittle flew from his foaming lips. He threw a fearsome scowl to the others, whirled and flew back up the steps.

Nimrood stood again in the torchlight, looking like a phantom out of the darkness around him. He hesitated as he turned to leave, and then turned back. "I would begin at once with you," he smiled at the captives, again that treacherous grimace. "But that will have to wait," he continued. "I have a coronation to attend—it might interest you to know. There will be time enough for our diversions when that is done."

"What coronation?" asked Durwin.

"Oh, you pretend not to know. I will tell you—Prince Jaspin, of course. Midsummer's Day. Very soon Askelon will have a new king! Ha, ha, ha! I leave at once. I shall relay to him your warmest regards. And you, Queen Alinea—you think I did not recognize you? The Prince has wondered after your disappearance. I will tell him what you have been up to—tell him about all of you, *and* my plans for you."

Nimrood turned at once and vanished through the doorway followed by the stooped man and the soldiers. The prisoners could hear his insane laughter as he fled down the corridor. His voice echoed back to them like a thunder of doom.

"Ha, ha, ha! I shall soon return and we can begin. Ha, ha! Askelon's new king will be pleased! Ha, ha, ha! 'Till then, sleep well, my children. Ha, ha, ha. Sleep well!"

THIRTY-SEVEN

THE SOUNDS of men working, laboring to unload the ship's stores, had died down. Quentin pressed his ear against the side of the barrel and listened. He could hear nothing but the gentle slap of waves against the hull of the ship, as if far in the distance, but no doubt very close by. Occasionally he heard the squawk of a seabird soaring high above. All sounds reaching him from outside the heavy oaken barrel were muffled and indistinct.

He had filled the hours aboard the ship dozing and waiting, listening in the dark of his small prison and aching to stretch his legs, but daring not to move a muscle. At last, when every nerve and fiber cried out for relief, he had allowed himself to change position. Finding room enough, and having once braved the move with no dire result, he allowed more frequent repositionings, still remaining as quiet as he could.

Periodically, he had pushed the cap from the bunghole and let fresh air rush into the stuffy confines of his barrel. He pressed his face to the hole and peered out, but could see nothing of the ship's activity. This was both good and bad, thought Quentin. For it permitted him to draw air more frequently without fear of anyone noticing the slight movement of the cap. But it also meant that he could have no hint of warning if he *were* discovered, and no view of the deck to see when they reached their destination.

So he relied upon his ears to tell him what was taking place around him. He had been sleeping when the barrel was heaved up and carried off the ship. The sensation of being lifted, without warning, and jostled awake while swinging through space so surprised him he had stifled a startled shout.

But then he had been bumped down upon the beach—there had been no resounding thump, as on the deck of the ship when he had been thrown down—so he guessed they had unloaded the cargo upon the sand.

He waited then for the sounds of unloading, and the noise of the men grunting and cursing their duty, to diminish until plucking up his courage to risk another peep through the bunghole.

This new view from his tiny window was more encouraging. His barrel seemed to be situated close by a wooden ramp, seen from below as it slanted down from the top of his peekhole. This, he guessed, formed the crude dock which teetered out into the bay used as a harbor by Nimrood's men. Beyond the ramp he could see a length of shoreline where waves washed in gently, amidst the roar of breakers further out. A few standing rocks marked the beach, and Quentin could see from the long shadows reaching out in the bay from these stones that the sun was well down and sliding toward evening.

He could see no sailors or guards nor anything that would indicate another human presence nearby. Very well, he said to himself, wait for darkness.

Quentin had just closed up the bunghole and settled back into his curled position in the barrel when he heard a slight jingling sound—which grew steadily louder—and then the dull murmur of voices. Two men, he imagined, talking together. Then the snort of a horse and the grinding creak of a wheel upon the sand. A wagon, he thought, they've brought a wagon.

"Well, let's to it then," one voice said, muffled through the sides of the keg. Quentin removed the cap to hear them better.

"Not so fast!" said the other voice. "The others will be along in a little. They can help."

"But it will be dark soon. I do not fancy driving this wagon back up there in the dark. It is bad enough in daylight."

"Then we'll stay the night here. What difference does it make? Don't be so skittish."

"Well for you to say. You've not been here as long as I have; heard the things I've heard; seen the things I've seen. I tell you . . ."

"There you go again. Shut up, will you? I don't need to hear your tales. By Zoar! You're a weak one, you are."

"I know things, I tell you. If I'm afeared of this place at night it's because I've seen things . . ."

"You've seen nothing that can't be seen anywhere else. Now, shut up! I don't want to hear it."

The other man fell to mumbling to himself after that angry exchange. Quentin could not make out the words, but he knew that he now had to think quickly. He'd been offered a new choice. Either to wait and be loaded upon the wagon with the rest of the supplies, or to try making an escape now before the others returned. He replaced the cap slowly and hung for a moment in indecision: wait or go.

Quentin decided to wait. A clean entrance into the castle unsuspected would be better than floundering around outside the enemy's lair. But just as he reached this decision the choice was snatched from him.

"Hey!" cried one of the men at the wagon. "Something moved over there by one of the barrels."

"There you go again! Be quiet! I'm trying to sleep," the other snapped angrily.

"It moved, I tell you! One of the barrels moved!" the first protested.

"To Hoeth with you and your moving barrel! I'll show you there's nothing there. Which one was it?"

Quentin heard the tread of the man shuffling through the sand, coming closer. "There, that one on the end," pointed out the frightened worker, following the brave one.

Three steps closer. Quentin's heart pounded loud in his ears. He imagined it a drum beat that could be heard all along the beach.

He heard the man breathing. The footsteps had stopped right beside him. He could hear the rustle of the man's clothing as he stood looking down upon him. "There's nothing here, by Zoar!"

"I saw something. It was here a moment ago."

"A shadow."

"It was no shadow. There's something strange about these barrels."

"Look, will you! There's not a blasted thing here! By the gods! Do I have to open the barrels and prove it to you?"

Quentin's heart seized in his chest as if it had been squeezed in a giant's fist.

He heard the scrape of something heavy upon the lid of the keg. They were taking off the lid.

Quentin drew his feet up underneath him and crouched.

The lid wobbled loose.

"Well, look at that," said the worker. "This lid is hardly fastened."

At that instant Quentin shot up out of the barrel throwing the wooden covering into the man's face and shouting as loud as he could.

As he came leaping out of the barrel he caught a glimpse of the terrified worker as he turned and tumbled over himself in an effort to flee. The other, startled almost as badly by this strange, screaming creature which leaped out of barrels, fell backwards in the sand, the keg lid catching him on the side of the head.

"Toli!" Quentin yelled, "Run for it! We are discovered!"

Toli, well aware of what had been taking place, burst from his keg in an instant and started across the strand and into the wooded tract ahead.

The worker sitting among the barrels came to his senses as the two raced off. The other cowered beneath the wagon, his head buried in the sand. "Here come the others! Nimrood's soldiers—they'll get 'em," the first cried.

Quentin glanced over his shoulder as he ran. Marching down the beach he saw a dozen soldiers, some with long spears, others with swords drawn, not far behind the two workers who were now gesturing wildly and pointing in their direction.

He turned, put his head down and sped into the woods. "Run, Toli! Run! They're right behind us! Lead us away from here!"

With barely a pause in mid-flight Toli's quick eyes scanned the thinly wooded area. Then, like a deer before the arrow, he was off, heading into the deeper, more thickly grown regions beyond.

It was all Quentin could do to keep up. Toli, alert and every instinct keen, was back in his own element. He seemed to flicker through the dense undergrowth effortlessly, dodging, feinting, slipping through small openings and sliding over rocks and trunks of fallen trees.

At first Quentin stumbled and fell over his own feet, sprawling, lurching, and pounding along behind. But then, by imitating Toli, by dodging where he dodged and ducking where he ducked, Quentin found the going easier. He forgot his fear and ran completely free. His heart soared with the cool exhilaration of flight.

Behind them he could hear the soldiers crashing through the woods after them. They had fanned out to keep better sight of their quarry. They cursed as they came, thrashing through thickets and brush, entangling themselves in briars and low hanging branches.

Twice Toli stopped for a brief rest, and to listen. Each time the sounds of pursuit were farther away, receding into the evening sounds of the woods.

"It will be dark soon," said Toli. He lifted his eyes to the sky which still held a glimmer of light. But all around them the deeper woods were sinking rapidly into darkness. Already Quentin found it difficult to tell the column of a tree trunk from its dark surroundings.

"They cannot follow us much longer . . . we seem to be losing them." Both thoughts were questions; Quentin asked for reassurance.

"They will not catch us now," offered Toli. "But we must keep going. We will find a place to camp tonight." He turned and swiveled his head this way and that. He listened for the sounds of their pursuers, cocking his head to one side. "Stay close," he said, and raced off again.

This time they changed directions and began ascending the rise of a hill. The path rose steadily, and each step grew a little shorter. Toli slowed to allow for the climb, but pushed steadily on.

The noises in the woods behind them died away. Quentin guessed that either the soldiers had given up or they had lost them completely.

But now Quentin trained his ears on other sounds, the sounds of the deep woods coming to life with the night. For the greens of leaves and moss, the browns of trees and earth, and the blues of shadow had merged into one confused hue. He followed Toli now with his ears instead of his eyes as he trailed blindly along.

"Ooff!" Quentin went down with a grunt. He had caught his toe on a root across the path and pitched forward onto his face. Toli heard him fall and came back. "Let us stop," suggested Quentin. "Just for a little while. It is too dark to run like this."

"I forgot, Kenta—you do not have night eyes." Toli stood still and turned his head, listening. Quentin heard a strange snuffling sound. Toli seemed to be smelling the air.

"This is a very bad place. We cannot stay here," the Jher said at last. He reached down a hand and hoisted Quentin to his feet and struck off again, but slower this time.

Still the path continued to climb; then, without any sign, it descended steeply. They reached the bottom of a gorge, cut into the earth by the rain. A small, turgid stream flowed nearby. Quentin could hear it. A foul-smelling mist was beginning to rise, seeping out of the ground around them, clinging to their legs in tattered wisps as they moved through its grasping tendrils.

An owl called from somewhere overhead and was answered by its mate far away. Other sounds—sly chirruppings, furtive rustles in the dry leaves beneath bushes as they passed, the whir of unseen wings—crept out of the woods as the night took hold of the land.

Once Quentin heard a faint whiz in the air close by and felt a flutter on his cheek. He recoiled from the soft contact as from a blow. When he reached his hand up to feel where the touch occurred, his cheek was wet with a sticky substance. He wiped it off with a grimace and trudged on.

The malodorous mist thickened and rose higher, swirling in eddies upon the pools of air. Quentin imagined that it dragged at his legs as if to hold him back. He could no longer see his feet below him.

He followed Toli, who seemed to take no unusual notice of all that went on around him, with a fragile resolve. He longed to turn aside from this wretched path and climb again into the woods.

But he moved on.

His foot struck a rotting limb which snapped with a hollow crack that seemed to fill the gorge. Suddenly, from right beneath his feet, a wild shape came screaming up at him: white and formless as the mist, and screeching in long ringing cries that echoed through the woods. It flew straight up at him, and Quentin threw his hands in front of his face as the creature lunged at him. But, at the moment of collision, Quentin felt nothing. He parted his hands to see the white wings of a bird lifting away into the gorge ahead.

"Toli, is there no better trail we can follow?"

Toli stopped and looked around, gauging the distance they had come. "Yes. Soon we leave this path. Only a little farther."

True to his word, in a short while Toli led them up a steep, vine-covered bank. They climbed out at a murky juncture where a small stream through the wood emptied into the gorge in a sickly little trickle which dripped its fetid water over stones slimy with black moss.

Quentin slipped, losing his footing in the muck. He caught himself and grimly dug in, pulling himself up by handfuls of weeds.

Then at last they were out of the gorge and standing on a broad level space rimmed in by trees. Behind them, the gorge, with its stinking mist; before them, a densely wooded hill.

Without a word Toli began the long climb of the hill. Quentin fell in mutely behind him. It was no use to ask where they were going, or why. Toli would have his reasons; and anyway, Quentin had nothing better to suggest.

They had walked freely for several hours, the dark trees closing out the deeper darkness beyond, when Quentin saw something that startled him, though he did not know why.

He said nothing about it, but walked on, his eyes fastened on the spot far up ahead on the hill above where he had seen this thing. Presently, he saw it again. Just a wink.

He bobbed his head and saw it again—a thin glowing in the air far up ahead. He bobbed his head and it blinked. It flickered and danced and seemed to move away even as he approached.

The path mounted steadily upward and soon Quentin was certain he was not seeing a ghost. "See there," he pointed through the crowding branches. "Up ahead. Something glowing."

In ten more steps he knew what it was: a fire. Someone had built a campfire.

They approached the campfire cautiously. Toli was all for skirting the area entirely, but Quentin felt differently; he wanted to investigate. So they crept in close, moving slowly with infinite care, making not the slightest sound.

After an hour's aching crawl they were right next to the cozy little camp, just beyond the small circle of light. They watched and waited. There was no one anywhere to be seen. Whoever had started the fire was not around.

"The soldiers?"

Toli shook his head. "Not here. Not so small a fire for all of them."

They heard the warning tread too late.

From behind them on the path came a rustle and a heavy footfall. Then suddenly a huge shape was upon them, forcing them forward. Toli dived to one side, but Quentin was caught and thrown forward into the camp. The monster roared, as if in pain, and Quentin went down as numerous blows rained down upon him.

He twisted under the blows, his head close to the fire. He saw a flash streak by him—a face. And then a voice said, "Stay where you are!"

The command was stern and evenly spoken. There was a trace of fright, but that vanished quickly. Quentin slowly raised his eyes to meet the bulky form of a large man towering over him, with what appeared to be a club raised in his hand.

Quentin was struck by something which seemed somehow familiar about this imposing figure who stood over and threatened to dash out his brains with the club.

He peered up again and sought the face which wavered uncertainly in the light of the dancing flames.

Impossible! he thought. It cannot be! But he reflected in the same instant that encountering a ghost on this inhuman place was far from impossible; it was to be expected. Following hard upon that observation, so as to be almost one and the same thought, Quentin remembered that shades did not carry clubs, or strike their victims, as far as he knew.

But the face, there was something very familiar about that face. He had seen it somewhere before. In another place long ago.

Then it came to him. He struggled with the memory, thrust it from him; he fought to disbelieve it. But the recognition remained, though Quentin was far from certain.

"Ronsard?" he said softly, his voice quaking.

He heard nothing for a heartbeat, but the crackle of the fire.

The man dropped to his knees beside him, bent his face toward Quentin's. He reached out a shaking hand.

"Ronsard, is that you?"

THIRTY-EIGHT

"I AM Ronsard," replied the man kneeling by the fire. "Who is it that knows my name in this forsaken place?" He spoke gently. But Quentin could see now, as he bent closer to the fire, the same angular features, the same jut of the jaw that told of strength and purpose. Yet, the knight seemed tired and worn. Heavy lines of fatigue were drawn at the corners of his mouth and etched around his eyes.

"Do you not know me?" answered Quentin. "I am Quentin, the acolyte. You gave me the message for the Queen. . . ."

The knight's face was suddenly transformed by a vigorous grin which banished the care and worry and sparked a light within his eyes.

"Can it be? Quentin? . . . yes, I remember . . . but how?" The questions came fast as the great knight, struck almost speechless, sought to make sense out of this apparent miracle.

"Come out, Toli," Quentin called. He knew his friend was lurking close at hand, out of sight, ready to spring forth in an instant.

The thickets parted and Toli slipped in to stand by Quentin. "All is well. This is Ronsard—the knight I told you about."

"The message bearer," answered Toli in his own tongue. "Yes, and a great warrior." Toli bowed deeply as Quentin had instructed him for occasions such as these. But the formality of the greeting in the rough setting made Ronsard smile and Quentin laugh. "Welcome, friend of the forest," said Ronsard. "I have never met one of your race. Truth to tell, I had not heard they were so well mannered."

"We are both at your service," laughed Quentin. He felt waves of relief running over him.

"And I at yours," said Ronsard. "So, good friends, we have much to talk about, much to discuss. First, how did you get here? Theido told me that you had been left at Dekra, gravely ill. They were worried you would not recover at all."

Quentin then launched into an account of all they had done since Dekra, and before that, right up to the time when he had left the temple. He thought even as he spoke that it all seemed slightly incredible, like it had happened to someone else entirely, and that he, Quentin, had remained at the temple. Thinking about the temple, and speaking about it again, made him a little wistful. Still, he knew in his heart nothing remained for him there.

Ronsard listened to all patiently, and yet eagerly, mulling it over in his head with a look of rapt attention. "You are a special one," said Ronsard when all was told. "You would make a fine knight."

Quentin blushed at this high praise. "I am only glad to see you alive and whole."

"Alive I am. Whole I shall be—and soon. I feel stronger every day. Were it not for shipwrecks and kidnapping I should be as hale as ever I was." Ronsard went on to tell how he had been snatched from the temple by Pyggin and his crew of scalawags right out of Biorkis' healing hands. "I had been there some time and was just beginning to mend when they took me. The temple guards were no match for swordsmen; they scarce put up a fight, and I could not defend myself. I was thrust into a wagon and near jostled to death from Naramoor to Bestou where their ship waited.

"How they managed to find Theido and Durwin and the others was an odd piece of luck—though I was grateful for the company." He explained about the storm and the shipwreck and his lonely vigil on the island.

"And tonight I meet once more my friend from the temple," Ronsard laughed. "To tell you the truth I thought I would never see you again—I was certain my message had miscarried. But it appears the gods have bound our fates together."

Toli, listening to their speech, pieced together as best he could a vague idea of what they said. But at last he grew tired and, yawning, put his head down and curled up close to the fire and went to sleep.

"Yes, I am for sleep myself," said Ronsard. "I was just collecting firewood to last through the night when I bumped into you on the trail. I did not see or hear you until I nearly fell over you—scattered all my firewood."

"Was that it?" Quentin remembered being struck many times as he fell to the ground. "We did not hear you either, coming up behind us on the trail."

"It bodes ill to let anyone know you are astir on this island. It is a strange place, and far from safe."

Quentin nodded. "What about the others?" He had been aching to ask that question all night, but had not dared to. The thought shocked him back to the present and the task at hand.

"We will discuss that tomorrow in the clear light of day." With that Ronsard yawned and lay himself down to rest.

"Good night." Quentin paused and added softly, "I am very glad to have found you again."

"And I as well. Good night."

It was obvious as soon as Quentin opened his eyes that Toli had been up with the dawn, and probably before. Arranged around the campfire were leaf baskets full of berries, and several kinds of edible roots which had been washed and neatly stacked. Over the fire two scrawny rabbits, skinned and spitted, roasted merrily away, nearly done. And, wonder of wonders, oozing out its golden nectar upon a fresh mat of leaves: a honeycomb.

"It seems your friend has made us a breakfast," observed Ronsard.

Quentin rubbed his eyes sleepily and sat up. "So I see. Where is he?"

Just then Toli, balancing three oblong green objects in one hand, and three apples in another, stepped into the camp.

"Here is water," he said, handing round cupfuls of clear, sparkling water in vessels he had made of large leaves, folded. He then swiftly attended to the rabbits.

They ate as if they had never seen food before, cramming their mouths full and savoring every bite. The honey, saved for last, drew the utmost commendation for Toli's woodcraft. "Never have I feasted in the wild this well," said Ronsard. "My strength returns on eagle's wings. And well may I need it. Today we must go up to Nimrood's nest."

Quentin had forgotten all about Nimrood, or had shut the black wizard out of his mind. The mention of the black lord's name sent an icy chill through his heart.

"Is the castle far from here?"

"It is of a distance, yes—though not more than a league or two as the crow flies. It is on the top of a mountain, and there will be much climbing to reach it. The way is well marked, however. I have seen that much."

"Then let us be off," said Quentin. Toli was already on his feet, having dowsed the fire and scattered the ashes, removing any sign that they had been there.

They struck out again along the path Quentin and Toli had followed the night before. In a short while it descended again and joined a wider way. This road bore the signs of recent use: footprints of soldiers going both ways, wheel marks of wagons, hoofprints.

"I will send Toli ahead," Quentin offered, "to watch for anyone coming this way. The trees are so close here that we would run smack into them before he could see them coming."

"A good idea. I will keep a watch behind, though I do not think we will have to worry much for being chased."

In this way they covered the distance quickly, reaching the mountain summit as the sun climbed toward midday. Then, as they rounded a last upward curve, Kazakh, the sorcerer's castle, swung into view.

"There it is." Ronsard shaded his eyes with his hand and took in the sight. "And not a lovely sight."

Quentin gazed upon it with the same dread fascination he would have felt in watching a deadly snake wreathe itself on a nearby rock. "It is awful," he said at length.

Toli ducked back around the corner of a bluff covered with a heavy tangle of vines. "The evil one's warriors come from the castle," he told Quentin. Quentin translated for Ronsard.

"Let us get off the road and see what they are up to." Ronsard leaped into the undergrowth beside the road, and Quentin found a well-covered place beside him which afforded a perfect view of the road.

There was a rustle beside him and then a rip, as of a branch being torn away. Quentin turned just in time to see Toli hopping back onto the road with a woody fern branch in his hand. He was wiping out the tracks where they had stood talking together in the trail. "This Jher leaves nothing to chance," whispered Ronsand. "He is both cunning and quick. I like him."

"The soldiers must be very close by now." Quentin fought down the impulse to yell at Toli, to warn him, but resisted for fear that the soldiers would hear. He bit his lip as he heard the tramp of many feet in the dust and the jingle of a horse's tack.

Then Toli was beside him again, and a second later the first soldier appeared on the road. He was riding a black spotted horse, and as he turned in the saddle to call a command back over his shoulder to his men, Quentin saw a raking scar which seemed to divide his face in two.

"Him I have seen before," whispered Ronsard. "On the beach."

Following the horseman came a horsedrawn wagon with high sides, and behind that a small force of perhaps forty men. The whole procession shuffled along carelessly. Two soldiers rode in the back of the wagon with their feet hanging out the back.

"Undisciplined," breathed Ronsard. "Cocky."

"They are looking for us." Quentin watched the company pass and remembered his fear of the day before.

"How do you know?"

"We were discovered on the beach last night and escaped into the woods."

The soldiers moved off down the road at a leisurely pace. When they had gone Ronsard waited a few minutes, and when no one else appeared, took the road again.

They came quickly to the long, winding road across the ridge. Ronsard, standing in the last of the protection offered by the trees said, "I don't like this at all. We will be seen the moment we set foot on the road."

Ronsard studied the terrain carefully, measuring and appraising the distance to the foul lord's den. "There is no other approach to the castle that I can detect." He turned to Quentin and Toli. "We have two choices—wait until darkness can hide us, or go now boldly in daylight and take the chance."

"If we wait the soldiers may come back. I would not like to be discovered in there creeping about by night." Quentin shivered at the thought.

"Well said. And I would not wish to wait a moment longer to be free of that place if I were captive there." Ronsard himself spoke up. "That settles it then. We go at once."

Quentin's hand sought the golden dagger at his belt. He clutched it as he hurried off to catch Ronsard, who was already striding toward the ridge.

"Well, so far, so good. Not a guard or watchman in sight," observed the knight.

They were crouched in the shadow of one of the mighty drawbridge's stone pylons at the end of the road where the bridge spanned the gulf between the castle and the ridge. There were two pylons, one at either side of the road, like the posts of a huge gate. Stone griffins smirked atop each pylon.

Sliding his head cautiously around the corner of the post, Quentin could see the black tunnel of the gatehouse across the bridge. It was, as near as he could tell, quite empty.

"No guards inside, either," he reported.

"Then let us begin!" said Ronsard. "We may not have a better chance."

Quentin wanted to protest. They should, after all, have a plan of some sort, he thought. That was the way to do it, not rushing in like this, unprepared. Who knew what they might encounter. Nimrood himself might be waiting for them as soon as they crossed the bridge.

But Ronsard was already away and dashing across the drawbridge. Toli, like a shadow, flew right behind. Quentin, in order to keep from being left behind, scrambled across, too.

They inched their way through the gatehouse tunnel and peered into the courtyard beyond when they had reached the end. "No one about," said Ronsard. "Strange." He wrinkled his nose. "What is that smell?"

A slightly acrid odor could be detected over the dark mustiness of the gatehouse tunnel. It seemed to be coming from the courtyard beyond.

"Well, stay close. Here we go—" Ronsard darted out of the mouth of the tunnel and into the light. Quentin, running a few steps behind him, saw the knight suddenly stop. Quentin stopped, too, wondering what had gone wrong. Had they at last been discovered? Ronsard turned, his face contorted as with agony unbearable.

"What?—" Quentin began. Then it hit him—an overpowering stench like a massive fist. He felt his gorge rising and began to choke. His knees buckled and he went down on his hands. As tears filled his eyes he heard Ronsard retching and Toli gasping for air.

When the waves of nausea passed, Quentin raised his head slowly to look around. The courtyard was decidedly unkempt. Weeds grew through cracks in the stone flagging, filth accumulated in every corner, stagnant water stood in troughs where flies buzzed in thick, dark clouds.

"Oh . . . no . . ." Quentin heard Ronsard moan and turned his head to where the knight stood gazing at some object. Quentin could not determine what it was. He crept closer.

"The foul fiend!" cursed Ronsard, turning away.

Quentin gazed down and saw the skeletal carcasses of two horses rotting in the sun. The horses were still tethered to iron rings set in the stone; they had starved to death where they stood. Birds had been at them and had torn away huge chunks from their flanks. This then was the source of the festering stench.

Quentin turned away and pulled Toli with him. The Jher said nothing, but his eyes had grown hard and dark as stone.

Inside the castle it was the same—deserted and reeking with neglect. Everywhere they turned some atrocity met the eye. "Stupid waste!" spat Ronsard as the three inched along. Quentin's skin crawled; he felt dirty, as if he had been contaminated by a wasting disease. He knew himself to be in the presence of impudent, arrogant evil, and it made his blood run cold.

They continued on in silence until they reached a great stone archway at the further end of a long, crooked corridor.

"This is odd," said Ronsard shaking his head in disbelief. "Where is everyone?"

"Nimrood cannot have many friends," quipped Quentin. Ronsard regarded him with a knowing look.

"The dungeon must lie beyond." He indicated a heavy iron-banded wooden door with an iron bolt. "Let us see."

Ronsard tried the bolt and found that it slid easily enough, if not as quietly as he would have wished. But the door swung open readily and they saw a spiral of stone steps circling down into the blackness below. A torch stood ready in a holder just inside the door, with a candle flickering beside it. Ronsard seized the torch and lit it with the candle, leading the way down. Quentin followed and Toli crept along behind.

Quentin thought the stairs would never end, but presently they came to a landing which opened onto a vast chamber. Below them the chamber was filled with stores and barrels, heaps of armor, and unused swords and spears.

"He must be outfitting an army!" said Ronsard. "This is the basement. The dungeon is below." They continued down the twisting stairs.

The steps ended at an arched entrance. Ronsard paused, handed Quentin the torch, and peered around the arch. A low, wide passage ran to the left and right, lined with cells, and ahead of them a shorter passageway ended in darkness.

Ronsard took back the torch and said, "We will have to search every cell. I will go to the left. You two go to the right."

It didn't take as long as it might have: every cell was empty. The three met back at the place where the corridors crossed. "There is only . . ." Ronsard stopped short. "Listen!"

Footsteps could be heard slapping along just around the corner of the arch. Then a voice called out, "Euric! Is that you? Bring your torch, man! Euric!"

For two heartbeats Quentin stood frozen to the spot, then threw himself against the wall. Ronsard placed a finger to his lips and winked. Then, just before the man turned the corner, Ronsard stepped into his path and, holding the torch high, swung his other fist into the man's face. The man went down and out cold. He never knew what, or who, had hit him.

"Must be the jailer," offered Quentin, pointing to the large truncheon which hung by a leather thong at his belt and next to it an iron ring with an assortment of keys.

"Yes, we are in luck," said Ronsard, already lifting the man below the arms and dragging him into the nearest empty cell. "Now, come along. The way should be clear."

They dashed quickly and quietly down the shorter corridor ahead and descended the stone steps.

The narrow iron door was heavily locked; the bolt had been thrown, and a great iron lock attached. The captives inside heard the fleeting steps in the passageway and then the scrape of a key in the lock and then another, and others, and suddenly the bolt was flung back and the door heaved open.

"Ronsard!" The Queen recognized him first. "Brave knight, you have found us!"

"I knew you would come," said Durwin. Trenn and Theido stood staring—speechless.

Then Quentin thrust his way in, followed by Toli. He stood looking down upon his friends, his eyes filling up with tears.

"Quentin!" shouted Durwin. The hermit rushed toward him, his arms outstretched. The next thing Quentin knew he was embracing Durwin as he would have embraced his own father. The others gathered around, pounding him on the back. Alinea kissed his cheek.

Everyone talked at once as the questions came tumbling out: how? when? where? they wanted to know. Quentin was oblivious to it all. He smeared away the tears that splashed down the side of his face and considered this to be the sweetest meeting he ever had.

It was a moment he would keep forever.

THIRTY-NINE

ESCAPE from Nimrood's castle could not have been easier, or more quickly accomplished—to Quentin's amazement. Up out of the dungeon and back through the castle corridors, across the stinking courtyard between the inner and outer curtain, into the gatehouse tunnel and over the drawbridge to freedom.

Quentin kept expecting Nimrood to appear at any moment, to trap and imprison them, or at least challenge their flight. But not a soul did they meet—though they did hear prodigious singing as they flitted past the corridor leading to the kitchens. "A revelry? Here?" questioned Ronsard.

"The snake is away," said Durwin, and explained that Nimrood had gone to attend the Prince's coronation.

"The Prince? Prince Jaspin—king? Then it is even worse than I expected," said Ronsard.

"So it is!" said Durwin.

"Well, it cannot be helped now," said Theido. "We will have to deal with that in its time. Right now we have to free the true King."

"Yes," replied Ronsard. "Time for a council of war."

They huddled under the pylons at the end of the drawbridge and discussed how best to locate and free the King. Quentin did not care much for his assignment, which was to lead the others back along the trail to where the wood joined the ridge and sheltered the road beyond. He was to wait there and offer a signal should the soldiers return before Ronsard and Theido could meet them.

"Waiting!" complained Quentin darkly to Durwin as they trudged back to the hiding place. "We have come all this way only to wait while they rescue him. It isn't fair."

Although he had not thought about it before, he had naturally assumed that he would be there when the King was rescued. Only now when that prospect was denied did he feel cheated.

"I dare say it *isn't* fair at all," sympathized Alinea. "But the Queen is glad for the company of her protectors."

"I am sorry," blustered Quentin. "I did not mean . . ."

"I understand," she cut him off. "You had every right to be there. But we must all play our part as we are given it. And I am grateful, really. I could not have endured that dungeon cell a moment longer. You have rendered your Queen a great service once again. I shall never forget it."

At this Quentin brightened somewhat, and took his task more seriously. But the walk back down along the ridge was uneventful, and they reached the shelter of the woods without incident. Trenn grumped along behind: he, too, was miffed at being led away with what he considered the old men, women, and children.

They stopped to wait in the small glade, off the road and well hidden, but within easy sight of the dreadful castle soaring above on its crag of rock. The spot afforded a clear view of both the ridge and the road below. Each settled down and Durwin closed his eyes and drifted promptly off to sleep.

They waited. The minutes dawdled along maddeningly. Then an hour. And another. It was too much for Quentin, who jumped out into the road at frequent intervals to see if anyone was coming. Trenn was certain something had gone wrong and that they should all go rushing back to the aid of their freshly-captured comrades.

Gradually, the sun slipped lower in the afternoon sky. Quentin watched as a long caravan of clouds made its way in from the west. He had decided to give the rescuers until the last cloud had passed over the castle before going after them—against all orders to the contrary.

He was saved from this dereliction of his duties by the appearance of figures on the ridge.

"Here they come!" he fairly shouted. Toli, who had been scouting the road below, came running back, and Trenn and Alinea jumped back into the road to see.

"Yes, someone is coming, all right. But I cannot see—how many are there? Can you tell?" Trenn squinted his eyes against the sun, now shining level along the ridge.

Quentin could not see that far either, so he turned to Toli who peered intently for a moment and then announced, "*Lea nol epra. Rhunsar en Teedo.*"

"What did he say?" asked Trenn, anxiously. The Queen said nothing, only clasped her hands under her chin and closed her eyes.

"He said there were only two. Ronsard and Theido. The King is not with them," replied Quentin. "I am sorry, my Lady."

Shortly, Theido and Ronsard drew up. Theido, puffing from his run down the steep path, said between gulps of air, "He is not there. The King is gone. We searched the entire castle—even forced the chamberlain, who we caught napping, to open all the closets. He said they had gone, all of them, with Nimrood. Though who 'all of them' were he did not know."

"Are you certain?" cried Trenn. His anguish was real enough and spoke for them all. "There might be ten thousand places to hide a man up there."

"And we searched ten thousand!" snapped Ronsard. Disappointment darkened his brow. "He was not there, I tell you."

"Yes, you are right," replied Durwin who had been unusually quiet all this time. Quentin thought he had gone to sleep.

"I have been sifting the ether for a sign. I sense no trace of the King's presence. The chamberlain, it seems, is telling the truth. The devious Nimrood has taken his prize with him. I should have guessed as much."

"It makes sense," Ronsard admitted grudgingly. "That is why we met with no resistance when entering the castle."

"And none leaving," said Theido. "Now we have to find a way off this accursed isle."

"That, too, should not prove difficult," offered Quentin. "Perhaps the ship that brought Toli and me still lays in the bay."

"Excellent! Quentin has provided us with a ship. To the beach."

"It is not a large ship," said Quentin apologetically.

"I don't care if it is a bucket with oars," crowed Theido. "As long as it takes us far away, it will suit me. Lead the way."

Quentin and Toli led them off at once, Toli darting ahead along the trail to scout the path ahead, lest they meet the returning soldiers. But the path was clear, and by the time their shadows had grown long upon the dust of the trail they reached the thinly wooded area rimming the bay.

"It is beyond here a little way," whispered Quentin. "Just beyond those trees. Toli will go see what is to be seen." He threw Toli a quick sign and the forest dweller vanished in the wink of an eye, melting into the dappled patches of light and dark thrown down by the oncoming dusk.

In a moment he was back. He spoke a few words to Quentin while the others looked on anxiously. Quentin turned and said, "The ship is there . . ." Then he squelched the kindled hopes of the former captives. "But so are the soldiers. Toli says they have set up camp on the beach."

"Strange," wondered Theido. "Why would they do that?"

"That, at least is why they were not to be seen at the castle," offered Ronsard.

"Hmph!" snorted Trenn. "How many are there? We are more than a match for them be they ten to one."

"I would agree with you, but for the fact that we have no weapons."

"We have not long to wait until darkness," said Durwin.

"Perhaps something will present itself between now and then."

The fellowship settled down to await the cover of night. But no sooner had they made themselves comfortable than Durwin jumped up. "I have it! The perfect diversion!"

"Shhh! We will not require a diversion if you tell the dogs where we are," snapped Trenn.

Durwin paid him no attention. He cast an eye at a patch of sky overhead. "Quickly! We have but little time. We need to gather some things." He assigned each one an item to fetch from the woods: bark from certain trees, leaves of a certain type, stones which might be found, and other ordinary items. "Hurry now! And bring me all you find."

By the time the sun had set Durwin had amassed a small mountain of these raw materials. He set to work shredding and pulverizing, breaking and husking, mixing and sorting the substances into appropriate piles. As the first star of the evening appeared, he announced, "So it is! We are ready at last.

"Theido and Ronsard, creep to the edge of the wood to the sand. Dig a hole, so," he indicated the size, "three of them—one on either side of the path leading into the wood from the beach, and one in the center of the path.

"Quentin and Toli, each of you take some of this," he scooped up an armload of the stuff, "and follow me. Trenn, Alinea—gather firewood and come to the edge of the beach where we will dig."

At these words everyone leapt to action. When the holes were dug in the sand and approved by Durwin, the shallow depressions were filled with the things Durwin had requested, carefully arranged in layers with painstaking patience. Then Durwin took his leather pouch and emptied the contents over the three mounds.

On the beach, the soldiers had started a fire and were cooking an evening meal. Coarse laughter and snatches of their crude conversation drifted to where the party worked in silence under the watchful eye of Trenn who had been posted to watch lest any of the men on the beach take it into their heads to pass into the woods.

"Now," said Durwin, "to light it."

"Wait a moment," pleaded Ronsard. "Tell us what is to happen here."

"Did I not tell you? We have created a dragon for the amusement of the soldiers yonder. It will send them screaming into the night, I assure you. Light the pyres we have made here and then hide yourselves well away. When the soldiers scatter, make for the boat. I will join you there."

"But where are you going?" Theido asked.

Just then Trenn sounded the alarm. "Someone is coming!"

"The dragon must have a voice!" said Durwin as he turned to hurry off into the woods.

"Wait!" Ronsard rasped, his voice a strained whisper. "We have nothing to make a fire with."

"What?" cried Durwin with a startled expression. "Oh, very well. I suppose there are still some things I may do." With that he stooped and removed a twig from one of the miniature pyres. He held the twig before him and raised his other hand high over his head, mumbling the words of an ancient charm with his eyes closed. He brought the hand down swiftly and a blue spark leaped from his finger to the twig. The twig fizzled into flame.

"So it is! Light them with this at once. No time to explain. Get to the ship and cast off as soon as the way is clear."

"Hurry!" warned Trenn. "They are getting closer. They will see us."

Theido held the flame and lit the first pyre. "Hide, all of you! Get ready. When I give the signal run for the boat."

He lit the other fires and hid himself beside the trail. Raucous laughter floated up from the beach. It was quite apparent that the soldiers had helped themselves to a firkin of wine and were beginning to feel its effects. A few others had joined the first and were making their way to the woods to relieve themselves.

Quentin looked at the pyres in their dishes of sand. Nothing was happening that he could see. A few wisps of smoke drifted upward, all but invisible in the darkness which had settled over the wood.

Then, as he watched, a great bubble of smoke rose from the central pyre, followed by a bubble from each of the others. The bubble flattened and spread, snaking out over the sand toward the beach.

"Look!" said Quentin to Toli, who crouched at his shoulder. "The dragon's breath!"

Bluish smoke now billowed from the pyres and poured onto the beach, creeping low along the ground like a mist spreading over the sand. The smoke boiled forth, lit by green fire from the burning pyre below. It writhed in curling tendrils as it stretched down along the slope of the beach reaching toward the water.

The first soldier, stumbling up the path, singing a rude ditty at the top of his lungs, stopped and peered drunkenly down at the path as the snaking smoke curled about his feet and licked at his legs. He stepped back, almost falling into the two coming up behind him. For a moment they all stood staring as the mysterious mist swirled about them, thickening, racing on.

Quentin felt it before he heard it—a low thrumming note which vibrated in his chest. He fancied the rock beside him quivered in response to the sound.

The note grew in volume, becoming louder and louder still. To it was added a shrill hiss, the sound of steam escaping from a fissure in the earth, or of a monstrous snake coiling to strike. Then all at once the woods shook with a roar. The bushes rustled as if in the wind, but there was no wind. Leaves fell from the trees.

A thrill of excitement raced along Quentin's ribs. He turned wide-eyed to Toli who returned his gaze with a grin. "The dragon's roar."

The three soldiers on the beach, at first puzzled, and now alarmed, faltered and fell back. They turned as if to run, but remained anchored to the spot where they stood. The singing around the fire by the shore had stopped. Several stood looking into the woods.

Again the roar. Louder this time. From somewhere back in the woods a great light flashed—a bolt of lightning out of a clear sky. In that brief flare Quentin saw the terrified faces of the men on the beach; the look of unspeakable horror which appeared magically upon each brow sent a tingle of fear through his stomach. What if there *were* a dragon?

The flash of light was followed by a strange sound, the weeping creak of trees snapping off at the trunk, and the muffled crash as they fell to earth.

"The gods save us!" came a cry of dismay from the shore. "The dragon is coming!"

The slithering smoke had reached the huddled knot of men on the beach. "The dragon's breath! We're doomed!"

Two who had been entering the wood ran screaming back to the campfire, leaving the other collapsed on his knees with his hands clamped over his ears and his eyes squeezed tight in terror. He sobbed mournfully and then pitched over, face down in the sand.

"We'll all be killed," someone screamed. The horses, tethered to the back of the wagon, broke free and whinnied wild-eyed with fright, lashing out with their hooves at anyone who came near. Men began rushing to and fro upon the sand, arming themselves.

Then, from the smoking pyres, a weird glow went up, bathing the scene in a lurid green cast. The roar sounded again, rattling the branches overhead and, Quentin was certain of it this time, shaking the rocks in the earth. He cast a timid glance over his shoulder and fancied that he saw the huge black shape of a nameless dread moving through the deep shadows of the wood. The rending of trees and the crush of the undergrowth increased. The stench of burning sulfur filled the air.

The pyres, casting an eerie hue over all, now suddenly erupted in a shower of sparks and tiny cinders, becoming fountains of sparkling flame.

The soldiers, scattered and confused, shrieked as one. The horses bolted and ran down the beach. In an instant of hesitation, the men dropped their weapons and melted away, some to flounder in the ocean, calling for the waves to cover them. Others streaked away along the strand to hide among the rocks. Within the space of three heartbeats there was not a man to be seen upon the beach save the soldiers who had collapsed in the sand.

"Move out!" cried Theido. Quentin found that when the call came his legs were already moving as fast as they would go down the beach to the water's edge.

He threw himself up the rickety wooden ramp and over the rail of the small ship. He floundered across the deck to the mooring rope which he struggled to unloose from its post. He did not look up when he felt Toli's hands upon the rope working feverishly with his own.

"Are all on board?" called Theido. Ronsard, standing at the bottom of the ramp, his arms holding a load of swords and a shield or two, hollered back, "I cannot see Durwin. He must be coming . . ."

Quentin glanced back up the strand toward the wood. In the green glare of the smoking pyres he imagined he saw the great shape of a black dragon lumbering into the clearing. Two great circles of eyes burned into the night. Once more the water-freezing roar thundered. And then, inexplicably, Durwin emerged from the smoke, dancing down the path to the boat.

FORTY

FROM HIS high parapet Prince Jaspin watched the last-minute preparations for his coronation. Below, on the greens of Askelon, a hundred brightly colored pavilions had blossomed like early summer flowers. Lords and their ladies strolled the lawn while servants fluttered among them on errands of pending importance.

The air fairly billowed with the fragrance of a thousand bouquets and the savory aroma of meat roasting in the pits and sweet delicacies being prepared for the high feast. Everywhere he looked, color and festivity met his gaze, and even to Jaspin's jaded eye the sight dazzled and delighted.

He rubbed his pudgy hands and hugged himself in paroxysms of pleasure.

Jaspin had readily assumed the appearance of a king. Rings rattled on every finger; gold chains hung about his neck; his rotund form fleshed out a handsome brocaded jacket with wide lacy sleeves; a flattened cap, embroidered with gold, perched upon his head, and his long brown hair had been curled for the occasion. On his feet he wore boots of gilded leather; his legs were stuffed into the finest stockings which issued forth from his short velvet trousers fastened at the knee with silver buttons. He appeared the perfect picture of kingly grace.

His entrance into the city the day before had been no less grand and majestic. All his lords, bedecked in their finest armor, astride their best horses, rode with him in triumphant procession through the town. The streets were thick with throngs of on-lookers who sent their cheers aloft as the occasion required. To an objective ear the cheers might have been more effusive and heartfelt; nevertheless, to Jaspin, caught up as he was in his own pomp and circumstance, the tidings seemed the greatest possible adulation. In fact, the perceived acclaim so overwhelmed Prince Jaspin that he unaccountably loosened the strings of his purse and began flinging ducats of gold and silver into the throngs. This, of course, produced a heightened approval from the populace, most of whom made up the lower echelons of the realm. Those who had no great love for Jaspin, the more sincere citizens, stayed away from the procession altogether.

A more objective eye would have noticed that his praise poured forth from the throats of what might be termed a scruffy rabble. But to Jaspin, they were lords and ladies, peers of nobility every one.

That night there had been mummery and feasting and drinking far into the night. Jaspin, quite unlike himself, had retired early so as not to spoil his happy day with the wrath of the grape.

And now he beamed down upon the scene of his glory as the sun itself, sending down a rare beneficence to all that passed beneath his scan.

A shadow slipped fleetingly over his eyes, and he looked up to see a great bird gliding overhead. He turned and went back into his apartment to finish readying himself for the ceremonies soon to commence and to continue for several days. He heard a croak from outside on the parapet and turned to see the bird he had glimpsed moments before alighting on the balustrade. Before he could think or speak the bird changed, grew larger, its shape shifting and transforming. In a blink the dread form of Nimrood stood in the doorway, blocking out the sunlight streaming in. A cold finger of fear touched Jaspin's heart.

"What do you want?" the Prince gasped.

"Come, now. We both know what I want. Why pretend otherwise?" the sorcerer smiled his serpent's smile. "I want what was promised me." His tone had become an insinuating hiss.

"What I promised? I promised you nothing more than I have already given. You wanted the King—I gave him to you. That was our agreement."

"And did you think I would be satisfied with that? How innocent you are." Nimrood's black eyes flashed fire. His wild hair waved as if in a wind. "No! You promised a piece of your realm to any who would help you gain the throne. I have given you the throne. *Given* it to you, do you hear?" The wizard paced and raved. "Now I demand payment!"

"And what payment would you have?" the Prince asked cautiously. If pressed he was prepared to rave as loudly as any mad magician, where it concerned his wealth.

"Half your realm." Nimrood smiled grotesquely. "Half your realm, my Princeling."

"That you shall not have, by Azrael! You dare ask that? Be gone, you miserable—"

The words suddenly clenched in his throat. Jaspin gazed in terror into Nimrood's narrowed eyes, which flashed red in their depths. "I could crush you like a bug, Prince. Do not play with me. *I* am your master.

"You wish to be king? Very well. You shall be king—but at my price."

"And if I refuse?" Jaspin whined miserably.

"You cannot refuse."

"Can I not?" The Prince became sullen. "What can stop me? In two days hence I will wear the crown. I will be king regardless."

"I wonder if your pretty regents would hand you the crown so readily if Eskevar suddenly appeared?"

"You said he was dead. You sent his ring. . . ."

"As good as dead. He is close by; well-hidden—you cannot find him. But he may be revived to claim his throne once more. Of that I assure you."

"You would not," sneered the Prince. "It would undo all you have done; all your schemes would come to naught."

"Ah, but the sight of two brothers locked in mortal combat would greatly cheer me. And I need not tell you who would win." Nimrood's eyes shone in triumph as he drew himself up full height. "So, which shall it be? The crown, or Eskevar's return at a most inopportune moment?"

"You black serpent!" Jaspin threw his hands into the air. "All right! All right! You shall have what you ask. But what am I to have of your surety? How will I know that you will do as you say?"

"You have, Prince Jackal, the surety of what I will do if you cross me. Beyond that? Nothing. Nimrood does not condescend to any mortal."

Jaspin's countenance reddened with rage, yet he dared not express his anger toward the necromancer. His fear formed the greater part of his discretion; he held his tongue.

"So it is agreed," soothed Nimrood. "I will return in a fortnight to receive the necessary titles to my new lands. And I will bring you a token, a reminder of your pledge . . . and what may be your fate if you renege."

Nimrood spun round, his cloak flying in tatters behind him. He hopped upon the casement step, leapt to the balustrade and hurled himself off, to Jaspin's horrified stare. But in the instant of his falling his form again changed, so quickly it seemed he had not changed at all, but had always been the huge black raven which lifted its wings to the sky.

FORTY-ONE

QUENTIN had slept but little, and that had been restive. He had tossed and rolled in his sleep as if in a fever. He heard voices call his name, and when he awoke and sat up, the voices vanished, leaving only the splash of the prow slicing the waves.

He soon despaired of getting any rest and went to sit beside Durwin at the helm. "Steering by the stars is not difficult when you learn the knack," Durwin replied to Quentin's question. "Like everything else, it is all in knowing what to look for."

"Was there really a dragon on the beach tonight? I mean, I saw something. I cannot say what it was."

"It was an illusion. A vapor. Nothing more."

"Only that? But the terrible roaring, the lights, the smell." Quentin wrinkled up his nose at the memory of it. "How did you accomplish that?"

"As I said before—there are a few things a former wizard may do who has laid aside his power. It is permitted for me to intercede for good in times of need, but even then there is a price. Power always exacts its price. No, my greater powers are beyond my reach forever now, and it is for the best that I put it off."

Quentin was silent for a time considering this. When he spoke again he asked, "Why did you?"

"Lay aside my power? Very simple; a man may not serve two masters. The Power is a terrible master. It demands nothing less than the whole of your life."

"Who is the other master?"

"That you already know. The other is the Most High God, the One. He demands your life as well. But in him there *is* life, rather than death—which is where the Power always leads in the end."

"Cannot the Power be used for good? Like tonight on the beach?"

"Ah, yes. But that was only a very little power, that. The temptation is to use more and more, to give more and more of yourself to its mastery. But though you wield it, the Power is still your master. There can be no end but slavery and death. Sooner or later it destroys whatever it touches."

"Will it destroy you?" Quentin hated the thought, but he had to know.

Durwin laughed softly. "Who knows? Perhaps."

"But you said you had given it up."

"So I have. But the Power was strong in me for many years. I used it as I desired for my own ends and, as I said, the Power exacts its price. I would have taken it up again at Dekra, but wiser heads than mine counselled against this. They saw that even though a kingdom fell, it was not worth a soul. Even such a sorry soul as mine!" He laughed again.

"But if you have put it aside, how can it harm you?"

"Who is to say? Tonight on the beach I used but a remnant of my former abilities. Already I feel the urge to use more—it eats at your soul until there is nothing left. But the god is jealous. I have given over much that could have been his. Who is to say what I could have become if I had not wasted so much in the pursuit of the black arts." Though Durwin spoke without sadness, Quentin thought he could sense a longing in the hermit's voice. A longing for something once lost and never again to be recovered.

"Now you, for example," Durwin continued. He held the tiller in his hand and rested both easily across his knee as he spoke. "You have the best opportunity—you are still young. For me it is too late."

This saddened Quentin, but he knew what the hermit meant. "I know about the god," he said. "The One."

"Do you? How?"

"I met him in a vision. At Dekra. I received the Blessing of the Ariga from Yeseph and the elders. It was the night before we left."

"Tell me about it."

Quentin related all that had happened to him at Dekra, culminating in the ceremony of the Blessing. Durwin listened to Quentin's story with full attention, nodding and making sounds of agreement.

Quentin entered a second time into the feeling he had experienced that night. So long ago it seemed now. He described the Man of Light and the words he had spoken. " 'Your arm will be righteousness and your hand justice,' " quoted Quentin. In a sudden vivid flash he entered again into the spirit of his vision. " 'I will be your strength and the light at your feet. Forsake me not and I will give you peace forever.' "

"So it is," breathed Durwin at last. "You have seen him. Now you know. Any who truly meet him cannot go back to the way they were before."

"Do you see him often?"

"I have never seen him," answered Durwin simply.

"Never?" This shocked Quentin. He had assumed the hermit, of all people, to be on the most intimate terms with the Most High One.

"No, never. But I do not need to see him to know of his presence, to learn his ways. It is enough for me that he has accepted me to be his servant. I am content."

"But I thought. . . . You know so much about him."

"I suppose I do—know about him. He gives each man a special task in life, and a blessing to carry it out. You have been chosen for a great work, and yours is a special blessing. He has never appeared to me. Yes, yours is a Blessing of Power, as Yeseph would say."

Quentin was dumbfounded. Durwin had never seen the god

he served so faithfully. Durwin's words echoed in his mind: It is enough, I am content.

Quentin wrapped himself in these thoughts. He stirred only when he heard the creak of footsteps coming up beside him. "You two must get some sleep before this night is through," said Theido. "I will take over now. Go get some rest. It will be morning soon and we will enter the port of Valdai at midday." He laughed, "That is, *if* this dragon-slaying hermit has not steered us out to sea."

"Keep her bow aligned with that lowest star—that is our port star—and the moon over your right shoulder as it descends. That will bring us to our destination. Good night."

Three great ships dwarfed the harbor at Valdai. War ships, Ronsard said, though who they belonged to he could not tell; they were still too far out to see anything but the tall masts and wide hulls silhouetted against the hazy background of the port. But Ronsard and Trenn hung eagerly over the side of the ship anxiously watching for the first symbol to present itself: a pennon, a banner, some insignia of color or shape they could recognize.

"King Selric!" shouted Ronsard, as they at last drew near enough to make out the flag which flew from the topmost mast. "That is his battle sign. I know it as well as my own."

"Aye, it looks to be Selric's," affirmed Trenn. "How long had it been since I've heard that name?"

"What do you think?" asked Theido. "The first of the returning armies?"

"Yes, yes! I had nearly forgotten," shouted Ronsard jubilantly. Quentin, though he did not know why, was seized by the same spirit of elation which swept through his comrades. He watched as their small ship came about and entered the mouth of the harbor and drifted to its mooring place. Alongside the mighty warships their tiny vessel with the black sails seemed like a clumsy toy. Quentin gawked openly at the huge hull and at the towering masts. He had never seen anything in the water so big. And there were three of them, each an exact copy of the other, showing in every bold and graceful line the strength and prowess of their owner.

"How long have they been here?" wondered Theido.

"Not long, I think," replied Ronsard. "They could not have been there when Quentin was here. He would have remembered." Quentin nodded his agreement.

"Aye, not long indeed!" shouted Trenn. "Look! The wherries are still unloading men. Selric's army is going ashore." He waved an arm and those at the rail saw that he was right. The long rowboats were still carrying soldiers to the wharf as the last ship was being unloaded.

"If I know Selric," cried Ronsard, "That is where he will be!" He nodded at the furthest ship. "He will be aboard until the last man has gone ashore. A commander to the end."

They wasted no time in seeking Selric out. And they found him, as Ronsard predicted, watching over the disembarkation of his men from the taffrail of his ship. Upon seeing Theido, Ronsard, and the Queen he dashed down the ship's ladder himself to welcome them aboard. At a word from Alinea he invited them to join him in conference in his personal quarters. There Alinea told him the story of Jaspin's treachery and the King's distress.

Although no one had spoken it aloud, all assumed that Selric would be sympathetic to their plight. He was very much more than sympathetic. Selric, King of Drin, was beside himself with fury when he learned what had taken place while he and his armies endured the winter on the coast of Pelagia, waiting for the first fair winds of spring to sail for home.

"The impudent rogue!" Selric shouted, smacking his fist into his outstretched palm as he paced about his commander's quarters aboard ship. "His ambition has raced far ahead of his ability. This will cost him his head if I have anything to do with it!"

"Then you will help us, my Lord?" asked Alinea.

"Help you! Of course I will help you, by all the gods of earth and sky!" Selric swore. The color had risen to his cheeks, matching his fiery red hair, and inflaming his legendary temper.

He continued, pacing furiously all the while, "Do you not

know that Eskevar saved my life, and the lives of my men many more times than I care to remember? Not a man who fought Gorr would turn his hand from helping him now, by Zoar!"

Quentin watched the drama intently. Selric was the first king he had ever seen. He was fascinated by this slim, commanding figure with the shocking red hair, who absolutely burst with restless energy. Selric could not remain still for an instant. Even sitting, which he seldom did, his hands were reaching, gesturing; and all the while his eyes darted everywhere, never missing any detail, no matter how trivial.

Now Selric was an angry lion on the prowl. Quentin shuddered within, wondering what it would be like to face this intense commander.

"When can we leave?" asked Theido.

"Why—at once! We will leave at once! Tonight!"

"But your men have only just gone ashore," observed Ronsard.

"Bah!" Selric snorted. "They have been ashore all winter! I will send my trumpeters to sound the call at once!"

The king moved to the door in two long strides. "Kellaris!" he called. Instantly a tall man with a deeply pock-marked face appeared at the door. He bent his head and entered the crowded quarters of his king.

"At your service, Sire," he said, bowing with but a slight tilt of the head.

"Kellaris, I have just received dire news. Send trumpeters ashore to sound the rally call throughout the town. We must board the men as soon as may be. I will explain later. Bring me word when all is ready."

"As you will, my Lord." Again the tilt of the head, and Kellaris was gone.

Quentin leaned close to Toli and whispered in his ear. Toli nodded and both left the room unnoticed by the others who turned again to discussing what lay ahead.

FORTY-TWO

THE EVENING sky was ablaze with the glittering light of a billion pin-point flares of tiny stars, each one a jewel resplendent against the royal blue of the heavens.

It had been a long day, thought Jaspin. A long and glorious day. His coronation was everything he could have wished—a brilliant, dazzling display. A spectacle of pomp and power. And now he was king at last. He turned the thought over in his head endlessly as he sauntered along the balcony overlooking the magnificent gardens below the great hall. The night still breathed the warmth of the day and offered the heady perfume of a thousand garlands which festooned the hall and everywhere the eye chanced to stray.

King Jaspin sighed with deep contentment as he strolled, hands folded behind him, humming to himself. His guests, thousands in all, still feasted and danced in the great hall, or strolled, as he did, the balcony or the gardens below in the soft moonlight.

But Jaspin, wishing to be alone for a time, turned away from the high festivity and sought a more private place. He ascended a short flight of steps, leading to a low barbican nestled in the wall and overlooking the balcony below. Here, in times of war, a soldier would stand guard, watching over the inner ward.

He had no sooner gained the top step of the platform when

he heard a distinct hissing sound and a slight rustle upon the cool stone. Jaspin froze, afraid to move. The hair on the back of his neck pricked up.

There in the silver moonlight, a thick black snake drew its length along the gray stone balustrade. Jaspin could see clearly the sharp angular head and the glimmering beads of its eyes watching him as it slithered closer.

Then, as Jaspin watched, the snake coiled itself into a heap and disappeared, becoming a thin wisp of writhing vapor. The vapor coalesced into an amorphous mass which hung just before Jaspin's horrified face. Within the mist Jaspin made out the vague outline of a countenance he knew too well. In a moment there was no doubt.

"Nimrood!" cried Jaspin in a stricken whisper, not wishing to attract the attention of anyone who might happen by.

The face in the mist grew steadily more distinct, and the dread visage of the sorcerer glared out at Jaspin and snapped, "I have no time to exchange pleasantries with you." The voice was thin and far away.

"When did you ever?" wondered Jaspin to himself.

"I only come to warn you that the prisoners have escaped."

"What is that to me?"

"Do not make the mistake of toying with me, King Jackal!" Even in the form of a night mist, the wizard's eyes flashed lightning. Jaspin could feel the necromancer's awful power and stiffened in silence.

"That's better. You and I are partners, my obtuse friend. Never forget that. After all, I share one half your throne. Half of all Mensandor is mine—or soon will be. When I take the trouble to warn you, you may be certain that it tokens your concern. Oh yes, it does indeed."

"The prisoners, you were saying?" Jaspin tried to look appropriately concerned, which was difficult under the circumstances.

"Have you forgotten so soon? Or did you not even guess?" Nimrood's quick eyes saw the answer to his question. "You fool,

I credit you with more intelligence than you deserve. Did you not know that I had within my dungeon that rebel Theido, and some of his friends: Queen Alinea, and several others; your warder, for one, and a hermit, Durwin by name. Ronsard was to have been among them, although he was presumed drowned."

Try as he might, Jaspin could not make any connection between these people and any possible threat they might hold for him, though the group certainly seemed most suspicious. He blinked blankly back into Nimrood's questioning gaze. "I thought they were hiding at Dekra."

"Bah! I don't know why I bother with you! They have escaped and are returning here. Guess the rest—if you can. In the meantime, heed my warning to secure your crown. I will hasten to apprehend them. My spies are already abroad seeking their whereabouts. They will not remain free for long."

"But . . ." Jaspin blurted. The vapor which had held the depraved wizard's image was unraveling and seeping away into the night, vanishing on the breeze.

A cold shudder of fear rattled Jaspin's frame. He turned and hurried away, casting a furtive glance over both shoulders as he ran, lest anyone witness what had just taken place.

"How stupid I have been!" Jaspin cursed himself as he hurried to his chambers. "I did not need that poisonous sorcerer—I could have managed on my own! Now he involves me in his schemes."

So, they are returning here, he thought. Theido and the Queen; Ronsard, too, and alive after all. But who was this Durwin? Were there others he did not know about? Still, what difference did it make? How could they possibly hamper him now? The coronation was over; he was king. Very well, let them come. He would be ready for anything.

All these things Jaspin mulled in his head as he ran along. But arriving at his conclusion, he stopped and turned back to rejoin his own celebration. Secure in the knowledge that nothing could go wrong, he entered again the great hall of Askelon and was immediately swarmed by doters and well-wishers.

A steady breeze billowed the sails of Selric's foremost ship, Windrunner. Quentin stood at the starboard rail and watched the moon slide slowly into the sea.

He breathed deeply the tang of the salt air and listened to the gentle churning of the water as it passed beneath the prow of the warship. Then he heard the murmur of voices coming closer and turned to see Theido and Ronsard with King Selric walking toward him across the deck. He turned back to watch the glistening spray of stars rise and fall with the gentle motion of the ship.

The men came to stand a little way off from where Quentin waited. He could hear them talking quite clearly, though they spoke low and confidentially. He did not much like the tone of their conversation.

Presently, he grew weary of listening. A melancholy mood stole over him and he sighed and moved away.

"What is the matter, young sir?" A voice sought him from the shadow of the mast.

Quentin turned and peered into the shadow, but could distinguish nothing. He moved into the darkness himself and found Kellaris sitting on a carefully coiled pile of rope, with his back propped against a keg. "Oh, it's you," he said.

"I have been more heartily hailed in my day," remarked King Selric's most trusted knight.

"I am sorry," muttered Quentin, but his apology lacked conviction.

"There is something ailing you, that I can tell. Seasick?"

"No."

"What, then?"

"I was listening to the others just now; I overheard them talking," admitted Quentin.

"Nothing good comes from listening to another's conversation uninvited."

"I couldn't help it. Anyway, what they said about the King—about Eskevar. I mean . . ." Quentin broke off. He could not find the words to express himself as he wished.

"They think our hope is in vain, that he may be already past help. Is that it?"

Quentin, sinking down to sit cross-legged on the deck, only nodded. He felt as if someone had taken a spoon and hollowed him out. He did not raise his head when he heard footsteps approaching softly across the deck.

"Is this parley for men only, or may a lady join?" It was Alinea. Kellaris jumped to his feet, and Quentin rose slowly to his.

"Please, remain seated. Both of you. I will not stay if you are engaged."

"Not at all. Please join us, your Majesty. I would welcome the counsel of a queen in the matter we have been discussing."

"You are very kind. I will stop a while, then. Now," she said, settling herself beside Quentin, her slim arms drawing her knees to her breast, "what is it that requires my counsel?"

"Quentin here fears for his King. That the worst may have too soon befallen him." Although the knight spoke gently, Quentin jerked his head up and shot a warning glance as if he had given away a deep secret, or trespassed upon a sacred trust.

"That is something greatly to be feared. I fear it as well."

Quentin raised his eyes from the darkness of the shadows to look upon the beautiful Alinea sitting so calmly beside him. Though she had echoed his concern, her voice lacked the resignation that he felt within himself.

"But, it is Midsummer's already. Jaspin has been crowned king . . ." The words failed.

"And we know not where Eskevar may be?" she asked.

Again Quentin only nodded.

"Take heart, dear friend. The tale is not all told. There is much that may yet be done. If only we could see a little ahead into tomorrow, as Durwin sometimes seems to, we might see a very different prospect than we now contemplate. Though we cannot see what may be, we have hope. Hope has not abandoned us; nor should we abandon it."

"My Lady speaks well," agreed Kellaris. "Those are words from a courageous heart."

Quentin had to agree. Alinea showed remarkable courage, had shown it all along. Suddenly he was glad for the cover of night, for it hid the blush of shame which had risen to his cheeks.

He got slowly to his feet and said, "I thank you for your kind words, my Lady." That was all he could manage before he moved off again, walking slowly away across the deck.

"That young man carries the world on his young shoulders," said Kellaris, watching Quentin's form meld into the darkness.

"Yes, and he complains not for himself," murmured Alinea. "There beats a most noble heart, and proof against any evil."

That night, as Quentin lay upon his mattress in his shared quarters, he offered up his second prayer.

"Most High God, let your servant see but a little ahead. Or, if not, give me the hope that drives out fear." Then he drifted off to sleep.

FORTY-THREE

QUENTIN awoke to the sound of voices calling and feet pounding upon the deck. From the slanting beams of sunlight pouring into the sleeping quarters he could see that the day was speeding away. He threw off the coverlet and jumped nimbly to his feet, experiencing that momentary weaving sensation he always had when waking at sea.

Making his way out onto the main deck, Quentin noticed that the calls and sounds of activity were becoming more frantic. Something was wrong.

His curiosity alerted, he dashed out onto deck, nearly colliding with Trenn who stood just outside the cabin door.

"Look at that, young master," said Trenn, squinting up his eyes and jutting his jaw forward. "Aye, an evil sign if I ever saw one."

At first Quentin did not see what he was looking at. Then, as the sight overwhelmed him, he did not see how he had missed it.

Dead ahead and closing in on three sides, loomed a tremendous fog bank scudding swiftly toward them over the water. The sea was calm; the breeze light. The thick, curling fog seemed driven from behind.

The fog was a dirty gray mass: heavy, dark, its churning walls rose high overhead. And even as Quentin watched, the first leading wisps trailed across the sun.

Quentin ran to the rail and leaned over. Behind them Selric's two sister ships had drawn close, and the crew was trying unsuccessfully to throw lines from one ship to another so that none would be lost in the fog. That was the explanation for the sounds of urgency he had heard. For, though the other ships still sailed in clear weather, a wondrous blue sky arching overhead and the sun spilling down a generous light, Selric's vessel in the lead was now almost engulfed in the fog.

Quentin watched as the towering billows closed overhead, blotting out the last patch of spotless blue above. The sun became a dull hot spot overhead, then dimmed and was extinguished altogether. This *was* an evil sign, thought Quentin, as the rolling clouds swallowed the ship and removed the other ships from his sight.

He turned and was astonished to find that he could not see even as far as across the deck. So thick was the fog that he could not say for certain exactly where he was at that moment. If he had not had a fairly good idea of the lay of the ship, he could have been completely lost.

"Trenn," he called, and was surprised to hear an answer close at hand.

"Here, sir!" The warder had stepped close to the rail when the fog closed in. "I like this little enough. It is a trick of that wicked wizard Nimrood. Mark my words; he is behind this right enough. Even *I* can feel that."

Trenn's voice, though close by, sounded removed and muffled. His face floated in and out of view in the veiling mist: a pale apparition uttering dire pronouncements. Quentin shivered and said, "It is just a fog, Trenn. I am sure we sail through it soon."

"I am inclined to agree with Trenn," said a voice behind them. Quentin nearly leaped overboard. The voice had come out of nowhere, with no warning of approaching steps. But the voice was familiar and Quentin could make out the dim outline of Durwin's round shape standing before them.

"This is not the normal season for mists upon the sea," said the hermit. A long pause ensued. "I believe there is magic behind this. Evil magic. There are signs—one can tell. This is no ordinary fog. It is sorcery."

Durwin did not say more; he did not need to. There was only one who would cause such an enchantment to overtake them. Trenn had spoken his name aloud, though Quentin dared not.

The day wore on and the fog became every hour more foul.

It grew steadily darker and cooler, so by midafternoon it appeared as twilight, and the cloying air held a damp chill which seeped into the clothing of any who ventured out into it. Strange blasts of icy wind blew suddenly out of nowhere, striking the surprised victim on the face, first from one direction then from another. Selric's men, well-trained and seasoned, said nothing, their mouths clamped shut in grim determination. But their eyes revealed a mounting fear.

Quentin sat upon his mattress munching an apple. He did not feel like eating; the apple was merely an exercise against the creeping uneasiness they all felt. Only Toli, who dozed upon his pallet, seemed unconcerned. But the Jher had not spoken all day.

Then the voices began.

Quentin became aware of them as one becomes aware that the wind has risen. All at once it is there, though it must have been present and building in force for a long time unnoticed. That was how the voices started. First a whisper, barely audible. Then a little louder, growing until the long, rattling wails could be heard echoing across the sea.

Quentin and Toli tiptoed out on deck and crept forward to the main mast where they found a tight knot of sailors huddled together, and among them Theido, Ronsard, King Selric and Durwin.

All around them shrieks and moans filled the fetid air. Rasping calls and booming shouts echoed overhead. Whispers and cries and whimpering groans surrounded them. The eerie cacophony of voices assailed them on every side—a chorus of all the unhappy spirits that roamed the nether places of the world.

Amidst the bawling and the bellows, the raking screams and screeches, the bone chilling howls and absurd whooping arose a sound which made Quentin's blood run to water.

A laugh. A chuckle sounding small and far away began to grow. It swelled uncontrollably and insanely, booming louder and louder, a sharp, hacking cackle which shook the rigging and rattled the gear on board the ship. Quentin could feel that madman's laugh through the soles of his feet as he stood on deck with his hands clamped over his ears.

He couldn't shut it out; the sound had gotten inside his head. He began to think that if the laughter did not soon stop he would end it by leaping overboard and letting the waves cover him in silence.

"Courage, men!" a shout rang out, bold and true. "Courage!" King Selric, who had been in consultation with Durwin when Quentin had joined them, had climbed up in the rigging of the mast and was rallying his men to the sound of his voice as he would in battle.

"These cries are but the augury of a magician. They are not spirits of the dead; they are illusion, nothing more. Courage!"

King Selric's strong words seemed to help. Quentin noticed the fear subside in the eyes of those around him. Selric climbed down and resumed his place. Quentin and Toli, who had both stood stiff as stone, now inched forward to join the group.

"How long can this go on?" The questioner was Ronsard, though Quentin could barely see him through the filthy fog.

"Indefinitely," replied Durwin, closer to hand. "Until its purpose is accomplished. Though what that is I am not sure."

"To slow us down? Put us off course?" asked Theido.

"Perhaps, though I am more of a mind that there is another reason behind it."

Quentin felt a shift in the fog and a cold wind stirring the waves.

"*Partro!*" cried Toli. Quentin interpreted.

"Enchanted voices all around, and he says 'listen,' " mocked Trenn.

"No! He is right," shouted Durwin. "Listen! What do you hear?—beyond the voices?"

Quentin listened and heard a thrashing sound, the wash of water upon rocks. The rocks!

"We are heading for the rocks!" cried Theido.

"We'll crash!" shouted Selric, dashing forward. "Helmsman! Steer away hard to larboard!"

"No, stay!" shouted Durwin. "Selric, tell your helmsman to keep his course. Do not turn aside."

The king turned a puzzled visage to the hermit. He started to object. "We will be smashed upon the rocks. We are coming closer. Any second. . . ."

"It is a trick! Hold your course."

For an instant King Selric hesitated and then announced, "Helmsman, hold your course."

The company stood huddled, waiting for the awful sound of their wooden beams splintering upon the treacherous rocks of one of the Mystic Islands they seemed to be drifting so near. They waited for the grinding halt and the rapidly tilting deck as they grazed by, then struck and were pitched into the sea.

But though the sound of waves riven upon unseen rocks encompassed them round about, the anticipated wreck did not occur. The ship held steady, feeling its way through the oppressive vapor with the crash of waves breaking all around.

Several long hours dragged away. The group on deck sat now in a tense circle of worried faces. Periodically, someone would leave and another take his place, but throughout the evening the vigil continued.

As night took hold—adjudging by the darkness creeping rapidly through the mists, a general deepening of the darkness already present—King Selric ordered torches to be placed along the rails lest anyone fall overboard. Squatting upon the deck in the quivering light of the sulky torches, the miserable company waited.

Quentin, dozing fitfully as he slumped upon the damp planks of the deck, was suddenly aware of a great confusion. Nearby, the slap of running feet on the deck, shouts of alarm. And, more distant, the terrible sound of shipwreck.

He jumped to his feet, shaking his head to clear it, and followed the others to the stern.

"One of our ships has struck a rock!" cried a sailor. "It is sinking!"

Peering into the fog, as peering into mud, revealed nothing. But the anguished cries of men and the horrible tearing of the ship as it hung on the rock and battered itself to pieces filled the dank air. Quentin could hear the mast crashing to the deck and the screams of the men it crushed beneath its weight—cut short as it fell. He heard men in the water, drowning. A sickening, helpless feeling spread through Quentin's frame as he stood gripping the taffrail with whitened knuckles. Someone do something—save them!

King Selric called for the ship to turn about, to lower boats to save the crew of the distressed ship and pick up survivors. But Durwin, standing close beside him, a warning hand on his arm, said, "No, withdraw your orders. There is nothing out there. Hold firm to your course."

The king looked around in the swirling fog, appealing to the others for opinions. Theido said nothing and Ronsard turned away. Selric had his answer; he pounded his fists into the rail and cancelled his order for rescue.

"If you like, have your trumpeter sound a call to the other ships—if they are close they will hear that we proceed un-averted."

Selric did as Durwin suggested and the trumpeter, aloft in the rigging, blew a long, strong call on his horn. He repeated it as if to say, "Hold steady. All is well. Hold steady."

The ship continued on as before, and the cries of the men from the wreck were gradually lost in the muffling mist.

FORTY-FOUR

"WE SHOULD have done something," insisted Quentin. "It was not right to let them die; we could have helped. We should have done something."

"We did," said Alinea gently. "We trusted Durwin."

"But you did not hear it! Horrible! The cries of the men . . ."

Quentin had found the Queen emerging from the cabin below deck. Though her voice was strong and soothing, he could see by her red-rimmed eyes that she had been as much affected by the ordeal as anyone, though she had chosen to endure it alone in her quarters.

"Durwin had a reason for what he did; I doubt it not. Come, would you like to rest for a while?" Alinea had turned, about to usher Quentin to her own quarters where he might rest and relieve his troubled mind of its burden. "You need sleep."

Quentin nodded as one in a trance. His limbs wore leaden weights and his eyes burned in his head. Sleep. The word sounded so peaceful. Still, he wondered if any of them would find peace again. It had been so long since he had had any real rest, and sleep had become a torment of dreams and half-real horrors.

But as he stepped across the threshold and started down to the cabin below he heard the helmsman call out. "Clear way ahead! Clear way!"

He turned and saw the fog straggling in tatters, driven before a fresh wind. Stepping back on deck he raised his eyes toward the heavens and could see the thinning vapors receding as if some giant hand were drawing aside a veil.

Overhead the stars shimmered merrily, and Quentin thought he had never seen them burn more brightly. Now the ship plowed through the last bank of trailing mist and suddenly they were free.

Quentin filled his lungs with sweet fresh air. He could not stop himself from grasping the Queen's hand and squeezing it hard as he fairly danced with joy. "It is gone!" he cried. "We are free!"

There was not a more happy person on deck the next morning than Quentin himself. The hideous events of the day before had been wiped away with a solid night's sleep and now, in the clear light of a crystalline day, seemed remote and unreal—shadows only. Dreams of a tired mind, he thought. And yet he knew it had happened.

The most surprising revelation, and the one that cheered him most, took place the moment he climbed on deck. He could not believe his eyes when, as he scanned the blue horizon, noting the few frothy white clouds puffing their way across the sun-washed dome of the sky, he fastened on a most remarkable sight: two ships trailing out behind them. King Selric's ships.

For an explanation of this miracle he ran to Durwin, whom he found at the taffrail over the stern, placidly meditating as he gazed out to sea.

"So it is! As you see, no ships were lost last night," he replied to Quentin's inquiry.

"But I heard it. The wreck, the pleas for help, the breaking timbers. I heard it all. Everyone did."

"Yes, I should say we did. But, as the fog itself and the absurd screams, the shipwreck was sorcery. No doubt 'twas meant to draw us away from our course to confuse us and bring about a real collision. If we had turned aside we would have struck one of the other ships."

"There was no wreck, and no rocks either."

"Does that surprise you? Why were you so ready to believe the fog a work of magic, and the voices, but not the shipwreck?"

"That was different somehow—more subtle. It seemed so real."

"And so did the dragon on the beach seem to the soldiers." Durwin smiled mysteriously. "Much lies in the willingness to believe."

"I am sorry," said Quentin abruptly, after considering the sorcery at length.

"Sorry? Why should you be sorry?"

"I thought you were. . . ." Quentin couldn't make himself say it.

"You thought I was hard-hearted—not turning back after the drowning men. For a moment you thought me as loathsome as Nimrood ever was. So?"

Quentin nodded, avoiding Durwin's eyes.

"Bah! Think nothing of it. You were right to want to help."

"How did you know? How did you know it *was* sorcery?"

"I had a presentiment—a wizard can tell wizardry. It would be like Nimrood to throw something like that in our path. I trusted my heart to tell me the rest."

"Then you did not know, not for certain."

"No, not for certain. There is very little certain in this world. But, Quentin, you must learn to trust that small voice inside you, to stop and listen. The god leads by such hunches and nudges. Very rarely by direct command."

Quentin went away pondering Durwin's words. So much to learn. This god was very different from those he knew well, who spoke in riddles, surely, but they at least spoke in understandable words—and in signs, omens, and tokens. Not in nudges and vague hunches. At least when you received an oracle, there was something to point to.

But even as he held this thought he remembered all the times in the temple when he had seen a priest give a hopeful pilgrim a false oracle, having fabricated it only moments before. Yes, he thought ruefully, very little was certain. Then he remembered Alinea's words of comfort. "We did, we trusted . . ." Trust then was something one could do, no matter how one felt.

The rest of the day passed uneventually. As did the next and the next, and the one after. More and more, Quentin felt that all that had happened to him since leaving the temple had been a dream, or had happened to someone else. But he knew, from the firm feel of the deck beneath his feet, that it was all very real.

As time wore on and the ship plowed a wide furrow through many leagues of the sea, Quentin drifted into a moody humor. He alternated on a shifting course, rising to lofty light-hearted heights for the moment, and plunging into dark troughs of contemplation where he imagined a host of horrors yet to face. Too soon the flights of gladness dwindled.

Though he did not know what to expect when they reached Askelon, Quentin guessed it would be unpleasant and, more than likely, deadly as well. Nimrood's power had been defied thus far. Soon they would have to face him; the very thought filled him with an ominous forboding.

Toli followed him around deck, a mute companion; the devoted Jher had given up trying to interest his master in any activity which might soothe his troubled spirit. For, as soon as they would contrive a moment's respite, Quentin would lapse again into melancholy.

At last a faint reddish-brown smudge on the horizon let them know that Mensandor lay ahead. Despite the fog, where direction became meaningless, they were right on course and had made remarkable time. The close navigation of the Seven Mystic Islands had proved again the truth of the proverb: "The men of Drin are born of the sea."

In the council of war that followed the sighting of land, it was decided that, rather than landing and making the journey from Lindalia to Askelon afoot, or continuing on around the peninsula and striking in from Hinsenby, the best and most daring plan, and therefore the most unsuspected, would be not to land at all. They would come inland by ship up the wide sluggish west branch of the lazy Wilst.

"Can such a thing be done?" wondered Theido. They sat in the King's quarters, staring at a large map painted upon a parchment. Each face was blank under the pressure of heavy thought.

"By ordinary seamen, no. But with my sailors it is possible. My ships, though large and wide of hull, are shallow keeled. They are warships, after all. One never knows in war what will be required; there are times when river travel becomes necessary."

"I will vouch for the skill of his sailors and the craft of his shipwrights," said Ronsard. "I have seen much in the wars against Gorr to recommend them. There are none better."

"So it is! We shall head inland along the river from Lindalia. But can we make the fork where the Wilst joins the Herwydd? If not it would be better, though it would take time, to sail around and come up from Hinsenby."

"I am confident it can be accomplished," assured Selric.

"Yes," offered Theido. "I know that region well. The Herwydd is old and deep. Where it joins the Wilst the waters have carved out a broad cleft. High cliffs rise up on either side. The waters mingle here," he traced the route on the map, "stirred by deep currents. If we have no trouble reaching the fork we will have no trouble after."

Quentin, curled in a corner, said nothing, though it pleased him that at last something was being done, if only more talk and planning.

With every hour the coast of Mensandor became clearer and more distinct. The approach of land lifted his spirits, as did the council, but he still experienced great shudders of dread as he contemplated what lay ahead. In his mind's eye he could see nothing but blood and doom, the clash of sword against sword, fire, pain, and death.

"Stop your whining! You are king—act like it!" Nimrood waved a long, bony finger in Jaspin's face. Jaspin cringed and fell back once more into his throne.

Jaspin whimpered sullenly, "This would not have happened if . . ."

"You do not sit in judgment over me! It was that blasted holy man—that Durwin. He ruined my spell. And he shall pay for it;

you will see how he squirms. They will all squirm. They will wish they had gone to their graves at the bottom of the sea."

Nimrood, his wild hair streaming, flew about Jaspin's throne room in a maddened frenzy. He seethed and boiled, his temper finding imperfect vent in Jaspin's spineless blubbering.

All at once he stopped and glowered at Jaspin, who returned the wilting glare with fearful, hooded eyes, not daring to look the angry wizard full in the face.

"What? Why do you look at me so? Stop it! I don't like it!" bawled Jaspin. He shifted uneasily in his seat, hands gripping the arms of his golden throne.

"Let them come," purred Nimrood. A snaky smile slid across his lips. His black eyes cracked fire.

"What?" Jaspin was almost afraid to ask.

"Let them come. If we cannot stop them with magic we will stop them with force. You, King Jackal! How many men do you have?"

"Why, only three thousand or so . . ."

"How many knights among them?"

"Forty, fifty, maybe more. I have not attended to details yet; there has been no time for . . ."

"Enough!" The malevolent sorcerer had begun pacing again. He called the questions over his shoulder. "How many nobles have you in your pocket?"

"At least a dozen. I have no doubt others could be persuaded, now that I am king," Jaspin boasted.

"Save your idle vanity—it wearies me." Nimrood crossed his arms over his chest and came to stand before Jaspin. "Now, we have three days to marshal our forces. Gather your nobles and all their men-at-arms. We must have sufficient strength to crush them quickly." He clutched up a large green apple from a bowl of fruit on a nearby table and raised it with his gnarled fist into the air. He squeezed it, and to Jaspin's astonishment the apple exploded into yellow flames. In moments ashes drifted down like snowflakes.

"Ha, ha! You see how it is!" The sorcerer dashed a shriveled, blackened cinder, all that remained of the shining apple, to the floor.

Jaspin had been doing some rapid calculating. "That would be over ten thousand men—knights and footmen. It cannot be done. There is not enough time."

"It *will* be done!"

"But who would command such a force? I do not believe I. . . ."

"No, not you, my worm. I have a commander at the ready. He has only to join my immortal Legion."

At the word a ghostly pallor tinged Jaspin's slack features; his flesh became mealy. "Not the Legion of the Dead; there is no need for that."

"Silence! We will do this my way this time, and there will be an end. If I were to leave it to you, you would bungle it again." The wicked wizard fixed Jaspin with his slithering smile.

"Yes, my little poppet," Nimrood chuckled menacingly. "This time there will be an end."

FORTY-FIVE

BY NIGHTFALL the three warships had reached the ruddy coastline of Mensandor. The reddish color came from the rock cliffs rising abruptly from the strand on either side of the turgid Wilst. The smooth, red, sandstone bluffs glimmered scarlet in the dying light as the chattering calls of gulls and terns echoed among the cliffs.

They anchored for the night just off the large triangular crag guarding the mouth of the river. The crag, Carthwait, or "The Guardian," stood sentinel—a soldier standing eternal watch, and providing refuge for countless seabirds. Around its base the dusky waters of the Wilst stained the green of the sea—called Gerfallon by the earliest inhabitants of the region.

The next day saw the ships slowly making their way up river under the stares of the curious townspeople of Lindalia, who had come to see the spectacle of three warships pulling themselves along the cliffs by the straining muscles of the oarsmen.

By the end of the second day Selric's navy had reached the fork Durwin had described. They found it to be as Theido had said: the commingling waters of the two mighty branches had carved out a hollow bowl, rimmed around by high palisades. Plunging over the brink of these steep banks in green profusion, vines and vegetation splashed down like leafy waterfalls to trail away in the current.

One by one the ships turned into the deeper waters, shipped oars, and were carried along in the flow. Silently, along the wide expanse of the Herwydd, the invaders descended toward the plains. A calm hung over all—almost visible—like the honeyed light filtering down upon them from above.

Gradually, league by winding league, the high banks receded back into the land from which they had sprung. The ships, keeping to the deep center channel of the Herwydd, passed in silence along far slopes crowded with trees. Occasionally, they slid by a cluster of rude huts where peasants peered fearfully out of darkened doorways while spotted mongrels barked their defiance from the shore.

To Quentin time seemed to pass as a vision as he stood on deck, detached, watching the world wend away, feeling nothing in particular. The dull, aching dread had settled into a vague anticipation. He was being propelled toward something. Something he knew, but could not name. He would catch glimpses of it in the way the light moved upon the water, or through the trees. Golden light and silver-blue shadow. Darkness. Always the darkness at the end.

He thought to watch for an omen, but he had given up reading portents. Or had he? He did not remember it as a conscious decision, but he could not think of the last time he had seriously considered seeking one. The practice had fallen from him without notice. And until now, he had not missed it.

So, more had changed at Dekra than he supposed. In what other ways was he changing? he wondered. Quentin spent the rest of the day in contemplation of the god who had the power to change his followers—a thing unique in the lore of all the gods he had ever known.

On the third day the ships reached the plains of Askelon. The level flatland ranged below the heights of Askelon Castle a full league to the river. It was a broad expanse, the scene of many battles, the cradle and grave of numerous campaigns.

Fringing the plain, bordering it to the south and along the Herwydd, stood the furthest reaches of Pelgrin Forest. It was here, under the protection of the trees along the river, that Selric determined to establish his base. They would camp just within the trees overlooking the plain.

When the vessels touched land, the days of waiting and in-activity were abruptly ended. Swarms of men boiled forth from the ships, carrying supplies, weapons, tents, and utensils. Horses were led ashore bearing large bundles of armor and weapons. As the ships gave forth their cargo a small city sprang up in the trees. The woods rang with the calls of men working to raise tents and axes clearing the underbrush.

"This is a good place," remarked King Selric to Theido as they stood watching the activity. "We are protected at our back with the river behind. There is only the plain ahead. We will not be easily surprised."

"Walk with me a little; we may be able to see the castle from here."

They walked through the woods a short way, amidst the bustle of Selric's men readying the camp. At the edge of the trees they could see the plain and above it, hovering like a motionless cloud, the misty bulk of Castle Askelon on its mountain. But the two had scarcely arrived when they lost all interest in viewing the scenery. Before them lay the whole of Jaspin's army deployed upon the plain.

"Azrael take him!" cursed the king, "the fox is waiting for us!" He turned eyes wide with shock and dismay toward Theido. At the moment they heard the snap of a twig behind them and both men turned.

"So it is!" replied Durwin, taking in the sight of a thousand tents spread abroad, and the twinkling lights of evening fires beginning to dance in the dusk. "It was to be expected. They have known of our coming all along."

"We'll not surprise them now," said Theido.

"And we cannot go against a force that large with the men we have. How many do you think there are?" His eyes scanned north and south as far as he could see.

"Near ten thousand by the look of it."

"To our thousand . . ." King Selric's voice trailed off.

Without speaking further the three walked back to camp.

Fires had been lit and smoke, with the tang of roasting meat and bubbling stew, drifted throughout the darkening wood. Quentin and Toli, who had been strangely occupied from the moment the ships touched land, now came forward leading a great chestnut charger.

They found Theido, Durwin, Ronsard, and the others reclined around a crackling fire in front of King Selric's blue-and-white striped tent.

Quentin beamed brightly. "Is there a knight of this excellent fellowship who answers to the name Ronsard?"

Ronsard raised his head, a questioning look in his eye. "You know that there is, young sir. I am he."

Quentin laughed, "Then, sir knight, stand and claim your horse!" He handed the reins to the bewildered Ronsard and stepped back to watch the effect of his jest.

"Balder!" Ronsard shouted, his face shining with unexpected happiness. "Can it be?" He threw an arm around the horse's thick-sinewed neck and slapped the animal's shoulder affectionately. Then he stepped away and patted his charger's forehead saying, "You have cared for him all this time? You've kept him for me?"

Quentin nodded, for the first time feeling a twinge of loss at giving up the horse.

"But I have a secret to tell." The rugged knight gazed steadily at Quentin. "Balder is not mine. My own courser was lost in the ambush of the King. This good mount belonged to one of my companions . . ." He faltered, but his voice was steady when he continued. "He will not be needing his horse anymore."

"But you were his last master. He is yours all the more since his owner is gone."

"No, I cannot take him. An animal like this one," he patted the sleek jaw, "chooses his own master. I think he has chosen you."

Quentin could not believe his ears. But the others sitting nearby agreed with Ronsard. Theido said, "Every brave knight should have a charger just as brave. Balder is the only horse for you, I think."

Durwin added, "You have grown much and have become a real horseman—very different from the young acolyte I found curled upon my hearth," he laughed, "who left his horse to fend for himself while he slept!"

Quentin colored with the memory, but he gratefully accepted the reins back from Ronsard and eagerly led his horse away to be bedded for the night.

The company ate a simple meal in silence, which Quentin thought unusual. There had not been a quiet mealtime among the high-spirited companions since they had sighted land. Queen Alinea did not even come out of her tent to eat, but remained within. Trenn ate quickly, grumbled, and left to attend to her.

One by one the others went away to their rest. Quentin knew something was wrong, but he did not have the heart or the nerve to ask outright what it was, feeling that it would only further dampen already depressed spirits. He wondered if the mood around the campfire was a reflection of his own of the last few days. He turned this over in his head as he lay under the low evergreen where Toli had prepared their places near the horses.

He rested, but he could not sleep. After a while the noises of the camp died down as the soldiers went to sleep. Quentin rose and returned to the fire where he found Durwin sitting all alone, stroking his beard and gazing into the dwindling flames.

"What is it?" he asked the hermit softly.

"Do you not know?" asked Durwin. His eyes did not leave the fire. "Go and see for yourself." He waved his arm toward the plain.

Quentin got up and made his way through the wood and came to stand at the very edge. There, spread out upon the plain, light from hundreds of fires twinkled like stars in the sky. For a moment he wondered what it could mean, but then the significance hit him. He felt a catch in his throat and a sharp pang arrowed through his chest. He stumbled disheartened back to the place where Durwin kept his vigil.

"There are thousands of them. Thousands . . ."

"So it is. I should have foreseen this. I should have known." He fell silent again.

"Why did they not swoop down upon us the moment we landed?" asked Quentin a few minutes later. He too had become absorbed in watching the fire, though his thoughts were very far away.

"I wondered the same thing. I have been thinking about it all night. Why not, indeed?

"I will tell you!" the hermit said suddenly. "They are waiting for someone. Yes, that must be it. They already possess the advantage of superior numbers; they could destroy us without delay. Yet, they hesitate. Why? Because someone's presence is required. A commander? Perhaps. But someone who must arrive before the battle begins."

It seemed perfectly obvious the way Durwin said it just then. Quentin wondered that he himself had not thought of it. His eyes sought Durwin's face, red in the glow of the fire's embers. Durwin seemed blind to the world as he sought an answer within the glowing coals. Quentin got up and placed another log on the fire, and presently yellow flames were flitting and crackling once more.

But the hermit remained unmoved, as if he were boring into the very heart of the earth for an answer. Quentin watched, his senses tingling. Gradually, Durwin's calm features were changing, little by little becoming a mask of terror.

At that moment Quentin felt the tingle of a chill, as if an icy finger had licked the length of his spine. He shivered in spite of himself.

With an effort Durwin tore his eyes away from the fire. He turned a horror-stricken countenance toward Quentin—flesh pale from the exertion, eyes showing white all around. "There. You felt it, too, just then. They are coming . . . the Legion of the Dead. They come."

Quentin's heart fluttered in his chest. He glanced toward the moon hanging ripe over the treetops, spilling a cold, comfortless light down upon them. To Quentin it seemed to have shrunk inward as if oppressed, or drawn back by some unseen hand. He shivered again.

Then Durwin was on his feet, grasping a long straight branch like a wizard's staff, his face frightful in the red light. "King Selric!" his voice boomed a summons in the quiet darkness. He strode toward the tent calling for the king and others to awaken.

"Send your swiftest rider to the south, to Hinsenby," he told the king who met him as he stumbled from his tent half-asleep.

"What is it?" The question came from all who had gathered instantly around the hermit. "What have you seen?" asked Theido.

"The Legion of the Dead. Send your swiftest courier to the coast. Mayhaps he shall meet with Eskevar's returning forces. It is our only chance."

"Help would be welcome in any case," replied Selric, "But this . . ."

"I am not afraid of Nimrood's foul Legion," swore Ronsard.

"That is because you do not know them," answered Durwin. He shook his head slowly, as if remembering a great tragedy. "They are terrible to behold: the greatest knights of the age. In death they serve him. Immortal. They cannot be killed in battle by blade or bolt. They fight and do not grow weary, for they are strengthened by the power of their dark lord."

"Then what good are numbers against them? Were we ten times as many could they be defeated?" Selric sighed, bewildered.

"With aid we may find an advantage. Without it we will not last long enough to try," said Ronsard.

"Kellaris will go," said Selric. "Call him," he ordered one of his men away. And to another he commanded, "Make ready a horse. The swiftest. Better give him my own." The man darted away and Selric turned to the others. "The choice agrees with you?"

"I would go," offered Ronsard.

"Stay, sir, we will need you here the more, most like."

"If his horse had wings, still I wonder if it were fast enough," said Theido. "How long do you think they will remain encamped on the plain yonder?" He turned to Durwin whose brow wrinkled in speculation.

"I cannot say for certain. A day I think. Yes, perhaps more. I can feel them coming, but they are a long way off. There is a little time yet."

"Then tomorrow at dawn Ronsard and I will ride out to scout the enemy's position," said Theido. "We may find a weakness in their defenses which we can turn to our advantage."

"Yes, an excellent idea." The impatient stamp of a horse and the jingle of his bridle interrupted Selric. "Ah! Here is Kellaris! Go with the wind, brave knight. Bring back good tidings."

"I would rather remain here with you, my King," the knight replied.

"And I would have no one else by my side. But the need is great. On your way and do not fail."

The knight raised his hand in salute and, turning the horse, leapt away and was lost in the darkness. For a long while Quentin imagined he could hear the horse's hooves pounding away in the night.

The others dispersed then, each his own way. Quentin sought Durwin's side as they walked back to the fire.

"What is the Legion of the Dead?" Quentin asked when they were once again seated before the dancing flames. "I have never heard of it before."

" 'Twere better no one ever heard of it." Durwin sighed. He had just about reached the depths of exhaustion. He licked his lips, as if about to bite into a bitter fruit.

"Nimrood's sorcery knows no bounds. He dares all and fears nothing. Where others quail he treads boldly. He has looked upon the face of evil from the time he was young. He has delved to the very heart of evil itself and has grasped it in his hand.

"He has long been about his specialty: weaving spells over the dead. With this art he has assembled the most skilled warriors, the most courageous knights the world has ever seen. When they fell in battle he somehow knew of it and, by one means or another, spirited the body away to his castle. There he keeps them, and has kept them ever ready, preserved in death to serve his will.

"There are six or seven of them, maybe more by now. I do not know. I have heard reports from time to time, but nothing for many years. I dared not even consider that such a thing was possible—even for Nimrood. But when we were there, in his dungeon, I felt their presence. I knew then . . ." Durwin's voice lapsed as he gazed into the fire, shrinking away from it as though from some hideous memory too horrible to contemplate.

"And you said nothing?"

"I said nothing. Selric, Theido, and the others already know about it, of course. There was no need to trouble anyone else. And I had hoped there was a chance that Nimrood would withhold them for some other purpose—though that, I admit, now seems rather foolish."

"Is there nothing to be done against them?"

"If there is, I do not know it—that is, short of Nimrood's death. If he were to die they would perhaps be released. It is his power which binds them still to this earth. But, as you saw yourself, the enemy is ten thousand strong. Against such odds—well, Nimrood is quite safe. Had I my power . . ." Durwin gazed forlornly into the fire. Quentin saw the depths of hopelessness written in the hermit's face.

Then Durwin stirred himself and stood slowly, smiling wanly at Quentin. "Still, I will watch through the night. It may be that I will discover something," he tapped his shaggy head, "that will be useful to us. Good night, Quentin."

"Good night." Quentin wanted to go to Durwin, to throw his arms around the priest's knees, to cry with him, to comfort him and be comforted. But he remained seated by the fire, and the hermit wandered off already deep in thought.

A loneliness crept over him as he sat before the snapping flames. When at last he arose to return to his bed, he felt more alone than he had ever felt in his life.

FORTY-SIX

THE SUN was a hazy red globe barely peeping above the far hills when Quentin awakened. He lay and listened to the beginning day: the lone call of a bird to its mate, the clank and rattle of iron pots in the hands of the cooks, the swish of the horses' tails and their gentle snuffling and snoring.

He lay and listened, sifting the sound for he knew not what, seeking an answer to the meaning of his dreams.

He had dreamed through the night. A strange, disjointed vision which he had dreamed before. But this time it was clearer more distinct than before, yet he was no closer to an answer to its riddle.

He saw it mostly as a play of color: brilliant greens of all shades infused with sparkling gold; cool white, flecked with green-gray splotches; silver-blue shadows deepening to utter black. The colors swirled and interchanged, mixing, melting into one another, but always ending in deepest darkness.

Through it all he heard a kind of music, a high-pitched ringing. A bell? Perhaps; he was not certain. Beneath the sound there lay something vague and unsettling. He cared not to look too far for its source for fear of what he might find.

The dream also carried with it a sharp feeling of longing, a beautiful loneliness, a yearning unrequited. It was an emotion which left a hollow feeling in his breast upon waking.

After some minutes he rolled himself up and went down to wash in the river. The water's chill sting quickened him fully, and he began by degrees to forget his dream, though the strange hollow feeling remained.

As Quentin dipped his cupped hands into the clear water, splashing it over his neck and arms, he heard a commotion in the camp behind him. He jumped up, dripping, from the flat rock on which he lay and hurried back along the trail.

He arrived as a large group gathered around a rider on a foaming horse. He could not see through the crowd who the rider could be. Then he caught sight of Toli hurrying away from the scene.

"Who is it, Toli? What is the news?"

His friend fixed him with a worried look. "It is Kellaris, King Selric's messenger. He has returned . . ."

"But how? He cannot have come back so soon."

"He did not get through," said a voice behind him. Quentin turned and met Trenn shuffling away from the crowd. "Jaspin has forces moving in on all sides. Kellaris met them in the night. He was pursued—there is no way out. We are trapped."

The words were a pronouncement of doom in Quentin's ears. Trenn stumbled off to inform Queen Alinea. Quentin turned again to Toli who merely stared back with his round, dark eyes. What the Jher was thinking made no impression on his face that Quentin could read.

He was about to suggest they go find some breakfast when he remembered something that stopped him where he stood. "Theido and Ronsard—where are they?" he asked.

Toli blinked back at him for a moment. "Why, they have gone to scout the enemy. They left before dawn with five knights. They rode to the south along the river."

"That is where Kellaris has just returned from!" Quentin said, a note of alarm rising in his voice. "They will be ambushed and killed! Someone must warn them! Quickly, ready Balder!"

At first Toli hesitated, as if to object to his master's command. He opened his mouth, then closed it again, turned and hurried off with Quentin on his heels.

In a twinkling Balder stood ready, and as Quentin bounded into the saddle of the mighty courser he saw Toli spring lightly onto his own mount's bare back. "Come along, then," cried Quentin. "We will go together."

They trotted through the camp from behind the ring of tents. Durwin and Selric were standing in conference with Kellaris, and Quentin called out to them as he spurred his horse away. "We go to warn Theido and Ronsard!"

"No! Wait!" shouted Durwin after them. King Selric barked an order. "Somebody stop them! Come back!"

But they were already bounding away through the woods and were gone. "The god be with them," sighed Durwin.

Toli led the way, following the trail of the scouting party with his tracker's sharp eyes. They rode, it seemed, for hours. The initial excitement of the moment quieted to a drumming sense of urgency. Quentin feared that if they did not find them soon, it would be too late.

The sun was up and throwing bright light into the wood, sending slanting rays of yellow beams through the ground mist which wafted over the path to vanish as it touched the light. The woods smelled of damp earth and growing things. A patch of mint grew somewhere nearby; its cool scent tinted the air as Balder moved on.

Then, just ahead, they heard a sound: horses moving through the underbrush, the clink of their harnesses and the soft creak of leather. The low tones of a rider talking with his companion came to them as Toli reined his spotted black and white to a halt. Quentin bumped up beside him. "Have we found them, do you think?" he asked hopefully.

Toli frowned. "We must find a place to see them where they cannot see us." He led them off the trail and around to a place where the trail would again pass in front of them. They waited. The unknown party came closer. Quentin could hear their voices, though he could not make out the words.

Toli slid from his mount and crept to the edge of the trail. Then they were within sight. Quentin could see a white shape moving through the trees, followed closely by another, and then another. As they approached Quentin lost sight of them; the surrounding trees which protected him cut them off from view.

Quietly he urged Balder forward a few steps. The dark leaves shaded his face. Toli stood beside him.

The riders, four in all, had stopped in a small clearing along the trail. They seemed to be looking for something. One of their party was kneeling along the path and the others swung their eyes through the surrounding trees, as if seeking a sign.

"The enemy," whispered Toli.

They had run into a party of Jaspin's men who were evidently searching for someone. "They are after Theido and the others," answered Quentin. "Come. We may reach them ahead of these hunters." With that he turned Balder and drew away from their hiding place along the path. They dodged along the track for a while and then rejoined it far ahead of the enemy soldiers behind them. No sooner had they joined the path and proceeded a little along it when they again heard the sounds of horses and men moving just ahead of them. "This will be Theido!" said Quentin, a smile lighting his face.

He spurred Balder ahead and came around a tree-lined bend in the trail. Suddenly they were face to face with five strange knights, coming directly toward them on the trail.

Quentin froze. Toli turned his horse aside and pulled Quentin's arm. At first the unknown knights did not seem to see them. They came on a pace or two, talking among themselves, eyes down along the track.

Then, even as Quentin turned Balder off the path, one of the riders glanced up. Quentin met the other's eyes and in the briefest instant read the surprise there.

"Look!" the enemy knight shouted to his companions. But Quentin, with Toli ahead of him, was already dashing away.

"Spies!" he heard another shout. A third yelled, "After them! We must not let them get away."

Toli was already a blur bobbing ahead of him as Quentin flung himself forward. Balder put his head down and leaped off the trail. Quentin ducked the branches which struck out to unhorse him, keeping himself low in the saddle, laying along Balder's surging shoulders.

Behind him he could hear the sound of pursuit through the tangled woods. Voices rang out sharp and steel-edged in the quiet morning air. Toli shot fleeting glances over his hunched shoulders to make sure that Quentin was keeping up.

Balder's iron hooves flung the soft turf high into the air. Brambles snatched at Quentin's bare legs, scratching them, though he did not feel a thing.

On they rode, dashing ahead of their pursuers, flying over fallen trunks of trees and dodging low-hanging limbs.

Quentin heard a crash behind him, the high whinny of a horse, and a curse. One of the knights had been swept off his horse by a branch. There was a shout as another knight sought to avoid piling into the sprawling rider. Quentin turned slightly to see a horse struggling to its feet and a knight rolling in the grass. He smiled darkly to himself.

But when he turned back Toli was nowhere to be seen.

He reined Balder to a shuddering halt, almost pitching himself forward. For a heartbeat he stopped to listen and heard nothing. Then came the swish of brush and the hollow clop of Toli's mount darting through the wood just ahead and to the left. He had dodged onto another track.

Quentin leaned and threw the reins to the side and Balder reared back, gathering his legs beneath him. He snorted and jumped. From somewhere Quentin heard a whistling in the air and suddenly felt a piercing sting in his leg. Balder screamed and jolted away.

He turned in the direction of the sound and saw one of the knights lowering a crossbow from his shoulder, making ready to load and shoot again.

He glanced down at his leg to see the crossbow's bolt sticking out from the side of his leg. The vicious dart had arrowed through the fleshy part of his calf and had stuck in Balder's thick-muscled shoulder. He was pinned neatly to his horse.

Balder, urged by the sting, and lacking a direct command from Quentin, dashed off in the opposite direction from Toli. Quentin squeezed his eyes shut as the pain exploded in his brain in a burning flash of red brilliance.

Balder raced through the forest, his mane and tail streaming out behind him. Quentin fought to stay in the saddle. The great courser had his own head now and plummeted along a sharply descending trail.

The swiftly passing wood began to blur. The bright blue sky and yellow sun, the dark green earth and gray tree trunks all melded together. Behind him he could hear the shouts of the knights urging their steeds to the chase. But the sounds diminished and faded as Balder, running freely, outdistanced them with his great strides.

The trail turned and fell away. Quentin thought they must be near the river again, but he did not know which direction they were heading. A narrow brook lay directly before him—he heard it rather than saw it as Balder sailed over it and galloped up the bank.

The charger pounded along the path, and through eyes bleary with pain Quentin noticed the forest deepen, becoming darker and more dense. They were flying into the heart of Pelgrin. Quentin recognized the venerable old oaks spreading their branches above him. The light shone down green around them through the leaves which formed a living thatch overhead.

Then, without warning, dead ahead of them in the trail, an earthen embankment jutted out of the forest floor like a green wall topped by thick, wiry holly hedge. There was no time to stop. Quentin threw himself forward and clenched the reins in his hands as he gritted his teeth.

Lightly as a deer Balder lifted himself up into the air and sailed over the top, the hedges barely brushing his belly. The animal recovered from the jump gracefully as he skidded down the opposite side of the embankment and into a large ringed depression, a vast hollow bowl carved in the middle of the forest. There he stopped.

Quentin hung limply to his reins, spun in the saddle, and with an effort seized the bolt projecting cruelly out of his leg.

He pulled with a force and felt the dart give to his grasp. Another tug and it was wrenched free. Quentin straightened and before he could see where he was, black, formless shapes gathered before his eyes. He felt suddenly lightheaded. He could not breathe. He gasped, reeled in the saddle, and then toppled to the ground.

He saw Balder's dark eye regarding him with a calm, liquid stare. The sky spun. Then all went black.

FORTY-SEVEN

DURWIN sat with his head in his hands upon a log. It had been hours since Quentin and Toli had raced off into the wood alone. He feared the worst.

"Ease your fears, good hermit," Alinea said lightly. "It is you who say we are to trust in all things. We will trust their safety, as we trust our own, to the god."

"Your words are true, my Lady," answered Durwin, raising his eyes to her lovely face. "But my heart hears not."

"But look!" she said, springing up. "Here is something! Riders are coming in! Theido and Ronsard! They have returned, alive and safe!"

"Yes, that is good news," said Durwin rising slowly. He walked over to where a group was already gathering to hear what the scouts had to report. In a moment Durwin's hopeful expression was once again exchanged for one of despair.

Theido came through the crush without speaking; Ronsard

followed close behind. "Come," he said. "Let us go to Selric's tent. You come too, my Lady."

They gathered in Selric's tent where they found the monarch pouring over detailed maps of the area drawn on skins and parchment.

"You are back, the gods be thanked! What news? What did you find?"

"Nothing good," replied Ronsard. His face was flushed and sweat trickled down his neck into his tunic. "We have ridden far and find that all approaches are cut off. We are surrounded."

"Jaspin is strengthening his forces on all sides."

King Selric received the information with calm acceptance. "I see," he said.

"So it is!" said Durwin. "No more than we already know."

"What?" demanded Theido.

"Kellaris returned just after dawn," replied King Selric evenly. "He did not get through. Your words confirm his own." He pointed to the maps. "I have been studying these charts to see if there may be some vantage we may defend." He sighed heavily. "I find none."

"What will happen?" asked Alinea. Her voice, though steady, held a note of anguish.

"We will fight them," said Theido simply. "They mean to destroy us. That is certain. Jaspin will offer no mercy. He has not left us even a means of honorable retreat."

"He means to cut us down where we stand," said Ronsard, hotly.

"When?" asked Alinea.

"That I cannot say," replied Theido. "The enemy is still building his position. He may attack at any moment."

"Nimrood's dread Legion has not yet arrived," replied Durwin. "That is what they are waiting for."

"I have put my men to work excavating a ditch just beyond the trees. It may be they will have time to finish it. That will offer some defense," said King Selric. "We must keep our backs protected in order to retreat to the ships when the time comes."

"Must we talk of retreat so soon?" demanded Ronsard. "I will die rather than retreat."

"Yes, of course," replied Selric evenly. "I was thinking of the Queen." He glanced at Alinea's dark eyes which flashed defiantly. "I am sorry, my Lady . . ."

"I will fight side by side with my comrades, and die with them if necessary. I will not fly. If my King has not life left in him, of what use is my crown? Without my King I am no Queen and there is no kingdom. I will fight."

The stouthearted companions looked to one another around the tight circle, silently pledging their lives to the cause. "Then it is settled," said Theido softly.

At that moment a shout went up from the men outside and a messenger came running. King Selric stepped from his tent to receive the runner. "The enemy approaches, sire. They march hither—half a league distant."

"To arms! To arms!" Selric bellowed. He called to his trumpeter. "Sound the alarm! Call the men to arms!"

Within moments the scene was a flurry of flashing steel and shouting voices as the king's men took up sword and shield and the knights buckled on their armor.

"Assemble the knights before me!" shouted Theido above the tumult. "I have a plan that may buy us time." He himself had donned his armor in a flash and was standing before the king's tent with shield slung over his shoulder, his sword raised high in the air.

In a few minutes the furious activity subsided. The soldiers ranged themselves behind the earthen wall they had that morning constructed and lined with sharpened pikes. The knights under Theido and Ronsard's command, sixty in all, formed two groups which would take up positions to the right and to the left as the enemy approached the field of battle. It was Theido's plan to cross these two mobile forces back and forth between each other, scissorlike, and thus wear down the enemy, blunting his attack before he could reach the footmen behind the ditch.

King Selric commanded the footmen and, with Trenn, kept

watch over the Queen, despite her protests. For her part, she appeared hard of nerve and eye, armed with a slim sword and a buckler, more fitted to her hand than the heavier shields of the knights. She wore a corselet of plaited mail and a helm with a visor, as did all the king's men-at-arms.

They waited.

Far in the distance could be heard the trumpets of King Jaspin's army signalling their convergence. Dust from horses and tramping feet spiraled up into the noonday sky. Bright banners fluttering on long poles and pennons streaming from the lances of the knights, the far-off glint of a blade drawn, the sun's rays catching the visor of a helmet: these could be seen by the soldiers awaiting the clash.

Closer. The steady thump of the drums and the rumble of five thousand soldiers marching as one carried on the wind. The sun darkened under the cloud of dust sent up by the advancing soldiers. Carrion birds soared overhead, gathering for a feast.

Trenn twisted his stout neck around, sniffing the wind. "There it is!" he muttered to King Selric. "I knew I smelled something. Look yonder."

The first faint wisps of smoke drifted overhead. Selric noted the condition with a quick nod. "They burn the forest behind us." He gripped the pommel of his sword tighter in his grasp. "So be it!"

"Where is Durwin?" asked the Queen, looking around. "I have not seen him."

"I saw him making off behind the tents. I do not see him now," answered Trenn. "He will be up to his tricks if I know him."

The tempo of the drums increased. A mighty shout arose from the plain.

"They come!" cried King Selric. He flourished his sword in the air above his curly red head. "For honor! For glory! For King and Kingdom!" His soldiers returned the battle cry.

The swiftly advancing front was a wedge of knights on horseback racing ahead of the larger body of men on foot who hurried behind. The rest of the assembled armies held back, waiting for their turn to bolt into the fray.

As the wedge thundered down upon the waiting troops, a shout went up from the woods on either side. Theido and Ronsard and their knights darted forth and caught the hurtling chargers in midflight. They came on from both sides at once; the advancing knights did not have time to turn or even to meet them as one. The charge faltered and then dissolved in confusion. Horses went down, rolling over their heavily armored riders.

Theido and Ronsard closed the gap and leaped to the attack. Instantly the heavens were rent with the ring of swords and the cries of the dying.

The footmen, seeing their advancing protection stymied, fell upon themselves and drew back. Theido turned his force after them as Ronsard contended with Jaspin's knights. Many went down into the dust, never to rise again.

Jaspin's warriors buckled before the fury of Ronsard's knights and retreated, leaving half their number upon the ground.

Theido and Ronsard quickly called off the attack and rode back to the ditch to the cheers of the soldiers waiting there.

"Did you see them?" asked Selric anxiously.

"No, the Legion was not among them," answered Theido.

"Where are they?"

"Most likely, they will wait to see how we acquit ourselves on the field," answered Ronsard, raising his visor. "We surprised them just now; we may not be so lucky again. But I have a trick I learned before Gorr." They fell into a quick discussion, then the knights mounted their coursers once more.

"Remember," called Theido. "Tell your men to watch for any of the Legion. Stay out of their reach; melt before them and attack behind them. I think the soldiers will try to use them as protection and follow in their wake."

Theido and his contingent ranged themselves behind Ronsard's knights, one group forming a wall in front of the other. Then they waited.

The second attack came shortly. Two groups of knights charged, expecting to be met from either side as before. Instead, they encountered a wall of armored bodies waiting placidly for their onslaught. The foot soldiers advanced behind them over the dead upon the field.

As soon as the hurtling knights realized they were not going to be met on the flanks as before, they swerved inward and changed course to meet Ronsard's wall. It was the precise moment Ronsard sought. He called a charge and dived to the left, followed by Theido who dived to the right at the last instant.

The charging horses were once again thrown into confusion, carrying their riders headlong into the ditch and the sharpened pikes which seemed to spring up before them like quills. King Selric's men there made short work of them.

Theido and Ronsard fell once more upon the men-at-arms and punished them severely. Once more Jaspin's troops staggered back before the fury of their hungry swords.

"Twice we have turned them away," beamed Ronsard when they had again rejoined before the king. "What scheme can we hold to next to beat them back?"

"I have one," replied Theido. Even after two sallies he was scarcely breathing hard. "If they send not too many among us it may work."

Again the charge came, and again the small cohort was successful in disadvantaging the superior forces of Jaspin and his nobles. When they at last withdrew, the field of battle lay cluttered with fallen men and horses. The ground beneath them was stained dark with their blood.

In a pavilion of blue sendal constructed above the field on a high scaffold so to command the best view of the battle sat King Jaspin upon his traveling throne, sputtering with rage.

"Sir Bran! Sir Grenett!" Jaspin shouted, his face blackened with anger. "Lord Orwen! Lord Enmore!" The knights and nobles, grimy with sweat and dirt, their armor bearing deep gashes and crimson smudges, approached the pavilion on horseback.

Jaspin leaped out of his seat and threw a shaking finger into their faces. "You fools!" he screamed. "They are making sport of you! Cut them down! Crush them!"

" 'Twere easier to crush a stone, than a stream," answered Sir Bran. "Or to cut down a sapling as a shadow."

"They do not stand and fight," complained Sir Grenett. "They vanish before the charge and appear in our midst. They have our bumbling, ill-trained foot soldiers attacking one another."

"Do something! Soon Nimrood will be here, and I had hoped to win this campaign on my own."

"It is too late," whispered Ontescue from behind him. "He of whom you speak is already here." Jaspin turned to see the black shape of Nimrood ride around the far side of his pavilion. The necromancer sat astride a black horse that looked half wild and pawed the ground as it snorted. Nimrood wore a black, crowned helm with wings sweeping back from either side, and a long black cloak edged with silver. In his hand he carried a rod of ebony marble inlaid with silver tracery in strange, convoluted patterns.

"Nimrood!" said Jaspin. His breath rattled in his throat. "We were waiting for you."

"Were you indeed? I see dead stacked upon the field like kindling—they died of boredom, no doubt."

"The fiends attacked us without warning. We had to retaliate. Th-there was no choice," Jaspin stuttered.

"From the look of it, I would say they displayed the most remarkable luck," the sorcerer sneered. "A thousand attacking ten thousand and holding them at bay. Ha!" Nimrood turned stiffly in his high-backed saddle and spat out orders to the knights and nobles gathered before the pavilion.

"Go back to your men at once. Nurse their courage, revive their spirit. And wait. When I return I will bring my Legion to show you how to fight. I go now to bring my commander."

"He is here?" Jaspin gasped and sank back into his throne limp and trembling.

"Close by," hissed Nimrood. "I return within the hour. Meanwhile, do nothing. This battle will be over ere long. It should have been finished long ago. But never mind. You will all see a spectacle you will never forget."

With that the wizard spurred his jittery steed forward and galloped off across the plain and into the wood beyond.

"What is this Legion that the mad magician speaks of, sire?" asked Sir Bran. "Why should we wait? We can finish them now, ourselves. The victory is ours!"

Jaspin waved the suggestion aside with a damp hand. His jaw hung slack and his eyes remained focused on some far distant view. When he came to his senses he looked around feebly and said, "You will see soon enough. You will all see soon enough."

"We can finish them this time. I know it," insisted Bran.

"No!" shouted Jaspin, leaping to his feet. Spittle drooled from his lips; he looked like an enraged bull. "It is too late! Too late! We will wait!" He waved them away and hunched back into his throne. He passed a kerchief over his face and gestured for Ontescue to draw the curtain of his pavilion for privacy. He would wait alone.

"Oh!" he cried out in utter anguish. Sobs racked his body. "What have I done? What have I done?"

FORTY-EIGHT

FROM SOMEWHERE far away Quentin heard the sharp tinkling of bells, high pitched and floating overhead, as if the sound was carried on the wind. And another sound—a low murmur, like laughter.

Light danced above him; he could trace its movement through his eyelids. He felt warm and dreamy, and realized that something was tickling his cheek and the hollow of his neck.

He opened his eyes.

For the briefest instant he thought he must be back at Dekra. The feeling passed even as it formed. Above him a green canopy caught the sun and dashed its golden light into a thousand shifting patterns. The bells he had heard were tiny twittering birds flittering from branch to branch in the great, spreading oak upon whose roots he lay. He absently placed his hand to his cheek and brought it away wet. Then he turned and saw Balder lower his nose to nudge him once more.

"All right, old boy. I am awake," Quentin murmured.

He pushed himself up slowly on his elbows. In a few seconds the dizziness subsided, to be replaced by a dull, throbbing ache which spread throughout his body, but seemed localized in his left leg. He felt the leg, suddenly remembering how he came to be lying on the ground gazing up at the leafy roof above.

The wound had stopped bleeding and the blood had dried. Quentin surmised that he had been unconscious for some time. He reached out a hand and grabbed a strap of Balder's harness and hoisted himself to his feet. With a little effort he found he could walk, though stiffly at first and with some pain.

He scanned his surroundings. Though utterly strange to him, he felt the place was familiar somehow. Yet he knew he had never seen it before. He was, as near as he could make out, at one side of a gigantic earthen ring. His eyes followed the smooth grassy embankment around its circumference until he lost it behind a stand of ancient oaks which occupied the center of the ring.

All around the inside of the circle stood white carven stones, thick slabs as tall as Quentin, now pockmarked with age and flecked with green and gray lichen.

The standing stones threw shadows upon the lawn at odd angles as some of the stones were tilted and leaning precariously.

His eyes swept inward and only then noticed the mysterious mounds standing like so many gigantic, grass-covered beehives. All was peaceful; all quiet. But Quentin felt a thrill of something like fear race up the back of his neck and set his scalp tingling.

He *had* been here before: in his dream.

He had seen it all in his dream; and not once but many times.

It appeared very different, to be sure; the reality formed the opposite side of the coin. But it was the same coin—of that Quentin was certain. The inner feeling of remembrance told him as much.

But where was he? And what were the odd-shaped earthen beehives?

All sense of urgency—still nagging at the back of his mind—diminished in light of the singular feeling which washed over him like a cold stream. Quentin stood gazing around him. *I am supposed to be here,* he thought aloud.

Leaving Balder to nibble the grass at the base of the oak, Quentin hobbled toward the center of the ring, descending down into the bowl. It was ancient; he could see that. The cracked faces of the standing stones were worn, the inscriptions nearly obliterated by time and the elements.

Whoever had made it, Quentin was sure, had lived long ago. Back in the age of the mysterious mound builders, perhaps. Remnants of the mound builders' work still existed, tucked away in far corners of the land. Spirals, hillocks, rings—queer shapes all.

He heard a gurgling sound and the splash of water trickling over stone. He parted a leafy bower and stepped into a shaded spot where a small spring bubbled, pouring up its water into a clear, gemlike pool. Quentin knelt and dipped his cupped hand into the icy liquid. He drank and noticed the white stones placed around the perimeter of the pool, and just above the pool where the spring delivered its water the shrine to the god of the spring. A carved stone image of the god the peasants called Pol stood in the shrine. Once he would have poured a libation to the god, but Quentin merely nodded to the idol's perpetual stare and continued again on his way.

He made for the nearest mound and examined it carefully. Grass-covered, it stood at twice his height, perfectly smooth and symmetrical on all sides.

Some of the mounds, he could see now, were larger than others. And some had a slightly flattened or sunken appearance at the dome, as if they had collapsed within—the way graves sometimes do.

Graves. He held the word on his tongue and turned it over as if hearing it for the first time. Then, as sunlight slowly chased the night, he knew where he was. Quentin had stumbled into the Ring of the Kings, or the Kings' Ring, as it was sometimes called in stories and songs. It was the ancient burial place of Mensandor's first kings; the empire builders were buried here, their barrows dug within the ring. It was a most sacred place.

Quentin paused and then turned to make his way back painfully to Balder and then away. But something held him to the spot. He shrugged off his unaccountable reluctance and moved on, turning back again not four paces from where he had stopped before.

A thought came to him. If he was to make it back to camp alive he would need a weapon of some sort, at least a shield. The kings were customarily buried with their armor and weapons—outfitted for their trials in the underworld.

Surely, he thought, there would be no harm in obtaining a sword or shield from one of the barrows. Though taboo, and likely to upset the spirits of the dead—neither problem Quentin held in any great regard—he decided to try and find a weapon.

The first barrow he examined had no entrance that he could find, nor did the second or the third. Whatever means of entering the vaults had been contrived, they had long ago grown over, or had been carefully erased.

He was about to give up and return to Balder when he saw a large barrow situated in the midst of the others. Very well, he would try just one more, he thought. He limped toward it, moving between the eerie mounds like a giant passing between green-domed mountains.

The barrow which had caught his attention was different from the others he had examined—rounder, a more gentle arc all around, as if the tip of a large sphere bulged from below ground. He walked around it and neatly tripped over a small bush growing at the base of the shaded side of the hill.

He fell, plunging headlong to the turf and banging his injured left leg on the ground. Quentin winced in pain as he slammed down and felt something hard give way beneath him. There was an odd muffled crack, like the tearing of a root, and Quentin tumbled into the yawning blackness which had suddenly opened up beneath him.

He let out a surprised yell as he landed upon something hard. He coughed and sputtered in the dirt that caved in around him and wiped the dust from his eyes as small pebbles rattled away below him.

When the dust had cleared and he had taken stock of himself, Quentin saw that he had not fallen very far—less than three paces. The sunlight slanted down into the crevice he had opened up and illuminated a small patch of the floor on which he was standing. He saw one straight edge and then darkness: steps. He had stumbled into the entrance of the burial place which someone had been at great pains to conceal.

Steadying his quivering nerves, Quentin stepped cautiously down onto the step and then the next. The steps fell away sharply, and Quentin soon found himself in complete darkness, except for the patch of light through the hole where he had fallen. He thrust his hands out in front of him and continued.

The stairs stopped after only a few more steps and Quentin, his eyes becoming used to the darkness now, perceived a stone door barring the entrance to the subterranean chamber. The door, black with age, was carved with the intricate designs and runes of the ancients. Yet, from chips and scratches which showed white in the dim light along the left side of the narrow slab, he could see that someone had used tools to pry open the tomb's door, and not so very long ago.

Quentin placed his palms on the cool moist rock and pushed. Unexpectedly, the door moved with very little effort, grinding open on its unseen hinges.

He stepped into the tomb.

The interior of the tomb was cool and silent. In the feeble light of the open door, Quentin saw the glint of gold and silver vessels stacked along the walls. The dust of time lay thick upon the floor, dimming the colored mosaic tiles which there proclaimed in quaint pictures the exploits of the deceased monarch. A row of silver-tipped spears and bearskin shields—now mouldering to ashes—stood in ranks to his left. A saddle, with a horse's bard and chamfron supported by crossed lances, stood on his right.

Whatever else lay in the ancient burial vault Quentin never discovered. For his eyes found the stone table standing in the center of the chamber. And there, still and serene, as if in peaceful slumber, lay King Eskevar, his form bathed in an eerie blue luminescence.

Though Quentin had never seen his King, he knew in his heart he had found him, for it could be no one else. The bearded chin jutted up defiantly; the smooth, high brow suggested wisdom; the deep-set eyes, closed in repose, spoke of character; and the straight firm mouth of royalty.

Quentin, in a daze of wondrous disbelief, slowly approached the stone bier as one walking in a dream. The figure before him, dressed in shining armor, its arms folded across its unmoving chest, appeared the picture of death itself. And yet . . .

Quentin, holding his breath, stepped closer, daring not to breathe for fear that the vision before him might prove too insubstantial.

One step and then another and he would be there.

With a trembling foot he took the step. Shifting his weight, he raised his foot . . .

Something moved behind him. He felt the air rush by him, heard a metallic whisper, and caught the flash of two glowing points of yellow light arcing through the air as he instinctively turned to meet the blow and then he was struck down.

FORTY-NINE

THE BATTLEFIELD had grown as quiet as the dead men upon it. A hush crept over the plain which still echoed with the ring of steel and the cries of warriors. The carrion birds soared above, searching for an opportunity to begin their gruesome feast; their cries pierced the silence which now covered Askelon Plain like a shroud.

In respite from battle, the wounded had been carried from the field and taken to the river where Selric's surgeons offered what aid and comfort could be given. Those still able to bear sword or pike were bandaged and returned to the ditch to await the next onslaught.

Durwin, arms bared and robes drawn up between his legs and tucked in his belt, hurried among the litters to aid with word or skill as many as he could. Wherever he went the pain was eased and healing begun. Those who could not recover were comforted and their passage to the next world lighted with hope.

As he bent over the unconscious form of a soldier lying on the grassy river bank, Durwin felt a tug at his belt. He turned away from his patient to see a young man, sweaty and besmeared with blood, motioning him away.

"What is it, lad?" asked the hermit.

"A knight yonder would see you, sir," replied the young physician.

"Then take me to him," replied Durwin, and they both hurried off through the ranks of wounded lying along the bank.

"Here is the holy hermit, sir knight. I have brought him as you bade me." The boy bent close to the knight's ear. Durwin, thinking that he had come too late, for so it appeared, was surprised to see the knight awaken and the clear blue eyes regard him knowingly.

"They tell me I must die," said the knight. He was a young man, not yet beyond his twentieth year. "What say you?"

Durwin bent to examine the wound, an ugly, jagged slash in his side where an axe had sliced through his hauberk and driven pieces of his mail deep into his flesh. He shook his head slowly.

"Yes, 'tis true. The wound is mortal, brave friend. How may I help you?"

"It is as I feared," said the knight. His voice was growing weaker. "I have watched you going among the wounded and have seen you comfort men in screaming agony and calm those whom Manes had purchased."

"I do what I can," said Durwin softly.

"Then tell me what I must know of death, for I am not a religious man. It is said that you can look into the world beyond, sir. Look for me and tell me what you see."

Durwin, though he already knew what he would tell the young knight, bowed his head and closed his eyes as he placed one hand over the knight's heart. After a moment he began to speak.

"I see two paths that may be taken—one into darkness and one into light. The dark path is an unhappy one. There is no peace to be found wherever it does lead, and those who travel thereon never find rest or comfort for their soul's pain. It is a lonely, bitter road.

"The other way, the road of light, leads to a magnificent city wherein all who come rejoice in the presence of a loving king who reigns forever without end. It is a realm of peace where hardship and death are conquered, and none who abide there know fear anymore.

"These two paths are open to you, but you must choose now which one you will tread."

"The choice is easily made, good hermit. I would go to the great city and there pledge my service to the honorable king. If he has need of such as I, there would I be. But I know not how this may be accomplished, and fear I may yet go wrong."

"Worry not on it. Only believe and it will be so. Believe in the king, the King of all kings, and God Most High. He will meet you on the path and lead you himself into his city."

"Sir, I do want to believe. But your words are strange. They are unlike any words I have ever heard a priest speak. Are you a priest?"

"Yes, fair friend. I am a priest of the king I have told you about. He turns none aside who would come to him; it is a promise he makes to all men."

"Then I go to him at once." The knight's voice was a whisper. "Thank you, good hermit. I shall remember this kindness and shall greet your King for you. Farewell."

"Farewell, brave sir. We shall meet again."

At these words the knight closed his eyes and breathed his last. Durwin stood over the young man's body and marvelled at his courage and the firmness of his faith. "The Most High has won a faithful servant this day," he said to himself. "And none more valiant."

When Durwin had done all he could for the wounded and dying he returned to the ditch where Selric, Theido, and Ronsard stood in council.

"We have lost many good men," said Ronsard. "We cannot withstand another attack if they choose to make an end of it."

"Why do they wait?" wondered Selric. "Perhaps they will not challenge us again."

"No," said Theido. "They will come again. They are waiting for—"

"Waiting for Nimrood to bring his foul brood," said Durwin as he joined them. "They have not yet come. But they are close by."

"Then Jaspin hoped to win the day for himself without Nimrood?"

"So it is! But now he will be forced to acknowledge Nimrood as his master before all who call him king."

"It is no better than he deserves," observed Ronsard. "I believe he will yet rue the day he ever laid eyes upon that sorcerer."

"This waiting is worse than the fighting. Is there nothing we can do?" asked Selric.

"Yes," said Durwin. "Pray to the Most High. He is the only one who can save us now."

The unseen blow caught Quentin as he rolled away, grazing his shoulder and lifting him off his feet. He was flung headlong into the darkness to land sprawling on the floor of the tomb.

He squirmed to his knees in an effort to rise, pulling himself along the edge of the stone bier. But before he could regain his feet he felt something pulling him back, dragging him down with a sinuous weight. Something hard grasped him by the waist. Quentin grabbed at it and touched a smooth, yet rigid surface undulating under his grasp.

A wave of horror and revulsion swept through him as he realized that he was locked in the crushing coils of a gigantic serpent.

A coil shot around his arms, binding them to his sides. Another loop wrapped itself across his chest, and Quentin, struggling feebly to free himself, saw the terrible angular head rise slowly up before his face.

Hideous yellow eyes burned with an unearthly light, regarding him with extreme menace. He could feel the coils tightening around him, squeezing the breath from his body.

His hands scrabbled for a hold on the heavy scales of the serpent's skin; his nails raked the snaky armor ineffectually. Each breath was a labor fraught with pain now. Very soon he would suffocate. He heard the rasping hiss of the snake as it leered closer, showing cruel double rows of needle-like teeth and two great curving fangs.

Quentin's mind raced in a frenzy verging on panic. There

must be a weapon, he thought. Lifting his eyes, which felt as if they would burst from the pressure of the serpent's ever-tightening embrace, he chanced to see the shimmer of the King's sword lying at his side along the slab.

Quentin, growing weaker by the heartbeat, threw himself onto his side beneath the bier. The coils shifted momentarily as he went down. He gulped air and forced his arm free before the relentless coils squeezed again.

Slowly drawing his feet up under him, Quentin placed them against the stone trestle of the King's bier. With a kick he sent himself tumbling heels over head as the serpent, hissing with a fury, struck.

Quentin heard the monstrous jaws snap shut just above his ear. But he had gained his objective. His free arm was now on top as he lay on his side. He raised it toward the sword.

The serpent noticed the movement. A lashing tail flicked out and lashed a coil around Quentin's wrist and pulled it down in an iron grip.

In the shimmering glow of the blue radiance Quentin saw the awful outline of the black head rearing again, readying for the killing strike.

Forcing every fiber of muscle to obey, he lifted his hand once more. His fingers ached as he stretched them toward the sword. He felt the serpent squeezing his wrist; his fingers became numb. He closed his eyes and cried out with the effort, feeling that his heart would rend. Then he felt the edge of the bier under his grasp. He held on.

Inch by precious inch he clawed forward, his finger nails splitting as they tore against the stone. He could no longer breathe. His arm shook violently. Dizziness overwhelmed him, but he fought to remain clearheaded.

Then, miraculously, the sword was in his hand. He grasped the cold steel blade and pulled it down. But his strength was gone. He could not raise the sword or strike out with it. Instead, the honed blade lay in his benumbed hand, and he merely looked at it glinting in the darkness as he felt the black mists of death gathering over him.

in Jaspin's ears like the clang of a funeral knell. The pale usurper winced and shrank away from the black knight's address.

"The day is ours!" shouted the necromancer boldly, so all gathered on the plain could hear. Then, turning to Jaspin he said, "Look upon the face of death, and despair!"

Jaspin watched in horror—his heart trembled within his breast, his blood ran to ice in his veins—as the appalling spectre placed a black gauntlet to its visor and slowly raised it. Jaspin closed his eyes and looked away.

"See my handiwork!" cried the wizard.

Jaspin turned again to meet the apparition's gray, bloodless face. And as he cowered before it, the knight's ashen lids slowly opened to regard Jaspin with a chilling stare. Jaspin gripped the carved arms of his throne and uttered a low cry: the knight had no eyes!

"Away!" sobbed Jaspin.

Durwin turned his face into the streaming wind. His knowing eyes watched the great black clouds rolling over the plains of Askelon and regarded the sky growing murky as the unnatural, gloomy twilight descended upon the battlefield.

"Nimrood has arrived. He is here, and his Legion with him," said the hermit. "We must ready ourselves for the final assault."

"I am ready," said Ronsard. His strong tone held no trace of fear. "I have faced death many times: he is too old an adversary for me to quail in his sight now."

"Well said, noble Ronsard," replied Theido. "I, too, am ready. Come what may, I see glory waiting for us all out there." He nodded with eyes squinted toward the plain. "I mean to earn my share."

"Aye," agreed King Selric, "and a place in men's hearts wherever deeds of valor are storied round the fire."

Alinea, who had been long silent, now lifted her eyes to the horizon and looked her last upon the shimmering shape of Askelon's far walls, misty in the distance. Trenn, his mouth set in a defiant frown, stood resolutely beside her.

"I am a woman," said the Queen softly, "and no soldier. But for the love of my King I will gladly stand beside my gallant comrades till the enemy's cruel blade sends my spirit to its rest."

Trenn said nothing, but his thick neck bulged as he tightened his grip on his sword and touched its hilt to his heart.

Toli, who had returned from the forest after searching fruitless hours for his missing master, grasped a long bow and notched an arrow onto the taut gut. Beneath his dark aspect a smoldering fire kindled against those who had cut his master down.

Into the stillness that had settled over the plain the comrades-at-arms heard the growl of distant thunder marching through the heavens toward them. King Selric took his place at the head of his soldiers and sprang up onto a rock to address them, raising his hands and voice into the air.

"Men of Drin, my warriors! Hear me! You have made me proud to be your king, and though our time grows short, I would ask no greater boon than to lead you into battle one last time.

"The enemy is great, but though he break our bodies he will never vanquish the proud spirit that strengthens us to our end. Fight well, my friends. Look not behind, but look ahead. Glory and honor will you earn this day. Be worthy of it. Be strong. Be not afraid."

The soldiers, still as statues, now raised sword and spear, and with a mighty shout a thousand voices rang out, "For glory! For honor! For our King!"

Then, taking their swords, they began to beat upon their shields and sing a battle song, chanting to the rhythmic cadence. With Selric in the lead, they ranged themselves into the shape of a spearhead and marched out upon the plain, there to await the foe.

Theido and Ronsard took their knights and drew up beside their fearless comrades, flanking either side of the formation. The war horses tossed their heads and snorted as the wind gusted smoke from the burning woods across the battlefield.

Again they heard the sound of drums as the enemy came forth. Theido looked round to catch the eye of Durwin to bid his friend a last farewell, but saw that the hermit had vanished again.

Then, through the smoke rolling across the plain, the enemy emerged once more. This time they were led in close procession by the six black riders of Nimrood's Legion of the Dead.

They stopped. The drums quickened their tempo. The six lowered their lances, and at the trumpet's blast they spurred their chargers forward.

The Legion flew across the plain, their horses' hooves striking sparks as they hurtled across the gap. Behind them came the knights of Jaspin's forces, followed by the foot soldiers who now began to run with a mighty shout.

King Selric's army, rattling sword upon shield, steeled themselves for the clash. Theido and Ronsard launched their coursers to meet the charge.

There was an enormous crash. The earth trembled with the shock.

Dust billowed up to shroud the combatants from view. Horses screamed and the cold clang of steel rang out. When the dust parted Selric saw that Theido and Ronsard and their riders had succeeded in lancing through their opponents with but little hurt to their numbers; what is more, they had succeeded in unhorsing one of the Legion. His horse lay screaming in agony on the field, but he on foot came on.

Theido, ignoring the sable knights, turned his attack inward upon the more assailable enemy. Jaspin's own knights, surprised at this strategy, nevertheless joined battle with the onrushing knights. Instantly, all were surrounded by the foot soldiers who thronged to the fight.

"Away!" cried King Selric, and the trumpeter sounded the call as the stalwart thousand rushed to join the combat.

Footmen struggled to pull down the armored knights—for as long as a knight held horse he proved well-nigh invincible.

The knights rained blows upon the ill-protected heads of the footmen and took on each other in turn. Unsaddled knights grouped their comrades behind them and advanced like living shields once more into the struggle.

Theido hacked his way into the thick of the strife, but his

followers failed to keep pace and were cut off. He became stranded in an angry sea of enemy soldiers. Throwing his shield before him he bore down, his arm rising and falling upon the necks of his attackers. Then he felt a jolt and glanced down to see an enemy spear jutting from his mount's side. The horse reared screaming and plunged down, hooves flashing out, destroying the face of its assailant. Theido slumped to the ground with his dying horse as eager hands thrust out to haul him from the saddle.

Ronsard saw his comrade fall and turned his charger into the thick of the fray. His sword sang through the air and the whistling blade became a flashing rampart before him. Enemies flung themselves down to the ground rather than face his terrible sting.

The fearless knight plunged into the tumult surrounding Theido and in an instant three of the foe crumpled to the earth. As the enemy drew back, Ronsard reached down a hand and pulled Theido to his feet and up behind him on his horse. "Your hand is much appreciated, good friend," said Theido.

"A knight without a mount is a sorry sight. I do not like to see my friends looking so forlorn," Ronsard replied as they bounded away.

King Selric hewed a swath before him as he and his men advanced to where Ronsard's dauntless forces labored valiantly, though sorely beset. Many brave knights had fallen as their bodies felt the fatal sting of a blade thrust into some crease in their protection. By the time Selric reached the place only one remained upon his steed, his reddened mace dripping with the gore of his luckless opponents. He saluted his king and his fallen brothers and turned once more to the havoc.

Little by little the superior numbers of Jaspin's troops and Nimrood's black Legion wore down the stout defenders. The cruel end approaching swiftly, King Selric signalled the remains of his tattered army to circle and form a wall of shields to stay the destroyer's hand as long as possible.

Theido, having regained a horse, led his cohort wading through the tangle in an effort to join Selric, who stood within the circle of the shields next to Alinea. "Fight on, brave knights!" he urged them forward.

Suddenly, two of the dark Legion appeared side by side in his path. Theido dodged to the side to avoid them, but too late. A blade flicked out and caught him a raking blow on the arm. A deep gash opened up and his sword spun to the ground as Theido felt strength leave his hand.

He spurred his mount and jerked the reins back, causing the horse to rear; the well-schooled animal lashed out with its forelegs. But the sable knights ducked aside. A blade flashed; Theido threw himself upon the horse's neck and heard the swish of the sword as it chopped the empty air where his head had been only an instant before.

Theido desperately searched the ground for a weapon, throwing his buckler over his head to protect him. A blow struck the small shield, nearly wrenching it from his grasp. Another hit home, rending the metal in two. Another blow and the buckler would be useless protection. Theido reeled in the saddle.

Out of the corner of his eye he saw a curious sight. The sable knight to his left raised his sword above his head to deliver the killing stroke. But as the black hand began the downward arc, the arm suddenly went askew, careening off like a branch struck from a tree. An axe had severed it completely. Bloodlessly.

He heard a whoop and saw Trenn's blustery face beaming back at him. The next thing he knew the axe had been thrust into his hand.

The black rider on his right, heedless of his comrade's plight, came on with whistling mace. Once, twice the mace battered into Theido's poor shield. The third time it struck; the mace bit through the metal and snagged the buckler away. Theido let it fly. In the moment of confusion while the fouled mace hung down with the weight of the crumpled buckler, Theido swung the axe up, and with a mighty heave flung it into the foul knight's breastplate.

The war axe bit deep, cleaving the armor and neatly burying its head deep in the knight's chest. No cry of pain came forth, no sign of weakening. Theido could not believe his eyes—an ordinary man would have dropped like a stone.

But the blow did have effect, for Theido was able to spring away as the black creature tugged at the axe sticking out of its chest.

Now Prince Jaspin's army began to crush Selric's dwindling numbers as they staunchly stood their ground. Again the courageous king rallied his men, but strength flagged and still the enemy came on.

"I fear it is the end," said Selric when Ronsard and Theido, abandoning their horses, came to stand beside the valiant war lord.

"We have fought a good fight," said Ronsard. "I am not shamed to die this way."

"Nor I," replied Theido. He gripped the hands of his friends as the foe opened a breach in the wall of shields. "To the death!" he shouted.

At that moment an uncanny sound reached the battered comrades' ears: the sound of hearty voices lifted in song. Then someone cried out, "It is the Dragon King!"

The words struck their hearts like living sparks. Could it be true?

"I *see* him," someone called. "The Dragon King comes with his army!"

All at once a shout went up. "The Dragon King lives! He has returned!" Then they heard the song streaming forth:

> See the armies so arrayed,
> Line on line, ten thousand strong.
> See the Dragon King's sharp blade,
> Rising to a song!

The attackers faltered and cast worried looks from one to another. Before they could think or move there arose a whooshing sound, as of a mighty wind. Instantly the sky burst open The gloom which hung like death over the field of combat fled as a brilliant ball of white light roared into the heavens.

Then he was there: King Eskevar, sitting astride a great white charger, armor glittering in the blinding light, sword held high above his head.

The sight was too much for Jaspin's warriors. They cried out in terror and threw down their weapons. Some fell to the ground as if they had been struck down, others backed away stumbling over those behind them.

Jaspin's commanders sought vainly to rally their cowering soldiers. Another streak tore through the air and another fireball exploded in the sky, transforming the scene to deepest crimson. This decided the wavering forces; the line broke and Jaspin's army retreated. Thousands fled into the forest, shrieking as they ran.

In moments the plain was in turmoil. The nobles who had traded their loyalty to Jaspin for heavy favors held to their grim task, but the men-at-arms, who had nothing to gain by staying, bolted and ran.

Into this panic the Dragon King descended with his peasant army at his back. In the violent red glare of the fireball these simple peasants with their rakes and hoes were suddenly transformed into armed giants, every one a knight in the eyes of the stricken attackers.

A cry of terror rose from Jaspin's forces as the Dragon King and his mysterious men-at-arms waded into battle.

Nimrood, watching the contest from a distance, shrieked, "Stop, you dogs! They are only peasants! The victory is ours!" He spurred his horse onto the field in an effort to halt the rout. "Turn! Victory is ours, I say! Turn back and fight!"

The wizard's screams went unheeded. Pinched between stubborn defiance of Selric's soldiers and the Dragon King's fierce vengeance, Jaspin's army abandoned the field and fled to the woods and the river beyond. Only the nobles and their knights, and Nimrood and his Legion, remained to settle the issue so surely won bare moments before.

The knights and nobles came together and formed a wedge to thunder down upon Selric, hoping to scatter his men before turning their full attention upon Eskevar and his peasants.

The wedge assembled and hurtled down the battlefield to crush the staunch defenders. A great whirring sound went up and suddenly the air prickled with arrows. Voss and his foresters had taken up a position parallel to the flying wedge, where they loosed a stunning volley of arrows from their longbows.

The arrows, thick as hail, rattled off the knight's armor for the most part, though some by force or luck found a chink or a soft spot and did their work. The poor horses caught some of the missiles aimed for their riders, floundered, and dragged others down with them.

The wedge broke apart and melted away.

Nimrood saw this last attempt to turn the tide of battle falter and knew then that all was lost. He turned his horse and galloped away. He had not run far when a rider, darting out of the nearby wood, intercepted him.

"Halt! wicked one!" cried the cloaked rider.

"Ah, Durwin—failed wizard, failed priest. I should have recognized your childish tricks," Nimrood hissed as the other's horse flew up to bar his escape. "Out of my way or I will shrivel you like a piece of rotten fruit! You, I should have disposed of long ago. I should have destroyed you all when I had you in my keep."

"Save your breath, Nimrood. There is nothing more you can do."

"No? Watch me!" The necromancer pointed his finger and drew a circle around himself in the air. Instantly fire blazed up to form a wall around him. Durwin toppled to the ground as his frightened mount, eyes showing white with terror, bucked and bounded away.

"Ha, ha, ha!" cackled the sorcerer. "There is much this magician can do. Now, you will taste the death your meddling has earned!"

Nimrood raised his black stone rod and uttered a quick incantation. From outside the shimmering curtain of flames Durwin saw the sorcerer's rod begin to glow red as new-forged iron. Then cruel Nimrood lowered the rod and leveled it upon the hermit. "Say farewell to this world, hermit! Let your friends save you now! Ha, ha, ha!" he spat bitterly.

Sparks like lightning bolts hissed from the rod, striking Durwin, who was instantly dashed to the ground. He fought back to his knees as the sorcerer laughed with glee. "That was just a foretaste. Now, for the . . ." His voice faltered as he lowered the rod a second time to deliver the fatal stroke. From out of nowhere an arrow sang through the air and pierced the foul lord's arm. The rod tumbled from his hand.

Before Nimrood could turn, another arrow found its mark in his shoulder and he fell from his horse. In two heartbeats Toli was standing over Durwin, notching yet another arrow onto his bowstring.

He raised the bow and bent its long length.

"No! No!" the sorcerer screamed. "Don't kill me! Ahh!"

But the Jher ignored the necromancer's pleas. The arrow flashed through the wall of flames and sank into the wizard's black heart.

The old sorcerer crumpled inward and became a black heap upon the field. He quivered and lay still.

"At last he is gone," said Durwin, dragging himself to his feet. His mantle smoked where the firebolt had seared into his flesh. Toli offered his arm to the hermit, and together they turned to rejoin their comrades as the clash of battle, now diminishing rapidly, came quickly to an end.

They had not walked ten paces when they heard a great sizzling sound. They turned to where Nimrood lay and saw his huddled black form burst into crackling flame; thick black soot rolled into the air. Then, impossibly, in the sputtering flames, they made out the form of a great black bird rising in the smoke.

A moment later they watched as huge black wings slowly lifted away and flew into the wood. Drifting back to them came the rasping call of a raven.

FIFTY-ONE

AT THE demise of Nimrood an uncanny transformation took place. The Legion of the Dead, bearing down upon King Selric and his men with flashing swords and whistling maces, suddenly faltered in their swift course. Their black gauntleted hands went slack at the reins; they swung weakly in the saddle and plummeted to earth in a tempest of dust and horses' flying hooves. The six black stallions galloped away across the plain, free at last. The terrible Legion lay still upon the earth.

King Selric was the first to approach the six armored bodies as they lay. He crept close, his reddened blade held at the ready. Kneeling down over the first of the fallen knights, he glanced at the wondering faces of his men, now gathered around him, and slowly raised the helmet's visor.

The empty sockets of a skeleton's skull stared back at him. Death's Legion was no more.

For a long time the battlefield lay wrapped in silence; a deep and reverent hush had fallen upon the ground hallowed with the blood of brave men. Then, one by one, they raised their heads to a jingling sound and all beheld a sight that made their hearts soar with a happiness long denied: there was the Dragon King upon his white charger prancing into their midst, and there was Alinea his Queen running toward him.

Eskevar threw off his helmet, Alinea threw aside her shield and blade, and then he caught her up in his strong arms and lifted her off her feet and onto his horse in a long embrace.

The plain reverberated in tremendous, tumultuous, joyous acclaim. Tears of happiness streamed down besmudged faces. The Dragon King and his beautiful Queen were at last reunited. The realm of Mensandor was secure.

To Quentin, who had followed in the King's wake, the scene seemed to take on the quality of one of his dreams. There was the King and Queen riding into the cheering throng of their most loyal subjects. She, sitting before him on his saddle, appeared more radiant and beautiful than any woman he had ever seen. And though her auburn tresses tumbled awry and her features were grimy with soot and tears, he thought she looked the more lovely for it all. And the King, armor shining in the golden light of a glorious afternoon sun suddenly burning through the gloom, held his great sword high overhead and proclaimed the victory in a clear, triumphant voice.

Then Quentin was in the arms of his friends. Toli was pulling him from his horse and crushing him in a fierce hug. Theido, one arm newly bandaged, was nevertheless pounding him on the back with the other, while Durwin gripped his face with both big hands and fairly danced for joy. Ronsard, Trenn, and King Selric shook his hands and laughed until tears ran from their eyes and their sides ached.

Quentin, too overcome to speak—his voice seemed to have dried up—just beamed at them all, peering through bleary eyes that sparkled with happy tears. Never had he felt so wonderful, so complete.

The King raised his voice to speak; the glad companions turned to hear him. His voice echoed over the plain saying, "Today will be a day of mourning for our fallen comrades. Tonight their funeral pyres will light their brave souls' homeward way. The armies of Heoth have this day claimed many fine soldiers—we will honor them as is befitting men of high valor."

"But tomorrow," the Dragon King continued. All eyes were

upon him in rapt wonder; many could still not believe that he had indeed returned. "Tomorrow will be a day of celebration throughout the realm of Mensandor! The victory has been won!"

At this the Plain of Askelon leaped to a shout, and songs of victory poured forth from all assembled there. Far into the night the songs continued, muted only during the lighting of the funeral pyres of the fallen countrymen.

When at last the pyres had dwindled to glowing embers, Quentin and the others started back to Askelon. Quentin watched as over the darkened field the funeral fires twinkled and winked out one by one as if they were stars extinguishing themselves forever.

The next day was a day Quentin treasured forever. He awakened to fine bright sunlight streaming in through an open window on a breeze perfumed by the fresh scent of wildflowers. He rubbed his eyes and remembered he had spent the night in Askelon Castle.

Jumping up he found that his clothes had been removed and in their place were the rich garments of a young prince: a tunic of white samite with silver buttons and royal blue trousers, and a richly embroidered cloak woven with threads of gold so that it sparkled in the sunlight as he turned it over in his hands. There was a golden brooch in the shape of a stag's head and a golden chain to fasten the cloak. He had never seen clothes this wonderful. And shoes!—fine leather boots that fit him perfectly.

A servant brought rose-scented water and waited on him while he washed. Quentin's hands trembled as he dressed himself and dashed out of his apartment fastening his cloak with the golden brooch as he ran, quite forgetting the aching stiffness in his leg. Theido and Durwin, both looking more noble than he had ever seen them, were just emerging from their chambers, directly across from his own.

"Ho! young sir, where are you dashing off to so early this morning?" cried Theido with a grin.

"Unless my eyes deceive me," said Durwin, "this must be the King's champion off on some new adventure!"

"It is wonderful! All this—" Words failed him.

"Yes, yes. Wonderful indeed," laughed Durwin. "But you have seen nothing yet until you have seen the hall of the Dragon King in high celebration!"

"Let us go there now!" cried Quentin. "I do want to see it!"

"Not so fast," said Theido. "Breakfast first—though I would hold back somewhat, for there are sure to be delicacies abounding throughout the day. We will join the others first."

"*Then* can we go?" asked Quentin anxiously.

"In due time," laughed Durwin. "You are impetuosity itself. I should have known when I saw you riding off into the wood after good Theido here that you would bring back the King. I should have seen it!"

"You must allow the King's stewards to prepare the hall properly. It will not be ready just yet. A celebration like this . . . well, you will not be disappointed," Theido explained. "But come. We will breakfast lightly and then take our places at court. For today the Dragon King dispenses justice for the treasons raised against him."

At breakfast the three joined Toli, Ronsard, and Trenn, all bedecked in appropriate finery. Toli looked the part of a royal squire, and insisted upon serving Quentin by his own hand. He would have attended Quentin in his chamber had he not been prevented by servants of his own—Toli, too, was a most honored guest.

Quentin blushed, faintly embarrassed by Toli's enthusiastic ministrations; for, although the Jher did not say a word, Quentin could see the light of a glowing pride kindled in Toli's wide, dark eyes. To Toli, Quentin appeared at last to have taken his rightful place as a prince of the realm.

In the massive chamber of court, King Eskevar sat upon his high throne looking grave and righteous as he heard the evidence of the misdeeds practiced against him and his people during his long absence.

Lord Larcott and Lord Weldon were released from prison and restored to full favor with their monarch. In their places went Sir Grenett and Sir Bran, until they should have a change of heart and be willing to swear allegiance and fidelity anew to their Monarch.

Jaspin appeared next before the throne. So feeble with remorse had he become that he had to be dragged forth by guards and propped up on a stool to hear his sentence.

"For your part, Jaspin," said Eskevar, not without compassion, "I will be lenient, though you will no doubt perceive your punishment as more harsh than you can bear. Be that as it may, I have decided.

"You shall be banished from this realm to wander the world and make a home wherever you may find men to receive you. You will never trouble Mensandor again."

Jaspin wailed as if he had been stuck with a hot poker. He cried to his brother for mercy. "Allow me to confine myself to my own castle. In time you shall forget this unpleasantness."

But Eskevar was firm in his resolve. "You may take with you one companion: Ontescue." He nodded and the wily Ontescue was brought forth, muttering darkly.

"Ontescue," the King pronounced, "You, who would be the king's companion, shall accompany your 'monarch' wherever he goes to guide him in exile as you sought to guide him on this throne."

Ontescue blanched, but he bowed low and said nothing, grateful at least to have saved his head.

A whole host of nobles and knights, prisoners taken on the battlefield, were ushered in. They were each made to pledge their oaths of loyalty once more to the Dragon King and each then promised a ransom for themselves and a heavy fine for their lands. But they were released at once.

"I have served my enemies as the law and mercy allow. Now let my friends receive justice as well," announced the King.

King Selric was called first and came to stand before Eskevar who, out of deference to his friend, stood as well. "I cannot reward your courage and valor upon the field nor repay the service you and your soldiers have rendered this crown. For this I shall call you brother, for you have shown yourself more true than any tie blood itself could purchase.

"But as a mere token of my gratitude let me offer you the worthy ransom with which these nobles have redeemed themselves. Take it and divide it among your men and the families of the brave soldiers who died in this duty. Please accept it—it is but little recompense."

"I thank you, good Eskevar. You are fair and just. But my men are my responsibility to reward and I have means and plenty to do it. They will not want who have served in this campaign, nor families lack for the loss of a provider.

"For myself, I am content with your friendship, and will rejoice to call you brother."

At this, King Eskevar descended from the dais and hugged King Selric to himself in a fond embrace. Then the two men raised their clasped hands in the air to the loud acclaim of all who gathered there.

Trenn was called next and came to kneel before the throne. When he stood up to leave, the city of Askelon had a new sheriff. Ronsard followed and was made Lord High Marshall of the realm.

Theido received back his title, which Jaspin had plundered, and his lands as well as those of Jaspin's at Erlott.

Then it was Durwin's turn. "Sir, I would reward you with anything in my power to grant: title, position, gold. You have only to name your reward and it is yours," said Eskevar.

"Your safe return to a just rule of your people is reward enough for me," said the Hermit of Pelgrin Forest. "For myself, I wish only to return to my cottage and there live in peace."

"Nothing else?"

"Nay, let me remain but a servant of a just and righteous king." He paused thoughtfully and added, "But if I could request one favor?"

"It is yours."

"A promise then that the Dragon King will never again leave his throne empty for so long."

Eskevar laughed and held up his hand. "So be it. I have promised."

"There is one more who I would reward," said the King,

glancing down the assembled ranks of onlookers. Quentin was shocked to hear his own name ring out.

"Quentin, step forward."

A thrill of excitement shot through him as he nervously stepped to the foot of the Dragon King's great throne. He knelt there as had the others, hands folded on his knee.

"You I would reward most profoundly," said the King, emotion rising in his voice. "For you it was who broke the bonds of sorcery which held me and snatched me back from death. Your blood and prayers freed me from the spell of the evil necromancer.

"All that I have, the treasures of my kingdom are yours. For on this day you shall become my ward, my son."

Quentin looked up in uncomprehending amazement and then saw Alinea, a Queen once more, with her golden circlet upon her brow, approaching him, her emerald eyes sparkling. The King descended toward Quentin and both then met him where he knelt. They raised him to his feet and then the King proclaimed in a loud voice that echoed through the court and corridors beyond, "Let the celebration begin!"

All at once the doors of the court were thrown open and trumpets blared the King's proclamation. The clarion call echoed and reechoed through the castle and through Askelon itself and through the countryside, and anyone within earshot knew that today they would be welcome in the hall of the Dragon King.

Then Quentin, walking between the King and Queen, his feet fairly touching the floor, was whisked into Askelon's great hall.

It was like a fantasy come true. The hall was hung with ten thousand bright pennons of red and gold. Streamers of flowers formed varicolored canopies overhead, and the windows had been thrown wide to let the sun itself pour gold upon all it touched. The garden beyond had been transformed into a vast dining arena where tables were set, and luscious food of every kind and description was being prepared in front of pavilions raised for the cooks and their scullions, who scampered along the tables with platters of meat and fruit and cakes.

A mood of joyous festivity floated on the breeze like the song of a lark. Then the gates were opened and the people flooded in to begin the most wonderful celebration any of them could remember.

The sun was beginning to set when Quentin and his personal shadow, Toli, at last had their fill of feasting and singing and laughing. In the glow of hundreds of torches flickering to light throughout the hall and on the lawn Quentin sought Durwin, standing alone on the long balcony overlooking the merriment below.

"What is wrong, Durwin?" asked Quentin softly. He had seen a melancholy glimmer in the hermit's eye when he approached. "Why do you not join in the festivity?"

"Ah, Quentin it is you. Oh, I have enjoyed myself quite as much as I feel able." He smiled a smile Quentin thought a little sad. He turned to watch the stars come out one by one in the vast blue vault of the heavens.

"We won," he breathed, his upturned face lit by glimmering torchlight. "We won at last."

"So it is! We won the battle . . . but the war is not over, I fear."

"Not over? What do you mean?"

"Look around you, Quentin. Think about all that has happened to you. The old gods of earth and sky are vanishing, the old order is passing away. The true god is making himself known; his rule is just beginning. But the old ways die hard.

"This is the twilight of the gods, and there is much darkness still ahead before the dawn comes. Ah, but the light will come. That I promise you!"

Then the hermit turned and fixed Quentin with a long and wondering gaze. "Remember your blessing, Quentin. You have some part to play in all of this—the god has his hand on you. Perhaps he has chosen you to help bring in his new order. What you have done is just the beginning; there is still much to do."

Quentin stood blinking back at the holy hermit.

"Durwin," he said with a sudden urgency. "I want to go back—back to Dekra. Is there anything to prevent me, do you think?"

"By no means! A ward of the King may go anywhere; all doors are open to you."

"Would you go with me?"

"I would love nothing better. There is much I would show you."

"Can we leave right away?"

"As soon as may be, my hasty young sir. However, it would be well to abide in Askelon for a time to allow Eskevar to express his gratitude. But we will go soon enough." Then, noticing Quentin's anxious look, "What? Is not one adventure enough for you? You have to begin another so soon?"

"But there is so much to do, so much to learn!"

"And plenty of time to accomplish what has been given us. We will think about all that some other time. Look! Here comes Toli with someone who would meet the hero of the day."

Quentin turned to see Toli hurrying up; a young girl followed demurely behind him. With a start Quentin realized that it was the girl he had met outside the furrier's shop that cold winter's day that now seemed so long ago. She smiled shyly as she approached, and Quentin realized how very much like Queen Alinea she looked. Their auburn hair and emerald eyes were identical. Before Toli could make the introduction, Theido, who came strolling up along the balcony, called out, "Ah, Bria! There you are! After pestering me all day to introduce you, I see you have managed on your own."

Quentin bowed low and said, none too certainly, "I am Quentin at your service, my Lady." The girl, her green eyes sparkling, rustled a deep curtsy in her pale blue beribboned dress.

"Well you say 'my Lady,'" said Theido, beaming. "Do you not know that you are addressing the Princess?" He and Durwin both laughed, and when Quentin turned they were already walking away arm in arm back to the garden where music had begun to play under the stars.

"I am Princess Bria," the girl confessed. "Would you like to listen to the music?"

Quentin was speechless, but his eyes spoke most eloquently for him. Toli fairly pranced for joy, his dark features shining with pleasure, as he ushered the bashful couple along. Bria's warm hand closed upon Quentin's as she drew him away into a night he suddenly wished would never end.